CW00584822

PURPLE STAIN

Book One of the Cardiff Rainbow Series

Nat Lewis

Copyright © 2022 by Nat Lewis
All rights reserved.

This is a work of fiction. Names, characters, places and incidents either are the
product of the author's imagination or are used fictitiously. Any resemblance to actual
persons, living or dead, events or locales are coincidental.

Editor

Dominic Wakeford

Welsh slang supervision

Gareth Howells

Cover art and graphics

Chiara Shkurtaj (instagram @hebes_drw)

Typeface Robotech GP by Gustavo Paz

http://creativecommons.org/licenses/by-sa/4.0/deed.en_US

To those who have supported me through this marvellous journey.

A THOUGHT

You, who have been free falling into empty space, deep down a cave of blackness.
You have cried and thought that there is no end – that this pain will spiral forever.
Look up.

PROLOGUE

HAYDEN

I'd made a thrash metal concert out of my life. The bass, screams and heavy percussion were the only things that could drown out the pained whines piercing through my head. At one with chaos, I raved in the rough circle of a metaphorical moshpit.

Everything changed on an especially hot day at the end of summer. The shift came fast and sharp, like an elbow to the guts. The crowd had cast me out onto a filthy street. Kneeling alone on the damp ground, I could still hear the music, but I was no longer part of the gig. Whatever illusion of enjoyment I'd created for myself, it was over.

This is how it all started.

I dashed all the way home from work, my throat parched and a heavy feeling in my stomach. My heart thumped a fast beat in my ears.

In the kitchen, I guzzled down a pint of orange squash before springing upstairs to my bedroom. Barely catching my breath, I rolled a cig on the desk with sweaty fingers and lit it with the feverish frenzy of a nicotine junkie.

The smoke filled my lungs, white swirls escaped my lips and swam lazily towards the discoloured ceiling. A stillness haunted the familiar shape of my computer, mixer, synth and the posters on my wall. The silence made my bleary thoughts sound louder, and the summer heat choked me like a hand squeezing around my neck.

I looked out the window through narrowed eyes; the sun was beating on a familiar maple tree that knocked on the glass with its gnarled limbs.

There was something about being alone in my empty house, soaked in sweat and fatigued, that unsettled me. An irrational feeling, sure, but the motherfucker became a stubborn tension in my shoulders that *would not leave.* If I closed my eyes, I could see it morphing into a snare of dark roots that wormed out of a hole deep inside my chest.

I pushed away the bad thoughts but felt them clawing at the edges all the same.

I put on the blackest Dimmu Borgir track I could think of; nothing better than Satanic metal to drown out my demons. Building notes, angry growls and thundering drums enraptured me as I slumped over the bed and took a long drag from my rollie.

I was deep in thought when my phone buzzed.

'Hiya, it's the girl from the pub. Katy.'

I blanked. *How many girls were there at the pub yesterday?* After a moment, I remembered. There were three of them: a hot blonde, a squat brunette with a cute face and a feline half-Filipino girl. They *all* took my number and I had no idea which one of them was Katy.

I replied, *'Hello beautiful!'* and added a winking emoji.

The exchange that followed represented a standard half-assed flirting routine, something that was good enough to keep me distracted.

At one point the conversation got pretty hot. I was adjusting a hard-on in my pants and smirking when Katy texted, *'Are you free this afternoon? You live close to uni, don't you? I'm chillin nearby. Wanna meet up?'*

I read the words and grinned. I didn't expect my family to be home until later; a rare opportunity that could not be wasted. We arranged for her to come round to my house. I secretly hoped it'd be the hot blonde showing up at my door since she was the best-looking of the lot.

To my slight disappointment, it was the Filipino girl who whipped me into a hug. She pushed me against the wall by the front door and plunged her tongue into my mouth, hands climbing under my shirt, feeling my chest. I certainly didn't object.

Moving from making out to racing upstairs, dry humping on my single bed and pulling off our clothes didn't take long.

Before I knew it, I was driving into her and she was moaning under me. She was a little too skinny for my taste, but I liked the flawlessness of her skin and her long black hair, as well as the welcoming tightness of her body.

My heart, which was already beating fast, thundered. Maybe it was the heat, or perhaps it was the testosterone pumping through my blood and into my cock.

At some point, somehow, something inside of me cracked. The world closed in around me while the black, crawling tendrils of fear suffocated my whole being.

Seconds passed and, rather than concentrating on the physical pleasure at hand, my mind focused on the new-found awareness that my body could shut down at any moment without notice.

After all, why not? Anybody could just *die*. My stepfather and my gran did. My mother came very close too.

I went rigid like a cadaver, heaving and scared shitless. I heard myself crying and screaming, and couldn't form the words to describe what was wrong.

Eventually I came to my senses, finding that I was sitting in a corner, hugging my legs and wetting my knees with tears.

'Are you OK? Better now?' Katy asked with a small voice. She sat next to me as she tried to offer some comfort, but there was something in her eyes that made me feel insignificant. It was as if she realised that I was a broken man and not the confident hunk she was being fucked by mere seconds ago. I was no longer something to be desired, but pitied.

As soon as I was back on my feet and my hands had gone from shaking uncontrollably to trembling slightly, she put on her clothes and scooted down the stairs, mumbling a hushed, 'See you around.'

I was left alone with my conscience, shocked to find out I wasn't in control of my life anymore. An invisible monster pulled my strings.

1

HAYDEN

'Haven't seen you round the gym, butt. What the fuck's happenin', like?'

Rhys took a long puff from his vape and sat back on the park bench next to me. He lifted his chin and let out a thick cloud of cucumber-scented vapour which joined the stark whiteness of the sky above us. With the mist surrounding him, plus his ginger quiff, trimmed copper beard and long red coat, he made me think of the Welsh dragon.

I placed a smidge of tobacco on the rolling paper that I carefully balanced on my knee, spread it through and gently flattened it. I didn't want to answer his question. Not truthfully at least. I wasn't ready.

'Got a filter?' I asked.

Though he was in love with his vape, Rhys's transition wasn't complete and I knew he enjoyed a rollie from time to time.

'You haven't got one, have you?' He sifted through his pockets, lifting his arse a little to reach the ones at the back. Not an easy thing to do when his trousers were skinnier than the oat-milk latte at his feet.

'Nah,' I said, 'Only a roach, son.'

'No worries, like.' He struggled for a moment longer before extracting a squished plastic sleeve with a lone filter from his back pocket.

'There ew are.' He handed it to me like a shit prize at a fairground.

'Nice one.' I plucked the filter out and positioned it carefully on my Rizla, licked the skin and rolled it, completing my little creation.

'You coming back?' Rhys asked.

I held my cig between my lips and lit it. 'Coming back where?'

'To the gym, like.'

'Ah.' My friend was persistent. 'I'm working out at home these days, mate.'

'*Whaat!*' His high-pitched exclamation pierced my ears. 'Fuck's sake. Whatcha doing working out at home for? The gym equipment's loads betta, like!'

How could I explain to this untroubled hipster that I couldn't handle crowded spaces anymore? How could I make him understand that every now and then I irrationally believed I was going to die? That unless the sky was above my head or a room was empty, I could not think straight? This was the guy who'd said, 'Well, he was old, like – fair play,' to his girlfriend when her grandfather passed away.

How could he *ever* understand?

'I'm happy with my shape as it is. Just need to keep it up, like. Maintain the fucker, innit,' I said.

Rhys spent the next ten minutes trying to convince me to go back to the gym while I inhaled the smoke from my cigarette, my eyes narrowing and my jaw clenching a little more by the minute.

I met Rhys on my way back from work; I was chilling by myself when he'd passed by. Though I was happy to catch up, I knew that prickly questions would arise and it wouldn't be easy to shake him off. He was a mate, and a good one too, but for the love of fuck, I wasn't up for sharing right now.

With each second that Rhys kept going on and on about chest presses, exasperation increasingly twisted my guts. *Fuck the gym. Who cares? I have way more important things to worry about.*

I looked at the time on my phone; quarter past three.

'Gotta go, bruv,' I mumbled as I threw the butt of my cigarette on the ground. I stepped on it to put it out of its misery.

'Already? That's cold, that is bro. I haven't seen you in ages!' Rhys whined.

'Sorry, I've got to pick up my sister.'

'Alright, sound.' He smiled in defeat. 'What you up to tonight? Ads and I are going to The Woodville. Fancy coming or wha?'

'Can't, sorry son. I've got stuff to do for the Old Girl. Sorry, man.' I wasn't exactly lying, but it was close enough.

He nodded to himself. 'No worries, like, no worries. Catch you in a bit. Ow, keep in touch yeah?'

'Will do, son.' We fist-bumped and I made my way down Cathays Park, pulling at the strap on my rucksack to keep it steady on my shoulder as I strode by the pretty bushes and trees.

It was a twenty minute-walk to my little sister's bestie's house, which gave me plenty of time to reflect on the recent events in my life.

If splitting up with the ninth girl in six months was a major offence, then I was guilty. I couldn't stop looking for hook-ups, since sex was a great way for me to forget about things I couldn't otherwise kick out of my brain. It was a welcome distraction that my dick thanked me for.

Since my panic attacks started, meaningless sexual encounters had stopped being a fun pastime. By meeting a lot of girls, I was only adding to the list of people who knew how mental I was. I couldn't stand to face another Katy who'd look at me as if I was a loony creep.

For the first time in my life, I found myself wishing for something more meaningful; a girl who cared for me, even though I was a bit broken.

All I did in the past few years was sleep around and party,

which gave me little time to reflect on my inability to establish a deep bond with someone. It was clear to me that I didn't know where to start.

My most recent attempt at having a proper girlfriend had failed miserably. Cynthia had left me a long message where she said that we were not meant to be, that there was a physical attraction but we didn't click. She wasn't wrong; I wasn't into her personality all that much. I just thought she was hot.

Still, I felt pretty shit because everything I did felt insubstantial aside from my music. Putting tunes together was the only thing that had kept my head straight since that day with the Filipino girl. *How many times have I been overwhelmed by that dark feeling in the last six months?* I tried to recall but I'd pretty much lost count.

I had to hide in the bathroom and drown in my own despair at the pub once. Another time I collapsed on my way to work, and once in the kitchen at home. Both times I started shaking uncontrollably and cried as if someone had crushed my soul. One of the girls I was seeing briefly had to hold my hand as I wailed and screamed at the top of my lungs. That was embarrassing. We were watching a comedy, snuggling on her sofa, and still chaos managed to break loose inside me.

The worst time was when my friend Simon invited me to his club and I had too much to drink. While I was vomiting on the street, that dreadful feeling gripped me again. I shook like a scared little lamb, leaning on a pole between a bush and a stinky wheelie bin. I dropped on the ground then, quivering as I slouched over my sick.

The doctor had said it was a panic disorder, whatever the fuck that meant. The most disabling part of the problem was not knowing when the next episode would occur. He sent me to an anxiety specialist who prescribed some pills that did fuck-all.

'Well, fuck,' I grumbled to myself while listening to Chelsie Wolfe's 'Carrion Flowers' on my headphones. The low, growling guitar and the siren call of the singer soothed my mind, hitting all the right buttons.

A row of familiar terraced houses came into view. The whole area looked gloomy due to the overcast sky and dull sunlight of January. I glimpsed at Amelia's house. The dopey-looking gnome in the front garden was unmistakable. I pressed the doorbell and waited. After two minutes of standing in the biting wind, my phone rang. Amelia's number displayed on the screen and I picked up.

'Yello?'

Sophie said chirpily, 'Hello Hayden!'

'Hey Soph, I'm waiting outside.'

'Can I stay a bit longer, *pleeeease*?'

'Nah. Mum wants you home by four.'

She groaned and hung up.

A minute later Sophie stepped out of the house with a long face and her orange quilted coat zipped up to her chin. Amelia was next to her, holding her arm and jumping up and down like a cricket.

Dalia, Amelia's mum, tried to separate the two girls. 'Come on now, you pair! It's time for Sophie to go home.'

'But why?' Amelia pulled at Sophie's sleeve and I sighed; it was the same story every time.

'Enough now, the pair of ew,' Dalia said. 'You're going to see each other on Monday.'

The girls gave up and hugged each other. Sophie trotted to my side with a dramatic pout, her dark brown ponytails bouncing with each step. She was an eight-year-old girl through and through.

'How's your mother?' Dalia said, smiling cordially.

'She's good,' I said. 'Busy, like.'

'Still making vases?'

'Yep, still at it.' I smiled back, hoping the conversation would be over soon.

The corners of Dalia's eyes crinkled as her smile widened. 'Tell her I said hello.'

I shoved my hands in my pockets. 'Yeah, will do.'

Sophie and I headed home. I was knackered and longed for a hot shower, but Sophie was a ball of energy. She told me everything that had happened that day, starting from the unlikable girl in her class who bullied Amelia, to the secret BFF diary she and her friend were writing. Sophie recounted all this as if it was the most amazing thing in the world.

The small gate of our tiny front garden had been left ajar. I groaned at the sight of it. The shouts and thumping sounds of a rugby game on the telly came loud and clear, even through the barrier of the closed front door. Once inside, the cheering of a raging crowd and an excited commentator pierced my eardrums.

My brother stood by the table near the sliding door leading to the back garden. He stared at the screen, completely engrossed with the game and sipping an energy drink.

'Oi, numpty! I told you to shut the gate properly,' I said.

He turned to look at me coldly. 'You're home early, aren't ew?'

'I went to pick up Sophie, didn't I?' I studied him, noticing something was different. 'Did you get a haircut?'

Iwan gulped down the last of his drink. 'What do you think? I did what you told me. I asked the guy to shave the sides, like you have. Good boy me, see?'

I brushed off a bit of chopped hair that had stuck to his cheek.

'Suits you, fair play son.' He grinned and I smacked him upside the head. My brother looked surprised but the slap wasn't hard enough to give him a reason to argue.

I gave my best stern face. 'The gate. Remember what happened when you left it open last year?'

Iwan crunched the can between his hands and burped. 'They nicked the milk, yeah, yeah...'

'They cut off all the daffodils and broke Mum's vase!' Sophie butted in.

Iwan groaned. 'Ugh, alright, I'm sorry!'

I left my younger siblings to their own devices and headed upstairs. Sophie's tuneful voice was loud enough to echo all the way up the staircase. She was filling Iwan in with the news from the school too.

Iwan and I were very much alike, despite the fact we didn't share the same dad. We were both tall with curly dark blonde hair and a square jaw. In addition, we had some personality traits in common; neither of us liked to argue and had a lot of patience when it came to Sophie, no matter how much she chattered.

I followed the sound of a Celtic bodhrán and bagpipes coming from my mum's study. She sat by the window, surrounded by ceramics in various stages of completion. Her skinny white arms moved slightly, her hands shaping the clay as the wheel turned.

'Mum?'

She lifted her gaze from the wheel and smiled. 'Hiya love! Thank you for picking up Soph. It's nice to see you at home early for a change.'

I smiled back, though I was pretty sure happiness didn't reach my eyes. Spending so much time at home was not a wilful choice.

'I got your medication for you,' I said.

She looked appalled. 'I said I didn't need it!'

'Mum, you've got to take it, please?'

She huffed. 'That stuff makes my creativity slump!'

'Maybe. But you know it helps you in other ways, doesn't it?'

I went to the nearby sink where Mum usually washed her brushes. She always kept a bottle of elderflower cordial on the desk and a blue drinking glass next to it. I grabbed them both, made a drink and handed her a pill. 'Here.'

Mum shot me an annoyed glance before popping her pill in her mouth and taking a big gulp of her drink.

I smiled and crumpled the pharmacy bag with her meds inside, pocketing the bundle. 'I'll be in my room if you need me, alright?'

I scuttled to my beloved den, closed the door behind me and threw my rucksack on the bed. My room was a perfect example of modest comfort, a decent size with a touch of cool. I'd painted the walls some months ago in a dark shade of blue with a few odd white stripes here and there. I'd also lined the shelves with LED fuchsia lights and armed the place with fancy, glowing speakers and robotic props. It was the dopest background for my electronic show. My music equipment was arranged tidily on the desk: compact mixer and speakers, DJ console, synths, microphones and headphones. My electronic drums, guitar and bass were crammed in a corner nearby. Much of the stuff was covered with a sheet, or in the case of my guitars, a sleeve to protect them from dust.

Seeing I could barely step outside without gasping for breath, I had a lot of spare time to invest into promoting myself and my music. I went by the name of o-Drone and was known as a synthwave artist. I could say my efforts paid off as my first single released on Spotify, 'Arctic Cat', had done pretty well. The views on my YouTube videos were astonishingly high too; one of my fans once told me that the algorithm God had shone his divine light upon me. I subsequently put together a whole album, *Wired Minstrel*, and live-streamed weekly.

o-Drone was an homage to Daft Punk aesthetically, although my costume only went as far as being lined with wires and metallic components to look like an android and, rather than a helmet, I wore a cybernetic mask. I didn't like to show my face on video and my fans loved the concept. It was a win-win situation. I'd earned myself a fair following and a steady stream of earnings by now, setting up a Patreon account, selling a little bit of merch and even paying an artist to create an animation for a music video. Best decision ever.

I was hopeful my mental health would get better, since I was giving my mind an outlet and reducing my stress levels, but no – I was still under the thumb of my condition.

I considered whether I should turn on the computer or jump in the shower first but, as soon as I took off my coat, the sweaty odour of my armpits wafted to my nose. Shower it was, then.

Under the hot jets of water, I came up with a tune and thought of a cool sound effect I was going to make use of. I rubbed a towel over my face and picked up my phone. I searched Rightmove, for the umpteenth time that week, for a one-bedroom flat. Every time I did, it felt like I was doing something behind my mum's back. Even though I was a grown-ass twenty-four-year-old guy, I still lived with my family.

I'd set aside my independence to look after my siblings and Mum. My stepfather had been diagnosed with cancer five years ago and wasted away slowly for many agonising months, before finally leaving us. Mum had just recently achieved a semblance of stability and there was no way I was going to disturb her peace by telling her what was happening to me. If she found out I wasn't well she'd blame herself, as she always did.

Things were looking brighter recently, so why was I breaking down? I sighed; best not to dwell on it.

After putting on my boxers, I scrolled down the page with the listings, assessing the available properties. A shared house wouldn't cut it for me; I needed peace and quiet. On the other hand, one-bedroom flats were stupidly expensive, especially considering how run-down they looked.

I smacked my lips, feeling disgruntled. I went back to my room, still looking at my phone, and opened Cynthia's last message. She was so prim, never using an abbreviation in her texts. I read her words for the second time: '*We simply didn't click.*'

'Ugh, whatever.'

An electric guitar sound signalled that I received a new message, making me jerk in surprise. The text was from none other than Cynthia.

'*I'm sorry to bother you but I left something really important at your house. I thought I had it with me. It's a pink paper bag. I need it back by tomorrow.*'

I remembered seeing said bag somewhere, so I glanced around and yep, there it was under my computer desk.

'Fuck,' I said to the phone screen. I replied, '*U coming round to pick it up? I don't mind.*'

I did fucking mind but I wanted to sound as unbothered as I could. She was the one who dumped *me*. There was no way I was going to deliver the bag she'd left behind. Cynthia would have to drag her big ass to my house and come get it herself.

'*Actually, I asked my cousin if he could get it for me. He doesn't live far from you and he's meeting me tomorrow. He said he'd be coming round your house to pick it up in a few. Is that OK?*'

'Bla bla bla. Who gives a shit?' I grumbled as I typed my answer: '*Ye sure.*'

The phone chimed loudly again. '*Listen, he just texted me. He's on his way now.'*

I shook my head in disbelief and typed, *'Np.'*

I lounged for a few minutes, hair still wet, checking out my social media while waiting for Cynthia's cousin. Over the last two months my YouTube channel had really picked up steam, and I now had over fifty-thousand subscribers.

In the meantime, I received a few messages nagging me to get out of the house and get wasted at the pub.

My friend Lucas texted: *'It's Saturday and you're in your gaff, clearly doing sod all. If you want me to fuck off, just say like. But if you have some problem goin on, speak up bruv.'*

I stared at the words and gritted my teeth. I wondered if he was about to drop me like my other pals had done.

Six months ago, I had a ton of mates who insisted that I go out with them. After weeks of turning them down, only a few remained. I came up with an excuse every time: busy, tired, sick, meeting a girl. Anything was better than admitting that I couldn't deal with it all.

There was a soft knock at my door. 'Hello?'

Immersed in thinking about Lucas's text and the buzz of my social media, I forgot to make myself presentable for the stranger standing behind the door. I opened up with only my boxers on and a damp towel around my shoulders. Big, striking blue eyes met mine. *Oh, wow.* I gawked and the dude in front of me mirrored my expression.

The guy combed his dark fringe with his fingers, lowered his gaze to the floor and mumbled, 'Sorry to bother you. I came to pick up Cynthia's bag.'

'Ah, s-sure, yeah, no worries, like, no worries,' I spluttered in reply.

I wobbled to my desk and reached for the pink paper bag. I'd been caught by surprise; perhaps that's why my cheeks burned hot and my stomach tingled. A good number of friends from the gym had seen me shirtless and I was anything but shy, so I couldn't quite make sense of my reaction. Damn, had I spent that much time apart from people? Maybe it was because this guy was a complete stranger who had just stepped into my personal space that I felt so flustered.

I heard him swear under his breath. After picking up the bag, I turned to look at him. He stared at his right palm which was covered in purple ink. A large stain tarnished the grey and white pattern of his hoodie as it leaked out of his pocket.

'Aw, feck!' He extracted the culprit, a flowery purple gel pen, with two fingers. 'Shit, sorry,' he said. 'Do you have a tissue or a bin or something?'

I had a plastic bag where I collected all my crap and grabbed it, holding it open for him. He let go of the ink-sticky pen in the carrier bag, the purple mess landing on a pile of old cigarette butts and ripped paper.

'Oh no, don't tell me...' He carefully unzipped his hoodie and gasped. The hem of his T-shirt was covered and the purple ink looked black on the red background.

I gasped too, but for a very different reason.

The design was unmistakable: his T-shirt was one of my limited-edition o-Drone shirts! I'd only had eleven of them printed and I sent out ten of them four months ago as a giveaway. I'd kept the last T-shirt for myself as a memento.

I was flabbergasted. He was crushed.

'Bollocks! Ugh, I'm sorry but can I use your bathroom?'

'No worries. It's just over by there,' I muttered, pointing at the door left of mine.

'Cheers, and sorry. I'll be out of your hair in no time. I just need to wash my hands.'

I heard the water running behind the bathroom door, as well as his tutting, cursing and groaning. This *could not* be a random occurrence, could it? Was the guy a crazy fan-stalker?

I'd never shown my face or shared my address on any social media, and my accent wasn't that strong; if anything, I had a definite Hampshire twang. Nobody would make a random guess that I lived in Cardiff. How could he have known who I was? Maybe he hacked my personal info somehow. But then, would he have had a pen explode in his pocket just to have an excuse to show me his T-shirt and talk to me? Can you make a pen leak like that? Like, as a planned thing?

Then again, what were the odds of something like this happening? Unbelievably small. Did Cynthia have something to do with it? But how and why? My brain was going haywire.

Before I could reach a conclusion, he was out of the bathroom, looking depressed. His T-shirt was soaking wet and all scrunched up; clearly, he'd tried to wash off the stain but to no avail.

If he's a crazy fan, he'll try to keep the conversation going or maybe find an excuse to talk about my music.

The guy looked at me with big, sad eyes. 'Uh, yeah, so... the bag?'

I gave it to him, baffled. He turned on his heels and started to leave, heading for the door.

An inexplicable panic seized me. 'Hang on a sec!'

He glanced at me with a perplexed frown.

I knelt down again, this time to reach for a box stashed under my bed. There were many T-shirts there, all different colours and sizes, still wrapped in cellophane. The one I was looking for was red, like his. It was almost at the bottom, pretty wrinkled but all in one piece. I handed it to him and the guy stared at me, puzzled.

Before I could even think of what I was saying, I smiled and said, 'Thanks for supporting my channel.'

2

ANDY

I studied the T-shirt he held out to me, frowning.

'Oh,' the guy said. 'Maybe it's best if I bag it. You've got all that ink on you and if you get this one smudged too, that's it. I don't have another to give you.'

Was it me, or was this whole situation downright odd, to say the least?

Earlier, my cousin Cynthia had called me in a panic as I tried to enjoy my hot cheese and bean pasty in peace. She'd told me she left a pink paper bag at her ex's house and begged me to go retrieve it. I refused at first but *then* Cynthia added that her brother Mark's wedding rings were in the bag, and as we were going to his wedding tomorrow, we might need them. With a sigh, I left Greggs and got in my car.

Finding the house of the ex-boyfriend, a friendly little girl opened the door and sent me, a complete stranger, upstairs without any explanation, telling me her brother's room was the one with the Depeche Mode sticker on the door. I knocked and this Adonis opened up with his bulging arms, sculpted abs and chest glistening from the water dripping from his blonde curls. Not to mention the noteworthy package I'd glimpsed in his boxers! I had to look away, and it was only embarrassment and shock that saved me from an inappropriate erection.

When he knelt by his desk, his ass was semi-visible through the fabric of his boxers. I thought I was going to have an aneurysm or, perhaps, my nose would bleed as if I was some perverted anime character. Instead, it turned out that my vessels weren't the problem; my sister's pen exploded. I used it to make a note yesterday and left it in my pocket, forgetting all about it until now.

I'd made a fool of myself in front of Apollo incarnate. I was humiliated, sad, soaking wet and ready to retreat in shame.

'Thank you for supporting my channel,' was what he'd said. *What the hell...?*

'Wait, I'm confused,' I said.

The handsome bastard smirked at me. 'I'm o-Drone, innit.'

My jaw dropped. 'No way!'

He laughed. Heat rose up my cheeks and the more I was conscious of it, the closer I was to catching fire. 'You're joking?'

'When I saw you had that T-shirt on, I freaked out a bit, like. I thought you were a crazy stalker or something.'

'What? No! I swear I had no idea!' I said, waving my hands.

'I can tell from your reaction. This is mad, innit?'

I stared at the brand-new T-shirt in my hands. 'It is. I mean... are you really o-Drone? Like, *for real?*'

He grinned. 'The very same. Keep it on the downlow though, yeah?' He raised an eyebrow in amused challenge. 'My secret identity is a profitable gimmick.'

I chuckled. 'Yeah, I bet.'

I was struck by his looks at first. Now, I was also star-struck. My brain had taken over my dick, at least partially, and as I glimpsed at the room and the instrumental setup, I realised how familiar it looked; I'd seen it many times in o-Drone's streams.

'Amazing,' I said incredulously. 'Thank you for the T-shirt, dude. I love your stuff!'

'Nice one, cheers! You're the first fan I've met in person. It's awesome!' He offered his palm. 'I'm Hayden. Is it safe to shake your hand?'

I gave him the chance to squeeze a work of abstract art. 'Andy. I washed off the ink as best I could, but I can't make any promises.' He laughed and shook my hand anyway.

'So, this is where you make music?'

'Yeah. Wanna look?'

I tried to divert my gaze from his mostly naked body and looked right at his face. Every part of him was a sight for sore eyes. 'I don't want to disturb you.'

He snorted, 'You're not disturbing me! Or are you in a rush to give the bag back to Cynthia?'

Though I'd wanted to kick my self-centred cousin just fifteen minutes ago, right now she was suddenly my favourite person. 'No, I'll give it to her tomorrow morning.'

'Sound. Let me pop on some clothes.'

Before I could say another word, he put on a pair of grey jogs and a black Drab Majesty T-shirt with the Venus de Milo statue drifting through a virtual room. I liked Hayden more by the minute.

He looked at me expectantly. 'Coffee?'

Was I about to have a sit down with a drop-dead gorgeous guy who also happened to be one of my favourite synthwave artists? How could I ever refuse?

'Tea, please. One sugar, if that's alright.'

***

Tea and coffee. That summed up our differences.

'I love Pretty Hate Machine,' I said excitedly, 'It's got it all! The groove, the sad bits, the darkness, the twisted stuff. It's perfect!'

Hayden chuckled. 'What's your favourite song on the album?'

I tapped my chin. '"Sanctified". Possibly.'

A remix of the intro from *Stranger Things* played in the background. We agreed that only the first series was worth watching but that the soundtrack was awesome. This particular remix was Hayden's and it was exquisitely produced. It was more ominous compared to the original but sounded incredibly smooth, like ASMR.

'Call me obvious, but for me it's "Head Like a Hole",' he said with a wry smile.

'Why obvious? It's a really good song.'

He shrugged. 'It's the most well-known off the album, I guess.'

'That doesn't matter.'

He smiled. 'I guess not. So, do you play any instruments, like?'

'I play the piano and I sing a little bit. I guess it's useful to know which notes to press on my synth.' I chuckled at my bad joke.

His eyes widened. 'You make tunes as well?'

'I do, in my spare time. Nothing professional though, I just do it for fun.'

'Do you have anything with you that I could listen to? I'm curious.'

I scratched my head. 'I'm not confident enough to share my stuff online. To be honest, anything I put together is for my own enjoyment. But you can come round my house, if you want. It would be nice to hear your feedback. Maybe you can give me some tips on how to better use my equipment.' I realised how unsubtly I was trying to make friends with him a moment too late. 'I mean... like... whenever, you know. If you want to.' My face burned like a bowl of chilli.

Hayden smiled again. A single dimple formed in his right

cheek. 'Too right, I'd be up for that.'

Hot damn. This was a dangerous situation.

Everything about Hayden screamed, 'I like pussy'. His room décor said as much: there was a brunette on a poster showing a good portion of her boobs as she seductively lifted her top, plus skimpy figurines of Yuffie and Tifa from *Final Fantasy VII* lined the shelves, not to mention the anime girl on his computer background was a step away from being fully hentai.

Little did he know that I squirmed in my seat whenever he laughed or gazed at me with those intense brown eyes. I liked how he brushed his hair aside with his fingers, inevitably ending with a fringe of blonde curls falling back on his forehead.

He'd look at me intently while I talked, as if he didn't want to miss a single word. Most people I knew, including me at times, would check on their texts or social media while conversing. Instead, Hayden placed his phone face down on the desk. He picked it up only once after receiving a message, and even apologised for interrupting our chat. He must have set his phone on silent then, because it didn't make a sound after that; he dedicated his undivided attention to me.

Whenever he smiled, I felt like something in me was slowly melting. *God, why is he so perfect?*

Someone knocked on the door. The little girl from downstairs, who I'd presumed was Hayden's younger sister, peeked inside with a toothy grin. 'Hayden, it's takeaway night! Mum's asking what you want for dinner. I said either pizza or curry. What did you want?'

Hayden looked at me. 'Do you like pizza?'

I shook my head, saying, 'Oh! I don't want to intrude!'

'Why? You're not intruding at all and I'm not going to have you watching while everyone else's eating.' He said this like it was the most natural thing in the world, as if we were old friends. 'It's cool man, you're my guest,' he added.

His sister beamed. '*I'm* up for pizza!'

Hayden looked at me with a Prince Charming smile. 'What do you want to eat?'

'Uh... a small margherita's OK...'

He frowned. 'Sure? You can order something a bit jazzier if you want.'

Dirty mind, shush! 'Oh, no thanks. Margherita is good.'

Hayden turned to his sister. 'Right. One margherita and a meat feast for me please, Soph.'

'*Okaaaay!*' She closed the door behind her.

At that moment I noticed the sun had gone down and that Hayden and I were sitting in the dark. His eyes reflected the bluish light coming from the computer screen and his gaze focused on me. His lips curved and my heart drummed a fast beat in my chest. I willed myself to calm down, knowing that getting worked up wasn't going to lead to anything good.

Hayden put on a different track. It was a new piece he was working on; an exciting and somewhat sensual tune with low notes and slow, clean drums. Amazing.

'You're the first to listen to this. What you reckon?'

'It's awesome.' I closed my eyes, submerging myself in the sound. 'Only... no, never mind.'

He smirked. 'Nah, now you have to say it...'

'I just thought that if you added an element to the drums, it might improve this vaporwave-feel you have, something subtle.'

'Like a stronger snare?'

'More like a hi-hat.'

'Show me.' He opened the song in the sequencer, uncovered his mixer and turned it on.

I blinked in surprise. 'Wait. Are you sure?'

'You made me curious now. I want to understand what you mean.'

For the next twenty minutes we worked on the tune. He allowed me to tweak his track without hesitation. His trust in me made me feel weird; I was both flattered and embarrassed. I added a muted hi-hat sound as I'd suggested and that gave Hayden an idea. He implemented a cool sound effect that made the bass tremble and fizzle out. The piece took on a completely new dimension. It was way more vibrant and entrancing now. Hayden and I sat next to each other in silence for a while as we listened to the result. We exchanged a grin as the tune played. No words were needed; it was great and we both knew it.

The food arrived soon after – pizzas with a side of hot wings, chips and four Cokes that came with the meal deal. I joined Hayden and his younger siblings downstairs and I got introduced to them properly. Sophie had dark, wavy hair and sharp features that made her look quite different from her brothers. Iwan looked much like Hayden, with curly blonde hair and a strong jaw. He must have been fifteen or so, but he was taller and sturdier than twenty-three-year-old me, and mumbled the few words he spoke. Just like Hayden, Sophie and Iwan treated me as if I'd been there a thousand times.

'You've got a younger sister as well, have you?' Hayden asked, a pizza slice dangling from his hand. He opened his mouth, carefully capturing the melted cheese with his tongue.

I bit my lower lip and looked down, studying the small writing on my Coke can. 'Yeah, how'd you guess?'

'That pen in your pocket was pretty girly and tiny. I thought maybe it was your sister's or something.'

'You're very observant,' I said.

'Have you got a brother too?'

I laughed. 'An older one. Seriously? How the heck did you guess?'

'It looks like we have *a lot* in common, so...' he said with a chuckle.

We'd just finished eating when I glanced at my phone distractedly – it was half past eight! I'd gotten there before five! 'I better go. I promised a friend I'd go out with him for a pint. I really enjoyed myself, though.'

'OK dude, no worries.' Hayden gripped my hand, slammed me against his chest and patted my back in a way that I could only describe as utterly manly.

I wanted to laugh and cry at the same time because Hayden had such a potent, straight-guy vibe about him and there I was, getting all flustered at being in close contact with his body.

I offered to pay for my pizza and my Coke but Hayden was adamant I didn't have to.

'Well, next time dinner's on me then,' I said. *Oh God, was that too forward?*

Hayden only grinned and said, 'Sounds good, yeah.'

We exchanged contact details and added each other on every possible social media channel. I peeked at his Facebook page and he at mine. Hayden Morris, twenty-four years old. He laughed because he expected me to be born the same day and year as him. Instead, I was a year younger, born in December and not August like him.

Summer and winter; it suited us. We existed on the same wavelength, thought alike and had lots of stuff in common, but there was enough different too.

I left his house and was met by the freezing night air. My cheeks instantly cooled and my breath puffed and coiled against the dark background of the sky. Thank God my car was parked nearby.

'Hold up!'

My heart fluttered at the sound of his voice. I turned around.

Hayden grinned at me, handing over Cynthia's pink paper bag. 'You don't want to leave this behind! She'll kick right off!'

I took it from him. How could I have forgotten the very thing I went there for in the first place? The answer was in front of me, smiling and shivering from the cold. He hopped a little, trying to keep warm, and pushed both hands in his pockets.

'I've never got on with someone instantly like this, you know?' Hayden said. 'Honestly, bruv. You're proper sound, like.'

I smiled, feeling a bittersweet twinge in my chest. 'Same to you.'

'Catch you in a bit, yeah?' He half-hugged me again and rushed back inside.

'See you,' I murmured.

As I watched him go, I asked myself how come a person with his brains, looks and charisma was spending his Saturday night at home with his family and not out and about, drinking himself to oblivion and getting laid. Nothing wrong with a quiet night in, of course, but when I told Hayden that I was going to meet a friend for a pint, he looked a bit sad. Should have I invited him?
With these thoughts, I walked back to my car.

***

Cynthia was the maid of honour and she'd been very close to messing things up for her brother. She and I met near St. Peter's Church in Roath for the morning ceremony on Sunday.

I wore a long black coat over my freshly laundered suit and gazed at the greyish-white sky, hoping that it wouldn't drizzle while I stood out in the open. All the family was there, except for my older brother who couldn't make it since he was in America and buried in work.

Cynthia stood by a twiggy tree near the YMCA building and

puffed on her vape. Despite the temperature being below zero, she flaunted long, naked legs under the short skirt of a green dress.

'Here, dummy.' I gave her the bag.

She squeezed her eyes shut and smiled. 'Ahh, nice one! Cheers, you're a star!'

I shook my head. 'Seriously. You know how awkward I am with strangers, and still you had me go there.'

'It was an emergency!' Cynthia whined, her red lips pouting. 'It would have been way more awkward for me, trust me.'

I was curious enough to venture the question, 'Did he break up with you?'

She puffed on a popcorn-scented vape. 'Nah, I dumped him.'

'How come? He seems like a good guy.'

Cynthia squinted at the fat clouds above with a dreamy expression. 'Oh, he was good, alright? *So good.* Hayden's got a *huge* dick.' Her hands mimed an invisible eight-inch penis.

My cheeks heated at the memory of what I'd observed the day before, though I pretended I knew nothing of it and made a face. 'TMI.'

She clicked her tongue. 'At first I was really into him. He's hot and nice but, how can I say this, he wasn't putting in the effort. He was like... going out with me *just because*, you know? I don't want to fall for the guy and have to beg him to like me back. I can do better than that.'

'Yeah, I guess you're right,' I said.

Cynthia blew another white cloud of vape out. 'I heard he's a total man-whore anyway. I told him he had to get tested, otherwise it was going to be a no-go. All he wanted to do was shag. You remember Hanna, my college friend? She's slept with him, and Charlotte too. Maybe he was going to dump me in any case, 'cause you know... he's emotionally unavailable. It's better that I ended things first.'

'Yeah...'

She inhaled the vapour deeply. 'You know what? You'd get along with him better than me. He's into making music on the computer with the electric piano and stuff, like you. He likes all that eighties wave stuff, what's it called...?'

'Synthwave.'

'Yeah, that's the one.'

To say that Hayden liked synthwave was quite the understatement. His musical interests were broad, like mine. We even listened to 'Man of Constant Sorrow' from the *O Brother, Where Art Thou?* soundtrack and commented on the beauty of the piece. We both loved that movie too.

'Not that I'd want my cousin to hang around someone like him,' Cynthia added after a long pause.

I frowned. 'You said he's nice.'

'Yeah, but he's also a bit weird, like. He's got stuff going on with his family and he's not quite with it or something. I can't really say. Who knows, maybe it's only with his dates that he's cold like a bloody freezer. You'd be alright being around him, since he wouldn't want to fuck you.'

I glanced at Cynthia, trying not to show how much what she just said hurt me. 'Will it be OK to show that much skin during a wedding? Not that I care, though some priests are picky like that.'

Cynthia scrunched her nose. She considered the weather with a bemused expression, as if something odd hid behind the clouds. 'What about you, babes?'

I straightened my tie. 'What about me?'

'Have you met anybody interesting since breaking up with that two-timing cockhead? What was his name again?'

I groaned inwardly. 'Craig.'

'Yeah. How's it going in the hooking-up department?'

I sighed. 'I'm done with mindless sex. I pulled a couple of times at the club after Craig, and it was awful. My heart can't take it, you know? I hate one-night stands, casual stuff and all that. I can't bear that awkward feeling after doing the dirty deed. It makes me feel like crap.'

Her scarlet lips curved. 'You need to relax, hun. Don't take everything so *seriously*. Sometimes, mindless fun is a right laugh.'

I shook my head. 'Not for me.'

Uncle Jonah sauntered by, his bushy brows furrowed, and with a voice harsh like smoke he said, 'You two, get into church or the ceremony will start without you.'

The wedding began not long after our conversation. I sat next to my great-aunt Dorothy who gave me a lipstick-stained grin. Rather than looking at the bride and groom, my eyes were drawn to the mangled portrayal of Jesus on the cross.

I always wondered about the Catholic Church's need to depict death and pain so realistically. This particular crucifix was dark brown in colour, hanging in the centre of a pale-yellow vault and above an enormous triplicate of stained-glass windows. Jesus's head drooped in misery. I couldn't blame him; if I were stuck hovering by the ceiling and had to listen to the priest's litany every single day, hour after hour, I'd be miserable too.

I imagined Christ suddenly coming to life and shouting, 'Everyone, there's a sodomite in my house! What are you going to do about it?' Or, perhaps, he'd wink at me knowingly. I wasn't sure which scenario was worse.

I came out to my very Catholic parents when I was sixteen. They reacted stiffly, neither accepting nor openly condemning my sexual orientation. My father was OK with it as long as he didn't have to hear about it extensively, but my mother was nosey. Funnily enough, it wasn't gay sex she disapproved of, as such, but rather my 'loose morals'. She thought that gays didn't care about settling down.

So there I was, agnostic and completely out of place. Nevertheless, I was still a beloved member of the Nash family. I didn't get any dirty looks like Cynthia who stood proud by the altar with her heavy makeup, short skirt and high heels. The priest must have been too shy to say a word, or perhaps he was titillated.

My phone buzzed. I really wanted to see what the notification was, but the last thing I needed was the evil eye from under Dorothy's rococo hat. So I waited.

Once we were all out in the cold after the ceremony and headed for lunch, I looked at the message. It was from Hayden.

'*Check it out! We make a good team innit.*' There was a link to a song on Spotify and a smiling face with sunglasses.

I opened the link and my heart skipped a beat. He had published the tune we worked on together the day before. The cover was a dark grey background with a purple splotch. The title he'd chosen, written in a cool eighties font, made me gasp: 'Purple Stain'. I realised I was grinning like a buffoon and tried to compose my features. But then Cynthia's words rang in my ears: *He wouldn't want to fuck you.*

I grumbled to myself, 'Like I didn't already know that.'

3

HAYDEN

I'd been thinking about my encounter with Andy all weekend, which was odd. After sending him a text Sunday morning, I kept checking my phone in a restless state. I waited almost an hour before he answered my message.

I worried he'd think that calling the track 'Purple Stain' would be too cheesy, but no. He said the piece was incredible and found the choice for the title funny; he was happy and honoured to have worked on the track with me.

'If my bad luck inspired you, at least I can say something good came out of it!'

We messaged some more on Sunday evening and eventually I decided to call him because holding the phone up to text was getting tiring. I relaxed in my bed as we exchanged thoughts on speakerphone. We talked about bands, movies and books that we liked and disliked, places we wanted to travel to, our favourite foods and all sorts of meaningless stuff that simply drifted through our minds.

Sometimes the conversation would get serious and the topics deep, such as the possibility of life in the wider universe and the limitations of human understanding. Andy offered his theories in a serene tone and I imagined him lying in bed with his head on the pillow like I was. In a similar fashion to Saturday afternoon, we got along like magic. Whatever we disagreed on, which to be fair wasn't much, gave way to constructive discussion and, by the end of the call, I felt like I had a lot to think about.

Andy was the kind of guy who I'd ask for a second opinion on everything. He was super-chill and had a good sense of humour. We carried on talking until eventually the dim glow of dawn peeked through the slit between my drawn curtains.

I thought back on Cynthia's words – *We simply didn't click.*

Hell, I knew what she meant now. Andy and I? We clicked, alright. Spookily so.

When I woke up on Monday, around midday since Andy and I had spent the night talking, he was the first thing that came to mind and the thought of him made my stomach tingle with joy.

I sent him a text, '*You free at some point this week? Fancy meeting up?*'

After a moment, my notification tune broke the silence.

'*I have to study today. I've got to take an exam tomorrow morning. My last! But we could hang out tomorrow afternoon. I'm up for celebrating!*'

'*Congrats! You didn't tell me you were in uni! What u studying?*'

'*I'm doing my masters in classical literature, believe it or not,*' Andy replied.

I smiled. He did speak like a book sometimes and I knew he was well-read. There was nothing pretentious about him though; in fact, he was the humblest person I'd ever met.

'*Ah, so like, you know all about the Odyssey? Aristotle, Herodotus and all that stuff?*'

'*Did you just list the first three things you found on the Wikipedia classical literature page?*'

I chuckled. *'LOL, yep.'*

'I knew it! But thanks for the effort. To answer your question, no. Not all about it but I know more than most, I guess.' He added a grinning emoji so I pictured him grinning too and my smile broadened.

'You know, it's mental. I wanted to study literature too. But contemporary.'

'What's stopping you?'

I sighed. Not willing to make the conversation heavy with the mention of my depressing past and currently shitty mental health, I cut it short with a brief, *'It's complicated. Tell you another time.'*

After a minute, my phone buzzed again.

'Would you like to go out for a drink or a coffee then?'

I thought about it, then decided that I simply wasn't ready to hit the town unless it was for work.

'I was thinking it'd be nice to check out your equipment.'

Andy didn't reply for five minutes or so. Was I being too forward by asking to meet at his house? I typed again, *'You said you'd like to have me come round at some point. I must admit I'm curious to see your setup.'*

The reply came instantly. *'You mean my music setup? Sure, I'll give you my address. When do you fancy it?'*

Of course I was talking about the music equipment. What else could I have meant?

***

I should have known he was well-off. The address he gave me suggested that Andy lived in a fancy area and, when I got there, I found myself staring at this gorgeous white house with a snazzy front door, large windows and a smashing front garden with trimmed bushes and an enormous tree.

My brain analysed all the possibilities. The house was huge, four or five beds at least. He must have been living with his family, like me, which wasn't a farfetched scenario since he was a student and the uni was nearby. Why rent a room in a noisy dorm, live in a shared house or a tiny flat when your parents have a place like this?

I was a little intimidated because it was obvious that I was working-class and Andy was obviously not. If he introduced me to his parents, would they think badly of me? I wasn't exactly swank like I imagined them to be.

He led me inside and, as expected, the place was as sweet as heaven. The kitchen was large with sleek, marble tiles, a breakfast bar, range cooker and a humongous fridge. The sofas in the lounge were leather and there was a big grey, black and white rug with a minimalist pattern that screamed *expensive.*

Andy showed me some framed posters he'd hung on the walls; some from cool bands and others from movies, and other dope ornaments he'd bought. The bust of Arnie from *The Terminator* sat on top of a chest of drawers and I nodded as Andy spoke, thinking how much freedom his parents had given him to decorate.

Maybe it was because the lighting in the house was great, but I kept noticing things about him that I hadn't paid attention to before. Andy had smooth-looking skin with a light spread of freckles and barely any facial hair, though he was already twenty-three. His blue eyes were shadowed by long curved lashes that had to be a source of envy for many a girl. Dark brown hair fell messily over his head with a longish fringe that he kept brushing to the side with his fingers. It looked smooth to the touch and I had to stop myself from reaching to mess it up. He had such a lightness about him, despite the morbid *Cannibal Corpse* T-shirt he wore.

'Are the 'rents in?' I asked.

He raised his eyebrows. 'My parents? No, this is my house.'

I gasped. 'You live here *on your tod?*'

He smiled, showing a row of straight white teeth. 'Well, yeah. My grandfather was a rich guy. He owned loads of properties around Cardiff. He left a house to each of his grandchildren. My brother sold his and kept the money. My sister and I have a house each but, of course, she's a minor so hers is still in a trust.'

'Fuckin' hell,' I said. 'Lucky boy, ain't you?'

'With the housing crisis that we have nowadays? Yes! Very.'

I chuckled awkwardly. 'You aren't looking for a housemate, are you?'

His eyes widened. 'Why? Do you need a place?'

I ran a hand through my hair. 'Ah, well uh... kind of like... not massively though.'

'Let me know if you're interested. I've got plenty of room here! Right, the time has come to show you my kingdom.' His lips moved into an impish grin. 'Are you ready to see my music room?'

I beamed at him. 'Too right!'

He'd said *kingdom* and I could immediately see why. My bed and music equipment were crammed in the same, tiny space. *This* was a proper recording studio with sound-proofed walls and a sleek sofa, two computer screens, dope speakers, synths, microphones and several pairs of headphones...

I brushed my fingers over his digital mixer, astonished. Pretty sure my eyes were sparkling, I said, 'PreSonus StudioLive 32. Bruv, this is stuff of wet dreams.' I wasn't going to ask how much it all cost. I simply couldn't fathom it.

His cheeks turned pink. 'You like it?'

'You're having a laugh, yeah? This is...' I shook my head. 'It's just amazing. Proper mint.'

He smiled. 'You can come anytime you want.'

I shot him a grin back. 'I might just do that.'

'Fancy some coffee? I've got beer and orange juice too, if you would prefer?'

'White coffee for me please, if that's alright? No sugar. I'm sweet enough.'

He let me play with his setup while he made us both drinks. I felt like I was a little kid again and was getting over-excited.

'Can you play me some of the stuff you made?' I asked once he was back.

He bit his lower lip. 'OK, but don't laugh.' Andy searched for a track on the computer. 'Headphones or speakers?'

I flashed him a grin. 'Both. But speakers first.'

'OK.' He set up the speakers and told me he was going to play a tune called 'NOZ'.

'What does it stand for?'

'"Not On Zoom",' he said. 'It's an inside joke. Don't worry.'

Andy blushed. A lot. So much so that the crimson flush reached the tip of his ears. It must have been some sexual reference that he wasn't willing to share. I smiled at how coy he was being and decided not to prod further, but I watched as he attempted to conceal his embarrassment with a concentrated expression.

The room filled with the beating hum of a slow baseline. A flow of muted percussion followed, then the synths came in subtly. There was a deep open sound and a guitar line that he must have run through a pedal, modifying the riff to a gritty chug towards the end.

Andy smiled bashfully. 'What do you think?'

'It was fuckin' epic!' I glanced at him. 'What's there to laugh about?'

'I don't know, I just... I'm not sure it works as it is. It's not very original.'

'What do you mean? It's got a proper unique sound to it. Can I have another bash on the headphones?'

'Sure.' He plugged the wire to the computer and I put the headphones on.

I sighed with pleasure as the sound came beautifully to my ears. 'Man,' I said, 'these headphones are mint.'

Andy laughed.

With the headphones on, I picked up on different things and pointed them out to Andy. We tweaked the track for the next hour. The finished piece sounded purer, with the slow notes contrasting wittily with the chugs of the guitar.

'Wow, it's completely different,' he said after the final listen.

'It was already good at the start.'

'Can you listen to this one too? It's called "Asymmetric Altar", it's a little proggy...'

Time went by fast. We chilled out, listened to each other's music and stuff from other artists. Andy ordered a fancy Chinese takeaway and offered to pick it up as he saw how enthralled I was while listening to my tracks through his superior headphones.

'Is there somewhere I could have a quick cig?' I asked as he put on his coat.

Andy peeked out. 'I think it's about to rain. Maybe it's best if you go up to the balcony. Come on, I'll show you.'

Two minutes later I was looking out over the tidy back garden while the cold air nipped at my cheeks and knuckles. The plants were neatly trimmed, the garden was clearly well looked-after and, damn, he even had a huge barbecue, a table and a small gazebo.

I considered asking Andy if I could be his housemate more

seriously now. This place was lush and the company was awesome. I thought about it for another minute and realised that I couldn't move out, not yet. My mother and siblings still needed me around. I had to put them first.

Worries and unpleasant memories tugged on my thoughts – the agonising years spent dreading my stepdad's imminent death, my family dealing with grief, my attempts at trying to hold all the pieces together flooded my mind. I tried to push the depressing thoughts away but they kept returning, in the same way a flock of hungry pigeons go after a slice of bread. Before I knew it, my heart was racing and my breathing became irregular. *Fuuuck, fuck-fuck-fuck*. Calm. Down.

I went back inside and put on a relaxing tune. I sat on the sofa, hugged my knees and covered my head with both hands. I squeezed my eyes shut. *In and out. Just breathe. In and out*. I tried to think of something positive, something happy.

Out of all the things, Andy came to mind. I was in his house and I was safe. Where was he? Why wasn't he back yet? He said the Chinese takeaway was only five minutes' walk from his house. *I could die alone here, I...*

Tears pricked my eyes when the monster overtook me. *Oh God, where is Andy?* I gritted my teeth but began sobbing uncontrollably. I was so distraught and didn't even know why. I just wanted to let it out. The room was sound-proof so why not? I screamed so loud that I strained my vocal cords. I cried and grew weak all over, my hands going cold.

The door opened the very moment I let out a second shriek.

'Hayden!' Andy rushed towards me and placed his hands on my shoulders. 'What's wrong?' he asked shakily.

I didn't look up. Many others had seen me in this state and I couldn't care less what they thought of me. But Andy? I didn't want him to consider me a weirdo too. I hid my red, tear-streaked face from him, but of course he knew I'd been crying. There was no way he didn't. The thought made me weep even more. I shook hard as helplessness overtook me.

Moments passed where I could hear only the sound of my sobs and feel a warm hand on my back; a steady source of heat thawing my icebound heart. A thumb stroked my shoulder slowly, up and down. It was a comforting touch, and oddly intimate. I buried myself into silence.

Andy's voice broke through the walls of my muddled consciousness like lightning cracking the night sky. 'When the day is long...' he sang.

Oh... my God. His voice was incredible. Raspy, deep and soothing. I couldn't believe my ears.

There was a corner in my mind where I was still in control of myself, and that coherent part of me was stunned. The sound of his voice ran through me along with my blood.

I vaguely recognised the tune, a song by R.E.M., and though I remembered the notes going high and loud in the original version, Andy murmured through the verses as if not to disturb me, and then I was me again. My chest hurt and my heart, that had been drumming wildly, now thumped for a different reason; a warm emotion that I couldn't define enfolded me.

'You have the most beautiful voice I have ever heard. I mean it.'

Andy chuckled, worry casting a shadow over his smile. 'Do you think so? So, are you... are you feeling better?'

I sniffed. 'Yeah. Much better, ta. Just... uhm, my mouth is a bit dry, like.'

He patted my back. 'I'll go get you some water. I'll be right back. Won't be a sec.'

It was as if a huge bomb had exploded inside me and now all I could hear was a high-pitched ringing.

Andy sat next to me again a moment later, carrying a green tumbler which he handed over.

I sipped slowly and, after a few moments of silence, the urge to hide my face overwhelmed me. 'I... I am so sorry.'

He smiled. 'Why are you sorry? You've done nothing wrong.'

Shit, is he a saint, like? He must have been, or maybe an angel or something.

'I just have no control over this. I tried to sort myself out. I've been to a specialist but all he did was stuff me with meds that don't work. All they do is make me groggy and I'm no better than when it all started. I feel like life itself is weighing me down, and I can't... I can't breathe.'

I told him everything, starting with my mother's depression, my stepdad being diagnosed with cancer and his passing, followed by my gran's death. I recounted my lousy attempts to look after my siblings in their father's stead and explained my wish to move out and inability to do so, since my family needed me nearby.

'I can't even go to fuckin' Tesco if there's too many people inside. Pubs, clubs and restaurants are the worst, and forget going to gigs or the cinema... It really fucking sucks. I just want to hang out with people and do normal things like everyone else, innit. I'm scared I could have an episode at any time and I'm so fuckin' tired of being trapped in my own head, like. It's as if I'm drowning and there's never enough air for me to breathe, or enough water to actually die. It's like living in a fuckin' limbo.' My eyes filled with tears again. I was revealing things that I hadn't fully admitted even to myself. 'I feel as if I'm here but I'm not, ya know? I don't live. I just fuckin' *exist*.'

I'd never been one to offload on others and the realisation that I'd done exactly that with a dude who barely knew me made me feel exposed and embarrassed.

'Oh fuck,' I muttered, 'why am I telling you all this?'

Andy looked at me gravely. 'Hayden, I swear, you can talk to me about anything you want. You look like the kind of guy who keeps things to himself. You've been bottling it up, clearly. So please, don't worry. If you need to talk, I'll listen. I'm here for you mate, alright?'

I nodded and, before I could think about it twice, I bound him in a tight hug.

4

ANDY

I was done for. Hayden bared his soul to me, a stranger, and now my heart sorely ached for him.

He was so lost, vulnerable, though he came across as strong and self-assured – the kind of person who would easily shrug all worries off his shoulders. Instead, he harboured so much sadness and watching him cry had left me in pieces. I'd seen what he was going through in the past and knew how much solitude it brought.

Hayden had smiled at me sheepishly before leaving my house. 'I've never told anybody about all this. Shit, I sure need therapy, don't I?' He'd chuckled, but his smile didn't reach his eyes. 'Well, thank you for listening anyway. I feel much better now.'

When he walked through the front garden and waved at me while puffing on his cigarette, I knew that was it. I was falling for this guy. Hard and fast.

I met with my friend Tai Saturday afternoon, a week after my first meeting with Hayden, for a drink and a stroll. He was more than willing to hang out since he wanted a valet to accompany him on his shopping spree.

Tai was considered a bit of a guru amongst our friendship group and gave excellent advice, especially when it came to matters of the heart. He liked to put on a very unconvincing Chinese accent when he pronounced his pearls of wisdom. It was weird to hear a Chinese dude who spoke fluent Mandarin failing miserably at doing a stereotypical Chinese accent. Despite his ethnic background, Tai was more Welsh than a man eating a half-and-half while watching a rugby game.

My painful confession started in front of a mug of Earl Grey in Starbucks. 'So... I made friends with this really nice guy a week ago.'

Tai lifted his eyes from Grindr to purse his lips at me. 'Oh aye? Go on...'

'He's into the same stuff as me, you know,' I continued. 'Not only music, but also movies and video games. He's even read a lot of the same books I have! And we think alike.' I thought of Hayden's smiling face and my chest warmed. 'He makes synthwave as well, can you believe it? He's smart and he's... OK. Stunning-looking.' I let out the breath I didn't know I was holding.

Tai raised his eyebrows. 'And... he's a big gay, like you?'

'Uh, no. Straighter than an infinitely straight line.'

Tai laughed in that tinny way of his. 'Nobody's *that* straight love. Nobody.'

'He is. I'm positive.'

'Ewkay. So where's this conversation going?'

'Well, uh...' I sipped my tea. 'I guess I like him a bit? I dunno. Though I know I don't have a chance. And I should tell him I'm gay. I really should. I can't seem to find the right moment though.' I slurped my Earl Grey again, louder than necessary.

Gorillaz played in the café and I tapped along, accompanied by the harsh sound of steam from the espresso machine behind the counter and people babbling on about their lives, like we were.

'That's because you don't want to tell him,' Tai said. 'Are you scared he's going to hate you? What, is he a homophobe? Bit of a gay basher, is it?'

'No, not at all.' I shook my head to emphasise my words. I'd spoken long and often enough with Hayden to know he was very open minded. 'But you know how difficult it is for me to come out to my straight friends.'

'He'll find out eventually, babe. Might as well say it sooner rather than later?'

'Thing is,' I scrambled to find the words, 'we are really close already. Like, *really* close. We talk on the phone and message all the time. It's weird.'

Tai's eyes narrowed. 'Hmmm... all the time, like how? Come on. Spill to Tai.'

'Like, all the time. He sends me good morning texts with links to music I might like, stuff like that. Today we've been messaging non-stop since we woke up, and we spent an entire night on the phone talking about 28 *Days Later, Shaun of the Dead* and *From Dusk till Dawn*. Literally, from dusk till dawn.'

Tai squinted at me from behind his cappuccino cup. 'Yeeah. OK. That's weird.'

I took a bite of my flapjack. 'Yep.'

'Are you sure he isn't gay? I mean, to spend the whole night talking to you like that... That's not something straight blokes do with friends they just met. He probably wants your willy, babe.'

I groaned. 'Really though?'

'Maybe he just wants a mate. Is he lonely?'

'I think so.'

'It still doesn't explain why you're hiding the fact that you're gay.'

I sighed and raked my fringe. 'There's chemistry between us. I've never felt this connected to someone before. If I tell him that I'm gay, it's going to be on the table that I might be interested in him, seeing as I go along with his constant ping-pong of texts and calls.

And I don't want to make things weird.'

'But *you do* have a romantic interest though, yeah?'

I sighed again. 'I totally do. But I don't want to break the perfect balance we have. I'm so happy to have met a person like him. It was almost like fate, you know? When I get over the... uhh...'

'Crush? Sticky fantasies?'

'Y-yeah. I'll tell him then.'

Tai took a deep breath and let the wise-man voice roll out of his lips in all its contrived charm. 'First tenet of the Gay Bible: *Never fall for a straight guy.* It's only going to end badly for you. They're all the same. They don't know their arse from their elbow.' With that, Tai went back to flicking through pictures of men on his phone.

He'd just had a haircut and his black hair looked sleek, the curve of a perfect undercut fixed with a good spread of barber powder. I always thought, since he was a really good-looking guy, that he could afford to be as cocksure as he wanted.

I stirred my Earl Grey for no reason other than to keep my hands busy. 'What can I do? He's so amazing.'

'Mmhmm.' Tai turned his phone around. 'What ya reckon?'

The bloke he was looking at on Grindr was tanned, with a sculpted body and sunglasses.

'Not bad,' I mumbled, nibbling on my flapjack.

Tai chuckled. 'This is a definite *yes fucking please.* Anyway, have you got a picture?'

'A picture?

He rolled his eyes. 'Of the guy, silly.'

'No,' I replied, gulping down my last bit of tea.

'What about Facebook? Insta?'

'He's got no pictures of himself anywhere.'

'*Ahh,* he's one of those weirdos. I'm dying of curiosity now!'

'I'll introduce you some day.'

Tai smiled mischievously. 'Good. I need to scan him with my Taidar.'

I groaned. 'Still going on about that Taidar thing? You can't just look at someone and guess their sexual orientation. Come on, that's ridiculous!'

Tai batted his lashes innocently. 'And you can?'

'Look,' I said impatiently, 'he's Cynthia's ex-boyfriend *and* a known womaniser. Hear the word? *Woman-eyes-uh.*'

Tai gasped. 'The plot thickens! Also, the fact that he shags loads of women means fuck-all in this day and age, babe. Everyone's at it.'

I purposefully ignored his comment. 'He's so... incredibly... straight. I mean, most men are. It's always best to assume someone is straight rather than not. It's just maths.'

'Yeah, can't fault your logic, but my Taidar—'

'He's straight. End of,' I said, cutting him short.

I stared at my empty cup of tea and sighed. It'd been five days since Hayden and I last saw each other. Since then, I'd been dreaming about him almost every night, when we weren't awake talking, in not exactly innocent scenarios, although most of the time I struggled sleeping because my heart was beating too fast from the excitement. I'd slammed my head on the pillow every morning because I was being a complete idiot. This crush was not going to go anywhere. I distracted myself by walking through the town aimlessly, enabling my friend to lead me around instead.

Tai and I left the café and went for a walk. The Saturday buzz invaded St. Mary Street but, since Christmas had just passed, people were in no rush to go shopping and ambled around town.

The weather was undecided; sunlight poked through a cluster of fat, grey clouds that sputtered meagre droplets of rain as halfheartedly as my father gave compliments to his children.

A group of loud girls walked into us, and I almost crashed over a huge plant pot to avoid them. Tai did the complaining for me.

'Shall we go through the arcades, hun? I want to check out that vintage shop I told you about. It. Is. Fabulous,' he said, still glaring at the drunk girls behind us.

I followed Tai like a sad puppy. The truth was that Hayden had asked me to hang out tomorrow and I was both happy and worried about it. He had wondered if he could run some of his new stuff through my 'sweet equipment', and dang if that line didn't make my face heat up when it came from his lips. He apologised and said that in a different situation he would have asked me to go somewhere else, but with his current state of mind he simply couldn't bear crowded areas for long.

'The park is one of the few places where I can go without worrying, like. Busy spaces set me off a lot of the time,' he told me on the phone the night before. 'I can't avoid going to work innit, but it's as if my head knows that I can't do without money and so I don't flip out there. It's really weird.'

As for me, being alone in a room with him was going to be a problem. If I liked a guy, I was Mister Obvious and the last thing I wanted was to make things awkward. It was clear that Hayden needed a friend and, if friendship was all he wanted from me, that's what I would give.

Thinking about it, this wasn't the first time I'd fallen for a straight guy. I mean, who hasn't? One time that often came to mind was an infatuation I had during my first year in uni. The guy was chatty and cute, and I... well, I needed love. I'd blush like a timid schoolboy and smile, perhaps even gawk at him more often than I should. Of course he'd been weirded out. I was nineteen at the time and it took me *ages* to get over it. Once he found out I was gay, probably after asking around about me, our friendship was pretty much over.

The uni guy had nothing on Hayden, though, not even remotely close. Hayden was way more... everything. Smart, playful, thoughtful, funny and... *argh!* I was so scared of ruining the amazing thing we had going. Perhaps I didn't want to pop my bubble of hope just yet. I wasn't ready to hear I didn't have a chance, stupid as it was to delay the moment of truth.

Once in the vintage shop, Tai chatted ecstatically as he rummaged through a rack of denim jackets and furry coats. He was a proud and flamboyant everyone-knows-that-I'm-gay-right-away kind of guy.

It was a little different for me. I was more on the masculine side when it came to my fashion choices and didn't really like anything too girly, flashy or revealing. The same applied for my taste in most things. I guess my parents didn't expect a kid who liked playing with mini-bikes, watching martial arts and horror movies and who was obsessed with Batman, to also appreciate cock. I mean, Batman wasn't my hero as such, rather my earliest spank-bank protagonist. I mean, just *look* at those abs! And the deep, commanding voice? The mysterious dark aura? Thanks, Christian Bale, for making me realise how totally gay I am.

As Tai pirouetted and cat-walked through the shop, wearing a black and purple feather boa and teardrop-shaped sunglasses, I imagined once again what it would be like if Hayden and I had sex. Most straight guys who slept with dudes on a whim preferred topping, for obvious reasons, and so I expected Hayden to be the same. Also, he had a dominant, masculine air about him. Even with girls, I pictured him always being in control – pulling their hair with his big hands and pounding fast and hard. *Sigh.* I would have been a very happy bottom then. Not that he would *ever* have sex with me, aside from in my fantasies.

Tai tried on several hats and an out-of-place mesh top while I daydreamed of a scenario where Hayden pushed me against the wall and fucked me senseless, while whispering my name in my ear...

'Andy? Oi oi!'

I turned around and stumbled backward, almost falling over a rack of dresses and taking it down with me. It was incredible that my eyes didn't pop out of their sockets from the shock.

'Jesus Christ!' I yapped.

Hayden was there, grinning like me almost falling was the funniest thing he'd ever seen. 'I saw you from outside. I didn't know you were into vintage fashion.' Clearly, he was trying his hardest not to laugh at me.

'I-I'm not! My friend wanted to come here. What about you?'

He pointed at the right side of the arcade with his thumb. 'I work in an electronics shop. Didn't I tell you?'

'Ah! Near here? I didn't realise.' I could not believe this.

He raised an eyebrow. 'You sure you're not a stalker now?'

'I swear to God, I had no idea! If I were, I would be a pretty shit stalker, wouldn't I?' Needless to say, my face was on fire and my heart was beating a mile a minute. He was actually there, in front of me!

'Nah, not very stealthy,' he chuckled. 'I'm on my lunch break. Fancy getting something to eat?'

'Uhm...' I glanced around, searching for my friend.

Tai appeared in all his glory, wearing a neat black hat, waistcoat and sparkling scarf.

'Oh, hello there!' He visibly blinked, double-taking at Hayden's impressive appearance. He glanced at me, his wide eyes saying it all – *Who's this hot piece of ass?*

I bristled with tension. 'Hayden, this is Tai.'

'How's it going, mate?' Hayden offered his hand for a fist bump.

Tai smiled. I could see the cogs in his brain working; he was probably coming up with some cunning plan. They awkwardly fist-bumped and I hurried to break the silence.

'Hayden is on his lunch break. Would it be alright if I went with him? Just to, you know, catch up?'

'I don't mind if Tai wants to come with us. I don't want to get in the way like, if you've got plans,' Hayden said.

'No! No plans, no plans at all, babe!' Tai batted his lashes, mischief painted all over his face.

'Cool. There's a place nearby where they make really good coffee and amazing sandwiches. You'll love it,' Hayden said as he led the way.

While he wasn't looking, I turned to give Tai a warning look. My friend widened his eyes and gave me the most astonished look ever, mouthing, 'Oh my God!'

***

Hayden took us to a fancy café, found a deserted corner and threw his rucksack on a chair. The place was empty except for a short queue at the counter. An old jazz piece played in the background.

Tai grumbled because the café wasn't well-heated, probably the reason why nobody stayed there long – and why Hayden liked it. Even in a peaceful place like this, Hayden was uncomfortable. He glanced at the little crowd by the till nervously, trying to muster the courage to join the queue.

I took the initiative. 'I'll go order. What did you guys want?' Hayden looked surprised and a little uneasy. 'You sure?'

I raised an eyebrow and brought out our most recent private joke to help him relax his nerves. 'Yep. Latte for you, almighty Hades?'

He huffed a laugh and even blushed a little. 'Uh, yeah. I was going to grab a sandwich but uh, I don't know what they have on today...'

Tai scrutinised us, eyes flicking between Hayden and me. 'Why don't you both go? Cappuccino for me, Andy, and a chocolate cookie,' he grinned.

Hayden and I went to join the queue. It was cold enough that we both felt the need to keep our coats on. Maybe it was my imagination, but Hayden looked a little embarrassed. Perhaps it was the way he evaded my gaze and scratched his nose.

'What you having?' he asked.

'Tea and something light to eat? I don't know.'

Hayden chuckled. 'How very *refined*. What are you, an English prince?'

'I thought *you* were the English one here.' Hayden raised an eyebrow and I hurried to add, 'You've got a bit of an accent.'

His smile faltered. 'I suppose I am English if you consider that I was born and grew up in Southampton. My mum and all her family are Welsh, though. I moved to Cardiff when I was ten.'

'Oh really? How come you left England?'

Hayden's expression darkened. 'Long story.'

I cleared my throat. 'Do you miss Southampton?'

He scoffed. 'Nope. Not in the slightest.'

We chatted about our past for a while. Or, rather, *my* past. He was surprised to find out that, though I'd grown up in Cardiff, I had Irish origins and was born in Limerick.

'Both your parents are Irish?'

I grinned. 'Yeah.'

'Well, you have the looks for sure. Dark hair, blue eyes,

freckles... Do you know who you remind me of? That Murphy guy from *Peaky Blinders.*'

I laughed. 'You mean a poor copy of Cillian Murphy.'

'No.' He studied my face with a serious expression. 'You're better-looking than him. More delicate, like.'

'Thanks.' I urged my heart to slow down but a blush quickly slinked up my neck and cheeks. I knew his words meant nothing. I was fooling myself if I gave them a second thought, but darn it if Hayden wasn't sending mixed signals!

We returned to our table with a tray. Tai took his cookie and loaded his cappuccino with sugar while Hayden took a huge bite of his chicken cutlet, aubergine, cheese and lettuce ciabatta. I'd gone for a chicken cutlet salad that looked fancy.

It was so freaking cold in here that my fingers had gone numb, plus Hayden's presence next to me made me all tense and fidgety. While my friends enjoyed their meals, I was there fumbling with the vinegar sachets that came with my salad.

'You should open it from the side, not the top innit,' Hayden said.

I attempted to do as he suggested but failed, feeling so embarrassed that I couldn't refrain from making a cutting remark. 'My hands are frozen, that's why and... *argh!* These sachets are crap!'

'Here, let me.' He opened the sachets for me with an easy nonchalance and poured the vinegar on my salad.

Tai smirked and glanced at Hayden. 'You should toss his salad as well, now that you're at it.'

I almost choked on my tea. Hayden looked at me with a worried frown. 'Is it really that cold? Sorry for bringing you here.'

'No,' I half-wheezed, half-coughed. 'He's joking. Just ignore him.' I glared at Tai with all my furious might, but he just smiled like the Cheshire Cat.

A new jazz piece started in the background and Hayden went on about the ingenuity of the tune and the precision of the drums. Luckily, the sexual reference had been lost in translation. After a while, Hayden's phone alarm went off.

'Oh, time's up. See you tomorrow.' He fist-bumped me and patted my shoulder, then slap-shook Tai's hand.

'Bye Hayd!' I called behind him.

He parted from us with a smile but his back looked stiff and his cheeks flushed. Poor Hayden; even going to the café for a sandwich was a struggle for him.

I made sure he was gone before turning to Tai with a glower. 'You son of a bitch.'

Tai burst out laughing. 'He didn't get it, come on! It was funny.'

'Funny my ass!' I grumbled.

'Exactly! Give your ass some *fun*, honeybunny!' he said, wiggling his eyebrows.

I sighed. 'Well?'

'Well what?' Tai's eyes went back to his phone.

'What does your Taidar say? Go on, just put me out of my misery. *He's straight. End. Of.*'

Tai's jaw dropped. 'Hang on now. You mean Hayden was the guy you were on about?'

'Yeah. I thought you'd guessed.'

He stared at me in shock. '*Whaaaaat?* And he just showed up by chance?'

'I know, I couldn't believe it either. It's crazy coincidences one after another with him.'

Tai started counting on his fingers. 'So, let's have a think now. Let Tai break it down for you, babe. He messages you often and spends whole nights chatting on the phone with you. He invites you for dinner at his house, even though he barely knows you. He sends you cwtchy good morning texts, for heaven's sake! I mean, who needs a Taidar to guess it? Ask that chair over there. If it could speak it'd agree with me. He's *tooootally* and I mean *totally* into you.'

I bit my knuckles. 'But all this stuff could be interpreted either way.'

Tai sighed. 'Andy, open your eyes, for fuck's sake!'

'But... but...'

He rolled his eyes. 'Oh. My. God. You're unbelievable. The guy opened your vinegar sachets! All tender, like. What is he, your boyfriend or wha? He ignored me all this time and only had eyes for you. I'm not being funny but he was like... mesmerised. I was looking at the two of you queuing and gazing at each other lovingly, smiling at the same time, standing the same way... what's that called? Ah! Synchronising!'

'*What?* No way! It happens with friends too.'

Tai opened his hands. 'I was thinking, "Why is Andy wasting his time with a straight guy when he's got this hot piece of ass after him?" Seriously hun, I have no doubt that he's into you. There's nothing to misinterpret. The Taidar has spoken. That guy? *Not straight.* He'd bone you in an instant. Bet he's shit-hot in the sack too.'

'But there's nothing to... *confirm* these suppositions either. Some people are very friendly, you know. I think he's so nice to me because we share interests.'

Tai crossed his arms and leaned back in his chair. 'OK, let's make a bet. If he doesn't whip out his cock for you next time you're alone together, I will give you two hundred of our finest pounds.'

'Lower your voice!' I said even though there was no one around.

'If he does, I want you to go with me to The Golden Cross in drag.' He grinned mischievously. 'I'll choose the outfit and Crystal will do your makeup. Deal?'

'W-what!' I sputtered. 'Look, it's not going to happen! The... cock-whipping thing, I mean.'

Tai smirked. 'You look very confident that he's not interested in you, so why not accept?' He stretched his perfectly manicured fingers. 'Two hundred quid. Not a bad offer.'

I bit my lip. After a moment of hesitation, I shook his hand. 'Deal!'

5

HAYDEN

I staggered back to work, unable to take in what just happened.

My boss, James, smiled at me from behind the counter and a pyramid of vintage mini-radios, his dutifully trimmed moustache forming a seamless curve. 'It's about time! Come on, Hayden. I'm dying for a fag.'

I was left alone in the shop to deal with my jumbled thoughts. 'You Can't Hurry Love' played in the background, the happy tune mocking my confounded state.

The moment I spotted Andy by a rack of colourful clothes, looking lost in thought, my heart almost beat out of my chest in surprise.

It hadn't stopped thumping since then and, even though it was barely two degrees outside, my body burned hot. I couldn't even blame these feelings on the anxiety. The realisation had come to me full-throttle: Andy was most probably gay and maybe, just *maybe*, was into me.

I slumped on the counter, buried my face in the crook of my arm and exhaled a long breath.

I happened to know what 'tossing the salad' meant and damn, my relationship with Andy had taken on a whole new meaning because of it. I had to be downright idiotic not to pick up on the signs that something was brewing.

Andy's face had turned bright red at Tai's not-so-subtle suggestion and I got all flustered too, only I had been able to hide it. I congratulated myself for how smoothly I handled the situation by feigning total ignorance, though I was pretty sure my knees were buckling as I left the café.

Tai was blatantly queer and perhaps he found it funny to put Andy on the spot, seeing that he and I were obviously close. I guessed I wasn't supposed to get the joke because I was the dumb straight guy or something. But I wasn't dumb and perhaps I wasn't completely straight either.

During the last week or so I never questioned the nature of the happiness I felt after opening my eyes in the morning... Until last night.

***

I'd called Andy on the spur of the moment on Friday evening, around eight o'clock.

The phone rang long enough for me to get all tense and, before I could tell myself how much of a tit I was for calling him out of the blue, Andy's warm voice came through the line.

'What's up, Hayd?'

I laughed. 'I like that. Or you could go ahead and call me Hades, like the Greek god of the underworld. I'm all dark like that. See? Smooth, this time. Like fucking velvet.'

Andy snorted, 'Well done you!'

The fact that I was trying to impress him the same way I did when I hit on girls should have been a clue. That was the thing, though: *I wasn't thinking.*

We got into the zone of awesomeness right away; that's how it was with Andy. We went from talking about what we had for dinner, to the macabre scenario of having to eat the severed head of the pig in *Lord of the Flies.* Andy and I tried to decide which seasoning would mask the rotten flavour best.

We eventually started talking about our music. Andy had sampled the sound effect of the 'Continue' button from *Sonic 3.* He was using a slowed-down version of it to make a tune and told me he'd share the piece with me as soon as it was finished. The conversation went on and on.

'Fuck, it's already half past twelve!' I said, noticing the time on my computer screen. 'Have we been talking all this time, like?'

Andy yawned. 'Yeah. I don't think I can pull another all-nighter.'

'I've got work at eight tomorrow,' I said regretfully.

'Then go to sleep dude.'

Andy's voice sounded groggy and there was a rustle of blankets.

'Are you already in bed?' I asked.

'Yeah, I'm knackered. I've been working on my thesis all day but it's like I'm plucking my nose hairs one by one. It's a painful process. Anyway, my duvet is all messed up.' I could hear him fumbling with it on the phone. 'The padding is all on one side, like.'

I chuckled. 'Do you want me to come tuck you in?' I said it before I could think better of it.

'Yeah, sure,' Andy replied sleepily. 'I like it when it's tucked under my butt. I mean, the duvet. Sorry I'm talking shit 'cause I'm tired. Speak soon. Night, Hayd!'

'Night.'

Andy hung up. His words had conjured a flurry of dirty thoughts that would not shut up. The image of my cock tucked under his naked arse was flashing in my head like an intro to breaking news. I stood up and wobbled to my bed. Holy Christ, I was fucking rock hard!

Sitting on the edge of the mattress, I stared at my rigid dick poking my pyjamas and swallowed with a dry throat.

'OK,' I told myself. 'This just happened.'

I got into bed, still hard, and lay still on my back, too freaked out to do something about it. Sleep took care of things, though my mind went to the places where my hand didn't dare stray.

Andy invaded my dreams all night. He'd stretch his plump lips around my shaft, taking me deep and looking up at me with big, pleading blue eyes as he slobbered all over my cock. Then it was me sucking him or rubbing my erection against his. The porn-worthy fantasy ended with me pressing Andy's head against the mattress as I fucked him, pummelling him as if I meant to break the poor thing. All in all, it was a blur of utter filth.

It wasn't over though. New dreams came upon me, progressing like a rosy slideshow. Andy and I would be kissing by the beach, the sun setting in a spectacle of orange and pink that reflected on the waves. I could hear his voice and laughter in my head as if it was real. He'd blush after I told him he was cute, and would let me bury my face in the warmth of his neck.

When I opened my eyes on Saturday morning, I wasn't smiling. Instead, I slapped my face and groaned for a good ten seconds. My cock was up before I was. There was no way in hell I could ignore the signs.

I had a crush. On a dude.

I'd only ever dated girls before, but I knew deep inside that guys could be a turn-on too, occasionally. It was rare for me to be interested in men though, and I tended to suppress those feelings, telling myself that fancying a guy could get me in trouble. In fact, it was so uncommon for me to feel attracted to a man that sometimes I forgot I might want to swing that way. I'd ended up convincing myself that it had been a phase all along.

It was as if my libido was laughing at me now. I wasn't all about the pink; there was a tad bit of blue in my spectrum too...

'Purple,' I murmured, burying my face into the pillow and groaning.

***

What now? Does he like me too? Do I have a chance? The questions floated through my head all afternoon as I ripped boxes and priced some newly delivered items.

Concentrating on my work was difficult since Andy's pretty face kept appearing in my head like a shining poster. *Yes, he is cute.* Sue me. In fact, *gorgeous* was a more fitting term. I had thought that the very first moment we'd met, but had parked the notion at the back of my brain. His blue eyes were bright, big and expressive, his freckles adorable, his skin smooth and his mouth nicely shaped with white, perfect teeth. He was kind of girly with his constant blushing, soft laughter and delicate features, but that's where his feminine traits ended. He had a deep, warm voice, strong eyebrows, a lean body and good muscle definition.

I was distracted by my thoughts to the point that I almost fell face-down on the floor after tripping on a wire. In an attempt not to tumble to the ground, I held on to the counter edge and, to my horror, dropped an expensive retro gramophone. Thank fuck it was in a box packed with polystyrene and survived the impact unharmed.

I was still restless by the time I got home. I bolted up the stairs and went straight to my room, barely saying a word of greeting to Iwan and Mum who were watching the telly in the lounge.

Once in my room, I threw my rucksack and coat on the bed, locked the door and sat at the computer. I took a long, steadying breath.

I mustered the courage to type gay porn in my browser. I clicked on the first link. PornHub and an all-you-can-eat platter of options appeared on my screen. My choice landed on a video titled, 'Hot stud rims cute twink and fucks his tight ass bareback'.

I frowned. *What the fuck's a twink?*

Even though I wasn't sure what I was getting into, I clicked on the video since one of the two guys in the thumbnail looked remarkably like Andy. He was somewhat willowy, with an elegant air and light skin. He also had a spread of messy brown hair like the object of my fantasies, as well as his slender neck.

I swallowed hard as the Andy-lookalike started to make out with a muscular guy who helped him take off his clothes eagerly. The bigger bloke pushed him down on his knees and made him suck his cock with a forceful hand. My nostrils flared and my dick, already stirring and pulsing in my jeans, sprung up. I began to stroke myself lazily over the fabric, my eyes glued to the screen. After several minutes of the slim guy slurping on the other man's stiff cock, things got even hotter...

The big dude spread the dark-haired guy's legs apart and stuck his tongue up his arse. He was properly going for it, licking and dipping into the guy's hole tirelessly. The dark-haired guy threw his head back and moaned.

I sat back in the chair with a hanging mouth. This shit was hot! I had eaten ass before, but never a guy's. The idea of Andy panting and moaning as I feasted on his hole felt like the birth of the universe – a big boom of potential.

'Oh yeah, fuck yeah...' I unzipped my trousers and let my cock out before it could start screaming at me. It was hard and dripping with pre-cum, and my balls were growing tighter by the second.

As I stroked my cock I realised that, even though it felt good and all, something was missing. The dark-haired guy was good-looking but lacked the gentleness and warmth that Andy had in his eyes.

Heat crept up my face as I paused the porn video and opened Andy's Facebook page. Even though I was alone, this whole situation was nothing less than embarrassing. I had never wanked while looking at a picture of a friend before. Not to brag but, normally, I got to fuck every girl I liked without having to resort to jerking off over their photo. However, in Andy's case, I wanted to prod my feelings a little further before voicing the final verdict on my infatuation.

There was a particular photo in his summer album that I had leered over before and then told myself there was nothing unusual about staring at your friend's bare chest for five minutes straight. Andy had subtle abs, a narrow waist and small, light-brown nipples. In the pic he wore a pair of dark swim trunks and stood by a wall of rocks. He smiled broadly at the camera, one hand on his hip and the other holding a bottle of Beck's.

I drank in his body and bit my lower lip. My wank resumed, fast and furious. I whacked my dick and imagined I was going to spill over Andy's flawless skin...

My phone chimed, making me yelp and jump up in surprise. I now realised how tense I'd been while jerking off; my heart hammered in my throat and my forehead was beaded with sweat.

Seeing Andy's name on the phone only emphasised my vague feeling of shame. He'd sent me an email.

'*I just finished polishing my new track, the one with the Sonic 3 sample. Let me know what you think!*'

There was a WeTransfer link and I clicked on it. The piece was called 'NoNameYet' and I pressed play, my erection deflating.

I connected my phone to the speakers and set the tune on a high volume. A low, slow baseline filled the room. It was a relaxing sound that made me think of a magical trek through space. The *Sonic 3* sample was a subtle element in the background that had been tied to the other sounds seamlessly. I smiled. Not only was Andy amazing-looking but he was also smart, funny, kind and talented; an all-round incredible person.

My eyes went back to the seaside picture. Andy's smile was like the bashful grin of someone beautiful but who didn't really know it.

The vaporwave beats ran through my body and the hushed sounds of a fading synth trickled down my spine like warm water.

I went back to touching myself, imagining Andy standing next to me. I pictured him smiling with embarrassment and lifting his T-shirt just because I'd asked him to. He'd caress his abdomen and reach down into his trousers and waistband of his boxers...

'Oh,' I groaned. Percussion and cadenced beats gave a rhythm to the movements of my hand.

In my fantasy, Andy was stripping for me, taking off his zip hoodie and *Knight Rider* T-shirt, the one I saw him wearing that morning. His hair would get dishevelled after the fabric of his top slipped over his head and he'd give me a heated look as he tossed his clothes aside. I could see the bulge of his dick under his trousers and Andy would unzip them for me, to give me a better look. With slow, teasing movements he'd let his erection bounce free, leaking with desire. The music slammed into me and I writhed in the seduction of that image.

I wanted to feel the shape of his ass and rub my cock against his, pump us both with a lube-drenched hand, lick his chest, hold one of his nipples between my lips...

Would he hold on to me as I brought us both to climax? Would he kiss me and whisper my name against my cheek? I'd push my cock deep inside him to make him mine.

The music dropped. A minor curve, a change of tone, an open sound.

I came hard, and a load of cum squirted in my fist.

'Holy fuck!' I wheezed as my heartbeat thrummed in my ears.

Well, if I had any doubts before, they were gone now; I would have more than willingly tossed his goddamn salad!

The track was over and I sat back on the chair, swimming through the afterglow of the crazy orgasm I just had.

I spent a few minutes wiping my fingers and abs sluggishly with a couple of crumpled tissues. Once clarity returned, I asked myself once more: *What now?*

***

Around eleven o'clock I made myself a late cup of coffee and reflected some more. *So what if I like a dude? Whatever! I've had so much crap tossed my way from girls recently, that maybe a change of scenery is due.*

I made peace with myself, in a way, and accepted that things were the way they were and there wasn't much I could do about it. At least when it came to what my cock wanted, I was zen. I was into Andy and I was more than fine with it.

How long had we known each other? A week or so? And we'd only met three times! A week had been enough for me to bust a nut to this guy.

I crunched on a digestive biscuit and laughed to myself. If I thought about it, I had to admit that I liked Andy a lot, maybe more than I'd ever liked anyone else.

Even though I acknowledged my feelings, knowing how to go about making them real was another matter altogether.

Should I make a move on him? How should I hit on a dude? Is it the same as hitting on a girl?

The blurry memory of a pseudo-experiment with a male classmate in Year Eleven came to mind. We were good friends who wanked together sometimes and played video games afterwards. That wasn't a good comparison though, because what I wanted with Andy was totally different. I wanted us to be close, and this was completely uncharted territory for me.

I brought a hand to my face and dug my fingers into my cheek, saying aloud, 'Fuck. I don't know what I'm going to do.'

My phone chimed again. It was Andy and my heart skipped a beat.

'Did you listen to the track?'

Before I could reply, I received a second text.

'I mean, no rush.'

I smiled and tapped out a reply. *'Yeah, I did. It went beyond my expectations.'*

'Lol, what the hell does that mean?'

'It was amazing. You're proper talented.'

'Thank you!' He sent a smiling emoji.

'I noticed you don't have a title for the track yet.'

'No. Any ideas?'

I thought about it, although the words already danced over my lips. It was cheesy but described well how I felt about us. *'Synchronised Hearts.'*

As I waited for Andy's answer, I made up my mind. I was going to his house the following day and, once we were alone and the timing was right, I would just go for it. It was very possible that he liked me too. All I lacked was knowledge on gay sex, aside from the basics. I had the feeling that there was more than simple in-and-out of the dick involved, and I wasn't one who could stand being unprepared when it came to these things. I would do the most thorough internet research of my life and hope for the best.

Andy didn't reply to my message right away. I waited for a long ten minutes before my phone chimed again.

'Perfect title for a vaporwave track. I guess it does have a bit of a romantic vibe to it. Anyway, I'm going to jump in the bath. See you tomorrow!'

I stared at the screen. Did he just... bail off? Shit, did I misread things? I shook my head. I couldn't let my uncertainty get in the way: a decision had been made, and I wasn't going to hesitate. The idea of trying something with a guy was both scary and exciting.

I just hoped I wouldn't fuck it all up.

6

ANDY

It was ten to five on Sunday and I was impossibly nervous. I adjusted my hair in front of the mirror and, noticing how stupid I was acting, I dropped my hands to the sides. I frowned: why was I fooling myself? I was getting all worked up for nothing.

All the things Tai had told me the day before haunted me. What if Hayden *did* find me sexually attractive? Yeah, *as if.*

'Synchronised Hearts,' I murmured. I almost fell off the bed when I read it last night.

'Stop getting your hopes up, you waste of space!' I told my reflection.

I decided that Tai was right – I had to tell Hayden I was gay. Today. *If Hayden won't accept me, he isn't going to be worth my while.*

I honestly didn't think he'd care, but even the smallest possibility of rejection made my heart ache and twist. Yet it was a risk I had to take. Perhaps being open about my sexuality might be the only way to put an end to his unintended flirtations.

I'd made sure the house was well-heated before Hayden arrived. The fridge brimmed with beer and food. I'd gone to the shop in the morning and bought crisps and cheese savouries, as well as interesting snacks like seaweed crackers and cinnamon and maple popcorn.

I'd showered, shaved and spritzed some aftershave just in case Hayden happened to come close and smell me. *Because that's what friends do; they sniff each other!* I was officially an idiot. I put on a grey sweatshirt with the flux capacitor from *Back to the Future* on it, and fresh jeans from the dryer.

The plan was to work on some tunes, hang out and watch A *Clockwork Orange* which, to Hayden's astonishment, I had never seen.

It's like a date, my treacherous mind suggested. I banged my head on the cushioned armrest of the sofa in the lounge, forgetting that there was a sturdy wood frame underneath. My phone rang and my heart flipped in my chest.

When I saw who the caller was, I groaned. 'Hello Mum?'

'Happy to hear you're alive, ye little gomie!' she said, greeting me with a chuckle.

'What do you mean? I called you four days ago.'

'But ye said ye were going to ring me on Sunday, did ya not? Doesn't the dishwasher need replacing? I thought we were going out together today to buy a new one.'

I'd completely forgotten about it.

I sighed. 'I'm going to sort that out at some point this week, Mum. I'll get one online or something.'

'*What?* You should *look* at what ye're buying in person, eejit, not simply choose it from an online catalogue. Go out and peruse, for heaven's sake! Ye're always stuck in that house, mup out of it already!'

Just then, the doorbell rang.

'Mum I've gotta go. My friend's here.'

'Friend? What friend?'

I opened the door and let Hayden in.

'Hey...' he began, but my mum was still squawking on the phone.

'Mum, I'm going to hang up. I'll call you tomorrow, alright?'

'Is this friend yer lover? Is that why you're rushing?'

'A mate! Just a mate, OK? Jeez...'

She hung up, and I stared at the phone in shock. *A good start to the afternoon!*

Hayden grinned, and I'd almost forgotten just how fine he was. He wore a camo denim jacket under his coat and a dark-purple top with a really cool print; there was a blushing, cutesy smiling face on his chest and, underneath, a word in a chubby orange font: SATAN.

I inhaled deeply and wished Hayden was a little less my type. Instead, he was perfect from head to toe.

I reminded myself of my resolve for the day and cleared my throat. 'Sorry about that.'

'No worries.' He kept on smirking.

'What?'

'Did you know that when you get angry, your Irish accent comes out?'

'No, it doesn't!'

He laughed. 'It so does!'

How was I ever going to pretend I didn't like this guy?

We went upstairs to my mixing room. I put on an amazing 'Knife Party' remix by Purity Ring for Hayden who hadn't listened to it yet. As he sat back in the chair to watch the video, bobbing his head to the engrossing bass and slow beat, I popped downstairs to get us a drink.

When I got back, I found him wearing a concentrated expression and my Sennheisers on his ears. As always, he listened to everything twice: once through speakers and once with headphones.

'Wow,' he said as he watched the music video playing on the computer.

'Told you!' I beamed. 'These guys should do a whole remix

album. Nobody else has managed to make anything on this level.'

I handed him a cup of coffee and sat next to him. For a change, I enjoyed sipping grape-flavoured pop instead of the usual Earl Grey.

'These guys really get the Deftones' sound. As...' Hayden waved a hand in the air as he thought of the right words, 'they picked up on the idea behind the track, and reinterpreted it really well, like.'

I nodded. 'Yeah, I mean, their stuff is really good too. Have you heard any of their songs?'

He shook his head and lifted the cup to his lips. 'No... Mmm, this coffee is amazing, fair play.'

My body reacted when I heard him hum with pleasure. 'Glad you like it.'

I closed my legs a bit and compelled my heart to slow the fuck down.

'I have something for you to listen to as well,' he said. 'Headphones? The over-ear ones would work best, I think.'

I knew which pair he was referring to. I connected them to the audio input and he stood up, grabbed them and placed them on my head. His fingers brushed my cheeks for a moment longer than was socially acceptable. As he positioned the headphones over my ears, a choked sound escaped my throat.

'Good boy. Now listen carefully,' I overheard him say.

His skin on mine had felt incredible.

He put on a track on YouTube from a female artist I'd never heard of, Meg Myers. Right away the piece was enthralling. It was a reworking of Kate Bush's song, 'Running Up That Hill', complete with a full-on eighties vibe. The drums had a clean, engaging rhythm that accompanied the prolonged notes of the synth and open sounds. The passionate singing voice, the tune and the colourful, unique music video were a winning combination. I turned to look at Hayden to show appreciation with my eyes and found him staring at me intently, his thumb tracing the seam of his mouth.

Gosh, this is torture.

Once the track was over, I took off the headphones. 'Incredible! I have to admit I prefer this to the original. Don't call the music police on me for saying that though.'

'Yeah, I prefer it too,' Hayden said.

His eyes were still on me and his gaze intense.

I chewed on my lip, hard. 'What's up? You're staring at me, dude.'

Hayden stretched his arm and reached for my face. My breath caught in my throat as his fingers brushed my fringe.

He looked away. 'You had a bit of fluff. I'm going to the bathroom a sec. Won't be a min.'

'OK,' I muttered.

He rushed out of the room and I sagged on the light wood of my desk, hitting the spacebar of the keyboard with my forehead.

Was I wrong or was Hayden acting weird? Did he have any idea of the effect he had on me? He must have! The sexual tension was palpable, for Christ's sake! Maybe my mind was playing tricks on me... but no. *What was that just now?* I had to tell him I was gay, and as soon as possible.

I tried to regain my composure before he came back, but I found it virtually impossible; my legs shook from the nerves. I thought of something neutral to talk about to calm the waters before throwing the gay bombshell at him. Well, mostly *my* waters. I had a synthesiser that I wasn't really making use of, a Waldorf Nave. Perhaps Hayden might have a use for it.

The door opened suddenly and he strode in with an odd frown on his face. My heart leapt. I stood, my knees weak and barely holding me up. 'Hayden, I was thinking—'

I never got to offer him my Nave.

Hayden was on me. His hands enclosed my face and his open mouth landed on mine. My brain disconnected. I automatically responded to the movements of his tongue and the unexpected feel of his wet warmth overwhelmed me.

Hayden's hands moved down my ass briskly and squeezed, pulling me against his groin where his dick was hard and straining. I gasped against his lips. *Holy Christ, what the heck was happening?*

I held on to the fabric of his camo jacket to avoid collapsing, my legs wobblier than ever. He continued to press his lips to mine, his tongue alternating between teasing and scouring deep. Although the sensation was beyond amazing, my brain screamed for answers.

I broke the kiss and pushed him away enough to look him in the eyes. 'W-w-w-wait a minute!' I panted.

Hayden, who was equally breathless, looked at me in dismay. 'Fuck. Did I read the signals wrong?'

I gawked at him. 'What? No! I mean, you... you're into guys?' He licked his swollen lips and shrugged. 'Not normally, no. But I'm definitely into you.' Hayden chuckled and closed his arms tighter around me. 'Are you that surprised?' He leaned in, his mouth hovering over mine.

'Yeah,' I breathed out, 'very.'

Hayden laughed again, the sound deep, rumbly and delicious. He searched my expression. 'Can I kiss you some more, like?'

I swallowed and nodded weakly. Our mouths met again and *damn,* he was a good kisser. Hayden's tongue darted and teased rhythmically, reminding me of other activities that required thrusting.

His lips travelled south to trace my chin, suck gently on my neck and back to the sensitive skin of my ear. Needless to say, I was trembling with pure arousal.

I caressed his soft curls and sighed with pleasure as he found my neck with his lips again. He slowly lifted the fabric of my sweater and T-shirt underneath, ran a hand over my lower back and slipped his fingers in my jeans to grasp the flesh of my butt.

'How... did you know... I was... interested?' I asked between sighs.

He spoke ruggedly in my ear. 'Tossing the salad?'

'Ahh...' I closed my eyes. My heart was going to burst for sure.

Hayden kissed me again and I dared to feel his body. He was hard all over, his muscles defined, abs tantalising under the loose fabric of his long-sleeved top. The movement of his jaw under my hand as he lapped and sucked on my mouth was impossibly erotic. I could scarcely believe what was happening was real and not a daydream concocted by my libidinous brain.

Hayden grasped my hips and guided me against his hard-on, rubbing it against my jeans. My dick throbbed. I moaned, the rush of heat in my pelvis overpowering my senses. *Goodbye, rational side of my brain – it was nice knowing you!*

Hayden put his hands under each of my thighs and lifted me up in the air. I gasped in surprise. Strong as he may be, I wasn't a puny guy. He staggered, struggling to hold my weight. He dropped me on the nearby sofa and collapsed on top of me.

He laughed. 'Oops.'

Breathless, I stared into his eyes and waited for his next move. I felt like pretty much anything could happen. Hayden straddled my legs with eyes full of promise, gazing at me from above. He took off his jacket, grasped his top from his shoulders and slid it over his head in a smooth motion, giving me a full show of his ripped chest. The Greek god I had gazed at just over a week ago was there for me to touch, kiss and...

'Is this really happening?' I panted.

He bent over to kiss me. 'Looks like.' He unzipped his trousers and rubbed his large erection over my clothed groin through the fabric of his boxers.

As much as I wanted him, it suddenly dawned on me that messing about with Hayden wasn't an option for me. Straight guys experimenting never brought anything good to the gay recipient, aside from a fleeting sight of dick. Plus, my crush on him was already out of proportion as it was. If he and I crossed the line, I'd be stepping into an emotional danger zone and I was still recovering from a recent heartbreak. I couldn't afford to have another. As awful as it was to kill the mood with serious talk, I had to make things clear.

I pushed lightly on his chest and spoke breathlessly. 'Hayden, I... like you quite a bit.'

He stroked my cheek with his thumb and smiled softly. 'I like you too.'

Ahh, he wasn't going to make things easy, was he? It pained me to say the words, seeing how turned on I was and how awkward my speech was probably going to be. *You'll thank me later for saving your heart,* I told myself.

I said, 'W-what I mean is that I don't think I'm up for casual hook-ups. N-not only with you, just in general.' I avoided saying, 'Especially not with straight guys experimenting' and tried to think of something more universal. 'As things stand, sex and dating go hand in hand for me.'

I waited for the mountain to crumble into the sea and held my breath.

Hayden gazed at me with his intense brown eyes. 'OK.'

'OK...?'

'OK. Let's date.'

WTF? But I couldn't hand him the reins so easily. 'As in... being exclusive?' I blurted out. 'Because that's what I mean.'

Hayden frowned. 'Yes, exclusive. Do you normally date more than one person at a time then?'

'Ah, n-no,' I muttered. 'I mean, this is so sudden. You're OK with dating a guy... just like that?'

Hayden stooped over, resting his hands on the armrest behind my head and touching the tip of my nose with his. 'Just like that.'

He kissed me again and a flood of emotions hurtled through me. Hayden pulled at my clothes with the hurried hands of a giddy kid unwrapping a birthday present. He rolled the fabric of my sweater up to my armpits and exposed my perky nipples, covered one with his mouth and sucked. An embarrassing sound left my throat and I arched my back, my hands going to his hair.

As he licked my chest like a veteran in the field of nipple-teasing, making me gasp and moan helplessly, his hands moved to my trousers. Hayden easily removed the barriers of fabric separating my erection from the open air. Before I knew it my cock was out, straining upward and leaking pre-cum. He stared at my erection with wide, captivated eyes as if he'd found the Holy Grail. I had no idea what was going through his head but this was the moment of truth.

'A-are you sure you want to do this?' I asked with a small voice.

He exhaled a tremulous breath and rubbed his forehead. 'How can I say this? This is going to sound lame as hell.'

I gulped the lump in my throat. 'What?'

He gazed at me, eyes warmer than sunrise. 'It's like I'm not worthy. You're perfect.'

An instantaneous burst of heat made my body flush. *Holy shit! Who the hell says things like that?* I opened my mouth but could only say, 'Uhhh...'

Hayden covered his face with both hands, 'Oh fuck. I can't

believe I just said that.'

Neither could I. 'That... you really think that?'

He nodded and brushed a hand down my torso. 'You're beautiful.'

My cheeks burned. 'I... uh, I think we should kiss now.'

I reached to his chest and felt the hardness of his muscles under my fingers. Hayden bent down to meet my request. He coaxed my mouth open, pinning me down with a passion that left me breathless. My poor heart was running for the Olympics at this point, and I had the feeling I'd cum the moment Hayden breathed on my dick.

Time didn't exist until he broke the kiss and spoke with a husky voice. 'I'll need a bit of guidance.'

'For what?' I whispered.

His warm fingers went around my shaft and I stifled a moan.

He kissed my neck. 'I've never blown a guy and I might be shit at it.'

Had my heart been a volcano, it would have erupted. 'You... you want to do that?'

He thumbed my nipple with one hand as the other stroked my length. 'Yeah.'

Hayden scooted back and took better hold of my erection. With his hot breath on my dick, he said, 'You need to tell me if I do it wrong.'

I laid back on the sofa and exhaled ruggedly, 'O-OK.'

He sucked on the tip tentatively at first, tasting it, circling it with his tongue. I gasped at the feel of his hot mouth on my cock. At any rate, I was anxious he'd change his mind and stop. I was squeaky-clean and thanked the superior forces of the universe that my hopeful preparation had worked in my favour. Even so, surely a guy didn't have the same flavour as a girl there. I awaited with dread the moment

Hayden would freak out and draw back from me.

Luckily, none of that happened. Instead, his movements grew confident. He took me in deeper, worked his lips and tongue on the underside of my dick and my body tensed. My fingers clasped his curls and I whimpered. His mouth felt so good and damn, I wasn't going to last another heartbeat.

He might be new to going down on a man, but I thought he was great at it. Though maybe I was biased. After all, I was the guy dreaming about Hayden every night and would have rejoiced even if he tickled me with a feather.

His big fist and thick fingers were warm around my length. He stroked me up and down with controlled pressure as he fed me into his mouth. His lips rubbed on my crown seductively, and every one of my breaths was a gasp. Hayden lifted his head to look at me, a string of saliva stretching from my tip to his tongue. His arm moved swiftly under his stomach and I had a glimpse of his large dick sticking out of his jeans, his strong hand wielding it like a weapon.

I stared. And then stared some more. Cynthia wasn't exaggerating; he was hung and thick to boot, with a dark pink tip, long veins and a chestnut darkness of trimmed pubes crowning round balls that begged for a good suck. My mouth went dry.

Hayden took me in his mouth again and after a galvanising, thorough slurp he glanced up at me. 'Am... Am I doing alright? You've gone quiet.'

I flung a hand over my forehead and peered at him from under the shadow of my wrist. 'I'm trying really hard not to cum too fast,' I said shakily.

His eyes grew heavy with lust. 'But I want to see you cum.' He swooped down, mouth, tongue and fist working in perfect sync.

I threw my head back. 'Oh God. Hayden, I'm so fucking close...'

He sucked again, at the right moment, in that perfect way that I couldn't resist.

I came so hard that it felt like my soul was leaving my body. I moaned embarrassingly loudly. Hayden groaned his pleasure too and a choked whimper rose up my throat when I realised that he'd swallowed every last drop of me.

As I lay on the sofa, breathless and boneless, my fingers still gripping the cream leather, Hayden sat up. He studied his palm and wrist which were drenched with his cum, gave me a quick peck on the lips and disappeared to the bathroom, probably to wash his hands.

When he got back he looked at me and asked, 'Are you still there?'

'I need... a moment... longer...' I heaved.

Hayden laughed. After recovering his cup of coffee, he went to sit on the armrest of the sofa. From that perch he gazed at me with a bright expression. His upturned mouth formed that dimple that made me swoon every time it appeared.

He sipped his drink. 'Oh... it's gone cold. Oh well, still good.'

I brought my hands to my eyes. 'Did you... finish at the same time as me? While I was... you know, in your mouth...?'

'Yep.' He sounded very pleased with himself.

I exhaled the words, 'Oh my God.'

Hayden's phone on the computer desk rang, the notes of a Jimi Hendrix solo coming between his heated gaze and me.

He picked up, still smiling. 'Hello, Aunt Christie?' He turned to me and wiggled his eyebrows, a promising signal that told me we weren't done quite yet. Hayden glanced down at my indecent state. I squeezed the fabric of my sweatshirt and blushed.

Just then, his sultry expression changed to one of serious concern. 'What! Fuck. Is she alright? What happened?'

I could hear a voice fumbling through words at the other side of the phone. Suddenly, Hayden was looking for his clothes.

He managed to slip into his long-sleeve while holding the phone with his chin. 'I'll be there right away.'

I sat up on the sofa. 'What's wrong?'

A worried frown creased his face. 'My mum, she's... collapsed. I've got to go. I'm so sorry.' He shot out of the room, looking as if he was about to cry and scream at the same time.

'I'll drive you!' I said, putting on my boxers, trousers and shoes in three nanoseconds and following after him.

In a few moments we were outside, opening the car doors and getting in.

I drove at a steady speed, only occasionally glancing at Hayden. He looked out the window, lightly biting his finger and frowning as the neighbourhood hurtled by.

7

HAYDEN

When we arrived, the ambulance was already outside my house. Daylight had abandoned the sky. It was pitch black even though it was only six o'clock. Invisible talons clawed at my ribcage and it was difficult to breathe. It was fear animating me, not air.

I jumped out of Andy's car in a hurry and unlocked the seatbelt carelessly; the buckle whacked the plastic cover at the top. I didn't even have the time to feel bad about it. The little gate had been left unlocked and for once I wasn't annoyed about it. I strode to the front door.

Andy came after me and stood by like a silent guardian angel as I rang the doorbell. When nobody came right away, I banged on the white-painted wood. 'Open up!'

As I extracted the house keys from my pocket, the door cracked open. The distraught face of Aunt Christie appeared through the open gap. 'Hey, come in.'

Like my mother she was pale and had long, dark hair falling freely down her shoulders. The main difference between them was that Aunt Christie didn't have a haunted look in her eyes. Mum always gave the impression that she was about to break in a thousand pieces, like a porcelain doll falling off a shelf. Was it today, then? The day she would break for good?

'They're saying she will have to go to the hospital for a check-up, OK? She's hit her head on the floor pretty hard, but she's alright,' Aunt Christie said.

I turned to look at the small group of people standing at the bottom of the staircase.

Mum stared at her lap while two paramedics helped her. She sat on an old black stool that we usually kept in the lounge to leave keys or change on. I watched with a heavy, painful heart as one of the paramedics, a lady with red hair and a kind voice, took Mum's blood pressure while a man kept an ice bag pressed on her forehead. Mum's expression was vacant, her former joyful self lost and an empty shell was all that was left behind.

I stepped forward, desperate to reach her. 'Mum...'

She looked up, eyes wide and lips trembling. There was no relief in her expression, nor sadness. Only terror. Her fearful gaze was fixed on mine, devoid of reason or explanation, *begging* me to step the fuck away.

Once again, I hadn't been there for my mother when she needed me.

Aunt Christie took me by the arm. 'Come on boyo, we need to talk.'

She led me to the kitchen while Mum's rejection flashed before me.

After trying so hard to be a good son, and many attempts to remedy my mistakes and to be there for her, Sophie and Iwan no matter what, Mum was pushing me away. Rationally, I knew I couldn't watch her back at every given second, yet inside I couldn't help but ask myself if her being in this state was my fault. Maybe I hadn't been as present as I should have been.

I glanced over my shoulder. Andy stood by the entrance with a pinched look on his face. He followed the paramedics with his eyes as they prepared to help Mum to the ambulance. Was he going to leave the moment I turned around? He drove me home but he didn't owe me as much as to stay. A pang inside my chest set me off and I began heaving. I stopped in my tracks and leaned against the frame of the kitchen archway to keep steady.

Mum hates me. Of course she does. I should have been there for her.

A hollow, unbearable pain stemmed from the centre of my ribcage; it was as if a phantom fist had gripped my soul and was trying to rip it out of my body. I tried to breathe slowly but all I managed was a raspy gasp and a shaky exhale.

'Hayden?' Aunt Christie touched my shoulder.

I could hear her but I couldn't see her. I could see nothing. I was trapped in limbo.

'Hayden,' Andy called through the fog. 'Hayden, are you alright?' His voice was deep and gentle. A rope to safety.

His fingers touched my arm and I immediately captured his hand. 'P-please,' I sobbed, 'please, don't leave! Please!'

Andy put an arm around my shoulder and said softly, 'I'm not going anywhere. I'm going to stay with you.'

I shook uncontrollably. 'Please... please...' Hot tears streamed down my cheeks and, somewhere in the back of my mind, I asked myself, *is this really me?*

'Let's get him to a chair,' I heard Andy say.

It was as if I'd teleported to the chair by the small table in the kitchen. Andy sat next to me, his palm stroking my back with slow, soothing motions. His other hand held mine over the chequered pattern of the tablecloth, our fingers interlaced tightly like a Celtic knot.

'Would you like some water?' Andy enquired, probably remembering I'd asked for a drink last time I got into this state.

I hid my face in shame. 'Y-yes please.' My mouth was completely dry and the words came out like a weird hiss.

I told him where he could find a glass and he filled it with tap water. As I took small sips, my hands trembled around the glass.

'I-I'm sorry...' I muttered.

'I have no idea why you're apologising, but if you want my forgiveness so bad then I'll give it to you. I forgive you. How's that?' he said with a smile.

I half-sobbed, half-laughed. 'I need to see my mother... and my brother, and my sister! Where are they?' I suddenly remembered that they were my priority; I couldn't wallow in anxiety when I needed to be strong for my family.

In a clumsy attempt to stand, my legs wobbled and buckled under my weight.

'Hayden, sit down, come on.' Andy's words were both the kindest and the most imperative I'd ever heard.

I plopped back on the chair. 'But—'

'They've taken her to the hospital,' Aunt Christie said. 'Aunt Katrina is on her way there too, so your mum isn't going to be alone.' She hunched over the table and studied my face with a concerned frown. 'Are you feeling better?'

I nodded and gruffly wiped any remaining traces of wetness from my face. 'Where's Sophie and Iwan?'

Aunt Christie smiled. 'Uncle Bobi took them to our house, it's OK. Your cousins are there too so they should be kept entertained, especially Iwan. He gets bored easily, doesn't he? That boy, Christ almighty.' She was obviously trying to lighten the mood.

I looked her in the eye. 'What happened?'

Her serene expression faltered. She shot a quick glance at Andy. 'Right now, it might not be a good time to—'

'Please, just say it! This tension is fuckin' killing me.'

She took a deep breath. 'OK, but maybe we should wait until you calm down a bit more.'

'No, just say it now,' I repeated, wringing the tablecloth with my hands.

She clasped her hands. 'Well... earlier today, your father showed up.'

The revelation was like a wrecking ball. '*What?*'

'Your mum gave me a ring right away,' she hurriedly explained. 'She said she opened the door and he was there with a bunch of flowers.' Aunt Christie chuckled mirthlessly. 'He tried to get into the house but she managed to lock him out, thank God. I brought Uncle Bobi here with me, you know, just in case John was still lurking around. A bit of muscle, like.'

'You have got to be fuckin' shitting me! What are restraining orders for?'

'I know. I called the police. They're on their way now.'

I swallowed hard as anger swelled in my chest. 'Is he the one who pushed her, then? Is that why she fell? Fuckin' wanker!'

My aunt shook her head. 'No, apparently not. She was up and fine when she called me, a bit shaken though, but when me and Bobi got here she was on the floor, with Iwan fussing all over her.'

We all fell silent until I broke it with a whispered question. 'Does that mean John is hanging around Cardiff?'

'Probably,' Aunt Christie replied in the same hushed tone of voice.

I gripped two fistfuls of my hair. 'Oh my God! The fuckin' cheek of him, like!'

'I'll talk to the police, don't worry.'

'But how did he find us?'

Aunt Christie's face darkened. 'It's difficult to say but maybe when your mum appeared on the telly for that thing about Cardiff's ceramics? Maybe he saw that? Then again, all her family is here. It's not exactly difficult to find out where she is, if someone *really* wanted to look for her.'

'But to know the address too? God, he's a fuckin' stalker!'

'Hayden...'

Someone knocked forcibly at the door and the bell rang too. A deep voice boomed from outside, 'Police!'

The following hour swept by. Aunt Christie spoke to the officers at length and explained the situation so precisely that it was as if she was in charge of the investigation, not them. She handled everything like a champ, providing the most recent picture of John she could find and even telling them what he was wearing that day, about the bouquet of flowers and so on. Apparently, she had gained all this information from my mother when she had first called her.

Aunt Christie was always on top of things; a trait that I thoroughly wished I inherited.

While she spoke to the police, Andy and I sat on the sofa like quiet spectators. His presence was the only thing that stopped me from sinking into the darkness stirring within me. We held hands like school kids afraid of the adult world – he was the courageous friend and I the wimpy one.

His thumb, warm and a little clammy, stroked the back of my hand rhythmically, keeping me above the surface. I'd never needed a person in my life as much as I needed him now. I wasn't the clingy type, not at all. If anything, people always clung to me. Girls fawned over me and guys flooded my phone with texts, inviting me to hang out. Andy didn't suck up to me. He always spoke with his heart and somehow managed to say just the right thing. And it was all natural.

I could not comprehend how this day could be so great and so harrowing at the same time. The black cloud of John's return in my life cast a shadow over the radiance emanated by the person sitting next to me – the two opposing forces fighting for control.

When I thought I was falling back into oblivion, Andy's touch brought me back to life. This happened over and over, at every stroke of his thumb, until all I wanted was to bask in his otherworldly light.

8

ANDY

Shouldn't I go to the hospital as well?' Hayden asked.

His aunt put a hand on his shoulder, having to stretch quite a bit because of their impressive difference in height. 'She'll be fine. Katrina will look after her and keep us up to date. Besides, I'm sure she'll be back by the morning. Maybe even earlier!'

Her bright tone couldn't dispel the sadness on Hayden's face. A muscle twitched under his skin as he clenched his jaw.

He inhaled deeply. 'What if he shows up again?'

'Well, about that,' Christie said, biting her lower lip. 'I thought you, your mum and the kids could stay at our house until the police catch the bugger. Maybe you could help me tomorrow, get some stuff packed? Having the family around will be a huge relief, won't it? I promise you, hun.'

Hayden's eyes gleamed with unshed tears. 'Thanks, Auntie. You're amazing.'

She planted her hands on her hips and cocked her head, grinning. 'Well, what would you like to do? Do you want to come down to Llanishen with me? Grab a change of clothes for tonight and head off, is it?'

Hayden's brow creased. 'You're going to be squeezed in tight as it is.'

Christie's eyes widened. 'What does it matter? You cannot stay here! The police are patrolling the area but who knows what he's up to? He might still be around, you know, hiding behind the bushes! The evil bastard!'

As she spoke, a police officer glanced at us from across the road while speaking through the radio.

I tentatively touched Hayden's wrist. 'You could stay at my house, if you want. I've got plenty of space.'

Hayden glanced at me with uncertainty. 'You sure?'

'Of course! And don't worry. I've got a top-notch security system.'

Hayden's aunt looked at me and smiled. 'I didn't catch your name earlier, love.'

'Andy.'

'Andy,' she beamed. 'Sorry for not introducing myself. Call me Christie. Thank you for today, you've been an absolute star, my love!' Christie clasped my hand. 'Are you guys close friends?'

'Yes,' I said simply.

It wasn't exactly a lie. We *were* close but the *friend* line was pretty blurry.

'I'm entrusting my nephew to you, then. I can tell you're a sweet boy.'

Boy? Maybe I was a boy in her eyes, seeing that streaks of grey tinted her long hair. Her face was youthful and full of life though. Had she dyed her hair, I wouldn't have said she was older than thirty-five.

I smiled back. 'Leave it to me.' I patted Hayden's shoulder to demonstrate my dedication.

Christie laughed and I saw her resemblance with Hayden then. 'OK. If you have any problems, don't hesitate to call me, alright love?'

We stood by the entrance as she got in her car. After turning on the engine, she waved by the passenger window and made a phone gesture, mouthing 'Call me' and giving us a thumbs-up. She drove away and her dark-green Volvo disappeared behind the next turn.

'Your aunt is really cool,' I commented.

'Yeah, she's great. I think...' Hayden hesitated, 'if it wasn't for her, my mum wouldn't have been with us today. She helped us a lot in the past.'

Something twisted painfully in my abdomen. The situation was more delicate than I first imagined. I reached for his hand and lightly stroked his palm with my fingers as I had no words that could make do.

He nodded to himself a couple times, looking thoughtful. 'I'll chuck a couple of things in a bag and we can get going. Do you want to come in for a minute?'

I nodded back at him and felt the eyes of the police officer standing nearby on my shoulders.

I closed the door and Hayden was in the hall waiting for me. His heavy-lidded gaze met mine. My breath caught when his arms slid around my waist and his fingers travelled under my clothes, as if wanting to connect with my bare skin. He gently pushed me against the wall and meshed his lips with mine. I touched his hair and ran my thumb over his cheekbone, holding him close.

When he broke the kiss to look at me and press his forehead against mine, it was as if a bubble had burst. There was sadness in his eyes, as well as need.

'Thank you for staying,' he murmured.

'Don't mention it.'

'I won't be a minute. I'll go grab a change of clothes and my toothbrush.'

'Alright.' I watched him go up the narrow staircase, each step making the wood creak under the carpet. As I gazed at his back, for some reason, a lump formed in my throat.

He came down with a small gym bag and gave a shy smile.

When we went out the door and walked to my car, the policeman who'd been hanging around the street approached us.

'Sorry lads. I couldn't avoid overhearing your conversation earlier,' he said. 'Where are you headed?'

'I'm taking him to my place,' I explained.

The policeman, a big bloke with a round face, put out his lower lip and clicked his tongue. 'Can't blame you. It might be a little unsettling for you to stay here tonight. Where is it you going to?'

I gave him an idea of where I lived while the man asked questions about us, and Hayden begrudgingly revealed that he was related to 'the aggressor', but luckily the officer didn't press for more info.

'Tell you what,' he said. 'I'm going to escort you, just in case.' He spoke to a colleague on the radio and then we were on our way.

The officer followed as I drove Hayden to my house. He and I were quiet throughout the journey, the constant presence of the police car behind us a reminder of the dismal situation Hayden's family was in. I knew the guy was doing us a favour but I kind of wished he wasn't there. Hayden was upset enough as it was.

When I led Hayden to the front door of my house and pulled out the keys, the round-faced officer slowed down his car, lowered his window and bid us farewell. 'Alright lads, keep an eye open tonight, ey? And if you see anything suspicious, contact us immediately.'

'Thank you, sir,' I replied.

Hayden didn't say *anything*, staring down at his feet. The policeman drove away and we got inside.

***

I stepped out of the shower and, after drying myself and getting dressed, I went downstairs. I found Hayden hunched on the sofa, gazing at the television screen in the lounge with a vacant expression. The colours of the programme he was watching flickered and flashed, highlighting his features.

'Are you hungry?' I asked.

He turned to look at me. His eyes took me in slowly, then flicked back to the television. 'Nah, not really.'

I sat next to him and joined him in his absentminded state for a while. A YouTube video about Japanese metalheads played in the background but I barely registered it. He was adrift in a place where nobody could reach him.

I wanted to touch him, to hold him and tell him that everything was going to be alright, to kiss his mouth slowly, gently. I wanted to tell him he wasn't alone. But I didn't do any of those things. I waited for him to reach out to me, but the evening went on and Hayden remained quiet.

Unable to bear the silence any longer, I spoke again. 'Would you like a hot drink?'

He hid his face behind his folded arms. 'A... cup of coffee. I guess.'

Happy to have a purpose, I scooted to the kitchen and got out two large mugs from the cupboard. I put extra effort in making Hayden's coffee since I felt that was all I could do to make him feel better. I wasn't a coffee drinker myself but my ex, Craig, preferred it to tea like Hayden. I'd bought a fancy coffee machine to impress him when we first started dating. What a lame piece of work I had been in trying so hard, seeing how things had turned out in the end. The coffee machine had fallen into disuse for a while but now it had a whole new lease of life. If freshly ground Blue Mountain beans and frothy milk could bring a smile to Hayden's face, I'd give it my all to make the best latte I could whip up.

I transferred the espresso in a mug, frothed the milk and poured it with care. I made a Horlicks for myself.

I went back to the lounge and the TV blinked flashes of colour in the dark room. Hayden sat immobile on the sofa. The live Rammstein performance he was watching played at a low volume. When I approached and offered him the mug, he looked up. My heart ached when I saw the solitary trail of a tear gleaming on his cheek. Hayden wiped it quickly and sniffed.

He accepted the drink with a sheepish smile. 'Cheers.'

I sat next to him and watched as he took a sip.

Hayden beamed. 'Oh, wow! Your coffee's the best.' He took a long swig of his drink and stared at the foam for a long moment. He pressed his palm to his eye, as if to push back tears. 'Sorry, I didn't mean to get you involved with all this shit, like.'

'Sometimes, life just happens.'

He snorted, 'Too fuckin' right.' He drank more of his coffee and sighed. 'I told you about my stepfather, him getting cancer and stuff, how he died and left us to fend for ourselves. Well, when it comes to my biological father, he hasn't been part of my life for years. He's a piece of shit, to be honest. Abusive as fuck, but not enough that you could call the police on him, if that makes sense? He fucked with my mum's head and gaslighted her and shit. My dad was like a god to her for some reason. She would *always* defend him, whatever stupid thing he did or said. Sometimes, he'd pinch her arm hard enough to leave bruises and tell her, "You do what I say", things like that. He made her think she was nothing. She accepted everything because she was brainwashed, and she covered up her arms to keep him out of trouble.'

He clenched a fist, his nostrils flaring in anger. 'He had a little more fuckin' trouble manipulating me though. I would stand up to him, you know, but I was a little kid. I could only do so much. When I was about eight or nine, my father's business failed and he found whisky. He was chugging down bottles like a fuckin' black hole sucking in dark matter.' Hayden sighed. 'He started to beat me. It was slaps and beltings at first, then one day he twisted my arm so hard that he dislocated my shoulder.' He scoffed. 'Predictable, innit? Drunk abusive father. Everyone's heard it before.'

I remained silent. Both my hands and spirit had gone cold after listening to his words. I closed my fingers around the Horlicks mug to warm them.

Hayden cleared his throat. 'Anyway, the hitting had been going on for about a year before the shoulder thing happened. I wonder if my mother had been so scared of him that she couldn't react sooner. She was probably convinced that everything he did was for a good reason, until he'd sent me to hospital. I hated my mother too, then, but I didn't know what gaslighting was. And yeah, my mother wasn't strong-willed. But my old man, he... he had this fuckin' charm about him. Before he started drinking he was this great-looking bloke. Tall, blonde hair, blue eyes... he always knew the right thing to say, you know. People ate out of his hand all the fuckin' time.' He swigged some more coffee, angry eyes staring at nothing.

The rainbow of light coming from the murmuring telly outlined the curve of his nose and the flat of his cheeks.

'Seeing me wrapped up in a bandage was the tipping point, I guess,' Hayden said, shaking his head. 'I shouted at her, told her she was a shit mother and left the house. I just wandered through Southampton all afternoon and went to a mate's house. It was hot as fuck, I still remember. At that point, something in my mother finally snapped. She... just reacted. She called the police on my old man, like, suddenly. That's what I heard, anyway and John... heard her making the phone call.'

I gasped.

Hayden's face tightened. 'When I got back home I found Mum on the floor. Her hair was all tangled with blood and there was a massive red splatter on the wall. I thought she...' A sob made his voice crack. Hayden stooped over, covered his face with a hand and exhaled a shaky breath.

I put my mug on the coffee table and hugged him. 'Hey, hey. Don't force yourself to speak. It's fine. *Shhh*. It's OK.'

Hayden didn't cry but trembled as if a frozen wind howled around us.

He wiped his eyes. 'Anyway,' he said with a broken voice. 'The fucker went to prison for that, and for what he did to me. Fifteen years. As if that would be enough for him.' Hayden snorted. 'Mum and I moved to Wales, she met a new guy, got married, had two more kids. You get the gist. Life was good and then Gareth got sick. Mum's depression spiralled and now that she is finally getting better...' He gritted his teeth. 'That fucking cunt shows up again. How fucking dare he, like!' Hayden squeezed his eyes shut.

I rubbed his shoulder. 'The police are after him now.'

He sighed heavily. 'I know, but that's not the point. He went to our house to fuck with her head and clearly succeeded. My mum, she... she's so fragile.'

Hayden still shook and sweat permeated his clothes. Silence fell, but for the heavy beating of our hearts. I kept stroking his back, finding it impossible to not seek a connection with his body.

In my head, I asked the question – *What about you, Hayden? Aren't you fragile too?*

9

HAYDEN

After spewing the story about my past, I was left empty, sluggish and sore. I swam through a cotton-wool version of reality – the television flashed colours and garbled sounds I could not register. It was like a come-down from a bad trip. Now I was... back, I guess. I'd finally landed.

Andy sat next to me on the sofa, watching the TV that offered us vague entertainment. In the semi-darkness I recognised the print on his black T-shirt, a vintage painted illustration of *The Frighteners*, with the ghosts from the movie, the haunted house and Michael J. Fox frowning into the night. Andy's clothing choices always made me smile. Without moving a single muscle, he had managed to cheer me up.

In a different situation, I would have asked him where he got the T-shirt from, but at that moment, all I wanted was to hold him close and lose myself in his body. Sex had always been my way to cope with shitty stuff since I'd started sleeping around at sixteen. Now it wasn't any different. Only this time, the person I wanted to do it with felt precious to me.

I was awed by him, by his kindness and sincerity. Andy got under my skin so fucking deep.

His curved lashes and tip of his nose, the moistness of his

lips, the slope of his throat and the rise and fall of his chest were enough to stir me. I knew his skin was soft and warm underneath his clothes, *mouth-wateringly* so, especially around his neck and under his arms and groin. The taste of his mouth, the silkiness of his hair, the enticing moans he'd exhaled and the salty flavour of his cum... they were all fresh memories in my mind.

Was it weird that, after pouring out my soul and destroying any possible sexy atmosphere as a result, I was the one emerging with a raging hard-on? Definitely. Another guy in my position might have been too depressed to get it up in this situation, but not me. That was not how I worked. If anything, my body and mind begged for release, to escape to somewhere where everything wasn't raw, sad and misshapen.

Also, I'd been seriously lusting after this guy! John and all that came with him? Having that out of my head for a while would be great. Not that having sex with Andy was meant to be a way to forget things. Although, if I jumped his bones out of the blue, he might think I was insane. Maybe I was. I opted for a soft approach.

'Can I hold you, like?' I broke the silence with my croaky murmur.

Andy turned to me, looking a little surprised. 'Sure.'

I slid closer, put an arm around his shoulders and cradled him to my chest so that his head rested on my pecs. Andy smelled freshly washed, he was warm and fuckin' beautiful. I drew him close enough that he had to put a hand on my thigh to steady himself.

Now what, Hayden? Now what?

I thought about it. *I could move his hand from my thigh and put it on my cock. That's probably a bad idea though, because that'd be like going from zero to hero. He's definitely going to think I'm nuts. I should go with something less... sudden, I guess.*

A muffled sound brought me out of my ruminations. Andy's

expression was taut as he lightly bit his lip. Was he nervous about being close to me?

I pressed a light kiss on his forehead. 'Are you comfortable?'

'Yes,' he squeaked.

I tried to decipher the situation. Was he... turned on too? I peeked at his jogs to inspect for suspicious bulges but with the poor lighting I couldn't see anything much. He didn't look like he was hating sitting against me though. Horlicks

OK, *let's experiment*. I moved my hand from his shoulder and snuck it under his sleeve, seeking the soft, sensitive skin. From there, slow and calculating, I caressed his arm up and down, up and down, up and down. A moan escaped Andy's throat and he made an obvious effort to muffle it.

'You OK?' I asked, holding back laughter.

'Yeah, all good.' His voice was strained and shaky.

Reassured I wasn't the only one in a frisky mood, I put a hand on his cheek and turned his face to mine, so that our eyes could meet. 'Can I kiss you?'

Andy's irises glimmered as if galaxies twinkled within. 'Yeah, of course.'

The moment our lips met, I got lost in the sensation. The tender slide of his tongue, his eagerness, the lean form of his body against mine. I wished I could dissolve and merge with his heat, to be saved by the holy grace of him.

Despite all the gay porn videos I'd watched and articles I'd read to educate myself, I still didn't know what to expect from the real thing. This was Andy we were talking about, not some random guy who slapped dicks on his face for a living. What if Andy wanted to fuck me? Would I let him do it and would I enjoy it? Was he one of those guys who didn't do arse play at all, and only liked to stroke cocks? *Oh damn,* that would be hot too! And why not – I would take it up the arse if he asked. Ordered, even. I didn't mind the idea of being tied down and getting plundered mercilessly. Or the other way round. I could push Andy's head on the mattress, like in my dream, and make him beg for my cock. *Oh shit!* I wanted it all!

Andy's hand moved to my desperate cock, rubbing, stroking and feeling its girth.

I groaned and slipped my hands under his clothes, grasped his body and brought Andy over to my lap with a quick, sudden movement. He yelped in surprise. I grinded my erection between his legs and squeezed his butt-cheeks like I really fucking meant it. I knew there was something I wanted to do more than anything, which was to eat his hole. Lick it and suck it, stick my tongue in and out and make him scream with pleasure. It would be amazing if Andy sat on my face and rubbed his hole over my lips, calling me names and punishing my dick with his hand, slapping it and shit. *Fuck!* I could cum just like that. *Hayden, Christ! Breathe!*

I wanted to rim his hole so bad, I was panting like a dog just thinking about it. For a while I was overwhelmed by lust and simply rocked my straining cock against his opening over the fabric, breathing hard as I tasted his mouth and was getting dangerously close to shooting in my pants.

'You're so hard,' Andy whispered as he pressed his arse against my bulge. He kissed me and put his arms around my shoulders, eyes soft and dark like he was melting.

Alright, clothes off. Priorities! I helped Andy out of his T-shirt and, as soon as his bare chest was before me, I gorged myself on it. I flicked my tongue and sucked on his nipple which grew hard under my touch. His skin tasted of spice and I went for more, paying a visit to the other nipple too and touching as much of him as I could.

Andy moaned deep in his throat, curled his fingers into my hair and murmured words of encouragement. The need to feel the naked heat of our bodies was as strong as the need to breathe. I laid him flat on the sofa, straddled his hips and made a show of pulling off my denim jacket and sliding my long-sleeve over my head. A Gaviscon advert ran on the telly, the colourful light delineating Andy's dreamy expression. One moment the soft planes of his cheeks and big eyes gleamed light blue, the next pink.

It's not that I exercised for the sole purpose of easily getting laid, though I had to admit it was an incentive, but I was aware of the effect I had on others when I took my clothes off. Guys asked me about my work-out routine and girls fancied me a lot of the time. Now, as Andy appraised me, my physique acquired a totally new purpose.

If only he'd look at me and no one else ever again. I can be beautiful for him. I can be strong. I can be anything he wants me to be. What I need is... fuck, I want him to be with me. I need this, I need—

Andy sat up, put his hands on my hips and gently placed his wet lips on my nipple, circling it with his hot tongue. I grasped his hair and sighed, '*Mmm...* yeah...'

Would he put his mouth on my cock like that? I really hoped so.

I lowered my hand to his groin, boldly stroked his length over the fabric and reached down to cup his balls and tease his opening.

'*Ohhh*,' Andy moaned.

Close to self-combusting with want, I pulled down Andy's jogs and underwear in one brash, fluid motion. His erection sprung upwards and he gasped as if I'd forcefully exposed a secret he hadn't been quite ready to share. That was enough for me – that little sound turning me into a wild, unbridled creature.

Andy's cock was dark, stiff and gleaming. He didn't have any pubes and his crotch was smooth and ready to be tasted.

I sat up again and pushed my jeans and boxer shorts down to my ankles, letting my throbbing cock out. In his eyes there was a question that I interpreted as, *Are you going to shove that big dick inside my tight little arse?*

I smiled and waggled my eyebrows at him because yes, I was, in fact, going to pound his tight hole *real* good. I dragged my body over his, letting our damp cocks touch. His was as hot and hard as mine, juicy and calling for me to sample its flavour.

Andy whimpered and moaned as I respectfully obliged and bent down to run my tongue from his balls to the tip of his straining dick. I suckled his slit and watched his aroused expression the whole time as I worked my mouth on his gorgeous, dripping cock. His pre-cum tasted divine, decadently salty and hot.

'I want you so bad,' I said huskily.

'S-same here,' Andy replied shakily. 'But... you sure you don't want to... take things slowly...?'

Oh, fuck. 'Am I going too fast?'

Andy stroked my arm tenderly, warmth in his kind eyes. 'Today has been rough for you.'

Of course he was going to point that out. Sighing, I lowered myself and hid my face in his neck. 'I'm tired of stressing,' I said honestly. 'I don't want to think about depressing stuff anymore and I'm horny as fuck.' I trailed languid kisses under his chin. 'If you don't want to carry on, just say.'

Please, please, say yes.

He put a hand on my cheek. 'If you're sure.'

I snorted, 'I am more than sure.'

Andy pecked my lips. 'Alright. Let's go to the bedroom.'

And by saying that, Andy opened the gates of heaven. I could hear angels singing and playing their harps, throwing rose petals at me and clapping their hands. Fucking hell, I was that close to skipping with joy up those bloody stairs.

Andy was naked, but I still had my jeans and boxers on, which was alright because I had at least five XL condoms in my back pocket that I very much wanted to take upstairs.

He took my hand and led the way. It was as if I surged forward, skimming along the soft carpet and the smooth surface of the wooden steps. I burned with desire and something else, something deeper that made my heart thump like never before.

Andy made it just in time to turn on the light in the room before I pushed him on the silken grey duvet and roughly removed my socks, trousers and boxers.

I prowled over him, grinning. We shared hungry kisses and warmed each other with the heat of our breath, hands exploring all over and bodies locking together. Reaching between us with my hand, I enclosed our cocks and stroked them, pressing our lengths together and riding pleasure like the ignited tail of a shooting star. The wet tip of his cock was hot, smooth... I couldn't believe how good it felt to have another guy's dick against mine.

I leaned in and kissed down his neck. 'Do you like me rubbing our cocks like this?'

'Yeah,' Andy whispered, cheeks flushed red. 'You?' He put his hand over mine and caressed my fingers as I stroked us.

I smiled. 'So good. I want your cum all over my dick.'

'Oh God,' Andy panted. 'Hayden, you're killing me.'

I brushed his lips with mine and teased his parted mouth with my tongue. Our joined erections dripped onto each other. I jerked us faster and Andy responded to my kiss with a muffled moan.

'Too much,' he said.

'You don't like it?'

'I do, but I don't want to cum too fast. Not like this.'

'How, then?'

He closed his eyes and murmured something.

'Hm?'

Andy chewed on his lip and looked up. 'I want to cum with your dick deep in my hole.'

I stared at him wide-eyed for a moment, then a groan escaped from me. I said in a rugged voice, 'That can be arranged.'

So that's what Andy wanted: to be fucked. I could do that. *Hell yeah,* I could. I knew all about nailing arses, even though I'd never done a guy's before. From what I'd seen online, it involved similar processes of softening and stretching, pushing my dick inside, waiting and thrusting slowly at first, then picking up a rhythm, just as with a woman's hole. Only... different. *Fuck.*

Go with the flow Hayden, I told myself.

After a few more strokes, I let go of us and asked, 'Have you got some lube?'

Andy slid off the bed and opened the first drawer of his bedside table. His hand rummaged inside a bit before he grabbed a couple things and chucked them on the bed. He'd brought out a large pack of wet wipes, a bottle of water-based lube, a bunch of condoms and a huge dildo.

I stared at the pack of wipes. 'Why have I never thought to keep these in my room?' Then I grabbed the sex toy and said, 'I've never seen a dildo like this.'

Andy rushed back over to the bed and wrapped his fingers around my cock, tugging it a bit and making me gasp.

'Lay down,' he said in a low voice.

'Yes sir,' I muttered and discarded the dildo. I lay flat on my back and folded my hands behind my head, my erection pointing upwards.

Andy sprawled between my legs, snuggled through my thighs and slurped me down all the way to the hilt. It didn't even make a sound; my cock kind of went and disappeared like the most erotic magic trick ever. The soft, hot and wet insides of his mouth and throat made me arch my back.

I clasped the pillow under my head. 'Fuck!'

Andy gripped my dick, wagged it and downed it all up again. His tongue... *ohh*, it was doing things to me, alright? *Things.* Like driving me insane for how good it felt. I watched in a state of amazement as he dived, bobbing his head a bit. My cock hit the back of his throat like it was nothing.

There's no easy way of saying this, but my cock was above average size. I was lucky, girls loved it and all, but deep-throating wasn't something I experienced often for that reason. A lot of the time I was put off by the excessive gagging sounds and preferred a hand-mouth co-operation on my shaft.

For some reason I never expected Andy, of all people, to be able to do this and so incredibly well. An expert, like. He looked so... innocent. Gentle. My mental image of him as one pure of soul was slightly shattered, but not in a bad way.

Andy lifted his sultry gaze but, a moment later, he abandoned my cock to hold his mouth and laugh. 'Dude! You should see your face!'

I must have been staring at him gaping because I was aware of closing my hanging mouth. 'How did you learn to suck cock like that?' Stupidest. Question. Ever.

Andy laughed even more. 'Practice, I guess.'

'Holy shit.' I slumped back on the bed and Andy continued to kill me softly with his sweet, sweet mouth. After a bit I thought that if I wanted to last at least a decent amount of time when we fucked, he probably had to stop.

Before I could tell him to take a break, he did it himself. Andy grabbed the lube and squirted a large dollop on his hand. He knelt on the duvet, widened his legs and slid a finger up his arse, moaning softly.

I was entranced by the amazingly hot sight and the squelching sound. 'What are you doing?'

Andy bit his swollen lip. 'Stretching myself up for you.'

'I want to do it,' I said immediately. 'Go down on all fours?' Andy looked unsure for a moment but did as asked. He stuck his gorgeous, perky and pale arse up for me and a hot shudder coursed through my abdomen, chest and arms. I hummed in trepidation. I was hungry... no, *ravenous*.

His hole was pink and wet, twitching a little. *God almighty give me strength,* I prayed inwardly as I placed my hands over the most gorgeous butt-cheeks I had ever seen. I prostrated myself over his magnificent arse like a worshipper upon a blessed altar.

'Do you need more lube?' he asked timidly.

'In a bit,' I managed to say. Saliva had collected in my cheeks and I spat on his hole to moisten it. Andy gasped loudly when my mouth landed on his opening. Finally I was where I was supposed to be. I could die in peace. The world may very well end and I wouldn't care because I was eating *this* marvellous butt. God might be there, hidden between the folds of the tight muscle; I could honestly believe it. The lube tasted fruity and I resented it because I wanted to savour Andy's skin, his *true* flavour. Had he been a little sweaty I would have hummed with pleasure while cleaning him, licking and sucking everywhere. I opened his butt-cheeks to plant my tongue deep inside his hole, dipping in and out with delirious glee. Andy gasped and moaned, calling each divine being in the universe by name...

I tickled him open with my tongue, spat more saliva and slid a finger inside him, then two. I knew I had to curve them downwards, as if attempting to touch his belly button from the inside... Thanks, Google. I stroked the small bulge I'd found. Andy whimpered and crumpled the sheets. I removed my fingers and went again with my mouth. I ate him *good*. Now that he was a bit more stretched for me, it was easier to reach deeper with my tongue. After a while I sat up, mostly to catch my breath and rest my tired jaw.

Andy pressed his face on the mattress and breathed heavily.

I caressed the curve of his arse. 'Are you alright?'

'Yeah,' he said weakly.

I chuckled and grabbed the dildo he'd dumped on the bed earlier. 'Should I put this in for you?' I said, tapping the soft plastic of the toy against his hole. 'Or would you like me to use my fingers again?'

'No...'

'Then... Do you want me to keep going with my tongue?'

'Please just... make me wet with lube and fuck me blind.'

I sucked in a breath and immediately took my cock in hand, jerking it to make it nice and stiff, not that it had gone soft. I was hot all over as I recovered the bottle of lube, squeezed some on the tip of my fingers and slid two inside him. Andy grunted and sighed with pleasure.

On the duvet there were a bunch of condoms. I picked up one and put it back down. As I thought, they were too small.

I got off the bed, went to recover the jeans I'd abandoned on the carpet and extracted one of my XL condoms from the pocket. Standing in the centre of the room, I put on the johnny. Andy watched me with big eyes all the while, laying on his side like a slender prince waiting to be attended to. An anxious-looking prince, but so very beautiful.

As soon as I was sheathed, I quickly moved over to the bed and covered him with my body, revelling in the feel of his warm, smooth skin. *Oh*, how could I say it? How could I put into words the feeling of gratitude that bloomed inside me?

Andy was a precious gift to me. That was it. If I deserved him or not, I couldn't be sure but I was certain I was going to keep him. It didn't even make sense that I wanted him so; we barely knew each other! And yet, and yet... it was as if I'd always known him. He'd walked inside my room, barging in my life big time. Andy had spoken to me, being just himself... and it was perfect. He'd glowed like a holy apparition. What was that about? It was as if inside me, an old mechanism had been reactivated, the gears creaking and finally, *finally* turning again. I was stupid but *God*, I didn't care.

I brushed my fingers all over his body and kissed him. I wanted to fuck him as much as I wanted to hold him close, escape the world as I hid in his selfless embrace.

'I want to do it while looking at your face,' I said.

He gave me an uncertain smile. 'OK.'

Andy lay flat on the bed, grabbed a pillow and placed it under his lower back. Heart beating fast, I positioned myself between his legs.

He studied my face. 'Hayden, have you *really* never done it with a guy before? You can be honest with me.'

'Never. Why?'

He turned his head to the side, a little sheepish. 'It's just that you're pretty good at this. I mean, you know how to touch a man.'

I broke into a grin and pecked his cheek. 'No, you're my first and I'm happy it's you.'

Our faces met again for a kiss – a slow, gliding dance.

Andy's hands trailed over my back. 'Hayden... Hayden, you feel so good...'

Damn, my body hummed with joy. I savoured Andy's soft lips, his reddened cheeks, continued pressing my mouth along the slope of his throat and lingered on his chest. My tongue found a nipple. I lapped at it seductively and down I went to his flat abdomen, kissing, sucking and biting lightly, until I reached the fold of his groin.

I positioned myself between his thighs, like Andy had done with me, and curved my fingers around his damp cock. It was a beautiful thing to hold, to revere. I gave it a long lick and chuckled. 'Funny. I was thinking the exact same about you.'

Andy whimpered softly and exhaled a low hum as my mouth closed around one of his testicles. He was completely hairless there, *Holy Christ*. I would have stuck my face in his pubes if he'd had any and thoroughly enjoyed it, because that's the kind of lewd guy I was, but with the bush out of the way I had more freedom to make him feel all of my mouth on his sensitive skin.

He wanted me to fuck him blind, but I wasn't in a rush. This was kind of special for me.

I was always this sex-machine dude; the girls I met with often saw me as such, or they wanted me to be their trophy boyfriend which was something I could do without. I was OK with the drifting, or at least I believed I was. I thought, *I'm young, I have all the time in the world for serious stuff.* I wanted to meet new people, to swish through my youth as if it were a colourful carousel, never staying in the same place, never looking at the same spot. Never thinking.

What was I now? *God,* I must have been seriously dysfunctional. There was this strange part of me that wanted to kneel, to rest my head on Andy's lap and feel his hands stroking my hair, hear him say with his gentle voice that everything was going to be alright. I could cry without shame and open myself without fear. I knew deep inside, with utmost certainty, that he would understand.

And so I gave him pleasure because I wanted him to stay with me.

I massaged his dick, the sound of wet skin tickling my ears, as I gently sucked his balls, encasing them in a liquid heat. His hole was soft and supple so my fingers dipped easily inside, in the hottest, most gorgeous place in the world.

Andy gasped, 'Hayden, I want... please...'

I slurped on his shaft, burning with new feelings. 'Say it. Ask me nicely.'

His Adam's apple bobbed. 'Please, put your cock inside me and fuck me.'

I'd made him wait enough. I slapped my dick against his thigh before positioning myself over him. Andy raised his hips readily and opened for me. I took my erection in hand, pressed the tip against his hole and he murmured, staring at my cock, 'So damn big.'

I burst out laughing.

Andy slapped me in the arm jokingly, smiling up at me. 'You smug prick! Bet you've heard that before.'

I kissed him. 'Can't say I haven't.'

I entered him slowly. My cock met the resistance of his tight muscle and Andy groaned, his cheeks turning even redder. *He is so, so beautiful.* Eventually, his body accepted me in all its heat and I was almost overwhelmed by the feel of him. In a way, I lost sense of who I was, but not at all in the same way I did when the monster engulfed me. Rather, it was a blissful soaring.

'Fuck,' I huffed in awe, 'you feel amazing. So tight.'

Andy wrung out several breaths and his body relaxed under me. Carefully, I moved, slipping inside the pocket of his soul. He'd let me. A rush of emotions pooled and rippled through me, outdoing everything else.

Oh God, oh God, why is it like this? Is it supposed to feel like this? I kissed him deep as I rocked inside him.

'P-please, do me hard,' Andy said.

I met his gaze through the haze of lust and absolutely everything else I was feeling. 'You sure?'

He closed his eyes. 'Yeah.'

I chuckled, because otherwise I might sob, which was weird, and steadied myself on the bed. 'OK, but don't ask me to carry you around later if you can't walk.'

I'd say his words broke my control, because what I did then was lift my hips and go down like a wooden ram bashing against a locked door.

Andy threw his head back and cried out, 'Holy shit! *Ohhh!*'

I fucked him deep, and at every thrust I chanted his name in my head. The wet slap of our bodies, huffs, groans and moans came together in a messy song.

Andy scrunched his eyes shut and pierced my biceps with his nails. 'Oh God, *ahh!*'

'Damn... you're so... fucking... tight...' I said as I sunk in him, over and over.

Sinking. That's what it was, not down into bottomless darkness but inside a deep lake of glistening water. My heart thumped steadily and my body exulted as if warm honey fuelled it. I wondered about it all.

Why is it so different from the other times? Andy put his arms around my shoulders and kissed my cheek. I sighed, sweetly. *Oh, why?*

Well, you know why, a voice in my head said and then, simply, I knew that Andy was *it* for me. A deep calm overtook me then.

Fuck, I closed my eyes and yielded, astonished. Andy held me tight and my name rattled out of his lips because I still pummelled into him, hard like he wanted it. Even though I was on top and his body lay at my mercy, he owned me. I was taken, dragged into the vast embrace he offered. I had to do something, change position or I was going to do stupid shit like confess my undying, everlasting love for this shining person I barely knew.

I slid out of him and smiled. 'I want to do it a different way.' Kneeling, I slapped my thighs. 'Come here.'

Andy sat up too but said, 'I'm a bit wobbly.'

I laughed because this was the result of his eagerness to be fucked hard. I drew him against my chest and helped him sit on my lap. We kissed for a while and I loved the feel of his cheeks and smooth jaw under my hands.

'Do you think you can ride me?' I asked.

Andy nodded, his cheeks flushed. He positioned himself above my cock and, since he was sleek and stretched, he easily guided me in. He plunged down hard, wet skin squelching, and steadied himself by holding on to my shoulders. We were both sweaty and hot like summer, peering into each other's eyes. I put my hands under Andy's arse and lifted him, helping him to put more weight into each sinuous movement. More kissing, more thirst for him to quench. I began pummelling his ass from underneath.

Andy pressed his face against my shoulder and gasped, 'Oh! *Oh* fuck! Oh fuck! *Mmm!*'

I grinned as if I'd conquered Everest and thrusted harder, faster.

Andy's eyes gleamed with passion and I watched his expression morphing as he revelled in it. It was incredible to know I could do this to him. I could make him look at me with such helplessness and disbelief, at how good I could make him feel.

Andy whimpered and looked down at the space between us. His prick was stiff, impossibly so, and dark. It slapped slightly on my abdomen, sloshing streaks of pre-cum on my skin.

'Are you about to cum?' I raised him and let him fall hard

on my cock.

'*Yes!* Yes, oh God!' He reached for his dick to set his orgasm free. I could see the urgency on his face but I stopped him.

'Let me.' I put a hand on his cock, pressed it against the dip of my abs and slid an arm under his butt-cheeks. Andy looked into my eyes as I pounded into him. At each thrust, his cock rubbed against my stomach and the palm of my warm hand.

He came, uttering a shapeless sound as ribbons of cum spewed freely from his cock and all over me. What a perfect thing.

I looked down at the streaks of cum on my chest, and ran a finger on my skin to bring a hot droplet to my lips. This was the taste of achievement. I flashed Andy with a heated look as he watched me in wonder.

I flipped him over and onto his back. He gasped in surprise. I pulled away, plucked off the condom and pumped my cock hard.

I squeezed my eyes shut and groaned, '*Ahhh...* fuck!'

I was going to bathe him with cum, like a wild fucking caveman, but then the shiny shape of his softening cock attracted my attention like a beacon. I shot all over his dick, balls and groin. My own testicles contracted as waves of bliss radiated through me, unfurling all over to reach the tip of my toes and end of my fingers, body tensing and soul swimming in glory. Semen flooded Andy's belly button as it spread over the flat of his stomach.

The sight of him covered in my cum was the thing dreams were made of; this image of him, flushed and sprawled on the bed. I'd given him was more than a splash of jizz. It was me. All of me.

When you know, you know. The notion was ridiculously massive and stupid and crazy and true. Absolutely true.

Decadent, beautiful, perfect... what else?

I collapsed next to Andy, surrendering to the vision. I rolled on

my side to kiss his shoulder endlessly. 'Oh, babe, you're so giving...'
Andy gasped softly and ran his fingers through my hair, rubbing my
scalp gently.

Eventually, the hormonal tempest subsided, leaving us limp
with languor and bliss. Andy grabbed the pack of wipes and probably
used half of them to clean us. We embraced, kissed and traced our
bodies with delicate fingers. Neither of us could stop smiling.

Andy stroked my cheek. 'Earlier, did you call me babe?'

I inhaled through my teeth. 'Yeah... was that too much?'

He moved my hair away from my face. The blue of his eyes
shone as he smiled. 'Not at all.'

Giddy with joy, I drew him to my chest, pulled the blankets
over our bodies and sighed contently. 'Can we stay like this for a bit?'

'Yeah,' he said.

I kissed Andy's smiling face, lips and cheeks, caressing and
stroking his warm form. He hugged my waist and buried his cool
nose in the crook of my neck. My heart was full.

10

ANDY

I'm not in love. I am not!

It's that thing, what's it called... endorphins! That's it! I am under the influence of endorphins. My heart wouldn't stop thumping and I begged for it to slow down. T*ake it easy. One breath in, one breath out...*

Then Hayden hugged me tighter under the duvet, surrounding me with his strong arms. He nuzzled my hair and, with a deep, husky voice said, 'You smell amazing.' *Super sexy*, like one of those hot aftershave models that say all that pretentious crap but with the best voice ever.

I closed my eyes, listening to my heartbeat. *Du-dum, du-dum, du-dum...*

I was the little spoon. The l*ittle flipping spoon* and a wall of warm, hard muscle encased my back, utter manliness weighing over me. Hayden's hand roamed over my abdomen and he brushed his lips onto my shoulders a million times over.

And now he was turning me over to kiss again and he was *so good* at it. He was sure of his movements, and that thing he did with his arms slipping under my body and calves folding into mine, as if he was slowly but, beyond doubt, capturing me...

He tantalised me with his lips, my mouth opening like a helpless flower. His tongue glided over mine and prodded at a steady rhythm. But I needed time to process things. I couldn't have sex with him again, not yet. What I should have had was a solid plan to put things into perspective.

Hayden pressed his nose onto my cheek, so close I could feel the flutter of his lashes on my skin.

'You know,' he said. 'You're so fuckin' beautiful, mind.' He chuckled like he was embarrassed.

Oh my God, how was I ever going to survive this? I replied, 'You're beautiful too.'

The corner of his mouth quirked as he stroked my cheek with a finger. 'I want to dream about you every night so I can see you even when I sleep.'

Oh man. Shit.

I closed my eyes again. I couldn't bear looking at him. He must have been under the effects of endorphins too, to come up with stuff like that! His words were like the sweetest blades, piercing through my barriers and filling me with warmth and colour.

He caressed my body for a while and kissed my face like he was marking each and every corner. Forehead, eyebrows, eyelids, nose, cheeks, lips and chin. Nobody had ever been so tender with me and I couldn't handle it.

'I need to pee,' I said.

He smiled and stretched. 'Alright.' Hayden let me go, but not before he kissed me so passionately that there was no way I wouldn't come back to him.

I waddled to the bathroom. My backside was positively sore; my butt cheeks, as well as the obvious spot. But it was a good kind of ache. It'd been so long since I'd had sex and doing it with Hayden had been a great way to start anew. The problem was that sex wasn't a word that could describe in full what had happened between us. Not even close.

And I was shocked. And happy.

I relieved myself, washed my hands and glimpsed at my reflection in the mirror. I had the dopey smile of someone who had enjoyed one hell of a dicking.

Most gay guys had no such luck with presumed straight men. The majority of them *stayed* straight; everybody knew that. It was rare to have one turn around and go, 'Oh, you know what? Your knob is alright. I'll have an order, please.'

Dudes in denial, trying the D out and throwing tantrums afterwards? Yes. Guys wanting their cocks sucked, no matter whose mouth is blowing? Once again, yes. An astonishingly good-looking man who's renowned for sleeping around with girls turning around and saying to someone like me, the king of dorks, 'You have a penis and I'm absolutely fine with it. I'm definitely into you. Oh, and yeah. Let's date.'

Not at all something you'd hear every day.

And damn, the things Hayden said, the way he looked at me, how lovingly he'd touched me – how could I possibly not... *Aaargh!*

I spent a longish time in the bathroom, giving myself a quick clean to get rid of the lingering stickiness on my pelvis. The image of Hayden towering over me and cumming all over my dick was *very* fresh. *Oh God.* I ended up swaying from side to side as I clung to the ceramic basin like a tormented Shakespearean hero. I padded down the stairs to retrieve my phone, which I'd left in my jogs. 'Twenty past eight,' I murmured to myself, my voice sounding loud in the large, empty lounge. I went back upstairs.

Upon entering the bedroom, which was now brightened

only by my bedside lamp, I found Hayden flat on his back and fast asleep. Most of his body lay bare, aside from a corner of the duvet covering his groin and one of his legs. He looked peaceful and... wow. Just wow.

His head lolled to one side and a muscled arm elegantly folded under it, the yellow light sculpting his body in a flawless play of shadows. The myth of Psyche and Cupid popped into my head. I could now imagine how Psyche must have felt as she crept into her bridal chambers, the flame of her oil lamp wavering as she resolved to see the true shape of her lover. *Thereupon lay the divine form of the god of love, young and exquisite, with his golden head drenched in ambrosia and soft skin that called for kisses.*

Not a direct quote but an accurate description. Hayden's beauty certainly met Ancient Greece's standards. His dark blonde curls, his strong but harmonious features and the definition of his lean muscle made him a worthy model for a nude statue.

This guy called *me* beautiful. Right. A joke. This was a joke. Then I remembered that Cupid had flown out the window and left Psyche when he'd discovered she had taken a good look at him, despite her promise not to. Hayden wouldn't have left just because I'd gazed at his naked body – I'd done a bit more than that – but who knew if he'd find another reason to be skittish and run away?

With an oddly heavy feeling, I snuck back under the duvet and my phone buzzed, catching my attention. It was Tai. What perfect timing – I was desperate for guidance.

His message read: *'Can you give me back the books I lent you at some point this week? Let me know when we can meet. Thx babes.'*

'Day after tomorrow?'

'Sounds good to me. I'll be finished with work after lunch. Meet u at 3 somewhere in town? We can decide where exactly tomorrow darl,

cheers xx'

I shuffled so that my head sank deep into the pillow and exhaled as I sent a new message. *'How do you know? How do you always know?'*

Tai replied with a sole question mark.

'Hayden. How did you know?'

Instant reply, 'WHAT HAPPEEEENND!!!???'

I cringed a little. I could hear Tai's voice shrieking in my head. As expected, my screen filled with astonished emojis and GIFs, my phone vibrating constantly and ready to take flight from my hands.

I quickly set it on 'do not disturb' and slipped deeper under the duvet.

'In short, a lot has happened. Just so you know, Hayden is sleeping next to me now, in my room, and we're both naked.'

'OMG!!!! OMG!!!! You've gotta tell me everything Andy! OH MY GOD I won't be able to sleep tonight if you don't spit every detail RIGHT THIS INSTANT!!!'

I knew he wasn't lying. Tai was going to bug me incessantly until I spilled the beans. Not that I was planning on keeping things from him, anyway. So I explained how Hayden had kissed me suddenly, confessed he was into me and how one thing had led to another.

Tai replied, *'OMG I knew it!'*

'I know that you knew, that's why I was asking how the feck did you?'

'It's my superpower.' Tai sent a glittery GIF of a rabbit smiling widely. *'But in this case, even an idiot would have noticed that Hayden had a thing for you. After all you said he did and the way he looked at you at the café? Sweetheart, it was SUPER OBVIOUS.'*

I told Tai how I tried to gauge Hayden's motivations, to understand if he was only wanting to experiment, and that Hayden accepted to date me on the spot.

'Did he say that only to have sex with you?' Tai asked.

'God, I hope not.' Worry seized me at the thought. I glimpsed at Hayden, who still slept comfortably next to me.

I typed speedily, 'Could that be the case? It all happened in the heat of the moment. Oh shit, I always get carried away. He looked like he really meant everything he said, though, but so did Craig when we first got together. Oh no, what do I do? What if he thinks he likes me, but he actually doesn't? I knew it was too good to be true!'

Tai replied, 'Calm down! I'm not saying that's necessarily the case. He really seemed to like you. In any case, even if he just wanted a shag, wouldn't that be OK? If that's all he has to offer, at least you got to have a good time, no? Think of it that way. xxx'

I sighed. 'I can't think that way. Something happened while we were doing it. Like... the dam flooded or something?'

'What u on about?'

'I like him a lot.'

'You fall in love too quickly bae. Take things slowly.'

I inhaled a sharp breath, cheeks blazing. 'I'm not in love! And in any case, how am I supposed to take things slowly when he came onto me like that? I almost had a heart attack! And it wasn't a simple shag, if you must know. He bonked my brains out!'

Another stream of elated GIFs and texts followed my message. 'Is he good in bed then? Does he have a big dick?' Of course Tai was going to ask that.

'It's not all about dick size, come on!'

'Oh shit. Does he have a small prick? Oh well, as long as it feels good for you.'

My eyes widened. 'No, his dick is fine! He's huge, if I'm honest, but that's not what I mean. What's going on between us doesn't feel *just physical. He was really sweet and we cuddled after. I still feel unsure, though. Everything happened so fast.'*

Tai sent a GIF with another glittery rabbit, this time with hearts in his eyes. *'Oh Andy, I'm so happy for you! Take my advice and give things time. So far, whatever you guys have seems promising! xxx'*

Tai didn't know a big part of the story – Hayden's family problems, his panic attacks or the reason why Hayden was spending the night with me in the first place. What if he just wanted someone to comfort him during a difficult time, and I just happened to be there? *That* was the intrusive thought going round and round in my head. I told myself it was paranoia, to set these stupid suspicions aside, but the notion stayed there, the kernel of doubt growing.

As I pondered how to give Tai more details and what I could reveal without being insensitive, Hayden stirred next to me and groaned. He began heaving, making slurred, incomprehensible sounds and then, out of the blue, he threw his head back and screamed.

11

HAYDEN

'You're a little shit as always, Hayden,' my father said.

John gave me that boastful, crooked smile he always had when he was drunk and about to rough me up. He sat on me, pressing down on my right arm.

'Fuck off of me you bastard!' I rasped out.

I couldn't move. My body was heavy and ungainly.

Dad picked up a large bottle and took a long swig from it, the emerald glass gleaming ominously in the darkness. He cackled, then lifted the whisky once more and chugged it all. Amber liquid streamed down his lips, neck and trickled down to his shirt, soaking it.

'Ah, that's better,' he said. 'Now, where were we?' He raised the bottle high in the air and I saw murder in his eyes.

'No! Nooo!' Tears filled my eyes.

The bottle swung down like the blade of an axe.

'Ahhhh!' The scream poured out of me.

I gasped for air and clutched my chest, trying to stop the flow of blood, but there was no wound on my bare skin, only a sheen of cold sweat. A deep ache clobbered at my ribs, my stomach in knots. I freed myself from the weight of the blankets and stumbled off the bed in a frenzy to escape. Whatever I could discern looked unfamiliar.

Was I back in my old house, in England?

I dropped to my knees and sobbed, 'No! No please, no... Oh God, please!'

'Hayden!' The voice was deep, mellow and soothing to my senses. Tender hands touched me, holding me tight.

'Hayden, what's wrong? Did you have a nightmare?'

I met a pair of big, worried blue eyes.

A nightmare. That's what it had been and Andy was there with me. This was his house, not John's.

I put my arms around him and held him like a lifeline. 'Thank fuck it's you. I'm so glad, oh God I'm so glad.' I kissed his cheek, his mouth, and tears won the battle against my scrunched eyelids.

'It's OK, it's over now,' he soothed.

Was it *really* over, though? John *was* back.

'Oh fuck, my phone. Where did I put my phone? Oh shit, what if the police have found him?' I stood up and looked around, heart pounding in my throat.

'Where did you last put it?' Andy asked.

'In my denim jacket. There's a zip pocket.'

'OK, stay here. I'll go get it for you.' He kissed me on the lips and hurried out the room.

The solitary moments that followed were agony. What was wrong with me? It had been years since I'd had these kinds of nightmares. 'Fucking John,' I muttered.

I sat at the edge of the bed and willed my body to stop shaking, clamped my hands together and squeezed them tight.

Andy came back, rushed to my side, handed me my phone and sat next to me. I quickly unlocked the screen and saw there was one lone message from Aunt Christie.

'I want you to take it easy tonight. You've had it rougher than us all

and it's just not fair that you and your mother must live in fear of that man like this. Your family supports you, you're not alone. If there's any news, I'll be the first to contact you. Enjoy your evening with your friend, sweetheart. Everything's under control here. Only give your brother a ring when you can. He was asking about you.'

I stared at the words and read them over a couple times, pressed the screen to my forehead and sighed. 'Fuck, I'm in pieces.'

Andy's hand was on my back. 'Any news?'

'No. My auntie told me to take it easy. I'm just really exhausted mentally, like.' I glanced at his troubled expression. 'I'm sorry I woke you. I didn't mean to freak out.'

Andy smiled. 'You didn't wake me, don't worry, though I admit I got scared for a moment.'

'Sorry,' I said sadly.

'It's fine!' Andy caressed my shoulders, his hand soft and warm.

After a bit he retracted his arm and I captured it, brought his hand to my mouth and pressed my lips to his palm for a long moment. Andy stared at me with a dazed expression. My blood seeped to my groin; the sight of his naked, smooth body made me want to do him dirty all over again. He must have seen the lust in my gaze because his cheeks reddened.

Andy freed his hand from my grasp. 'So... ahem, what would you like to do? Want to grab a bite?'

'Sure.' I studied his features, perplexed.

'Great! Let's get going,' He sprung off the bed and grabbed a dressing gown from his wardrobe, a *Doctor Who* robe with Tardises floating on a black background, and slid it on. What I was given was a *Ghostbusters* gown, black with a bright green belt and a big logo on the back. Andy was like some sort of upper-class geek who looked like he belonged to a black-tie party but preferred to stay home and watch sci-fi instead. I chuckled.

'What?' he asked.

I smiled. 'You're amazing, you know that?'

He looked away, as if uneasy. 'Thanks.'

I frowned. 'Something wrong?'

'No,' he said in a not-too-believable way. 'Why don't you have a shower while I make us something to eat?'

***

Once I dried myself after the shower, I put on some comfy clothes – a pair of jogs and a T-shirt. The *Ghostbusters* gown, as cool as it was, was definitely too small for me.

I tried to ring Iwan a few times but the sod didn't answer.

I texted instead, *'Call me back when you can. I'm at Andy's house. Remember Andy? If there's any changes, or you need to talk, I'm here for you.'*

After a minute or two, there was still no reply. I headed downstairs with a sigh.

Andy stood by the counter, carefully slicing a tomato and putting together a salad. He had put the clothes he'd been wearing earlier back on and discarded his dressing gown on the sofa. My eyes went straight to his ass. The way his butt filled his joggers was positively fine and the fabric of his black T-shirt, gently falling down his narrow waist, made my inner fire burn hotter.

It was surprising, bizarre even, how as soon as Andy and I had sex, it was as if a secret door in my subconscious had opened – one that could never be closed again. That morning, I had woken up thinking, 'I like guys.' Now, it was something more along the lines of, 'I definitely, *absolutely* love cock and arse, and I want more.'

I had a vision of myself, kneeling on the floor and lowering the elasticated waistband of his joggers and boxer shorts. I'd expose his pale, soft glutes and bite them, lick them and sneak my tongue through the crack. While diligently working his hole with my mouth, I'd beat his cock hard and fast. In the meantime, Andy would bend over the counter and moan, begging me not to stop as he pressed his cheek against a messy row of sliced cucumber. The image was so intense, so erotic that I actually had to lean on the wall to keep steady, as I reminded myself to shut my gaping mouth and gulp down my saliva before I started drooling.

Andy must have heard me exhaling steam like the kettle he'd just put on.

He turned around and looked at me with a startled expression. 'Why are you standing there?'

'I, uh... nothing...?' I ran a hand over my brow and found it slick with sweat.

'Why don't you have a seat? I'm almost done here.'

Andy turned his back to me again. I tracked his movements with a focused eye as he gathered some lettuce. I didn't do as he suggested. Instead, I approached him with the intent of a predator stalking a clueless deer. He must have been miles away because, when I put a hand on his back to run it down his butt, he started a little.

'A salad, eh? Need some help?' I positioned myself close, my hand still firmly parked on his arse.

'Oh no, it's fine. But I should have asked. You like salad, don't you? I thought you might want a side with the pizza, since it's not very big, and greens are good for you.'

Andy's face flushed. He had such pretty eyes, long curved lashes and soft cheeks that begged for kisses.

I squeezed his butt and leaned over to speak into his ear. 'That's very thoughtful of you babe,' I whispered. 'Though I can't help but wonder if this is your subtle way of suggesting I give you a good toss with my tongue. You know, all you have to do is ask.'

He sucked in a breath.

I stroked between his butt cheeks with two fingers and pressed on. 'I could do it all day, have my face buried right here like...' I placed a wet kiss on his ear.

'We sh-should eat first,' he stammered.

'If you're hungry, I've got something big to fill your mouth with,' I said, rubbing his hole more insistently and biting lightly on his neck.

'Ha-Hayden, b-before we do more, I...' Andy turned to look at me with big, sky-blue eyes. His tongue flicked to moisten his lips and the movement caught my attention. 'I have questions,' he said.

The statement was somewhat charged. Did he want to know more about my family drama? I really didn't want to darken the mood further but Andy had the right to get answers since I'd dragged him quite deep into my personal life.

I exhaled a long breath and slipped my hand back to his hip. 'Of course. Ask me anything.'

'OK,' Andy said, chopping a couple of radishes.

My palm strayed up and down his back, skimming over his body and feeling his shape. Andy's stance was a little rigid and his features taut. Whatever questions he had, they were certainly bothering him.

'Let's sit down,' he said, 'then we can talk.'

A few minutes later the pizza was ready. It smelled fantastic, miles away from the cheap stuff my family and I would often settle for. It had buffalo mozzarella and some fancy ham on top, olives and pesto. Andy cut the pizza into slices with a large pair of scissors, put some salad in a bowl, seasoned it and set it all on a tray which he handed me with a tight smile.

'Do you fancy a glass of something? I've got lemonade, fizzy grape, squash... I've got this one,' he said, reading the label on the bottle, 'crushed apple and cinnamon.'

'Squash sounds good.'

Andy offered the glass and the same flustered expression as before painted his face. His embarrassment was a turn-on but he looked so serious, worried even, that I felt I should hear what he had to say before thinking of jumping him again. I wasn't sure why the pizza was on my tray but I figured he'd take his slices from there. I waited patiently as he poured a packet of something in a mug, which he filled with boiling water.

Hot drink in hand, he took a seat next to me and smiled. 'Eat before it gets cold.'

'What about you? Are you not having any?'

'Ah, well.' His face reddened as he took a small sip from his mug. 'I'm just going to have this for now.'

I raised an eyebrow. 'Powdered soup?'

'Yeah, this will do me.'

Chewing on the delicious pizza, I frowned. 'Does this have to do with the sex?'

'What?'

Heat bloomed in my cheeks. 'Ah, it's just that yesterday I was reading about a bottom's preparation and that there's a specific *routine* to follow. I thought that maybe you're keeping your stomach empty just in case we do it again. Sorry, it was a really stupid question.'

Andy blinked in bewilderment and, a moment later, cracked up. He put a hand on his stomach and doubled up, laughing heartily. His amusement was contagious. 'Ugh, I get it. I'm not an expert on the topic alright?' I tutted, feigning annoyance, but my grin told a different story.

Andy wiped a tear from his eye. 'Sorry, sorry. Phew! That was unexpected.'

I shrugged. 'It seems like all I do is surprise you, for better or for worse.'

His smile was kind and there was a sparkle in his eyes that made me feel warm inside. 'You're a bit of a paradox, you know.'

'Am I?'

He took a sip of his soup. 'Mm, yeah, how can I explain? You say you never had sex with a guy nor have any interest in men usually, but you know how to touch a dude and flirt like a seasoned gay man.'

I snorted and gave him a saucy glance. 'Thanks.'

'I'm guessing you've done anal before.'

'Loads of times, yeah.'

Andy's expression tensed a little. 'With girls.'

'Yeah. That's why I researched about gay stuff. I wasn't sure that what I knew from experience would be enough. I wanted to be prepared, you know, in case we hooked up and stuff, which we did. There was a lot of conflicting information online and I got really confused. Porn is alright to an extent, so I found some interesting stuff I fancied trying and integrated it with what I already knew.'

Andy's eyebrows rose, his eyes wide. 'Wow. You thought about this a lot.'

I shrugged. 'I wanted to make a good impression. Did I succeed?'

'You did.' Andy tapped his mug and stared at its contents, looking absorbed.

I crunched on a mouthful of salad and waited for him to speak. Anxiety clenched at my insides like pliers twisting wires. I thought it was better to hear what he wanted, for him to ask immediately, for me to answer and be done with it. He probably thought I was a mental case already – it really couldn't get much worse.

'You said you have questions,' I mumbled.

'Yeah.' He played with his fringe that way he did every time he was nervous. 'So, about what we said earlier. The... dating thing.'

My ears perked up. So it wasn't about the depressing stuff that I didn't want to think about! *Hooray!*

I smiled with relief. 'Yeah?'

Andy looked genuinely troubled. His pretty eyebrows pointed down and I felt the urge to smooth his pinched expression with my lips.

'OK, so you said you've never slept with a guy, or given them head,' he said. 'Fair enough. What about other things? Kissing? Hand jobs? Sorry to ask, I just want to understand something.'

'No problem.' I took another pizza slice and devoured half of it with one bite. 'And no. None of those things. I had a wank-buddy once but we never touched each other. We watched porn and wanked off together. That's as far as my gay experience goes.' I grinned. 'Well, until now.'

Andy's answering smile was not as confident as mine, 'Then, what about attraction? Have you ever... fancied a guy before?'

I thought about it. 'A bit, yeah. I had fantasies, from time to time, about doing it with a guy, but never like this, innit. This is the first time I've had such a big crush on someone.'

'Someone of the same sex, you mean?'

My heart picked up a quickened rhythm for some reason. 'No,' I said, looking him in the eye. 'I've never liked anybody as much as I like you.'

It was difficult to interpret Andy's expression. His gaze was soft and his lips were parted. He slowly turned to put his mug on the coffee table with an almost trembling hand, and covered his face with his palms. 'You can't say things like that.'

'Why not?' My heart didn't slow down; rather, it beat faster. I placed my tray on the table, scooted closer and put an arm around his waist. 'It's true.'

His face remained hidden behind his hands. 'I want to get something off my chest, if that's alright.'

Why did he sound like he was about to break? 'Yeah, no worries, like.'

Andy's forearms flopped onto his knees. 'I broke up with a guy recently. OK, *maybe* recently is not the right word. It happened four months ago, but it ended badly. We were together for a year and he cheated on me.'

My heart ached. 'Oh, shit.' I caressed his shoulder gently like he did when I was feeling down.

'We started out a bit like you and I have,' Andy continued. 'He said he was bisexual but without much experience with guys. We were friends at first and then he said he felt something for me. He wanted more and I liked him too, so we got together.'

I was frozen inside, dreading the direction the story was taking.

Andy carried on. 'It was great at first, aside from the fact that he wanted to keep our relationship a secret. I mean, I'm the one with the Irish Catholic parents and I didn't have as many qualms as he did. Anyway, I respected his wishes. Nobody knew we were together, aside from our closest friends.

'At first it seemed like everything was good between us. You know how these things go. He grew distant and I was desperate to keep him close. I put all my effort into trying to make him happy, but it seemed that nothing I ever did was good enough. At some point I realised how often he was away from Cardiff. He said it was for work but it turns out he'd started seeing a girl. He drove all the way to London at least three times a month to meet her.

'The reason why I found out was that this girl had fallen for him too and suspected he was seeing someone else. She managed to take a peek at his phone and saw my texts. She wasn't aware he was two-timing us both when she started seeing him, or at least that's what she told me, and when she came to know her boyfriend was also *my* boyfriend, she contacted me straight away to explain what was happening.'

'Sounds like he's a right cunt,' I murmured.

Andy snorted. 'Yeah. Well, I might have some trust issues because of him now. I don't want his actions to affect every relationship I'll have in the future, but you can easily see why I became a bit biphobic. Rationally, I know that this has nothing to do with being attracted to both sexes. My ex might have had cheated on me even if he was totally gay, but still. It really did make me feel like I'd been used, that he'd never really fancied me in the first place, like it was all a lie.

'Our chemistry is amazing, Hayden, but sex and getting along are not everything. Not for me, at least. I fall easily for people and I might be the one at fault, but whatever. I've taken too many blows in the past and I'm tired of being treated like garbage. What I mean to ask is...' He sighed heavily. 'Do you think you could have a loving relationship with a man? Like, a boyfriend? Or is it just a spur-of-the-moment thing? You said you've never liked a guy before and suddenly it's OK to be with me...'

'It is,' I said honestly.

'But how can it be? Like, overnight?'

I studied Andy's expression; his eyebrows were downturned, and his eyes gleamed with hurt.

'It wasn't really overnight though, was it?'

Andy stared at his intertwined fingers. 'Was it not?'

I moved my arm over his shoulder and gathered him close. With the back of my finger I stroked the underside of his ear and kissed the opposite cheek. Andy exhaled a wavering breath.

'The first moment I saw you, I knew deep inside that meeting you was special,' I said. 'I didn't understand what was going on exactly, because I've never felt so attracted to a guy before, or anybody. I'm smitten, like. And sorry, but I really don't have a problem with you being a guy. They say, "Listen to your heart and *then* ask your cock for a second opinion."'

Andy laughed. 'Who says that?'

'Everyone,' I said seriously. 'And, in my case, my heart and my cock agree. I want you. You've been filling my mind for the whole fucking week. I even dreamt about you.'

Andy's expression softened. 'I dreamt about you too.'

'See?' I grinned, 'So, what's it gonna be? If you want me to call your parents and ask them for your hand, I will!'

Andy burst out laughing. 'Piss off!'

'But I would.'

'I know you would, you weirdo.'

I raised an outraged eyebrow. 'Hey!'

He pulled me by the shirt. 'Come here, you.'

We kissed and I stopped myself from saying, 'Finally!'

Andy's clothes were officially my enemies and my hands on a mission to uncover his skin. I rubbed his nipples under his T-shirt with my thumbs and Andy gasped. I lowered my head, ran my lips down his neck and sucked hard.

Andy groaned and tugged at my hair. 'H-Hayden...'

After a few seconds, I let go and smiled triumphantly at the dark red mark I'd left on his skin. Andy placed gentle kisses on my cheek, my jaw and looked at me with sweet, beautiful eyes. My heart did something strange, like a little flip, and warmth flooded me from within.

I hugged him tightly and met his gaze. 'Your ex was a blind prick. Oh well. All the more for me. Give me a couple days and you won't even remember he existed, don't worry.'

A wide smile broke across Andy's face. 'You really do always know the right thing to say, don't you?'

'One of my many talents.'

My phone, parked on the coffee table, rang and buzzed, making the glass underneath shake. I set it that way so that I wouldn't miss a call or a message. Even though I couldn't do without a mobile phone, there was something about it interrupting the good things in life that I couldn't stand, no matter the reason. When I saw who the caller was, my heart pounded in my chest.

'Mum?'

'Hello love.' She sounded tired, but as always tried to put a chirpy note in her voice, even if there wasn't much to be happy about.

'How are you feeling?'

'Oh you know, better, they said I can go home soon. The nurse just took a blood sample and asked me about the medication I'm taking. I couldn't remember the name...'

'Citalopram.'

'Oh yeah, that's the one.' I could almost hear her smile.

'Mum, I wanted to ask you, what did John—'

'Oh, the doctor's here. I'm going to tell him... Citalopram?'

'Yeah, twenty milligrams.'

'Oh, very quickly. Chrissy said you're staying with a friend tonight?'

'Andy. He's my boyfriend.'

'What you say, love?' A masculine voice mumbled something in the background. 'Sorry love, I've gotta go. I'm glad to know you're with a friend. Keep safe sweetie. See you tomorrow.'

'Alright. Love you, Mum.'

'Mwah! Love you lots,' she said, hanging up.

I sighed and put the phone back on the low table. Andy stared at me with a wide-eyed expression.

'My mum seems to be OK,' I quickly reassured him. 'She's avoiding talking about John, though. I guess I shouldn't have asked about him. At least she's in good hands and Katrina is with her. Mum just told me they're going to discharge her soon. Nothing to worry about, at least when it comes to her physical health. I bet she's not alright inside though.'

'Yeah, of course. It must be hard for her,' Andy murmured. He wouldn't meet my eyes.

'What's wrong?'

He played with his fringe and looked at his feet. 'Did you... come out to your mum on the phone?'

I frowned. 'You wha?'

'You said I'm your boyfriend.'

I raised my eyebrows. 'Yeah. Ain't you?'

He laughed awkwardly. 'I was thinking we'd take it slow.'

I put an arm around him. 'But you told me you wanted to be exclusive and date and all that. You asked me if I could have a loving relationship with a man. Aren't you basically saying that you want me to be your boyfriend?'

He chuckled. 'Can't fault your logic there. It's just funny that your mum found out I was your boyfriend before I did.'

'I don't think she heard, but I'll make sure she does next time.'

I gave Andy my most dazzling smile.

Andy grinned back, then laughed. He covered his face, laughed again. 'I can't believe this.'

I wrapped my arms around him and stamped a smacking kiss on his cheek. 'So, *boyfriend. What's happening first? Clockwork Orange or hot, hot sex?*'

12

ANDY

I woke up feeling fabulous. Achy, but fabulous. I couldn't remember the last time I had this much amazing sex. Oh, right: never. How many times did we do it? Five? Six, counting the sixty-nine? A little smile tugged at the corners of my lips as I rolled onto my back, stretching an arm and expecting to find Hayden next to me. Instead, the other side of the bed was cold and empty.

Oh. I sat up and rubbed my eyes.

I vaguely realised I was butt-naked as the duvet folded softly onto my lap. The room smelled of us, of our lovemaking.

Maybe Hayden had gone to the bathroom. I was a little disappointed that I didn't find him lying next to me as soon as I opened my eyes, but I was always too sappy like that.

I checked my phone: eight o'clock. Yawning, I got out of bed and toddled to my chest of drawers. I picked up a pair of green boxer shorts and an awesome *Evil Dead 2* T-shirt. Whatever I'd been wearing yesterday night, when we got frisky after dinner, had been left scattered somewhere on the way between the lounge and the bedroom. I grinned to myself, probably looking like an oaf and not caring one bit.

I went to the nearby bathroom; the door was open and the

room empty. I frowned at the vanilla tiles near the shower, since I was hoping to get a glimpse of Hayden's naked body and not a sleek wall.

A low voice reached my ears. I couldn't make out the words but it seemed to come from downstairs. As I descended the steps, my suspicions were confirmed – Hayden was talking to someone on the phone.

'Seriously, where the hell is he hiding?' he asked angrily.

The response was a muted babble on the other end of the line.

I reached the bottom of the staircase. Hayden stood in the wide space between the lounge and the dining area, wearing nothing but his underwear. His back was turned to me, offering a stunning view of his toned muscles and taut skin gleaming with sweat.

'Investigating what?' There was another pause and the low murmur of a feminine voice.

Hayden balled a hand into a fist. 'It sounds like the police don't have a clue and John is just walking around, waiting for the next chance to make our life fuckin' miserable.' He sighed. 'Well, at least Mum is with you. I just hope they find him soon, I really do.'

He turned around with a slight frown and saw me.

The moment our eyes met, his expression softened and his lips curved into a smile. 'One sec...'

He walked the few feet that separated us and slung an arm around my waist. 'Hello gorgeous,' he murmured huskily.

A rush of good feelings flooded me. Hayden leaned over to kiss me teasingly, the brief touch holding a trace of the passion we'd shared all night.

'Hey,' I said, still pressed against his chest, 'everything alright?'

'Is that Andy?' Christie's voice was loud and clear, even though she wasn't on speakerphone.

Hayden pressed the flat screen on his ear. 'Yeah.' He glanced at me, an eyebrow raised. 'She wants to speak to you.'

I met his gaze in puzzlement but took the phone from his hand. 'Hello?'

'Oh hello Andy! How are you?' Christie asked brightly.

'I'm very well. Yourself?'

Christie laughed. 'You're such a well-mannered boy! Your mum must be proud.'

'That's debatable.'

Christie laughed again. 'Listen love. Hayden is coming down for lunch and he's going to bring some stuff for his mum and siblings. I was wondering, would you like to join us too?'

'Uhh...'

'If you've got nothing else to do, of course.'

Hayden mouthed, 'What's she asking?'

'I don't want to impose,' I mumbled.

'Oh, don't be silly! We'd be more than happy to have you! Do you like steak and chips?'

'Uh, yeah...?'

'Perfect! I'll come pick you guys up in a few hours. We only live in Llanishen.'

'Uhm, well, there's no need. I can drive us to your place and stop at Hayden's house to get the stuff.'

'Are you sure? I really don't mind giving you a lift back.'

'I'm positive.'

'Great. Let me speak to Hayden. Ta.'

I handed back the phone with a rigid arm. Wow, it seemed I had zero ability to turn anything down, especially if it concerned Hayden. Persuasion must be a family trait.

Hayden looked at me with a questioning frown, but as soon as he was on the phone again, his eyes widened with understanding. 'Oh. Oh yeah?' He glanced at me and grinned roguishly.

I blushed.

'Right,' he continued. 'If he says he's OK with it... yeah. That's very kind of him. Yeah, he's a great guy. We'll see you just before midday, then. Bye. T'ra.' He hung up and looked at me with a bright smile on his face. 'She suckered you into it. Typical Christie. If you don't want to go just say. I'll send her a text.'

'No, I'd like to come along.' I ran my fingers through my hair. 'If... you want me to.'

Hayden drew me against his bare chest and slipped his arms around my torso, holding me tight. He kissed my neck over and over, making loud popping sounds each time.

'Are you an octopus?'

One of his hands moved down to my ass and squeezed. 'Is that the kind of thing you're into? Tentacle porn?'

I hugged him back. 'No, not really.'

Hayden licked his lips. 'What do you like, then?'

I thought about it. 'I don't mind risky stuff, sometimes. It's a bit of a fantasy of mine.'

His eyes widened. 'Ooh! What kind of risky stuff?'

'Sex in socially awkward situations. I like it when my hand is forced a little.' I flashed him a smile.

Hayden's eyes sparkled. 'Really?' He pressed me against his groin. My pulse quickened.

I ran my hands through his hair and found it warm and damp. 'Why are you so sweaty?'

'I've just finished my morning workout.'

'Oh, really? You should have woken me. I would have liked to watch you strain on my floor.'

At that moment, my stomach decided to growl in protest. No wonder, I'd barely eaten anything since the previous morning.

Hayden chuckled. 'Perfect timing. I ordered a McDonald's breakfast twenty minutes ago. I didn't know what you liked so I got one of everything.'

'One of *everything*?'

'You need to eat something substantial,' he said. 'You won't survive another day if all you feed on is powdered soup and salad.'

The delivery man handed us a humongous paper bag a few minutes later. Hayden put on one of my larger T-shirts and sat next to me on a stool by the breakfast bar. We gorged on what my mum would have called 'sinful food'. We chatted and listened to music through my hand-held speaker, the tunes ranging from metal to grunge, electronic music, alternative pop to the seventies prog vibe of Ghost BC.

Hayden took a huge bite from his sausage and bacon McMuffin and scrolled through his phone. 'Which one did you want to listen to now?'

'"Square Hammer", that's my favourite!' Hayden selected the track and pressed play.

I sang along the tune, harmonising, then mimed the guitar solo and Hayden laughed.

He popped a whole hash-brown in his mouth. 'You've got a great singing voice, but your air guitar? Nah.'

I raised an eyebrow. 'Well, can *you* do any better?'

He grinned. 'I'm an alright guitarist, actually.'

Hayden pretended to press chords in the air and plucked non-existent strings with a skill that undoubtedly surpassed mine. He played his invisible guitar while I kept on singing, and when the track ended we smiled at each other. His glance was unmistakably lewd. I averted my gaze and took a bite of my bacon bagel, shaken by the bolt of desire that overtook me, all because of a salacious look.

'Thank you for breakfast,' I murmured.

Warm fingers coasted inside the collar of my T-shirt, caressing the skin of my neck. My breath caught. I glanced at him. Hayden regarded me with that same sultry expression, eyes glinting.

My heart beat faster. 'What?'

'I was just checking, you know. It really shows.' He stroked my neck with his thumb.

'What shows?'

'The hickey.'

'What! *Where?*' I opened the camera on my phone and pointed it at my throat. There it was, the *huge* purplish branding, right on the crook of my neck.

Hayden's hand went to the back of my neck and dragged me towards his face. His hot tongue flicked between my teeth and upper lip before invading the rest of my mouth. My cock swelled in my pants.

Hayden was slipping a hand down my boxers and I moaned softly with anticipation when my phone, lying next to my cup of tea, rang. He wasn't fazed by the interruption and continued stroking my hard length, thumbing a nipple under my T-shirt and licking and sucking on my neck.

I saw three ominous letters on the screen and groaned. 'I think... I should answer that. It's my... *mmm*... mother...'

Hayden picked up my phone before I could. I thought he would hang up, instead he pressed the green icon, set the call on speaker and placed the phone back on the counter. I frowned at him, perplexed. He grinned wickedly and waggled his eyebrows, took a firm hold of my wrists with one hand and let my hard cock out of my boxers with the other.

'What are you doing?' I hissed under my breath.

Hayden didn't let go of me. He slid off his stool carefully and knelt on the floor in front of me, between my legs.

'Hello? Andrew, are ye there boy?' Mum said.

My gaze flicked from Hayden to the phone, then back to Hayden. He clutched each wrist with a strong hand now. His grip of steel was as firm as the bulge in his boxers looked. He tipped his head and lapped at the slit of my erect dick.

'Ah... ahhh, hey M-Mum, what's up?' I stammered.

'*What's up?* I'm yer mother, not yer mate! *Jaysus*!' she laughed.

'S-sorry,' I muttered.

Hayden smirked, stuck out his tongue again and slowly licked my shaft, balls to tip. He went back down and sucked on my foreskin, eyes blazing with lust. I bit back a groan and shuddered.

'I was expecting a call from ye, but it seems I'll have to wait forever unless it's me who calls first,' Mum said. 'So, what's happening with the dishwasher?'

'All s-sorted,' I lied.

'Oh really? What model did ye settle for then?'

Hayden took me in deep and tongued the underside of my crown. His hands gripped my wrists tight and the constriction, as well as the sticky situation he put me in, turned me on so much. He licked my slit again, dived in and slurped on my tip.

I closed my eyes. '*Mhhhh...*'

'Andrew boy? What's the matter?'

'Mum can you please... I... can I call you later...? *Ah!*'

'Why? What's wrong?'

Hayden sucked faster, harder. 'I've got... s-stomach cramps... oh... *ohhh...*'

'Oh really? Are ye alright? Do ye want me to come over?' She sounded seriously concerned.

'Mh *noo*... my... f-friend he... went to the pharmacy for me. To-to get a... mhh... medication...' Hayden chuckled with my cock deep in his mouth.

'Did he now? What friend? The one from last time?' Mum asked suspiciously.

Oh God. She knew what I was up to. She must have. I was leaking pre-cum and Hayden hummed in approval at the taste of me, gulping down my juices like a horny dog.

I whispered, '*Pervert...*'

'What d'ye say?'

'Y-yeah.' The word came out breathy. 'Hayden.'

'Do I know him?'

'N-no.' I bent over to murmur in Hayden's ear, 'I'm gonna cum.'

He lifted his head to say, 'Do it.' Hayden went back down to suck on my hard meat.

Oh shit! 'Mum... I... am going now... for a lay down.'

'Ye sure ye don't want me to come over?'

'Yeah. I'll be fine once... once... he's back.'

I could barely think. Hayden's hands held my wrists tighter and his tongue, his *fecking* tongue circled around my crown, and down again he went.

Mum was silent for a moment. 'Alright then, call me as soon as you can. Don't keep me waiting.'

'N-no. Thank you, Mum.'

'Bye darling.' The phone call ended.

'Oh God Hayden, oh God!' I panted.

He let go of my wrists and began tossing at the base of my erection while his mouth worked on my tip tirelessly. My hands went to his hair.

I clutched at his curls for dear life, almost ripping the strands off his skull.

I squeezed my eyes shut as my orgasm hurled out of me, wave after wave of intense sensation, the kind of pleasure that takes it all from you and leaves you limp like overcooked spaghetti. Hayden gulped down my cum and made a soft moan in his throat, like he was really turned on.

How could it be that this guy had never done this to other men before? Swallowing my load had been right up his street from the first time he went down on me. I myself didn't have the courage to let others come in my mouth in my early days of experimentation.

I drooped onto my folded arms over the counter and sighed. Hayden moved next to me.

'Was that risky enough for you, like?' he asked in a sultry tone.

I had just enough energy to lift my head and shoot him a glare. 'That was my *Catholic mother,* you dickhead!'

Hayden smiled lopsidedly, somewhere between guilt and amusement. He dropped his gaze to his interlaced hands. 'Sorry. Are you mad at me?'

'I bloody well should be!'

'And are you?'

I stuck my face in the crook of my elbow and said nothing.

'Andy, I need to ask you something.'

'What?' I said sharply.

'Can you... help me?'

I peeked at him to see what he was talking about. He raised his T-shirt and gave me a view of his abs and impossibly hard cock straining against his boxers.

He squeezed and stroked his length over the fabric, looking at me with a lecherous expression, soft eyes and reddened cheeks. 'I need to cum.'

I stared at his erection and swallowed. 'N-no,' I muttered. 'Sort it out yourself, p-pervert.' *Oh my God,* I was shaking.

His lips parted and his hand moved faster over his boxers.

'When you act all embarrassed and push me away, it turns me on.'

'I'm starting to think that everything turns you on!'

He bit his lip and released the pink flesh slowly through his teeth. 'If you're pissed at me, you could punish me.'

My voice wavered. 'What?'

'You could sit on my face and press your hole against my mouth, rub your ass on my face and call me names. If you're angry at me, you can be forceful. I'd like that.'

My jaw dropped. 'Holy shit.'

He stood up and put his hands on my shoulders. 'Do you want me to beg? I'm very good at begging.'

Hayden was right: he did surprise me, over and over. Also, I'd underestimated the power of hormones. My conscious mind officially had a new focus: sex... and more sex.

He bent over to kiss me and our tongues were quickly entwined. I was lost.

Sure enough, minutes later I was stark naked on the sofa, riding Hayden's face and gasping, 'That's it! Eat my fucking ass, just like that! Filthy fucking pervert!'

Hayden lapped, sucked and worked my opening with his tongue while furiously jerking himself off. He moaned, thoroughly enjoying it. I was so turned on and overwhelmed with amazement that all rational thought abandoned me completely. We were all instinct and raw need. I stroked myself too as I stared at his hand moving over his hard length. The situation was almost too much; so impossibly arousing. He hummed in a low voice, all because my ass was on his face, and I pressed and rubbed myself as he'd asked me to. Hayden came all over his stomach with a hoarse groan and I followed suit, my balls tightening. My jizz dribbled out of me, mixing with his and leaking down his side.

I closed my eyes, waiting for my frantic pulse to subside. Hayden's hand went limp. Panting, he placed tender kisses on my butt-cheeks and hole.

I sat up on my knees and he kept on stroking my backside with a reverent touch. 'I think that if I had a God, it'd be your arse.'

What could one say to that? 'I... I'll go grab a cloth, to clean us up. I mean, mostly you.'

Hayden folded an arm under his head and smirked. 'OK.'

I came back from the bathroom a moment later with a damp flannel and a large towel. I knelt by the sofa and cleaned him with care. In the meanwhile, he caressed my arm and hair with tender fingers, making my heart swell.

'Are you always like this?' I asked.

'What you mean?' he enquired softly.

What did I mean, indeed? Passionate? Amazing? Intense? Rule-breaking? I cleared my throat. 'Horny?'

Hayden laughed; a low, husky sound that made me all hot and bothered. 'I've always been a sexual person, like. I haven't felt this way for a long time, though.'

I dried his abdomen with the large towel. 'What way?'

He sat up and put a hand on my cheek. 'On fire.'

Hayden kissed me, sucked on my lips, teased me open. Heat flooded my chest and I recognised with dismay the nature of this feeling. He embraced me, his body warm and comforting like a cup of hot chocolate when the rain outside is tapping at your window. He exhaled a long breath against my neck.

'God, you really make me burn. Let's go have a shower together,' he whispered.

I pushed on the wall of muscle that was his chest. 'We have to get going!'

'I'm all sweaty and sticky with cum, I have to wash anyway. Won't you... join me? Wash my back?'

I stared at him in disbelief. Those pleading eyes, that beckoning gaze.

'We both know it's not your back you want me to wash,' I grumbled.

Laughing, he took my hand and led me upstairs. The fight in me died. He didn't even have to persuade me: I went down on my knees of my own volition, sucking him deep as the warm jet of the shower splashed over my shoulders. All the while he watched me intently, like that first time we spoke, as if he didn't want to miss a single thing. He called me babes, moved my fringe away and put a hand over my brow to keep the water from streaming into my eyes. That gesture, so attentive and caring, made my heart burst. Hayden came inside my mouth, helped me up and kissed me slowly.

'Andy... Andy, you're so giving,' he said.

He held me for a long time, lathered soap over my arms and back gently, carefully, as if I was meant to be cherished. Eventually he got hard again, worked my hole with his mouth and used the lubricant I had in the shower rack to make me sleek. He only left to get a condom and was back right away. He entered me, slow and deep, then took me against the tiled wall.

Hayden kissed my shoulders and whispered gentle words as he moved inside me. 'You're beautiful,' he said. 'You're perfect. You're so smooth, so sweet.'

I floated through the sensation, swept away by the whirlwind of heat and tenderness his words and body provided. I was spellbound. *He's making love to me*, I thought. *Oh this... is love. This is love.*

An hour later, Hayden and I finally got dressed. I existed somewhere between the physical world and paradise, both ecstatic and terrified.

While he was on the phone with his aunt, asking about some items he needed to pick up from his house, I checked on my messages. A couple of friends asked me if I was free at the weekend and congratulated me for finishing my exams. Then, there were two texts from Tai.

'*Don't think I have forgotten, btw. You have lost a bet BIG TIME.*'

The second message, which had been sent about half an hour later, stated:

'*You haven't replied to my last text which can only mean that you're busy fucking like a beast. I am so jealous! I have to say babe, you have pulled amazingly well. Hayden is seriously HOT and I'm so happy for you! Craig doesn't hold a fucking candle to your new man. You have it great. It's not going to be a big sacrifice to allow me to make you beautiful since you're in such a good place, right? So yeah. Wednesday karaoke at the Golden Cross, next week. It's definitely happening! We're going to perform as a duet!!! I bet Hayden's going to love seeing you in a mini skirt!! ;) xxx*'

'A duet? What?' My mouth went dry.

A gentle touch on the hip made me jump. 'Everything OK?' Hayden asked.

I quickly hid my phone screen. 'Y-yeah, all good.'

He put an arm around my shoulder and kissed my lips. 'Are we ready to go?'

I didn't know what was worse: the prospect of wearing a skimpy outfit and singing in front of lots of people, or to have fallen in love with a guy I'd known for just over a week.

13

HAYDEN

As Andy drove with a focused expression, I tried to memorise the small details of his body. The way his eyes caught the light of the sun as he waited for a car to give way and his elegant fingers, brushing over the steering wheel. A crease on his brow, his teeth biting his lip and the bend of his neck as he leaned over to scour the road. I itched to trail his bare back with my fingertips. Images of his mouth sucking on my cock and his sweet hole, squeezing my dick as water trickled down his spine filled my mind. I rubbed my forehead and inhaled deeply. Fuck, I was officially a sex addict.

'Turn left onto Station Road,' the robotic Google Maps voice suggested.

I was embarrassed to admit I was super happy that Andy was coming with me to see my family. I wanted him nearby and *could not* stray too far from his presence. Not today; my body and mind dictated so.

'It's really no trouble. I made sure I was free today anyway,' Andy said.

'Yeah?'

His cheeks flushed. 'I was meaning to spend some time with you if you fancied it, since you said you don't work on Mondays. We could have worked on some music together, played video games, watched a movie or something. I didn't know we were going to hook up at that point but, you know,' he smiled coyly, 'you were on my mind for sure.'

I sat back on the passenger seat and grinned. 'Were you hoping for *things* to happen?'

He chuckled. 'I didn't dare hope for that.'

I licked my lips, feeling the need to taste Andy's mouth. 'Because you thought I was straight?'

'Among other things.'

I frowned. 'What other things?'

He shrugged. 'Well, you're way out of my league.'

'Says *you*?'

Andy's smile was tight. 'I'm average.'

I wasn't going to hear this nonsense. As we continued for Heol Hir, I tapped on his shoulder. 'Turn right, here.'

'Uh? Are you sure?'

'Take this turn,' I said firmly.

Andy looked puzzled but followed my instructions. He led the car up a narrow side street to a virtually deserted car-park next to the cemetery.

'Go there.' I indicated that he should drive to a spot behind the cover of a line of trees.

'Do you want me to park here…?'

'Just here, yeah.'

Andy positioned the car, turned off the engine and pulled the handbrake.

He glanced at me with uncertainty. 'Are we getting out of the car?'

I undid my seatbelt and scuttled towards him, put a hand on his cheek and pressed my lips to his.

'You are the most wonderful person I have ever met,' I said. 'We've not known each other long, but you already mean a lot to me.' I took his hand and kissed his palm. 'You have no idea how much I... *how happy* I am that we've found each other. Trust me when I say that I'm serious about you, yeah?'

His expression softened. 'I'm serious about you too.'

'When you say that I'm out of your league, I feel... God, that feels ridiculous. You haven't got a clue of how beautiful you are. If only you could see yourself the way *I see you*... I mean, if someone is punching above their weight, that's not you. I guarantee it.'

The chirping of birds and children laughing somewhere nearby carried through the silence as we kissed. It was a slow, tender entwining of tongues, exploring and caressing.

A succession of rapid thumps at our window broke the spell. An oldish lady with a rye-coloured perm wagged her finger at us.

As she pushed her handbag against the glass, her droopy features contorted with indignation. 'Have you got no shame? There's a cemetery right here and children are walking by!'

There was another lady, a ghostly woman with a glum lilac dress and an aquiline face, standing a little further away and in line with the windscreen.

She gasped when she took a better look at us. 'Oh, good Lord! They're both men!'

The two ladies got into a white Daewoo I hadn't taken notice of before. I wished I could beam lasers through my eyes like Clark fucking Kent.

Instead, all I could say was, 'What absolute cunts.'

'Yeah, well, it happens,' Andy replied, caressing my face.

'Does it though?'

He smiled softly. 'You've never dated a guy so you might not have a grasp of how many homophobes are out and about in the world. To be fair, those two might have bothered us even if one of us had been a woman, since we're making out by the cemetery.' He chuckled. 'I'm up for doing it again at some point! Anything that offends religious nuts is right up my street.' He fondled my pecs and grinned.

I raised an eyebrow. 'Something will be right up your *butt* now in a minute, if you keep stroking my nipples like that.'

He moved his hands away and laughed. 'Right, OK! Your auntie is expecting us. Can we walk it from here?'

'Yeah. If Bobi and Katrina have parked in the front garden, there's not going to be any space left for us. Leaving the car here is our best bet.'

After grabbing Iwan's grey coat from the backseat and a bag full of clothing for the fam, we got out of the car. Busy as I was getting things straight with Andy, I had forgotten how apprehensive I felt about seeing my mum. John was going to come up and I dreaded the moment. The police hadn't found him yet; the memory of that fact made me shiver. They were 'investigating some unclear details', Aunt Christie had said. I called bullshit.

Where the hell is he hiding? Could he be... following us? Fear gripped my guts and I stopped in my tracks.

'What's wrong?' Andy asked.

'Nothing, I was just making sure I had my phone with me,' I muttered.

Timidly, he reached for my hand. I promptly took it and interlaced my fingers with his. Feeling heartened by his touch, I held on to his warmth as we walked alongside a metallic fence and up the slope of Heol Hir.

***

'Is this the house?' Andy asked.

I nodded. 'Yeah, that's it.'

Aunt Christie's front garden was mostly covered with thin gravel, with three little trees and a scrawny bush giving a splash of colour. Like most of the houses in the area, it was painted white with a dark roof and had a large bay window at the front. As I suspected, the little parking space available was already taken by Aunt Katrina and Uncle Bobi's cars.

As soon as we passed the low brick wall separating the pavement from the property, Andy's hand scrambled away from my grasp. I turned to look at him in silent question and he gave me a sheepish smile in response. Before either of us could make a move to press the doorbell, the front door opened.

The colossal figure of Uncle Bobi filled the open space of the doorframe. He was the very definition of a man-bear: chunky, strong, tall, hairy and cool.

He raised a straight eyebrow and rubbed his round stomach. 'I thought it was you. I've seen you from the window!'

'Hiya,' I greeted.

Bobi enfolded me into a tight hug and gripped my hand.

'Alright butt? Well look at you!' He gestured at my figure. 'What do you eat for breakfast? *Metal* or what?'

I chuckled. 'Uncle, this is Andy.' I indicated my smiling companion.

'Nice to meet you.' Andy shook Bobi's hand.

'Nice to meet ew. I'm Bobi.' My uncle flashed his trademark crooked smile. 'Come on in lads! Lunch is ready and I'm *starving!*'

As we followed Bobi inside the house, I wondered if Andy meant to keep our relationship a secret after all. Why would he let go of my hand in front of Uncle Bobi otherwise? I felt like it'd be natural to be open about things, but maybe I was wrong. He did look flustered when I told my mum we were boyfriends after all. Should I act more discreetly? We hadn't agreed on how to go about things, what we should share and with whom. Personally, I didn't give a fuck about what people had to say about who I slept with. I wanted to scream to the world how happy I was, tell them that I glowed with joy because Andy and I were together.

We crossed the small foyer and entered the lounge which was, to be fairly accurate, *very* lived in. Toys, shoes, clothes, DVDs and many other random things were scattered all over the carpet, sofa and coffee table. Sophie and my little cousins, Melissa and Eliza, were playing on the floor with dolls. Sophie, being the oldest, was leading the game and the two six-year-olds listened to her instructions eagerly.

Sophie beamed the moment our eyes met. 'Hayden!' She stood up, ran towards me and enveloped my waist into a hug.

I rubbed her little back. 'Hiya Soph! What have you been up to then?'

She grinned, shining brown eyes looking up at me. 'I've been playing with Melissa and Eliza. Auntie Christie said I had to miss school, so I didn't get to see Amelia.' She pouted. 'I promised to give her our BFF diary today 'cause it's her turn to write in it...'

I stroked her hair. 'You'll have the chance to give it to her soon, no worries.'

I'd received a text from Aunt Katrina that morning saying that, as long as John roamed free, neither Christie nor my mother felt comfortable sending Soph and Iwan to school alone, or have them walk around Cardiff by themselves. They were going to skip class altogether today, since yesterday had been a little traumatic for us all.

I couldn't agree more. As for Sophie, it was best if she was kept unaware of the adults' worries.

'Hey Sophie!' Andy waved his hand and smiled.

The corner of his eyes creased in a way that made me want to kiss him.

'*Andy?*' Sophie's eyes grew wide. 'What are you doing here?'

Andy's smile broadened. 'Just stopping by for lunch.'

'You're eating with us?' Her eyes gleamed with delight.

'Yeah. Your auntie invited me too,' Andy said.

Sophie threw her fists in the air and bounced up and down. '*Yeeah!*'

Andy's perplexed expression echoed my own feelings in seeing Sophie's reaction.

'Too much sugar for that one,' Uncle Bobi explained. 'One and a half packs of Skittles between the pair of them this morning. I managed to snatch the second pack before they could gobble the whole bloody lot. They cried their eyes out *for ages*. Only now they've started to calm down, aye.'

I shook my head. 'Did *you* give them the sweets?'

Bobi put up his hands. 'I had nothing to do with it.'

'It was my fault,' Aunt Katrina grumbled.

She swished toward us with her long, patterned dress, loose fluffy cardigan and flowing curls. Aunt Katrina was the youngest of the three sisters and made a point of being the flashiest too. Fluttering her fake eyelashes, she offered a gracious hand to Andy for a shake and they introduced themselves.

'Thank you for giving my darling nephew a place to stay the night,' Aunt Katrina said. 'Hayden is lucky to have a friend like you.'

I gnawed on my lower lip and glanced at Andy.

He smiled serenely, unperturbed. 'It was no trouble at all.'

Andy left the bag of clothes by the entrance and we headed to the dining room. Iwan and my cousin Ceri were already sitting at the laden table, munching on grapes and Red Leicester while chattering about sport.

The two lads were so enthralled in conversation that neither of them noticed me until I pinched Iwan's ear. 'What about answering my messages?'

'Ouch! I ran out of credit! *Oooowww!*'

I let go of his ear and hung the grey coat on his chair. 'What about *my phone* calls, hmm? Don't make me worry so much, innit!'

Ceri snickered and Iwan blushed. 'I was going to talk to you on the phone this morning but Christie said you sounded busy.' He turned back to look at the football game on Ceri's tablet.

A choked sound came from behind me. Andy combed his fringe nervously, trying to hide the redness of his cheeks. Heat rose up my face too. 'Just answer your phone next time, OK?'

I patted Iwan's shoulder gently but he didn't look up. I needed to have a talk with my brother but this was neither the time nor the place.

'Here you are!' Aunt Christie emerged with her frilly apron from the rustic arch leading to the kitchen and gave us an amused look. 'You boys had a late night?'

Ohh, if only she knew. Although, from the sounds of it, she actually did.

'Hiya Christie.' I looked around, searching for the obviously missing person. 'Where's Mum?' I glanced behind me, trying to remember where the staircase was. It had been a while since I came to visit Aunt Christie and even longer since I last went upstairs. 'Should I call her for lunch?'

Aunt Christie clutched my arm. 'She said she's not hungry at the moment. She's going to eat later, she is.' Her smile didn't meet her eyes. 'Your mother had a difficult night. She needs a bit of peace and quiet.'

An uncomfortable feeling knotted my guts. 'Yeah. I understand.'

'I am *hungry!*' Uncle Bobi slapped my shoulder with a powerful hand. My breath huffed out of my lungs and Andy chuckled.

It was a noisy meal. With three enthusiastic little girls, two teenage boys and my exuberant aunts – who had decided to interview Andy on everything regarding his life – I couldn't expect less. The only silent ones were Uncle Bobi and me. His steak and chips absorbed him completely and he threw the odd comment or a bark of laughter only here and there. I, on the other hand, focused on listening to the conversation taking place between Andy, who sat next to me, and my aunts. They asked him about his job, which was currently non-existent since Andy had just finished his studies.

'I have an MPhil in Philosophy and I began studying Classical Literature when I was twenty,' Andy said.

'Wait a minute, how old are you?' Aunt Katrina asked.

'Twenty-three.'

'I thought you weren't older than nineteen. Your features are so...' she made a gesture around her face, 'elegant.'

Andy laughed softly. 'Thank you.'

My uncle, who'd left to go to the kitchen, had come back holding a red bottle. 'Ketchup, anybody?'

Andy lifted a finger. 'Yes please.'

'You're handsome, smart and polite,' Aunt Katrina winked at Andy. 'I can see why the girls are after you.'

Andy smiled but his eyes widened with alarm. 'Pardon?'

Aunt Christie wiggled her eyebrows and pointed at her neck, the same spot where Andy showcased my not-so-small hickey which he'd clearly forgotten about. I hid a smirk behind my drinking glass.

Andy covered the mark with one hand and shook the ketchup bottle with the other. 'Ah, well...' He flushed bright red.

Iwan gasped and Ceri brought a hand to his mouth, smothering a chuckle. Before I could interpret the signs, a red explosion happened next to me. There was a general uproar of surprise; the girls and both my aunts screamed while Uncle Bobi exhaled a loud, 'Woah!'

My brother groaned in anguish and Ceri roared with laughter. As for me, I watched in horror as ketchup rained on Andy's face, hair and clothes, and over pretty much everyone else too. I grabbed a napkin and began wiping Andy's face.

'Are you alright? Did it go in your eyes?'

'Ah, no... just about everywhere but there,' he muttered.

There was ketchup all over him, even inside his nose! I straightened, my body tight with fury. I turned to look at Ceri and Iwan to give them a piece of my mind, but found that they, as well as everyone else at the table, stared at me with wide eyes and a slack jaw.

There were streaks of red on everyone's faces and on the walls, chairs...

My world stopped turning as a sick feeling grew at the base of my stomach.

I started shaking uncontrollably, my nails piercing my palms. Heaving, I leaned against the wall. My heart pounded so fast that I was amazed I wasn't dead already. I gritted my teeth.

'Hayden,' Aunt Christie began, her face pale.

A scream escaped my throat, so loud that it pierced my ears. Sophie, Melissa and Eliza shuddered in fear and they all began to cry. I clutched at my chest, a deep pain taking hold of my thrumming heart. My legs gave in and my vision blurred. The hardness of the tiled floor met the weight of my slack body.

'Hayden!' Aunt Christie called out.

I couldn't answer her. I was lost, drowning at the bottom of my inner well.

14

HAYDEN

I came to on the sofa in Aunt Christie's lounge. Silence surrounded me as I stared at the familiar ceiling above.

I hadn't passed out, not really. I had been there all along, but was hidden in a little corner of my mind where no one could hurt me. I sat up, my chest and back aching. Bile rose up my throat.

'Hayden! How are you feeling?' Andy asked. He was sitting on an armchair nearby.

I brought a hand to my mouth. 'Fuck. I'm going to be sick.'

He ran to the kitchen, yelling, 'Washing-up bowl! Quick!'

It was too late, though. I spewed up by the sofa and on the carpet. I stared in shock at the pool of sludge soaking through the brown pile.

Christie and Andy ran in, panting, a white bowl in her hands. I looked at them both and they at me.

'Oh,' Aunt Christie muttered.

The humiliation and shame were too much to bear. I covered my face and burst out crying.

Aunt Christie rushed to sit next to me and put a hand on my shoulder. 'Oh no, babe! Don't worry about it! It's fine! A bit of soap and a good scrub will do the job, nothing I haven't dealt with before, you know me.'

I shook my head. Though her words were kind, they didn't make me feel any better.

'Christie, could you give us a moment?' Andy asked.

She looked up at him. 'Eh?'

'Please.'

'No worries. I'll grab some towels and gloves...'

'I'll clean up my own mess,' I growled.

'Can we sort that out in a minute?' Andy pleaded. 'I need a word alone with Hayden.'

Her eyes flicked between the two of us. 'Alright. I'll be back in a bit now.'

Aunt Christie left us and Andy took her place next to me. He wrapped his fingers around my cold hand. His heat, pouring through my body, brought my senses back to life.

'I told them not to call an ambulance,' he said.

I exhaled with relief. 'Thank fuck for that!'

'Christie wasn't happy about it but I told her this happened before and that I knew that it wouldn't solve anything, only get you more stressed.'

'You're amazing,' I said. 'I meant to ask you, how do you know how to deal with... you know, this *shit* so well?'

His mouth curved into a sad smile. 'A friend of mine, in college, had loads of anxiety episodes. He hated it when people called 999 for him when there wasn't a real need for it. It only drew attention to him, which made him feel worse. It takes time to deal with these things. Being pitied and treated differently is not what a person who's feeling down needs.'

I took in the sight of his beautiful, ketchup-smeared face and brushed his cheek with my fingers.

He grinned. 'It's alright. You can lick it off me later.'

I slipped my arms around him in a hug and buried my face in his stained clothes. 'That sounds good.'

He chuckled, cupped my chin and leaned in to kiss me.

I backed away. 'Hang on a sec now, I've literally just thrown up!' Andy laughed.

I squeezed him against my chest, breathing his scent deeply. 'Andy, I—'

'Ah.' The sound was nothing more than a whisper, but loud enough to make us turn around and look.

Ceri stood at the base of the staircase with an awe-struck expression.

I slid out of my embrace with Andy just a little, but firmly kept a hand on his waist. 'Hey bro.'

'I uh... wanted to apologise to Andy for... the ketchup prank.' He fidgeted, avoiding our gaze. 'It was supposed to be for Dad, you know, for a laugh. He always uses the ketchup first and I thought there weren't going to be any mix-ups. I didn't know you were coming and that he bought this fifty percent less sugar ketchup that he was using today, instead of the normal one...'

'It's OK. All is forgiven,' Andy said with a smile.

Iwan came down the stairs too, followed by Uncle Bobi. Iwan looked at me with a strange expression; a mixture of fear and worry in his eyes.

Bobi leaned on the wall. 'How are you feeling?'

I plastered a smile on my face. 'Better. Where are the girls now?'

'With Katrina. Since you were crying and screaming like a banshee on the floor, she thought it was best to take them away.'

I frowned. 'Shit. Was I screaming on the floor?'

If a fly had sneezed, I would have heard it for how quiet the room went.

'You don't remember?' Iwan asked.

I ran a hand down my face and sighed. 'I... uh, I'm sorry about what happened. It's been going on for a while and...'

'What do you mean "for a while"?' Auntie Christie came in with a big bowl of soapy water, a bunch of old towels dangling from her arm and plastic gloves. Her face was a mask of concern. 'Do you mean that yesterday wasn't the first time you've been unwell?'

Uncle Bobi's eyes widened. 'What, it happened yesterday too?'

Aunt Christie nodded, brows creasing. 'Yes, but it was *nothing* like this.'

I rubbed my painful head. 'Anyway. I'm taking medication for it, but it's not helping all that much. I'm sleeping better, but that's it.'

'How long have you been having these attacks for?' Uncle Bobi enquired.

I pressed my palm against a throbbing vein on my forehead and exhaled. 'About six months.'

'Have you been hiding it all this time?' Iwan asked, a pained look on his face.

'I'm sorry, like, I didn't want to worry you.' I gave him a meaningful look. 'And you know how Mum is. The last thing she needs, especially now, is to deal with *my* problems. She's got enough on her plate as it is. You're old enough to understand this, mun.'

A bleak expression darkened my brother's features while an awkward confusion and concern glazed the eyes of the rest of my relatives. It was as if they wished they could help me but didn't quite know how.

I turned to Aunt Christie. 'I'll take that bowl from you, Auntie. I'll clean the carpet myself. Crack on with lunch, go on.' I attempted to stand but my legs wobbled like gelatine.

Andy helped me back down before I could fall over.

'Sit down, mun! Give yourself a minute!' Uncle Bobi said.

Andy put a hand on my shoulder. 'I'll go get you a glass of water.'

I tilted my head and pressed a lengthy kiss on his cheek. 'Thank you.'

Andy smiled and his face turned crimson. He stood up and skittered through the room, looking embarrassed. My relatives followed him with their gaze before turning to me with wide, astounded eyes. Iwan looked particularly flabbergasted and Uncle Bobi hummed deep in his throat, a perplexed frown rumpling his forehead.

I sat back on the sofa and sighed. 'Before you start wondering, I'll tell you straight. Andy's my boyfriend.'

Iwan openly gasped and Ceri brought a hand to his mouth.

'I knew something was up with you two!' Aunt Christie chuckled. 'He looks at you so tenderly.'

I perked up and grinned. 'Does he?'

'Oh yeah,' she said, a knowing gleam in her eyes. 'How long have you been together?'

'Since yesterday.'

Aunt Christie grinned. 'Oh?'

'Wait a minute! Wait a minute!' Iwan cut the air with his hands. 'Since when are *you* gay?'

I tightened my lips. 'Bro, seriously? Why are you asking me that?'

'Because I have never, *ever* seen you with a guy, like!'

I cocked my head. 'Does it bother you that I'm dating a guy?'

'Eh? No! It's just surprising. Like, sudden.'

Uncle Bobi and Ceri's creased brows seemed to support Iwan's sentiment.

I rubbed my aching ribs, my hands still clammy. Although weak and quivering, happiness warmed my heart.

I smiled. 'Tell me about it.'

Andy walked back into the lounge. 'Here,' he said, handing me the glass. A persistent blush coloured his cheeks.

'Thank you,' I accepted the drink with a dazzling smile, downed a good swig and patted the seat next to me.

Andy took his place on the sofa with slow apprehension, leaving a decorous seven-or-so inches between us. I remedied this immediately, scooting the distance, putting an arm around his shoulder and, after gulping down more water, nudging his face towards mine. A choked sound squeaked out of Andy's throat as I went to kiss him.

'Right!' Aunt Christie's shrill voice seized the moment. 'We're very happy that you've found love, Hayden, but I need to clean the stain off the carpet before it settles in.'

It was my turn to blush. 'I'm gonna take care of it, mun.'

She promptly ignored me and turned to the assembled onlookers. 'You boys, off with the pair of you. And Bobi, what we need now is *pizza*, so jump to it, come on.'

'Yes, alright.' Uncle Bobi turned to Andy and me. 'What pizza do you want?'

I smiled. 'We both like sausage-stuffed crust.'

Ceri groaned and Andy hid his face behind his palms, his ears bright red. My smirk widened into a full-blown grin. Aunt Christie raised an eyebrow and Uncle Bobi guffawed, holding his hard stomach as his body quaked with laughter.

As for Iwan, he slowly shook his head at me, his eyes half-shut in an unimpressed stare. 'You dirty bugger.'

15

ANDY

Warmth danced up my limbs, chest and face, as if I'd downed two or three shots of whisky on an empty stomach and the alcohol had gone straight to my head. Hayden wasn't the only one who didn't have the strength to get off the sofa. His hand interlaced with mine and his thumb, stroking the length of my index finger with repeated ease, sent ripples of pleasure through me. At every touch, it was as if my soul expanded and my body couldn't quite contain it.

At the same time, as I glimpsed at Hayden's profile, a prick of unease made me restless. I cared about this person more than I could understand. Seeing him overtaken by the dark side of his mind, witnessing the expression of some old, rooted pain, was almost unbearable. How I wished I could soothe him, take his troubles away, but all I was able to offer was a clammy hand to hold. Knowing Hayden, that was probably all he wanted right now.

'Auntie Chris, please.' Hayden perched his head on his hand, stooping over as he watched Christie gather the contents of his stomach into a tattered towel.

He had tried to convince her to let him clean his vomit off the floor several times, but she kept on ignoring him and quickly set out to do it herself. This was his umpteenth attempt to persuade her to let him take over. The more he asked, the weaker his resolve became.

Finally, Christie lifted her head and scowled. 'Look, love. You know what my job has been for the past twenty years, don't you?' Before Hayden could reply she continued, her frown deepening, '*Exactly*! I wipe old people's arses for a living. Do you really think that after *many* instances of shit explosions, urine pools and snot dangling from noses, this is going to bother me? And I have three children, for goodness' sake! As if this is my first time cleaning up sick! This is a piece of cake for me, so *stop worrying*. I'm pretty much done anyway, and I know where my products are and what to put on the stain so it doesn't *stink*.'

Bluntness was a family trait, it seemed. Her words were enough to shush him. Hayden kept on following her movements, looking dejected. I leaned over and kissed his cheek. He turned to look at me. We exchanged a brushing of lips, then another.

'You two, behave now.' Christie's warning was good-natured, and Hayden and I both broke into a smile. 'Andy, how do you deal with my nephew? Isn't he a right pain in the arse?'

Hayden cracked up.

Christie grabbed a towel, one of the unsoiled ones, and whipped it on Hayden's calf. 'You really are a dirty pig!'

A blush crept up my cheeks as I gave Hayden a disapproving glance.

He kept on chuckling, unrepentant. 'Sorry, sorry.'

We remained silent for a while, our linked hands a source of blissful contentment. Christie darted in and out of the room to get rid of the dirty towels and bring back a small container with a spoon. At this point, the vomit stain had mostly disappeared and Christie was intent on spreading a white paste over the remaining halo. Baking soda and warm water, she explained, to be left to soak up the dirt for an hour.

I put my head on Hayden's shoulder and every so often he'd steal a quiet kiss. To be able to act romantically towards another guy in front of his family was a new experience for me. Hayden's relatives had looked surprised, but accepted the nature of our relationship immediately. Though my parents let me do as I pleased when it came to my private life, they didn't approve of same-sex shows of affection anywhere near them and probably never would. As for my exes, my relationships had never been deep enough to lead to family involvement or, as in Craig's case, our being a couple was kept hushed. Right now, I was cuddling up with my boyfriend at his aunt's. *My boyfriend*. The thought made my heart flip with delight.

Hayden's grip tightened on my hand. 'So... what did Mum say?'

Christie raised a puzzled eyebrow. 'Hmm?'

'She must have heard me.'

Christie bundled up her cleaning stuff in a clean towel. She really did have a lot of them to spare.

'Your mum hasn't heard a peep,' she said.

Hayden straightened up. 'Really?'

She pulled off the plastic gloves. 'Your mother needs rest, peace and quiet. I had the kids making a racket all morning and Bobi tramping down the stairs like a boulder. There was no way she was going to get a wink of sleep, so I gave her a pill and some earplugs. She's snoozing soundly. Until they catch that cunt... oh, sorry Andy.'

'No problem,' I said.

Christie stood up, anger making her look fiercer than an Amazonian queen. 'Until they catch him, I won't leave her by herself. We almost lost her once.'

A shallow breath came out Hayden's throat.

Christie collected her things and looked away, uneasy. 'I don't know where he's hiding or what he thinks he's doing by worming his way back into your mum's life, but I will have none of it. Also,' she stared at Hayden with dark, intense eyes, 'you mustn't live your life in fear of him. John is a piece of shit, but he's human. He eats, shits and bleeds if you cut him, like any of us. What happened to you today, do you think it has some connection with—'

'I dunno.' Hayden's voice was low and sharp.

Silence grew heavy between them.

Christie exhaled, finally breaking the quiet. 'Anyway, I'm done here for now.'

Her eyes went to Hayden, who was staring blankly at a random spot in the room and playing with the curls on his forehead. 'Do you want a cup of tea or something else to drink while we wait for the pizzas to arrive?' she asked.

I gave her a polite smile. 'No, thank you.'

Hayden didn't reply. He closed his eyes and clenched his jaw, his foot tapping on the carpet.

***

Neither of us were particularly hungry, and we barely got through a pizza. I had eaten a third of my steak beforehand. Then, of course, ketchup had erupted on my face and I had no chance to decide if I wanted to eat more. The pizza was meant as a pacifying meal, as it were, to lighten the mood since... well, the end of the world happened.

The dining room was, as Christie put it, in a dreadful state. Instead, we sat in the lounge and ate relaxedly in a semi-circle, plucking assorted slices from the various boxes lined up on the coffee table. Us boys had dragged some ketchup-free chairs from the dining room since the three-seater sofa and armchair weren't enough for all of us.

I took a long gander at Hayden's family as they ate and chatted in good spirits. Nobody worried about conventions and that was a refreshing sight.

If only my relatives could be so chilled out about things. I guessed I couldn't complain; it was good enough that my Catholic parents didn't reject me outright. Still, my heart squeezed at the thought that it would never be like this with my family.

When I stretched to pick up a slice of the sausage-stuffed crust pizza, Ceri giggled. My cheeks burned every time I took a bite. Bobi slapped Ceri's arm as he chewed his four-cheese, piercing his son with a withering stare. Ceri rubbed the spot on the shoulder where his father had whacked him and grumbled.

Katrina came back with the three little girls who all sprinted to Hayden and hugged him.

They asked, 'Are you OK now?' and, 'Have you got baddies? Did you hurt? Is that why you were screaming?'

One of the little twins reached for his face and caressed his cheek. 'Don't be sad, it's OK.'

Hayden's face was a mask of shifting emotions. He looked as if he was about to cry but he bit his lower lip and held in whatever he was feeling.

After a while, Hayden leaned into Christie's ear and asked a murmured question which I, sitting next to him, happened to hear.

'Do you think it'll be OK to go upstairs to speak to Mum now?'

Christie chewed her mixed-veg pizza and regarded him before saying something in his ear too. The answer must have upset Hayden because he began to tap his foot again, gnawing at his lip.

'It's because I look like him,' he spat out, loud enough that Ceri turned to look with a worried frown.

Christie put a hand on his arm. 'Don't say stupid things like that. You know that's not the reason. She won't talk in detail about what happened with John to anyone, not just you, and you've suffered at his hand as much as she has. You're her son. She wants to keep you out of it, if she can manage. The less she thinks about him, the better.'

Judging from his expression, Hayden didn't seem to believe her. He hunched his shoulders and his back tensed. A concave dip on his cheek suggested he was biting on it.

Aunt Christie rubbed his back and regarded him with kind eyes. 'Give yourself another day to sort out your thoughts, innit. Why don't you come back again tomorrow? I'll tell Bobi to come pick you up. Who knows! The police might find John by the end of the day. Right now, we're all on edge, worrying that he might pop out of nowhere. Hopefully, we won't be worrying for long. In the meantime, though...' Christie glanced at me from over Hayden's shoulder and my cheeks heated as I'd been caught listening in. I nibbled on my pizza and looked away.

'...You could introduce her to your boyfriend.'

Hayden turned to look at me, his gaze soft and full of want. My breath caught in my throat as he slipped a hand up my nape, sliding his fingers through the short hair at the back of my head. He drew me in and, for a long, heart-racing second, I thought he would kiss me passionately, without reserve, in front of everyone. My body instantly grew weak... because *of course* it did, since it was Hayden's special ability to turn me helpless like a kitten. His lips brushed my face, travelled down the length of my neck and found their stop at the opening of my sweatshirt. He pulled the fabric of my collar with a sneaky finger and sucked on my skin gently. The circular sweep of his hot, wet tongue made me gasp.

'H-Hayden!' I screamed under my breath, almost dropping my slice of pizza.

That sly contact had my senses reeling and I recognised in horror the nature of the pulsing heat growing in my underwear.

'Phwo!' Bobi's eyes popped wide, his jaw chewing on a hot wing furiously. 'Hold your bloody horses, you two!'

Hayden hid his face in my neck and tickled my skin with the warm breath of his nose. 'Sorry.'

Katrina, until now oblivious to what kind of relationship Hayden and I entertained, stared at us.

Her features were unmoving, a ball of food in her cheek. 'Did I... miss something?'

***

Hayden and I slipped quietly up the stairs. He led me to a door on the left and knocked softly. As no response came, he turned the handle carefully and the white door creaked open. The small bedroom was a little stuffy and mostly dark. The light seeping through the curtains outlined the slim shape of a woman sleeping serenely on a bed, her arms hugging the pillow and long, dark hair spread over the light sheets. Hayden gazed at his mother for a few moments before closing the door as quietly as he had opened it.

He turned to me. 'I don't want to disturb her. I'll introduce you properly another time.'

I nodded in agreement. We could overhear the giggles of Hayden's little cousins coming from the lounge downstairs and Sophie singing 'Poker Face' for them. The adults chattered too and Bobi's whoops of laughter surpassed the other voices in volume by several notches.

In the quiet, semi-dark secrecy of the landing, Hayden and I gazed at each other. Just like that, the air grew thick with sexual tension; a pull so strong that my breath caught and my pulse beat loudly in my ears.

Holy crap, was it even normal to feel this attracted to another person? His hands sneaked under my clothes, felt the flat of my stomach and small of my back. While the fingers of one hand dipped through my trousers, squeezing my butt and travelling down the line of my crack, his other palm rubbed the bulge at the front. As Hayden did this, he pinned me with a hungry, resolute gaze. My hands shook too much to do more than stroke his chest and grip the fabric of his clothes. We were at his aunt's house, for goodness' sake! He teased my lips with his until I was open for him and took the hot thrusts of his tongue. I whimpered. He lifted my top and stroked my nipple as he kept fondling my straining cock through the fabric of my jeans.

'Stop!' I panted, 'stop, please.'

His arms moved to a less dangerous form of contact by resting around my waist. We were both breathless and sporting raging hard-ons. Hayden rocked slowly against my groin, pressing his hardness to mine.

'We shouldn't do this here.'

'I know,' he said hoarsely. 'Sorry.'

A male chuckle coming from the nearby staircase made me tense up. Hayden got off me just a moment before Iwan appeared in the landing, followed by Ceri.

'You guys alright?' Iwan asked.

'Yeah. Mum is fast asleep. I'll talk to her tomorrow,' Hayden said.

Iwan nodded thoughtfully. 'Are you... sure you're OK?'

Hayden ran a hand through his hair, 'Yeah. We're going to make a move now. I'll see you tomorrow, yeah?'

Iwan nodded again. After a moment of hesitation, he pulled Hayden into a hug and patted his wider shoulders in a brotherly gesture. 'I'd heard John was a twat, but that's all I knew since you and Mum never talk about him. I'm really sorry I didn't answer your texts. I was angry because you didn't show up all night yesterday, innit. I kinda thought you didn't take Mum fainting seriously and I didn't know what you were going through, or that Andy was your boyfriend.' Iwan let out a gasp and jumped back. 'Holy shit! Have you got a *boner*?'

If only I could have disappeared at that moment.

Hayden clicked his tongue. 'Yes,' he said simply. 'Don't worry, though. It's definitely not for you.'

I considered jumping down the stairs to put an end to my mortification. Instead, I slapped my forehead. 'Oh, God.'

'*Oookay*,' Iwan said, looking away. 'I'll leave you to... uh... *to it*.'

Both him and Ceri walked stiffly down the corridor, heading to a room at the very bottom.

'Oh and Iwan,' Hayden called after him, '*Diolch o'r galon. Ti'n frawd amazing.*'

Iwan's eyes widened in surprise and a smile curved the corner of his mouth. '*Wrth gwrs. Gallet ti ddibynnu arna i unrhyw amser.*'

Hayden replied, '*Mae hynny'n dda i wybod.*'

Iwan and Cori disappeared into the room and closed the door behind them.

I stared at Hayden wide-eyed. 'I didn't know you could speak Welsh!'

'Just a little bit like, but not as well as Iwan. Gareth used to speak in Welsh to us all the time.'

'Gareth...?'

His smile was soft. 'My stepdad.'

I sensed we had broached the border of a delicate topic.

He put his hands in his pockets and smirked. 'Let's go somewhere where I can fuck you proper raw.'

My heart tripped in my chest and I flushed hot. 'Jesus!'

'I've been thinking about it since we were in the car. You naked with your ass in the air and your hole pink and swollen, my cum all over it—'

I slapped a hand on his mouth. 'S-stop talking!' My heart thrummed in my chest.

His lips stretched into a grin under my palm, his teeth wetting my skin. Hayden gently removed my hand off his face and pressed a kiss on it. 'Shall we go, then?'

Once downstairs, Hayden mumbled his goodbyes, mentioning something about me being covered in ketchup and needing a shower and a change of clothes.

Bobi, who was comfortably sitting on an armchair and holding a can of beer, frowned. 'You mean you're not sneaking out to snuggle up with your boyfriend?'

Hayden grinned. 'Yeah, that too.'

Sophie appeared to be very perplexed. 'What boyfriend?'

Hayden pointed at me. 'This one. He's my boyfriend.'

She gasped. 'What?'

On our way out, Christie touched Hayden's shoulder. 'Watch your back, hun.'

He squeezed my hand and replied, 'Will do.'

16

HAYDEN

Andy lay sprawled on his back over his grey silky bedcovers, his legs spread and arse propped up with a pillow. His opening twitched, pink and moist, after the prolonged ministrations of my tongue.

Cheeks flushed, he glanced at me with his pretty eyes and murmured, 'Hayden, please...'

I put some lube on two of my fingers and inserted them in his hole, rubbed to moisten deep inside and sought out his prostate. My efforts must have had some effect because Andy gasped.

I licked my lips, stroking the sweet spot. 'You're loving this, aren't you? Tell me you do and I'll make it even better.'

Andy threw his head back and squeezed his eyes shut. 'God! *Ahnngh*! Yes! Yes, I fucking love it!'

I carried on working his hole, adding more lube and putting in three fingers.

Andy whimpered and clutched my wrist. 'P-please, Hayden! Put your cock inside me!'

I bit my lip. 'I want to fuck you hard. I need to make you nice and stretchy. Yeah?'

Andy threw an arm over his eyes and whispered something.

'Mh? What did you say?'

'I said,' Andy swallowed, 'I like it when it hurts a bit.'

Arousal surged inside me and my cock twitched in response. 'Alright, then. I hope you won't regret it, babe,' I said hoarsely while slipping on a condom.

I threw his body down the edge of the bed. He yelped in surprise and I chuckled, seeing his arse was now in line with my groin.

I sunk inside him in one savage, swift motion. Andy arched, a keening sound bursting out of his throat. I remained unmoving for a moment. Andy shook and, for a terrifying second, I thought I'd entered him too forcefully. I caressed his thigh, asking, 'You alright?'

'Oh yeah,' he breathed.

Encouraged, I thrust hard into his tightness, then stopped again. 'Is this what you want, yeah? Tell me.'

Andy reached for my hand which still lingered on his leg and dug his fingers into my flesh. 'Please, fuck me hard.'

I exhaled a fiery breath, my control forgotten. I plundered him, over and over, setting a rapid pace.

Andy cried out, '*Ah*! Fuck, you're so thick. Oh! Oh! *Ohhh*!'

His hot canal stretched and squeezed around my length. Pleasure shot up my groin, drowning me in its intensity. I broke into a sweat as I fought to prolong the time in which our bodies were joined. Andy kept his eyes on me, lips parted and eyes heavy-lidded in an insanely erotic expression. All the while, his calves bounced against my biceps and the wet sound of our bodies clashing was heavenly.

The sight of him turned me on so much that I had to avert my eyes, lest I cum too quickly. I tried to focus on things that weren't Andy and his tight hole, like the patter of heavy rain on the window, or the amazing Carpenter Brut print on the bedroom wall with a Satanic, neon-pink design and gorgeous artwork.

Speaking of gorgeous, Andy gasped and moaned under me,

pulling the sheets. 'Oh God, Hayden, it feels so good!'

I couldn't stop myself from folding over him to steal a long, demanding kiss. My emotions ignited like an out-of-control firework. I pushed Andy's legs forward until his knees touched his shoulders, squatted over his butt and pounded his hole. A possessive, dominant mood took over me. How could I want Andy so bad that, even though I was thrashing his body with my dick, it felt like it wasn't enough? I had been dancing at the edge of my own climax for a while but now hard fucking simply wasn't going to cut it. I *needed* to pummel his ass as fast and hard as I could. I descended like a meteor and our bodies slammed together. Andy's expression tightened, his eyes squeezed shut and his mouth opened.

Raspy moans escaped him as he crumpled the sheets and his body flushed red. *Oh yes.* I was so close. I bit hard on my lip in a desperate attempt to stretch out the imminent orgasm a little more.

Andy cried out. A string of semen spewed out his dick once, twice, three times, each in time with my thrusts. My eyes went wide in disbelief: he'd just shot his load without touching himself and I had forced an orgasm out of him with the sheer force of my cock.

I came inside him with a rasping growl. 'Fuck!'

The pleasure was ground-breaking and I had to plant my fists on the mattress to avoid collapsing over Andy and crushing him. 'Holy shit!' I panted.

Andy breathed heavily. His legs, now perched over my shoulders, quivered. I slid off his body and collapsed next to him, drenched in sweat and winded. Carefully, I extracted my condom from my softening cock and tied it up. It was certainly a good brand if it could sustain that kind of fuck.

Andy lay silent next to me. He'd brought his arms to his face, hiding it from my view. His chest rose and fell, gleaming with the droplets of his spill.

'Are you alright or wha?' I asked. His silence was starting to worry me.

'I think...' His arms slumped at his sides and Andy stared up at the ceiling. 'I think you just killed me with your dick.'

I laughed and shook with mirth even more when Andy turned to look at me with a troubled frown.

'You look alive enough to me,' I said.

His gaze went back to the lightshade above us. 'Your eyes deceive you.'

I rolled on my side to lean over and kiss him. Our lips brushed and our mouths meshed in a slow glide. After a while, we separated with a contented sigh.

Andy chuckled. 'Do you think you could grab a couple of wet wipes for me? In that drawer, over by there.'

I grinned. 'Not sure *a couple* will be enough.' I sat up and got off the bed, walked to the said chest of drawers and plucked some wipes from the packet.

I knelt by Andy and cleaned the cum off his chest and abdomen with careful strokes. 'I didn't know you could, uhm, cum just like that, without touching your dick.'

Andy exhaled. 'Yeah, that was... something I thought could never happen in real life.'

My eyes widened. 'You mean this is a first?'

He raised one of his dark eyebrows. Fuck. Even his eyebrows were pretty.

'Don't start bragging now,' he said.

'You can't expect me not to brag.'

'Alright, fine! It was amazing. Happy?'

I put my arms around him, laughing and kissing his lips.

'Yes, very happy.'

***

We lounged in his music room for a while, enjoying a beer and some cheese on toast.

I was overprotective of my own instruments, so when Andy offered to eat while working on some tunes near his computer, synths and mixer, I went rigid. 'What if the crumbs fall through the keys?'

He laughed. 'We're not *literally* going to eat on top of the synths, come on! What's a piece of toast going to do?'

He pointed out that I hadn't refused a cup of coffee in the music room in the past, and that was definitely more of a hazard. I couldn't argue with that.

Andy opened the sequencer. 'So, this is something I've been working on for a while, but I've been stuck for ages because I don't know how to end it. I have to warn you, though. As it is, it's pretty rough and probably nothing special.'

I pinched his cheek. 'Stop putting yourself down and let's hear it.'

The piece opened with long, reverberating notes and a deep bass. By now I had gathered that Andy preferred atmospheric sounds when it came to his music, though he occasionally put together something really groovy, or added a section with a little more rhythmic oomph in a slow track.

Another thing I noticed was that his synth compositions were much more interesting than mine, with creative changes and frills that my music totally lacked. Sometimes it seemed as if he was scared to be too experimental with the drums. The piece was rough, as he'd mentioned, but it was clear to me that, with the right adjustments, it was going to be incredible.

I turned to look at Andy to say something and spotted him biting his finger while staring at me with anxious eyes.

I chuckled. 'Why are you so nervous?'

'You have a super-serious expression. I can't tell what you're thinking.'

'I'm thinking that you're very, *very* kissable...' I leaned in and Andy pressed his hands on my chest to keep me away.

'No, really. What did you think?'

'I think it's a great start, honestly. Would you like me to help you finish it?'

Andy beamed. 'Could you? Thanks! I keep going back to this tune but I can't seem to decide what I want to do with it.'

We worked on the track for an hour or two. I suggested the piece needed a more captivating bass-line. It didn't have a leading instrument and, though the tune itself was good, the overall sound was a little flat. Once we established a solid bass-line, it was easy to come up with a satisfying ending. The tune needed more tweaking, but now it certainly had more character.

Andy listened to the final product, slightly bobbing his head in rhythm. 'Wow Hayden, you really are amazing!'

'I think every musician has these sinkhole tracks, so don't worry. Sometimes, like, taking a step back or having someone else look at them is really what you need, you know?'

'Sinkhole tracks?'

'Yeah, that's what I call them, innit. You get obsessed with them, spend hours trying to make them perfect and never succeed. They suck you in, like, forever.'

His big eyes studied the computer screen, a smile on his face. 'That makes total sense.'

I stretched my arm to put it around his shoulders. 'Well, I think

I deserve a kiss now, don't I? I worked proper hard.'

'OK...' Andy didn't fight this time.

Of course, our play of tongues wasn't enough for me and I trailed my hands under his clothes to feel the soft warmth of his body. I dragged him off his desk chair and onto my lap. I was already hard by the time his butt weighed on my legs.

'God, Hayden. Your libido is unstoppable,' Andy whispered.

I lifted his top and licked his nipple. 'It's not my fault you're so cute, mun.'

Life came knocking at my door in the form of a Jimi Hendrix guitar solo. I looked at my ringing phone on the desk, my stomach clenching. Auntie Christie.

I picked up. 'Hullo?'

'Hello Hayden. I've just spoken to the police.'

My guts twisted. 'And...?'

'John's vanished. As if... he was never there.'

A silent pause stretched for a time that seemed infinite. 'What do you... what you mean?'

Aunt Christie sighed. 'Hayden I... I don't know how to tell you this.'

'What is it? I'm going fuckin' mad here.'

'John, he... he died, three months after coming out of prison.'

My mouth hung open. 'W-what...?'

'He had an argument with his estranged brother, I've been told. Apparently, he set a brewery on fire while both of them were inside. Neither of them survived.'

My eyes widened. 'He did fuckin' *what*? He killed his brother, is that what you're saying? I didn't even know he had one, like!'

'Did you not?' Aunt Christie sounded surprised. 'John had turned everyone against him after he started drinking, even his closest family. It's terrible to think about. Bloody bastard, that's what he is.'

'But then if John is dead, who did Mum...?'

'We are trying to figure it out, but perhaps she... well... She might have imagined seeing him, Hayden. You know this wouldn't be the first time.'

I still couldn't make sense of her words. 'So John is... dead?' I could hardly breathe.

'Yes. Apparently this story was big in Bromley and all over the news, but somehow it didn't reach us here until three months after it happened. So really, we only found out because of your mum collapsing. The whole thing is spooky as hell, it is.'

'Yeah, wow. That's mental.' I was totally, utterly shocked.

'There's no reason to keep your mum cooped up here,' Christie continued after a moment of silence, 'so I'm going to drive her and the kids back home in the morning, yeah? Please, though, don't tell Grace about this. Not yet anyway. She's convinced John went to see her and to say it was all in her mind might not be a good idea, as things stand. You and I know she won't take it well. I told her he's gone for good and that she's got nothing to worry about. That's not a lie. He won't hurt anyone ever again.'

I swallowed, though my throat was impossibly dry. 'OK. Thank you for telling me.'

'Are you alright?'

'Yeah, sound, uh, yeah,' I said, though it really wasn't true.

'Is Andy with you?'

Andy was still on my lap, gazing at me with a dumbstruck expression.

'Yeah. He's here with me now.'

'That's great. Call your mum as soon as you can.'

'OK. Thank you for everything.'

'I'll always be here for you, sweetheart.' Children screeched in the background. 'I've gotta go now, the girls are playing up again. Call me if you need anything. I'm here for you love, OK?'

'Cheers. Speak soon.' She hung up and I stared at the phone screen. My hands shook.

'Hayden,' Andy began.

'I... I need a moment.' I helped him off of me and staggered to the nearby sofa. I sat down and put the weight of my head on my palms. 'Fuck.'

Andy came close. 'Do you want me to leave?'

'No, no please. Stay.' I shivered all over though it was warm in the room.

Andy sat next to me and put a hand on my back. I could not stop shaking. I took in deep breaths and let them out through my mouth. 'This shit is seriously messed up.'

'It sounds pretty rough and you don't have to talk about it if you don't want to.'

I sat up, my body still quaking. 'Just know that finding out my father is gone doesn't make me sad. Fuck, the opposite. He wasn't only a violent bastard and a manipulator. He's left this world with blood on his hands! Motherfucker! I can't believe I'm related to that piece of shit.' A sob rose to my throat. 'I wanted the fucker to die so many times and now it's really true. And Mum? She's having delusions again. She hasn't for years, so why now?'

'Oh, Hayden...' Andy hugged me and I buried my face in his chest.

'Why does it feel as if the universe wants to drag me down to hell, like? Even though I'm trying so hard to stay positive.' I snuggled into his arms even more and exhaled. 'Maybe it's best if I leave, I dunno.'

'Oh? How come?'

I took his hand and stroked his knuckles with my thumb. 'We

just got together and here I am, fuckin' burdening you with all this crap innit. I wish we'd met a year ago, like, when I wasn't an emotional wreck. Not as much as I am now, anyway.'

'I'm just glad we got to meet at all,' Andy said. 'Sometimes, it feels like it's unbelievable.'

I smiled. 'It *isn't* unbelievable, though. It happened and this is the best thing ever.'

We kissed and I enjoyed his taste, his warmth a little longer before I started to collect my things.

Andy didn't try to stop me and I was glad that he could read me well enough to know that I needed some space.

He accompanied me downstairs and stood by the entrance. 'You sure you don't want me to drive you?' he said, glancing at the rain.

'Nah. It's alright, like. I've got an umbrella in my rucksack and the walk will be good to clear my head, innit.' I bent over for a goodbye kiss. 'I'll text you when I get back. Promise. I want you to think of somewhere you'd wanna go for a date, yeah? A proper one. What about the cinema or the arcade by St. Mary Street? What you wanna do?'

He watched me wearily. 'I thought you didn't want to be in crowded places.'

I caressed his cheek. 'For you, I'll take the risk.'

Andy put his hand on mine. 'I'm happy even if we hang out here, or the park.'

'Andy this... anxiety thing is ruining my life. Even if it had to do with my past trauma, and perhaps it does, John's dead now, thank fuck, so I have no excuses. I have to move on. Simple as, innit. There'll always be something to be worried about, so might as well just face it. Only... I might need to take a walk in the rain to get over this one.' I gave him a crooked smile. 'And some counselling.'

He smiled, but concern veiled his eyes. 'OK.'

I grinned in return. 'Right. Think about what I said.'

Cold droplets fell through the collar of my top the moment I walked down the front steps, and water soaked one of my shoes which had a hole in the sole. I opened the umbrella and smiled at Andy one more time before meandering down the puddled pavement. His gaze was soft and part of me regretted leaving the shelter of his arms. A big part, actually. But tonight I had to be strong and leaning on others all the time wasn't my style.

I wanted to deal with my problems and get my life back. Only then could I truly enjoy what I had with Andy and take all the happiness I could get.

17

ANDY

On Monday night I went to bed with a heavy feeling in my chest. Hayden and I had only been together one day but I already missed him keenly. I wondered how he must have felt, lost and alone in his quiet house. All that business about his dad was terrible! I curled under the duvet around eleven and drew the pillow Hayden had slept on to my chest, hugging it and breathing it in. The sheets still smelled of him. Of us.

As I was about to doze off, my phone chimed. A message from Hayden.

'*Wow. I seriously miss you. Like, bad. Is this normal? xx*'

I smiled and replied, '*I'm hugging the pillow you slept on last night to fall asleep so I'm probably the wrong person to ask.*' After I sent the text Hayden didn't reply right away. For a long minute I got all stressy that I'd gone overboard with the cheese. Then the phone chimed again.

'*You are the most beautiful thing in the universe, babe.*'

I stared at the words with a thumping heart for ages. OK, so maybe I shouldn't worry about being corny because *clearly* Hayden had no reservations on that front. Another message came in.

'*I'm sorry, I know I'm crass as fuck. Maybe you won't even want* to talk to me again because I'm being so sappy.'

I composed my reply with trembling hands. *'That's never going to happen.'*

'OK then. I have another one. Prepare yourself.'

Swallowing the lump in my throat, I typed, *'I'm ready.'*

A few moments later, the phone chimed. *'I'm so incredibly happy that you're in my life. I'd thank God if I thought there was one. Instead, I'm going to thank you.'*

The dams opened. Love poured out of my eyes and nose in the form of tears and snot. I couldn't think of the last time I'd fallen for someone like this. An entire year with Craig hadn't been as enrapturing as my ten days with Hayden. I struggled to recompose myself.

We texted a bit more and then I must have fallen asleep because at some point I woke up to one of his messages.

'Goodnight beautiful. Dream of me. I am deffo gonna to dream of you <3'

I slept all night with Hayden's pillow squashed against my body. I stroked it and even spoke to it, imagining that Hayden was in my arms. I couldn't stop myself from getting teary.

'Don't be sad,' I'd tell my pillow boyfriend, 'or I'll be sad with you.' Eventually I had to get a tissue box, otherwise pillow-Hayden would be soaked in my tears.

When I finally dragged myself out of bed around eight the next morning, my eyes puffy and my soul pretty fecking blue, I went to type a message.

'Morning. Hope you're feeling better.'

I quickly deleted it. Of course he wasn't going to be better after what he'd learnt about his father; the issue was simply too big to be forgotten that quickly. I reworded it.

'*Hiya. Sorry I didn't reply to your last message last night. You OK?*'

I washed, dressed and made myself a bowl of cereal. Cinnamon squares – perfect for sweetening my mood. My phone chimed.

'*Good morning, beautiful. Much better thanks to you. You're like a beacon of pure light in this foggy darkness.*'

I let my head plunk on the breakfast counter. Oh my goodness, *again*! How could he say something this sweet so easily? What could I ever say back? My heart pounded hard and I took several deep breaths before writing a response.

'*No matter what, I'm here for you. Take as much time as you need to sort out your thoughts. What you're going through... I can't even imagine. I wish I was there to give you a hug.*'

Hayden sent me a smiling emoji. '*Since there's no need to go to my auntie's house after work after all, we can meet if you want. I finish about quarter past two.*'

I sent him a GIF with two bears hugging each other. '*Absolutely! I promised Tai I'd meet him at three to give him back a couple of books I borrowed. I'll quickly return them, if that's alright, and then we can hang out as long as you want after that. You can sleep over again, or I could come around your house.*'

The phone rang. Hayden's name was in the middle of the screen. My heart picked up a hurried beat and I answered with a trembling hand.

'Hello?'

'Hey gorgeous. I wanted to hear your voice.'

A warm, tingling flush ran through my body. I licked my lips, suddenly craving a kiss. 'I can't talk much.'

'Oh. Is this a bad moment?'

'No, it's just that my heart is beating so fast I can barely think.'

His laughter was soft and luscious, like a mug of malted milk. 'Yeah. Mine's beating fast too. I really want to see you. This shift is going to be fuckin' torture.'

'So, where would you like to meet?'

'Are you and Tai going to see each other in town?'

'Yeah, though we haven't decided where, exactly.'

'Would you mind if I joined you? I wanted to thank him personally.'

'For what?'

'For encouraging me to toss your salad. I'm glad I took his advice.'

My face burned hot. 'No way you're going to say that to him!'

He laughed. 'Are you embarrassed, babe?'

'If you tell him, I'm never going to live it down!'

'Well, don't you at least want to show off your boyfriend? Not that I'm a trophy, like,' he said with a laugh. 'But I kinda want to show you off too.'

I bit my lip. 'Only if you swear you won't say anything about the salad thing.'

'OK, I swear down.' I could picture him smiling.

'Alright then. I'll let him know you're coming too. Shall I meet you outside the electronic shop at quarter past two?'

'Actually, I need to go somewhere after work. It won't take long, but it'd be best if I met you wherever it is you guys are going, at three o'clock, yeah?'

'Alright then.' I was sadder to hang up than I should have been. 'See you in a few hours.'

'The longest hours ever, fuckin' hell,' Hayden said.

***

I stared at my computer screen. This thesis wasn't going to write itself, but there was no way I could concentrate.

Eleven-thirty. Three and a half hours before I could see him again. I glanced at my phone: no messages.

I slapped my cheeks. *Get a grip!*

My phone rang and I stiffened. The last thing I wanted was to have to explain to my mother how I'd overcome a stomach ache I never had and then talk about the dishwasher. Luckily, it was Tai.

I'd sent him a message earlier in the morning, after speaking with Hayden, and told him my boyfriend was going to join us at three.

What I didn't tell Tai was how worried I was about Hayden, his mental health and how I hoped he wouldn't push himself for me. There had been no reply to my messages and I figured that Tai was still asleep. I guessed he'd woken up now with a big surprise on his phone.

I cringed as I answered the call and waited for my eardrums to be sorely abused.

'Hey.'

'Andy! You're fucking joking, right?'

I sat back on my chair and sighed. 'Hello to you too.'

'What the hell do you mean that you are boyfriends? Like, proper shaggin' and all that jiggery-pokery? You've only just met, babe! You haven't even been on a proper date yet! Look at you par mun!'

'If you count all Sunday and Monday, then we've had two dates.'

'Are we talking about the guy straighter than an infinitely straight line? That same guy?'

'I know, I'm overwhelmed too.'

'Couldn't you tell him to slow the fuck down?'

'Not really.'

Tai made a weird, rumbly noise and I put him on speakerphone.

'It was unavoidable,' I grumbled. 'It was like a tsunami. You can't just run away when a tsunami comes, can you? You're not going to make it. It's too big of a wave. You can only... I dunno... Stare at the water engulfing you or something.'

'You call it a tsunami. I call it a nice fat cock up your arse, daring. Good fucks are known to cloud your judgment. Dr Tai checking in.'

I put my face down on the desk. 'I wish it was only the sex that got me.'

'Got you? Got you how? Oh no. Please, Andy.'

'What?'

'Don't tell me you've fallen in love with this bloke already, come on!'

My face heated. 'Pfft! What? No, of course not!'

'Bullshit! I know you too well! He's totally your type and... OK. Maybe Hayden is half of humanity's type, but whatever. I admit he's a head-sway and a hell of a pull, but looks and big throbbing dicks are not all that matters, babe.'

I scoffed. 'Wait. Is this Tai talking? We all know what your relationship with dick is.'

'We're not talking about me. I can survive on big dicks and good looks just fine, but not you!'

'That's not all there is. He said he's serious about me and that I'm the most wonderful person he's ever met.' My heart swelled at the memory. 'I'm the first guy he's ever been with but he's accepted our relationship completely and he's comfortable being open about it. He came out to his whole family, kissed me in front of them. I was so embarrassed I wished the earth would swallow me. I'm also stupidly happy and I don't know what to do.'

There was a long pause. 'Really?'

I made small circles on my desk with a finger. 'Yeah.'

'What if...' Tai fell silent.

'What if what?'

'What if he dicked you proper good but perhaps your cock-sucking skills burned his neurons too? It must be it.'

I grunted. 'Why can't we just be two guys who really like each other? Is it so impossible to believe?'

Tai chuckled. 'But it's crazy! He's this supposedly forever closeted bisexual guy who suddenly wants to be your boyfriend and is overwhelmed by the joys of gay sex. You've either made the "handsome straight guy turning gay" fantasy come true, or this is about something less romantic than that. Sorry for being so down to earth, hun, but more often than not, people aren't nice like you. I don't want to burst your balloon, babe, but I know you. Craig, that lying piece of shit, he got to you, emptied your fridge and lived the lush life while fucking a girl behind your back. I won't let another guy do the same again, you hear me?'

My voice wavered. 'It's not like that. Hayden is not like Craig at all.'

'Well, fine. I'll be seeing him today, right? I'm going to scan his ass, and if he dares to hurt you I'll skin him alive.'

Despite myself, I smiled. 'I'm sure it won't get to that.'

Tai huffed, 'We'll see.' The dragon had finally ceased to spit fire.

'Where are we meeting, then?'

'Wait there. You're not getting away with it, you know that don't you? I'm not just going to forget.'

'What?'

'Golden Cross. Karaoke Wednesday. Drag.'

'Oh for God's sake!'

'We're going to perform "Devil in Disguise" and we're going to be an angel-devil pair! I'm the devil, obviously.'

I clutched a handful of my hair. 'You've gotta be kidding me!'

'Not in the slightest!' Tai sang. 'Hold on. I'm going to show you the outfits I chose for us.'

I waited with dread. A moment later, I received a WhatsApp notification. Two pictures. The devil costume was a red corseted dress, shiny and short, with knee-high boots, high heels and laces everywhere; tail, diabolical wings and horns included. The skin-clothing ratio verged on sixty-forty. I swallowed hard and clicked on the second picture. Well, phew; *my* skin-clothing ratio was going to be fifty-fifty. *Hoo-fecking-ray*!

The picture showed a model wearing an embarrassingly short dress that required thorough leg depilation or death by shame, feathery mini-skirt, angel wings, golden halo, white stockings and high-heel boots with lace and frills all over them.

I groaned, 'Oh my God, I can't do this! Please, at least not the stockings!'

'Uh, the stockings are a must, actually babe.'

'But why?'

'Because they are.'

'I hate you so much.'

'You don't! And you're going to look amazing! Bet we're going to end up in a gay thirst TikTok compilation.'

'*Gaah*! Don't say another word, please.'

Tai giggled. 'See you at three, babe! Oh, burger place in Church Street. Honest Burger? And don't forget the books.'

He *was* the devil, no shadow of a doubt there.

***

Two thirty-three and I was still at home, checking myself in the mirror one last time before leaving the house. I'd chosen a zip hoodie with a funky design – black, orange and white, with octopus tentacles curling down my chest, shoulders and sleeves, grey jeans and Vans shoes. I made sure to have my rucksack with Tai's books, otherwise I was going to get a royal bollocking.

My heart pounded like crazy.

The phone bleeped – Hayden's name was on the screen. My heartbeat jumped an obstacle in its already frantic run.

'I can't wait to see you babe.'

Pretty sure there was a melty smile on my face.

'Me too. Tai said he wants to meet at the burger place on Church Street. If it's not alright with you please tell me. We can always find somewhere else to go.'

He replied quickly, *'Honest Burger, is it? Love that place. See you guys at three innit :)'*

I stared at his text with dread. Was he pushing himself to do something he was uncomfortable with for me?

My drive to the city centre was spent floating on a happy little cloud, Porter Robinson's 'Divinity' beating through the speakers. The joyous sounds rolled against the dull atmosphere of the damp winter day. A puffa jacket and scarf covered my snazzy hoodie and, somewhere between my house and the NCP car park, I ended up convincing myself that I looked like a bumpy sausage.

I paid for the parking and made my way through town. My cheeks tingled as the icy wind blew over my face. I lifted the scarf to cover my exposed skin the best I could. Maybe I should have worn the beanie my mum got me for my birthday, but I looked like a right tosser with that on my head. I was a barely acceptable shivering sausage, why make things worse?

My phone bleeped and I extracted it reluctantly from my pocket. Right away, the cold breeze bit on my knuckles. Gloves. That was going to be my next purchase. Would I look like a twat if I wore those ones that allow you to type on phone screens? I read the text from Tai.

'Jaxon is here too, btw. I'm not even going to ask you if you mind, since I know you do, but one – he overheard my conversation with you this mrng and has been bugging me to meet this hot boyfriend of yours. And two – me third-wheeling? No thank you babes x'

I groaned and shoved my phone back into my pocket.

Church Street was finally before me with the familiar tall grey tower of the Baptist Church looking dark against the overcast sky. Thank fecking goodness the meeting place was near – I was about to become eligible for permanent residency in the frozen section at the supermarket.

I walked inside the restaurant and was hit by a blast of warm air that made me sigh with relief. I looked around circumspectly. The place wasn't crowded but busy enough to make me wonder if Hayden could handle staying there without feeling uncomfortable.

The staff worked busily behind a bar counter above which was a large metallic rack stocked with colourful drinks, wine glasses and potted plants that brought cheeriness to the muted décor of the restaurant.

At the very back, close to the rustic wall, were my friends. Or rather, a friend and a barely tolerable acquaintance. Jaxon scrolled down his phone with his usual life-is-a-misery expression.

Tai saw me, beamed and began flapping his hand like an aristocratic lady. 'Yooo-hooo! Andyyy! Over here babycakes!'

I slipped on the chair at the table and met Tai's bemused smile. 'Hello pretty boy,' he said.

'Hi there.' I freed myself from the clamp of the scarf and coat, daring to look at Jaxon.

He lifted his eyes from the screen briefly and drawled out a flat, *'Haaai.'*

The first time I met Jaxon I thought he was very attractive. There was never anything interesting about me, and Jaxon had seemed to tick all the boxes of the things I wished I could be: cool, mysterious, fashionable, confident. As I got to know him, it became clear to me that he was all appearance without substance. In all honesty, his straight black and ice-blue hair, leather jacket, lip rings and neck tattoos were probably the only interesting things about him.

Jaxon went back to sift through his social media, looking utterly bored. How Tai could find having sex with this member of the living-dead pleasurable was a mystery to me.

'Is Prince Charming on his way, babe?' Tai asked.

'Yeah. He said he had to go somewhere before coming here.' I was arranging my coat, rucksack and scarf on my chair's backrest when Tai gasped sharply enough to make me jump. Even Jaxon looked up.

Tai brought a hand to his mouth and pointed, 'Oh my fucking God, what the hell is that?'

I frowned and looked down on my clothes; all seemed to be in order. 'What?'

Tai's expression remained unchanged. 'Did he suck you in other places like that?'

I slapped a hand on my neck, face burning. *How could I forget about my humongous hickey? How, exactly?* 'Tai! Lower your voice!'

I dragged my fingers down my cheek and glanced at a group of lads nearby. I met the eyes of a dude in the process of sinking his teeth into his burger. I avoided his gaze quickly.

'Alright, alright. Sorry,' Tai said with a conspiratorial grin.

Jaxon cocked his head and stretched his lips in a way that was probably meant to be a smile. 'I haven't seen you in a while, Andrew. How have you been?' Although he asked, he sounded like he really didn't give a shit.

'I've been well, just busy studying for my last exam.'

'Can't wait to see you at the Golden Cross next Wednesday,' Jaxon smirked.

I gawked at Tai, horrified.

Tai shrugged, a large grin brightening his face. 'Talk of the town, hun. It's a big event.'

My stomach flipped. 'How big?'

Tai thought about it for a moment, squinting into nothing and humming in his throat. 'Twenty?'

'Twenty what?'

'Twenty participants. We've decided to put together a little competition, just to spice things up. We spoke to the owners and they thought it'd be a great idea. It's still Karaoke Wednesday, but with a spin! It's a full-on fancy-dress event. Everyone is going to wear a themed costume and the singers are putting together a little show. We'll even have judges to crown the winning act, of course. I expect the place will be packed and, if it's popular enough, I'm sure there's going to be a repeat. This is all a big Facebook group thing...'

'Yeah, yeah.' I cut him off, crossing my arms in protest. 'This competition thing was not what I agreed to.'

Tai attempted to look guilty, pouting his lips and giving me the puppy eyes, but I knew better.

'I suppose I should have been a little more specific when we made that bet,' he said. 'But I was worried you'd say no. Come on babes, I know for a fact that we'll make a stellar duet! I can't imagine doing this with anybody else. Dream team, innit.'

I waved a hand. 'What about Dan Devine?'

Tai grinned. 'Devine's flying solo.'

'What about Jaxon, then?'

Jaxon snorted and lifted a hand in the air, holding the imaginary weight of his words. 'Oh please, Andrew, I cannot sing at all! I mean, I can barely blow through a whistle.'

I imagined all the ways Jaxon might suck at blowing.

Jaxon's eyes widened as his gaze fixed on something behind my shoulders. 'Oh. My. God.' His lips upturned and he gave Tai a little shove with his elbow. 'Serious hot piece of arse at twelve o'clock.'

I turned around to look and *of course* it was Hayden who stood by the entrance while typing on his phone. He wore a military green coat that I was familiar with, blonde curls falling down his forehead. He lifted his gaze, looked around and then, as if the pull of the universe made it so, our eyes met. His pinched expression morphed into a radiant, dazzling smile.

Hayden walked alongside the tables and I stood up to meet him, although my legs juddered like poorly built Jenga towers. I could hear the cheesy saxophone of 'Careless Whisper' playing in my head as Hayden strode assuredly like a majestic lion. For a magical moment, there was only the two of us on the planet. I was reminded of how much I cared about this guy and there was absolutely nothing I could do about it. I was, for better or for worse, fucked.

Hayden got close enough for me to catch a whiff of his scent; a mixture of aftershave, laundry detergent and just... Hayden. I'd read somewhere that a person's smell plays an important role when it comes to sexual attraction, and I could see why because his scent did something to my thinking process, like stopping it altogether. Not to mention the power his deep-set eyes had on me; they could hold me in place like a giant's hug.

'Hello,' I croaked.

Strong arms went around me and, *holy hell*, Hayden lowered his head and kissed me.

It wasn't a simple brush of lips, oh no. Rather, a full-on cave descent, ocean dive and water-slide kind of kiss. My heart thumped against my ribs furiously. All I could do was take all he had to give, let him drag me into the whirlwind of his embrace and worry about everything else later.

His mouth left mine eventually, but only to move to my cheek and everywhere else on my face. Hayden decorated the speechless me with kisses, nuzzled my shoulder and sighed. 'I missed you.'

'I... missed you too,' I mumbled, still pressed against his chest.

He moved away enough to look into my eyes. 'I got you a present.'

'You did?' I glanced to my right.

The group of lads had quieted down and they were openly staring at us, their cheeks full and unmoving. A cold shiver ran up my spine. *Oh God, what did we just do?*

Hayden nodded, grinning. 'Yeah, I'll show you in a bit. Let's not keep your friends waiting.'

He took me by the hand and led me to our table, which wasn't at all difficult to find; it was the one with the two guys with stupefied expressions. I couldn't blame them – I was pretty fecking overwhelmed myself.

'Tai, my dude! What's up man!' Hayden leaned over to offer his fist.

Tai chuckled awkwardly and reciprocated the greeting. Wow, embarrassed Tai; that was something I had never seen. Hayden gave his hand to the other slack-jawed member of our group.

'And you are...?'

'Jaxon.' The thousand-year-old immortal promptly clamped Hayden's palm and smiled.

'Nice to meet you, mate. I'm Hayden. Have you guys ordered yet or wha?' He interlaced his fingers with mine under the table and squeezed.

I had the strong feeling that eyes were boring into my back. I was too terrified to check if it was just my imagination or the blokes eating a step away from us were actually staring.

Tai's devious smile widened. 'No. We were waiting for you.'

'Oh, really? Cheers for that,' Hayden said.

A waiter showed up at the table with an electronic pad and took our orders. Hayden leaned in and pressed a light kiss on my cheek, close to my ear. My face burned. How could someone be so happy and frightened at the same time for something as small as a kiss? The prick of self-consciousness hadn't left me. *Don't look at them, don't look at them.*

Hayden spoke close to my ear. 'The waiter's asking what you would like to eat.'

'I, uh... the Tribute burger and a side salad please.'

A masculine laugh and whispers trickled in from behind us. I could still feel the probing eyes of the lads near our table. The hairs on my neck stood and a thin sheen of sweat dampened my hands.

Hayden scrutinised my expression. 'Are you OK?'

'Uh, yeah.'

After the waiter left, Tai, as promised, started his third-degree interrogation.

'So, how did everything come to be?' He gestured at me and Hayden. 'You were just friends four days ago and suddenly you're super lovey-dovey. What happened?' As if Tai hadn't envisaged me hooking up with Hayden before either of us did.

Hayden grinned. 'Andy seduced me, I guess?'

I raised an outraged eyebrow. 'Who seduced who?' I regretted speaking so loudly right away.

Tai pursed his lips and perched his chin on both hands. 'Is it true that you've never been with a guy before?'

My eyes widened and my back stiffened.

I glanced at Hayden, worried he'd be mad that I shared his secret with Tai, but he replied with a casual tilt of his head and a soft smile, both directed at me. 'Yeah.'

Shut up, Tai! I hoped my blazing gaze would relay the message but my friend continued with his questions.

'I'm sorry but I have to ask. What changed? Normally, bisexual people go through some kind of acceptance phase, especially guys who've only dated girls and don't *jump* in serious relationships like you have.' There was an unmistakable warning note in Tai's voice, mixed in with the honeyed words.

Hayden's face did something I rarely saw it do – it reddened.

He ran a finger over the tip of his nose. 'Well, you know, I couldn't really deny anything. It was too strong, like. You know that thing with Cupid shooting the arrow and all that. That's how it was when we met.' Hayden mimed holding a bow, taking aim and letting go of an invisible arrow. He even made a thwacking sound with his mouth. 'Straight to the heart,' he said.

I gaped at him and so did Tai and Jaxon, the latter chuckling awkwardly.

'Are you saying it was love at first sight?' Jaxon asked.

Hayden blushed even more. I could not believe what I was hearing or seeing.

Hayden cleared his throat. 'Well, uh...'

Before he could say another word, Jaxon burst into laughter. 'Oh my God, that's amazing! Although, even without asking, I would have said you're really into him. I'm surprised Andy let you get on with the PDA though.'

Hayden frowned and glanced between me and Jaxon. 'Why?'

Jaxon smiled. 'Oh, did he not tell you? I guess you have enough muscles to scare away any bellend who decides to bother you two. You're like the perfect bodyguard.'

I bristled. 'Alright, that's enough.'

'Hayden?' The voice came from somewhere near our table.

A guy holding a Coke stood there, looking down at us with a slight frown. He was strong-looking, of average height, with a chequered, buttoned-up shirt and a collection of vintage tattoos poking out his rolled-up sleeves.

'Oh shit, Lucas?' Hayden grinned.

I knew his expressions enough to recognise a forced smile. Hayden stood and the two exchanged a ridiculously blokeish handshake, where Lucas's hand dive-bombed on Hayden's palm, making a loud sound. Had it been me, I would have probably grimaced in pain, but Hayden didn't flinch. Instead, he patted his mate's shoulder, unperturbed.

'Fuck, bruv.' Lucas looked Hayden up and down. 'You're even bigger than the last time I saw you. Rhys said you're not even going to the gym anymore! What the fuck did you do to get like this?'

'You'd be surprised but a chair works great to put more weight on your push ups. I've got a bar for jumping pull-ups too, a box for stand-over burpees and I do a lot of kettlebell exercises for core workouts and strength gain.'

Lucas laughed. 'That sounds fucking hardcore.'

The two talked about muscle mass, protein shakes

and deadlifting for a short while. In that moment I saw a side of Hayden that I had only glimpsed in the past; that confident, charismatic person who attracted everyone around him. That's how he must have been before his panic attacks started.

'Let me introduce you, by the way,' Hayden said. After the initial tension, he seemed to have regained much of his cool. He turned to me and smiled. 'Andy, this is Lucas.'

'Alright?' I offered my palm.

'Andy's my boyfriend,' Hayden said.

Lucas bent over to clasp my hand and chuckled. 'Yeah, righto son, whatever.'

Blood drained away from my face as I grasped Lucas's fingers. I stared at the guy's face who, in all fairness, looked like a friendly bloke and all but... shit; he didn't consider that Hayden could be serious, not even for a split second.

Jaxon smothered a laugh behind his palm.

Lucas straightened and met Hayden's bemused expression. We were all looking at Lucas, waiting for the penny to drop.

Eventually, he joined the blushing club. 'Oh. Oh shit. You serious?'

'Yeah man,' Hayden said, drier than a rice cracker.

'Oh fuck, for real?' Lucas's face was close to being scarlet and his eyes were wide in disbelief. 'Sorry I'm just... shit Hayden, I didn't expect it. You've virtually fucked every girl I know, aside from my mother, like.'

More laughter from Jaxon. He was having the time of his life, the shithead, whereas Tai and I were following the exchange with an astounded look.

Hayden's jaw stiffened. 'Thank you, man. Remind me to say the same thing when you eventually introduce me to your girlfriend.'

I didn't think Lucas could blush more, but blimey if he didn't. 'Oh shit! Sorry, I didn't mean...' He looked at me apologetically.

'It's cool, no worries,' I quickly reassured him.

Actually, I felt sorry for him. Sexual orientation isn't something you see written on people's foreheads, and Hayden... well. I couldn't say he was hiding his. Shit, the opposite.

'So,' Lucas muttered, 'is this why... is this why you haven't been hanging out anymore? Because dude, I don't care if you're into men. I mean, whatever like. It's your gig, not mine, but we're mates and, honestly? I'm not that shallow. I wouldn't dump a friend just because they're seeing a guy. That's proper shitty.'

Hayden's expression dropped. 'No, Luc, it's got nothing to do with that.'

'I know there's a lot of homophobic cockheads out there, but I ain't one of 'em, like,' Lucas said heatedly, cutting Hayden off. 'If you and your boyfriend go to the pub with me and the guys and someone comes and gives you shit, I'll kick right off, like.'

Hayden smiled. 'I know. I know you're cool like that.'

Lucas grinned. 'Sound. Are these guys your mates too?'

There was another round of introductions between Lucas, my devilish mate and Lord Dracula. Lucas complimented Tai's tattoos, which consisted of a row of small, tidy ideograms on his bicep and a large one with a cool brush effect above his elbow crease.

'That's sick, mate,' Lucas said. 'What does it mean?'

'*If they spit at you behind your back, it means you're ahead of them.* Confucius,' Tai said. 'This here reads **shuōhuà de y ǒngqì**; the courage to speak up. And my name Tai is written here,' he said, pointing at an area above his elbow crease and traced the shape of a red ideogram. 'It means extreme, great, big... all things that are true about me.'

Lucas laughed. 'That's awesome! I'd love to get a tattoo in Chinese but I'm worried it would look daft, or that the tattoo artist gets it wrong, like you see on the internet, innit. Knowin' my luck it would probably say "GO FUCK YOURSELF", or something.'

Tai pouted his lips. 'I could translate for you. Just ask and I'll be at your service.'

'Nah, nah,' Lucas said, shaking his head. 'You're called "extreme". Bet you're the kind of guy who loves playing a prank. You're going to write "dickhead" in Chinese and then tell me that's a Tao principle and shit.'

Tai smirked. 'Busted.'

Apparently Lucas's sister worked in the burger place and that's why he was passing by. He made Hayden promise to hang out with him sometime and to bring us guys along. 'I'm gonna keep an eye on you. If you ignore me again I'm going to barge into your house.'

'Alright, alright, point taken son.' Hayden gave him a half-smile.

They dabbed, fist bumped and parted on good terms.

The food arrived and we ate enthusiastically. There was a sea of chips on our plates and the burgers smelled amazing. Tai went on praising Lucas, who had 'sussed him out right away', which apparently was a noteworthy achievement. Jaxon huffed and mumbled half-arsed replies. He didn't seem to like Lucas as much as Tai did.

Hayden smiled, laughed and handled Tai's teasing jokes with ease – he seemed to be having fun and my heart was light too. I watched him furtively, observed the creature in the wild to learn his nature.

At one point, his phone buzzed on the table and the strum of a guitar played blaringly loud.

'That's a hell of a text notification.' Jaxon folded a hand on his chest like a Victorian prince. 'It scared the fuck out of me.'

'Your fucks were scared away long ago, Jax,' Tai said with a grin. 'They ran away screaming.'

I glanced at Hayden, who'd busied himself reading the text message, and knew immediately that something was off. His jaws tightened and his eyes veiled with dread as they fixed on the screen.

I brushed his arm. 'Everything alright?'

'Y-yeah just... Iwan.' He rubbed a hand on my thigh, up and down, his fingers unusually warm and damp through the fabric of my jeans.

I peered at him and murmured, 'You sure? You're a bit pale.'

He nodded, but his eyes said otherwise. 'Can we go out for a breath of air, like?'

'Of course.' I turned to the others. 'We're going out for a bit.'

Tai tilted his head and smiled. 'OK lover-boys, we'll be here, being bored.'

I stood without even bothering to grab my coat and waited for Hayden to do the same. As he straightened, I noticed his legs buckling slightly. I took his hand and went for the exit. His sweaty hand gripped mine tightly.

'We're almost out, hold on,' I whispered.

Hayden gave a jerky nod, jaw clenched. We passed the table of lads, who thankfully didn't pay us any attention.

I breathed a sigh of relief, striding the rest of the distance with Hayden in toe. I was desperate to get him out of the restaurant before he could slump on the floor and cry out under the gaze of strangers. The episode in front of his family replayed in my head. I couldn't let that happen to him here. I knew how horrible it could be to have a crowd staring at you in a moment of crisis. Furthermore, the attention would only exacerbate the symptoms of anxiety.

'The shorter guy must be the girl. Hello fairies!' The comment, loud, clear and deliberate, split the air like the crash of a glass shattering on the ground.

I went to cross the open door, determined to ignore it, but Hayden stiffened next to me. He fixed his gaze on the table of students and onto the wide eyes of the chubby, obviously tipsy girl who had spoken.

He let go of my hand and wheeled around, faster and scarier than a black storm. 'What the fuck did you just say, you fat cunt?' he hissed.

The girl's face blanched. 'I-I'm sorry!'

Hayden heaved, his face a mask of ire. 'Mind your own fucking business! Go and shove another chip in your gob, you fuckin' whale!' he said venomously.

He picked up a stray chip and chucked it on the table with force, enough for it to bounce close to the girl's face and make the whole group flinch in fear. Had it been someone else doing it, it might have looked silly, but since it was Hayden, with his strong figure, deep voice and scowling features, nobody could have even considered laughing. He turned to me.

Colour had drained from his face but there was a fierce determination in his eyes. 'Let's go, come on.' He opened the door with a strength I lacked, took my hand again and led me out.

18

HAYDEN

Seat, a seat! Where's a fucking seat?

Panic clung to my chest like a slithering vine. I tramped down the paved street, grey under my feet. Grey church, grey sky... why did everything have to be so fucking grey? My head buzzed like a nest of angry hornets. I was there and I wasn't, the light switch of my mind going on and off, on and off. My heart was beating its way out of me.

My eyes flicked, right and left, legs speeding up. The rapid tapping of my shoes on the road grew loud in my ears like my quickened breathing, like the scream searing through my head.

'Hayden, slow down. You're scaring me.' Andy's hand squeezed mine.

My angel, dearest thing. Did I just think that? Fuck, I did.

'Sorry babe,' I heard myself say through parched lips.

I willed my legs to walk at a pace that was closer to normal, although at that moment I couldn't quite gauge what normal was. I stumbled and Andy caught me. His arm went around my waist and I was as grateful as I was ashamed. God, I wanted to cry. *Why is it always like this?*

'There's a bench there,' Andy said.

I looked and couldn't see, not quite. My eyes saw, but not

me. I was floating and breathing, holding on to a thread which was invariably tied to Andy's presence, to his warmth. Now I was sitting on a cold, hard surface which instantly froze my buttocks and cooled my nerves. Fuck, I was an absolute wreck, shaking and dizzy and sad. So sad.

My hands welcomed the shape of my face, becoming the only shelter where I could hide.

'I'm broken,' someone said. It was me. A lame, forlorn version of me.

'No babe, you're not,' Andy murmured. His cold hands stroked my neck gently, my shoulders, my arms. I'd dragged him out the restaurant without even giving him the time to wrap up warm. What an utter piece of shit I was.

I pulled at my hair, clutching it with the intent of causing pain but, compared to the heaviness in my chest, it was nothing. Hot, treacherous tears spilled. I scrunched my eyes shut but it was too late; salty water slipped free between my cheeks and palms.

My voice broke, 'Please, don't hate me.'

'Oh Hayden, I could never hate you.' He clasped my wrists gently and tried to pry my hands open to see my face, but I didn't budge.

'Hayden, look at me.'

'No mun,' I sobbed.

'Please.'

Slowly, I emerged from the darkness and saw the sun in Andy's eyes and gentle smile. 'There you are. See? It wasn't so hard.'

'I'm not sure about that, like,' I said.

Andy knelt on the cold stone in front of me, under the blow of the biting wind and leaned in to kiss me. His cool lips touched mine and his arms went around me.

How could I not love him, this shining being who'd descended from the sky to care for unworthy me? How could I not gaze at him in awe and thank whatever divinities may exist for allowing me to be with him in this world? Maybe I wasn't in the right state of mind – my thoughts and emotions were scattered like the fuming debris of a crashed plane, but I believed with all my heart that there was nothing I wouldn't do to make this person happy.

I held him tight into my arms and sunk into the warmth of his neck, breathed in his scent, stroked the softness of his hair. I had no words to express how I felt. Andy was oxygen, water, fire... the sun itself, for fuck's sake! *Not in the right state of mind,* I told myself.

'You guys alright?' I barely registered the question, but Andy turned around and the nippy breeze whooshed between us.

Tai stood nearby with a frown on his face, the bundle of our coats in his arms. 'I saw what happened, the row with the students and that fat bitch. What did they say?'

Andy replied, 'Nothing worth mentioning. But we really must go, Tai, sorry. Could you do me a favour and stay here with Hayden for a minute? I'll go grab our bags and pay for our food. I'll be right back.'

'There's no need, I'm alright like,' I said. My voice quavered and I tried to speak again, more firmly. 'I was going to pay for us today. I'll go...' I tried to stand and that was a mistake.

The world spun and nausea churned in my guts. The acid twinge of bile flooded my mouth, and I made it just in time to lean over the side of the marble seat and puke on the rectangular shape of a manhole.

Immediately, Andy was next to me, stroking my back and murmuring kind, worried words. I stared at the puddle of vomit in shock and tears threatened their way out of my eyes again. My body quaked with upset but I didn't let myself cry. A choked, painful sound squeezed out of my throat and that's all I'd allow it to be, although I wasn't brave enough to lift my gaze, because what polluted my body wasn't fear anymore, or queasiness – it was shame.

'I'll go get your bags and pay for your food,' Tai said. 'You can always give me back the money another time but, honestly? Don't worry about it, babes. Stay here with Hayden, yeah?'

Andy's hands swept up and down my shoulder blades like gentle waves, soothing me. I disappeared again – the walls of my consciousness shrouded me like curtains drawn over the window to the world.

'Hayden, sit up, put this on. Come on.'

I obeyed wordlessly. My chest hurt, my stomach too. My arm raised and Andy helped it through the sleeve of my coat, slinging the thick fabric over my back and sliding it over the other arm.

'You should zip it up,' he said. 'It's freezing.'

Andy helped me again and did it for me. He pulled the zip up to my collarbones and I was bundled up warm. Only then did he cover himself with a coat. He also had a scarf which he considered, glancing at it and then looking at me. He stepped forward and went to wrap it around my neck.

'No.' My voice was like a creaking hinge in desperate need of oiling. 'You wear it. I'm not cold.'

'You sure?' Andy's eyes were big with concern.

I slung an arm over his shoulder. 'Come here.'

I drew Andy to my chest and burrowed my nose into his hair. He hugged me back and sighed with pleasure against the crook of my neck. Then I remembered. I pulled back and brought a hand to my mouth. 'Oh shit, I'm sorry. I should really brush my teeth before putting my face in your hair.'

Andy hooked my waist with his arms tighter and huddled in my embrace, chuckling. 'I don't care about that. Just... hold me, please.'

I did and felt as blessed and content as I'd ever been.

Minutes flew by as we waited for Tai to come back with our bags and I wished time could stop in that perfect moment. Andy unzipped my coat and slipped his hands in the space between the heavy fabric and my back, seeking the warmth there. He let out a happy little sigh that brought a smile to my face.

'You're like a furnace,' he said.

I put my overheated palms on his cold cheekbones and he gasped in surprise. 'Oh my days!' He closed his eyes and groaned,. 'That feels so good.'

Laughing, I said, '*Oh my days?* Do people still say that?'

I continued stroking his cheeks and drowned in pleasure at the feel of his smooth, luscious skin. If only I could do this all day; trace his body with my lips and hands, have my cock deep inside his welcoming body. I wanted to press against him in a tangle of limbs and bury myself in his heat. At the back of my head, though, I reminded myself I had somewhere to be and that I couldn't stay.

Andy pressed small kisses on my neck. They were only pecks at first but they slowly became more insistent. He parted his lips, sucked on my throat gently and teased the skin with the tip of his hot tongue. That sweet tongue that had lapped at my cock and stuck out to take my cum, willing to taste me. I tightened my grip on his body, breathing heavily. My cock was hard in that lovesick way. I acknowledged the pulsing throb of arousal while unable to do anything about it, aside from riding the wave of sensation and keeping time with the fast drums of my heart. I returned Andy's kisses in mute desperation, brushing the tender skin under his ear with my mouth.

The city moved around us. Andy and I had cloaked ourselves with the length of our coats and hoods, hiding our faces from the curious gazes of others. Heat and skin, hair, saliva, tongues and the sleek pops of our mouths were the building blocks of our universe.

Fleeting voices and heels hitting the hard ground passed us by. Faraway laughter trickled and the rustle of leaves coming from the tree casting its shadow over us caressed my senses. It all existed beyond our shield of fabric. Two guys, embracing under the biting wind of deep winter, sat by the Baptist Church and a pool of vomit – somehow, it couldn't be more perfect.

Andy looked at me in that way every person wishes to be gazed upon at least once in their lives. He kissed my lips.

Someone cleared their voice nearby. 'Guys! I've got your bags.'

We separated and turned to glance at an awkward-looking Tai.

Andy let go of me and went to grab our rucksacks from his hands. 'Thank you so much!' Andy smiled at his friend. 'Oh, your books!'

Tai smiled. 'I've taken the liberty to grab them from your bag, babes.'

Tai had a strange expression on his face, somewhat soft and thoughtful, as if he'd solved a mystery and was now dealing with the truth. He looked at me and I cringed, expecting to find pity in his eyes, a replay of what I'd seen on the face of many others in the past months. *He's not right in the head, poor sod.* Something along those lines. But no. In Tai's gaze there was knowing. Relief, even.

'Take care, my bloody beauties,' Tai said. Lips upturned in a lopsided smile, he sauntered back to the restaurant with his hands sunk deep in the pocket of his tight leather trousers.

Andy said bye, sat back next to me and laced his fingers with mine. 'How are you feeling?'

I took in the details of his face, the curve of his expressive eyebrows, eyes rimmed with thick black lashes and irises blue like the summer sky everyone waits for the whole year round. The slight upturned tip of his nose and slender jaw. The sprinkle of chestnut freckles on his cheeks.

I exhaled slowly and smiled. 'Like I'm melting.'

I took his hand and brought it to my chest, right where my fast-beating heart was.

Andy bit his lip. Under my gaze, his cheeks turned pink. He sunk onto me, hiding his face between the base of my neck and the fold of my hood.

'Hayden,' he breathed on my skin.

'Yes baby?'

'I'm worried I'm falling in love with you too fast and we haven't even had a proper date yet. You haven't got my permission to... to make me... feel like that yet.'

My heart galloped at the meaning of his words. 'You're right, we should sort out this date, shouldn't we, yeah?'

Still snuggled on my chest, he nodded. 'Definitely.'

***

A catchy song played inside Andy's car. The guy singing was a marvel; his voice stretched, smooth and beckoning, and there I was, tapping my foot and falling under the rhythmic spell.

'This is gold, man,' I said. 'Who are they?'

Andy smirked, smug like a fox. 'The Black Queen. Never heard them?'

I thought about it, bringing my disposable cup to my lips and taking a gulp. 'No, I haven't, no. How the hell did a group like this slip under my radar, like?'

Andy and I had stopped to buy some hot chocolate on our way

to the car park and I was glad to have had the chance to pay for it, even if it was just a small thing – he'd done so much for me already.

He sipped his drink and a little dark semi-circle formed just above the bow of his lip. 'Do you know The Dillinger Escape Plan?'

I stared at that mark like a hungry dog would stare at a meaty bone. 'Oh yeah. *Under the Running Board* is a great album. I saw them supporting some noisecore band down the Barfly once.'

Andy adjusted the temperature of the heating and smiled. 'That's Greg Puciato singing. This is his side project.'

'For real? It's really good! He's into electronic music then?'

Andy nodded and leaned back on the driver's seat. 'Oh yeah, massively. Loves his eighties synth sound, as you can tell. The other two guys are Joshua Eustis and Steven Alexander.'

'What, from Nine Inch Nails?'

Andy said more about the band, how the Steven guy was in Dillinger at some point, but I was too distracted by his sweet little chocolate moustache. My need to do something about it was growing stronger by the second.

I put my hot chocolate on the dashboard and gave him a meaningful look. 'Andy, don't move.'

His eyes widened. 'Why, what's wrong?'

I leaned forward in a deliberate slowness. 'Stay as you are.'

Before he could ask any more questions, I had my open mouth pressed on the soft space between his lip and nose. I ran my tongue on it and lapped at his chocolate, which tasted sweeter than mine. He inhaled sharply and our eyes met. Just like that, I was hard like Floyd Mayweather's punch.

I hummed my need and licked my lips. Andy's big eyes half-closed with a swoop of arousal. My arms surrounded him. I was a hungry wolf and he a soft little lamb ready to be eaten. There was a mile of smooth warm skin under the barrier of his clothes and the thought of it made my mouth water. I stared into those eyes, blue like a cerulean sea and wide with expectation. His chest rose and fell fast and his lips parted. I licked and sucked on those lips, so soft, so juicy and *God*, I wanted them all over me.

'You do it on purpose, don't you?' I panted.

'Do what?'

I slid my hands under his baggy hoodie and felt the silky, warm surface of his sides and back. *So good*. 'Things that make me want to fuck you.'

Andy still clutched his hot chocolate, but grasped the fabric of my top with his free hand. 'I don't. It's you who's a pervert.' His voice was a shaky murmur.

I was happy to know I wasn't the only one affected by our nearness.

'Then I have it bad,' I said. 'It's as if I'm an addict, and you're my daily dose!'

Andy's breathing quickened. 'And what am I supposed to do about it?'

I brushed the soft flesh of his hips and squeezed. 'Let me fuck you continuously for a week in a row. Not sure that's going to be long enough to cure me, though, to be honest, like. Make it three weeks. We won't even need to get dressed, innit. We'll just hang around naked. All we'd do is fuck, make music, eat, fuck, listen to some good tunes, watch a film and then fuck again.' I broke into a smile. 'Basically, heaven.'

Andy chuckled and put his free arm around my neck. 'That does sound pretty amazing. What happens after three weeks, then?'

'We change the sheets and start over, of course.'

Andy laughed and kissed me. Our tongues met and the hot

contact sent a ripple of heat through my body. My hands roamed under his clothes and over the slight raise of his ribs and muscle. I skimmed a nipple with my fingers and toyed with it until Andy's breathy moans filled my mouth.

Lips swollen and cheeks flushed, he looked up at me. 'Want to go back to my place?'

I did, more than anything but *fuck,* I couldn't. In the past few years I'd learned that what I wanted always came second to my family's needs. And my family needed me right now, and badly.

I sighed painfully. 'Not this afternoon. I need to check up on my mum and I'm not sure how Iwan and Sophie are doing either. It's been a weird last couple of days.'

He traced my cheek with his fingers. 'Has something happened at home?'

I reached for my phone in the coat pocket, unlocked the screen and opened Iwan's last message.

Andy took the phone and read the words. The message only said that my mum was acting weird; a simple, frightening piece of information. A slight frown creased Andy's brow.

After a moment, he raised his eyes to me. 'She must still be in shock after what happened. I'm sorry you and your family have to go through all this.'

'I'm worried that my mum's having a relapse. For months after John went to prison she kept seeing him everywhere, like. Fuckin' everywhere. At the supermarket, at home. One afternoon she kept saying he was hiding behind the sofa and was terrified of going in the lounge for ages. After the trauma she'd suffered, it was more than understandable that her mind would be scarred somehow. She'd been fine after meeting my stepdad, but he...' Unpleasant memories of Gareth laying in bed, bold and dying but still bearing a smile, made my throat swell with sadness. I closed my eyes and pushed the image away. 'He's not with us anymore,' I murmured.

Andy's beautiful face was sombre. I reached for him and forced a smile. We shared a soft kiss and he hugged me. I hung on to his shoulders – the weight of the world didn't feel as unbearable in his arms.

'Sorry, I don't mean to bring all this crappy baggage between us. You got yourself a boyfriend with a few cracks.'

Andy snorted against my shoulder. 'The only crack you've got I can think of is the one on your ass.'

I broke into laughter and squeezed him tight against my chest.

Andy yapped in surprise. 'Ah, shit! Watch out, the hot chocolate—'

I took the cup from his hand and put it on the dashboard to keep its paper twin company. I kissed every inch of his exposed skin and Andy laughed when I pressed my lips between his eyebrows and on the tip of his nose. The sound of his glee was like a cool splash of water on a hot summer's day. The need to express how much he meant to me was so strong that it almost choked me. Words didn't come so I kissed him instead, slow and deep. Every stroke of my tongue said *I love you so fucking much*, over and over again, the movements of my mouth taking the lead since I wasn't brave enough to speak. I held him close, afraid to let the rare creature escape.

We broke our kiss but remained locked in our embrace, breathing each other's heat. The softness of Andy's hair through my fingers soothed me the same way music did.

He covered my neck in small kisses and exhaled against my skin. 'If I say something, promise you won't laugh?'

'Sure.'

He tugged at my hood and slid a hand down my nape. 'I cried a bit last night.'

My eyes widened. 'Why?'

He shrugged. 'I don't like to see you sad. It guts me.'

My heart sank. 'You cried for me?'

The corners of his mouth lifted in a tight smile. 'I guess, kind of. You deserve to be happy, that's what I think.'

Is he real?

I huffed a laugh, amazed once again at the sheer beauty of his person. 'You. You make me happy,' I said with a broken voice.

His eyes brightened. 'I do?'

I nodded, submerging in the warmth of his gaze. My phone buzzed and the text notification tune broke through the air. It was Iwan again. I read the message with a tang of dread.

'Mum's asking where you to now.'

I sighed. 'Gotta go. Fuck.'

'I'll drive you,' Andy said, turning on the ignition.

***

The moment we started heading for my neighbourhood, my stomach began to cramp. Nips of pain and nausea tore at my guts and Andy, once he was parked in front of my house, glanced at me with concern.

'Are you alright?'

I stooped, cupped my cheeks with trembling hands and shook my head. 'I'm scared.'

'Do you want me to come in with you?'

I wanted to introduce Andy to my mum but not like this, when neither she nor I were in a good place. 'Not today, nah.'

Andy nodded. 'OK, but if you need anything you know where to find me.'

We exchanged a parting kiss and I drew all the strength I could from it.

'I'll call you later, yeah?' I said, and let myself out.

Andy drove away and I followed the car with my eyes for a long moment, until it disappeared behind the next turn. The second he was gone from sight, a heavy feeling hung about my shoulders like a wet blanket and my heart ached. Now I was alone and the matter at hand felt huge and unbeatable; I was a mere mortal and my problems a hundred-headed hydra.

The gate was unlocked. Again. Sighing, I walked up the familiar two steps, slid my key three-quarters of the way through the dodgy keyhole and opened the door. The lounge was deserted and so was the kitchen. A muffled funk tune that I recognised as 'Redbone' by Childish Gambino came from upstairs, most likely from Iwan's room; he was home but he'd texted me saying that Sophie was at Amelia's again. The bass and slow beats bounced down the staircase like invisible balls. The music had an upbeat sound that made my skin crawl, since its slow, mundane joy deeply jarred with my state of mind. I went up the steps with heavy feet, my heartbeat running for its life.

'If you want it, you can have it...' Gambino sang. Have what? What did I want? *For the nightmare to end.*

Before coming face to face with Mum, I decided to make sure my brother was OK first. I knocked on his door, stickers of rugby players dotting the brown wood. 'Bro, it's me.'

No answer. I didn't know about other households, but here loud music blaring in a boy's room had a definite, unspoken meaning.

I pushed the door open just a little, letting my voice stray in but not my eyes. 'Bro?'

Iwan's choked answer broke me. 'Come in.'

He was sat on his bed, hands clutching blonde curls in a way that I sorely recognised.

I took him in my arms. 'Iwan, what's wrong, mate? Talk to me.' His body trembled. 'Mum, she's acting so weird, like,' he sniffed. 'I don't know what to do.'

My spirit groaned in pain. 'I'm here now, don't worry bro. I'm sorry I left you here by yourself.'

Iwan shook his head. 'No, it's not your fault. You're having it rough too, I saw it. I'm not a stupid little kid, you knows it, yeah?'

I hugged my baby brother tight to my chest and he clung to me like he did a few years ago, like when Gareth was too weak to speak, to eat, to breathe, and Iwan couldn't bear it.

'I know,' I managed to say, biting back my anguish. 'Where's Mum to now?'

'In her bedroom.'

I gave him a pat on the shoulder. 'I'm here now. Everything's gonna be alright, little bro.'

Iwan rubbed his eyes and smiled. Just then, he looked more like Gareth than ever before.

'OK,' he said.

'Right, I'll go see what's going on.'

'It's the man with the scar. He's everywhere, apparently.'

My blood froze at his words. I stepped out of his room with a ton of lead in each foot.

When I knocked on the slim door of Mum's bedroom, her hushed voice came softly. 'Iwan, Mum's busy love.'

I opened up. The room was dark, aside from the dim light of a dusty lightshade emanating a dull glow. Mum sat on a stool by the window and searched the houses across the road.

I cleared my throat. 'Mum?'

She turned to look at me. 'Hayden!' Unkempt, long dark hair framed her pale face, her light brown eyes haunted by a shadow.

A deep pain pulled at my insides at the sight of her. 'How are you feeling?'

She looked back out the window. 'I'm fine,' she said monotonously. She flashed me a strained smile. 'I haven't seen you since Sunday.'

'I went to visit you but you were kipping. Sorry. I should try to be here for you more.'

Mum chuckled. 'I don't expect you to be by my side all the time, you know? You're a big lad and you have your life to live. You used to go out all the time with your friends and sneak all your girlfriends in...'

I opened my mouth to speak but Mum interrupted me, a slim eyebrow raised. 'Don't deny it. I'm not blind. You're a looker and all the girls fall at your feet. The genes don't lie, my love.'

My throat tightened. 'My genes aren't all I am though.'

She smiled softly, 'I know.' Her eyes went back to the street.

'Have you taken your medication?'

'I did, believe it or not,' Mum scoffed. 'Your auntie threatened to snap my ear off if I didn't take it.'

'When did you take it?'

Mum sighed. 'Soon as she dropped us off.'

'But you're supposed to take it around this time...'

Her expression darkened. 'Hayden, love. It's done now, it's not the end of the world, mun.'

I bit my lip hard and took a deep breath. I was sure she expected me to ask about John but to bring it all up would be a terrible idea.

I tried to think of the right words. 'Mum...'

'Someone is following me, Hayden,' she whispered.

Mum's eyes were fixed on the road again but I could swear she was looking at nothing in particular. 'I thought it was your father. And it was, it was him but he couldn't be. I don't understand myself.'

My mouth went dry. 'But he's gone, Mum. They found him and now he's in prison.' The lie stung on my tongue but I continued. 'He's not going to bother you again, don't worry now.'

'Your aunt said so too but I saw him again today. He was looking up our window. I could see him clearly, even from here.' Her eyes gleamed with unshed tears. 'He's like a demon who's risen from hell to torment me. Have I not suffered enough, mun? I failed you as a mother, maybe that's why. I deserve to live in pain...'

I ran to her and hugged her shoulders. 'No, Mum, no. You deserve all the good things in the world, I promise you now.'

'I should have never let him touch you. He's a monster but I'm no better am I? God took Gareth away from me to teach me a lesson. I know it.'

Her words were like blunt knives plunging through my stomach. 'Mum, stop. Come on now.'

She sniffled and breathed in deep. 'You're my beautiful little man. Well, not so little anymore.' Mum looked me in the eye. 'You must be careful. I told Iwan to watch out for him too. He's got a large scar on his jaw. You know, a fire burn, all twisted and horrible. He's watching.'

Terror clutched at my guts. 'Fire burn?'

She nodded. 'Yes, but his face is as handsome as it always was. He's like a ghost from the past and he's out there. He's real.'

The doorbell rang. Once, twice. I didn't move. I couldn't.

Mum stood and slipped by me. 'That must be Katrina.'

I fixed my gaze on the dark blue of the sky through the glass, the evening broken by the glare of a streetlight, at the skeletal branches of the maple tree – a dark snare of twigs wagging and swaying under the wind. The pale-yellow curtains Grandma had made for Mum years ago cast a patterned shadow onto the carpet.

I stared at it all, body still and mind racing.

19

ANDY

I got home and put my keys in the usual spot, on a little glass plate on the breakfast counter. The house was unusually quiet, large and empty. Was my home always like this? Impersonal and cold? All this time I'd been fine with being here by myself, wearing my comfy slippers and living as lord of the manor. Now I felt like nothing mattered – nothing but his smile. I slumped on the sofa without even bothering to turn on the lights. Hot damn, maybe I was losing it.

I closed my eyes and what I saw was Hayden's face streaked with tears, his trembling hands. Slowly, I extracted my phone from my pocket.

'I'm in love with him,' I typed. I meant to send the message to Tai, mostly because I wanted to get the words off my chest and for someone to know how torn apart, how sweetly and terribly overwhelmed I was by my feelings. Love blazed within me – it was like a ball of hot energy pulsing inside my heart, making me dizzy with its intensity. I didn't send the text though. For several, long minutes I sat in silence in the semi-darkness.

Too fast. It's too fast.

The doorbell rang and I jumped off the couch in surprise. It rang again, a long shrill sound. Was it Hayden? Did something bad happen? It rang and rang and I rushed for the door, clasped the handle and opened up.

Cynthia stood at the threshold and her expression said it all. Blazing green-blue eyes, crowned with black mascara, flashed with accusation. Well, no matter what her face expressed, her mouth would certainly find a way to say more.

'Seriously?' she began.

'Hey,' I said mildly.

She whipped a hand in the air. 'No but, like, *seriously*?'

I sighed. 'Do you want to come in?'

She stomped inside, heels clacking and hair bouncing by her ears. I closed the door and Cynthia didn't even give me the time to offer her a drink before blurting it all out.

'OK first, let me just check. Is it true? Hanna literally just called and told me that she saw you making out with Hayden in, like, the middle of the street?'

I pinched the bridge of my nose. 'Look, I'm sorry for not telling you. It's a long story and Hayden and I kind of... happened.'

She laughed. 'What, like, you accidentally slipped and fell face down on his cock?'

I blushed. 'We became friends and then, I don't know, we got together. Anyway, why are you so interested in Hayden all of a sudden? *You* broke up with him and it's not like you were dating for long. You'd been seeing each other for what, like, three weeks?'

She wagged her hand. 'That's beside the point. I mean, there's a slight elephant in the room, I'm afraid to say. Babes, this dude,' she joined her fingers in a triangle, 'has shagged *sooo* many girls. It's, like, insane.'

'And?'

'And don't you think that this,' she gestured at me, 'is weird?

Isn't it suspicious that all of a sudden he's fine messing around with you? And wait, before you say anything else, even if you were a girl I would say the same. You hooking up with Hayden? Bad idea. And I can tell from your face that you think I'm being a dick just for the sake of it, but hear me out.'

I exhaled the anger that had risen up my chest through a tremulous breath and crossed my arms. 'Go on then.'

'Right. So I told you he's got family problems but there's more to that. How can I say this? He's not... right in the head. He's not the full shilling, like.'

'Bloody hell, Cynthia!' I growled. 'Hayden's got anxiety! Don't talk about his problems as if they make him less worthy of love, like people should stay away from him just because he suffers! Jesus, that's just cruel and horrible!'

She stared at me, stunned. 'Oh my God.'

'What?'

'You're in love with him, aren't you?'

I closed my eyes and took a steadying breath. 'So what if I am?'

'Andy,' she said pitifully, 'you *barely* know the guy, love. You're not thinking rationally.'

'*I don't care!*' I roared.

Cynthia shook her head. 'Babe, of all the people you could fall in love with—'

'Shut up!'

'But *listen* though. Hayden shags about to get over the stuff that's upsetting him.'

My soul started to crumble. 'Th... That's not how it is between us.'

'Andy, babes, I am so sorry but I have to tell you this, OK? I knew of Hayden for a while. Like, my friends knew of him and they'd go on and on about how he's a stunner, big cock, yada-yada, but I wanted nothing to do with him, right? Then he found me on Facebook and we started to talk. He was like, "Hello beautiful" and said he wanted to get to know me. I was standoffish and then, you know, he's got his way with words. He just does.'

Her latest statement felt like a kick in the stomach. 'What are you getting at?'

'I told you how it was, didn't I? He was seeing me *just because*. He said he wanted to date but then he was weird, like, he wouldn't go to public places. He only showed up to my house or invited me around to fuck, once or twice. He was all talk at first and then he wasn't. He had a weird-ass hysteric episode at the beginning of the third week we were dating. Like, serious crying and screaming, like. It was awful. I mean, mental-case scenario—'

'I know of his episodes,' I cut in like a blade. 'So what? I had the same, didn't I? Should I have been left behind too when I wasn't well?'

'Oh babe. What you had in college was nothing like this, come on mun.'

'Not far off!'

Cynthia huffed, 'Yeah but that was understandable, those guys beat you up—'

'Hayden has it way worse! *Waaay* worse! So yeah, you have no right to say what's understandable and what isn't!'

'What I mean is that his emotional issues are too big to allow for a healthy relationship.'

'Are you trying to scare me off? Do you really think that I'm going to turn away from him because he's having a hard time with his mental health? Hayden is... he's...' I swallowed back tears. 'He's the best person I've ever met, alright? It didn't work between you two and I'm sorry about that but this, what I have with him, I know it's special.'

Once again, there was pity in her eyes. 'You're so precious, hun, you really are. Like, I know you're super sweet and kind and that's probably what Hayden sees in you. What he's looking for is a crutch. I don't want you to become *that* for him, darl. You deserve way better.'

Knots of pain tightened and twisted inside my chest. I couldn't bear to hear anymore. 'Fine. You've said your piece. Now, would you so kindly get the *fuck* out of my house?' I stormed to the door and swung it open. 'Leg it!'

Cynthia's mouth dropped open, then closed again. 'Well, if that's what you want then.' She tramped out.

'And *don't you dare* text him or tell him any of the stupid shit you just told me, you hear me?' I yelled behind her as she scarpered to her car. 'Or I swear I'll never speak to you again!'

'Whatever!' she blustered.

I slammed the door shut as my heart thudded crazily. *Breathe, Andy, breathe*. I sat on the sofa again, this time shaking like my bones were made of jelly.

I don't care. I don't care about any of it.

20

HAYDEN

Coincidences. They were nothing new. For instance, the man I'd most loved and respected in my life and the one who ruined it had looked uncannily alike. I'd loathed Gareth when I first met him since he resembled the scum who happened to unload inside my mother and create me. Then Gareth started talking and laughing and being himself... and the hatred was gone, just like that. Gareth, who'd offended my young English pride by calling me 'butty' until I caught up with the fact that he wanted to be my friend. He had been so much more to me than that, though – a mentor and a father I could be proud of.

'Knowing you'll die soon helps you appreciate life,' he'd murmured once as he lay in bed, the sun shining through the bedroom window. 'Forget about the irrelevant stuff and focus on what's important. Everything changes, but the imprint of our existence stays forever.'

How'd he come up with that shit I didn't know. It must have been the morphine putting him on the path to enlightenment. I wrote down his words because they hit me deep. I kept an old notebook with our last conversations safe in my desk drawer. I brought it out and read Gareth's last words out loud while flat on my bed, looking for moral support on a sheet and a stretch of ink.

29th October 2017 – There are two types of men, Hayden. The bassists and the drummers. The bassists speak their mind calmly, sneaking their ideas through society without stirring up anything much. They change people's minds without anyone noticing. Sometimes, slow approaches are not enough, though, and that's when the drummers come in. Sometimes, you've got to make some noise to be heard, to break the habit, you get me?

I remember asking him to give me a second because I wanted to write down what he'd said. He'd joked that he'd be dead by the time I was done taking notes.

'So,' I'd asked, 'what kind of man are you then?'

'A bassist, of course.'

I liked the idea of being a drummer, 'cause that sounded cool. Gareth's cheeks were sunken and he had a pile of blankets layered over his body.

He looked at me and gave me a sparkling grin. 'Hayden, I've never said that a man can't be both. It's all a matter of occasion. The bassists are the ones running the world, really, and the drummers are there to speed things up. They stand out and they get a lot of flak for it. Most of the time, the big changes are invisible. Think about it. Sepultura. Great sound, right? But the vast majority of people can't really appreciate their music because it's loud, groovy, you know? It's aggressive, it is.'

'They're super famous, Ga.'

'Not more than Queen! "Bohemian Rhapsody" is everyone's favourite song, like. Not many can see the beauty through the noise. People want things explained easy to them, they do.'

I closed the notebook, got off my bed and selected 'Roots Bloody Roots' on Spotify, linked it to the speakers and let the song rage within the walls of my room. I threw myself back onto the duvet, closed my eyes and immersed myself in the sound – it dragged me down to the bottom of the Earth. Gareth's words from that day were indelible and replayed, clear in my memory, as if he was right next to me.

'Death is the same,' he had said. 'I think it's difficult to understand, that's why people don't like it. But there's beauty in death too. I'll own my own end, I will.'

Is death noisy, Gareth? Like a metal gig?

There was only me on the bed, my precious notebook with the memories it conjured and a sizzling silence. I remained unmoving, waiting for time to pass. I'd promised Andy I'd call him, but what should I say? *I was right. My mum is seeing shit and it's freaky as fuck.* Did she know John had died in a fire? Maybe she'd overheard it somewhere, but she was in denial and this was her way to cope? The *fuck should I know!*

My social media was like a traffic jam and I was the car accident that caused it. I replied to a quadrillion messages – posted and reposted shit until I went cross-eyed. I'd planned an epic stream for tomorrow and I seriously considered skipping it and taking a hiatus. I'd put together a tune while I was at Andy's, but since he'd had so much input in the piece it seemed unfair to advertise it as mine. Knowing Andy, he wouldn't have minded. Fuck me, what a guy.

I opened up his Facebook and creeped on his posts – 'cause that's the kind of dude I was now – and flicked through his pictures, fed off his smiles. I checked out his friends and relatives, including Cynthia who was tagged in a fair number of the photos. I wondered if Andy had told her about us; things had happened so fast we hadn't even had a chance to blink. Our relationship was like a fucking hurricane that had swept us off our feet, but in an awesome, sexy way.

I moved on to a different album where Andy posed with his parents. His dad was prim as fuck, as I'd expected; a man who likely used only the rational part of his brain. His mum was gorgeous, and it was clear where Andy got his lush blue eyes from. They were all lookers in his family. Cynthia had first caught my attention for that very reason, but Andy? Phew. He was *proper* beautiful.

My phone rang like a fire alarm and almost made me jump out of my skin. *I must remember to change my ringtone to something more bearable.*

I read Auntie Christie's name on the screen and answered. 'Hey.'

'Hiya love, I saw the missed calls. Everything OK?'

Sitting up, I exhaled a breath and rested my head on a palm. 'No, not really.'

Her tone was tense. 'What's wrong?'

'What do you do when a relative is hallucinating?'

Silence crept between us like a hiss of frigid air.

She whispered, 'What's she seeing?'

'John, with a large burn on his face. She said she'd spotted him looking up at her window, that he's following us around. Iwan got proper freaked out, as you can imagine, like.'

Christie made a choked noise, something between a groan and a whimper. 'I'll go to the GP tomorrow, see what he says, yeah?'

'Auntie, we need to tell her the truth. To keep the fact that John's dead from her isn't fair.'

'If the circumstances of his death were less unpleasant, I might have done it already. Before I break the news to her, I want to see the doctor. I wouldn't want to make things worse for her, you know? So you're saying she's seeing a man with a burn scar... but you didn't mention anything about the brewery?'

'No.' I lay back on my bed and hoped the mattress would swallow me.

'Mhm...'

'Does Aunt Katrina know about the fire?' I asked.

'Yes, but she promised she wouldn't say anything. She knows that if we approach the topic without the right precautions, the news could send Grace in a downward spiral. What if she thinks she's being cursed or something? She blames herself for Gareth's passing, says she's being punished for her bad deeds. I wouldn't be surprised if she blew things out of proportion.'

'Yeah, she mentioned that to me too, like. I *hate* lying to her.'

'I'll do what I can and, in the meantime, I want you to focus on yourself, yeah? You do you, babe. Have you spoken to someone about your episodes?'

'I haven't had the chance. I'll have a gander online tomorrow and call the doctor or something. Right now, my head is too cloudy. I can't handle it, like.'

'Alright love. What about Iwan, is he with you?'

I slipped my precious notebook back in its drawer, holding the phone with my shoulder. 'He said he's going to spend the night at his mate's. Can't really blame him for wanting to get out of the house.'

'And what about Sophie?'

I looked at the time on my phone: ten past seven. 'Katrina and Mum have gone to pick her up just now. I think Katrina is going to kip here.'

'Yes, I've asked her to,' Aunt Christie murmured. 'Right now, your mother needs her family around. This will hopefully be the last time we'll have to deal with John in our lives. Christ, even dead he's a nightmare!'

I closed my eyes. 'I know, innit.'

'I know things are difficult, but I promise it won't be like this forever,' Aunt Christie said kindly. 'Things will get better. John is gone, that chapter of your life is over and, Hayden, you're still so young. Since Gareth died you've been trying to pick up from where he left off, even though it's not on you to do so.'

'Of course it's on me. I'm the older brother, like.'

She snorted. 'You are and you've done an amazing job with looking after your siblings so far. You've also made yourself ill because of it.'

Her words swung at me like a punch. 'Is that what you think? That taking care of my family is driving me mental? I might as well call myself an ungrateful bastard, like!'

'Don't say things like that, you know as well as me that's not true. I think that you can help your mum and siblings by helping yourself first, babe. If what I saw in my house wasn't a mental breakdown, Hayden, I don't know what is, my boy. Your body is telling you that you need to give yourself a break. And I already said this but I'll say it again. You're not alone. You can rely on me, Bobi and Katrina. We are all here to support you. When your mum gets better, and she will, believe me, you'll be able to rely on her too.'

Whatever weight I had burdening my shoulders suddenly felt lighter. 'Ta. I'm so grateful, honestly.'

'That's what family's for.' Excited, childish laughter ran through the background. 'Hey you two! No more cookies, the pair of you!'

I chuckled. 'It sounds like you've got to go.'

'Yep. Speak soon sweetheart.'

'Bye.'

'Take care, hun.'

I stared at the ceiling of my room and spotted an old cobweb, dangling in the air like a tired ghost. I fixed my gaze there. How was I supposed to give myself a break, exactly? It wasn't that I didn't want to go out and meet my friends like I used to. I didn't have a clue what the fuck was making me flip out.

Heavy rain tapped at my window, its patter lolling me into a trance, when my phone came to life, buzzing and whining its text notification. Never had that sound been sweeter in my ears, since Andy's name was on the screen .

'I just want to know if everything's alright. You can ignore this if you want to. I'm a bit on edge, sorry. I'm not trying to invade your personal space or anything. I just want to make sure you're OK. Sorry. Again.'

I hugged the pillow and wished it was Andy instead. *'You said sorry twice in a row when you've done nothing wrong. It's me who should say sorry – I said I'd call you.'*

Andy sent a smiling emoji. *'I can wait.'*

'I can't.'

I pressed the call button and Andy answered his phone almost instantly. 'Hello?'

'Hello beautiful,' I breathed out.

'I'm still not used to that.'

'To what?'

'Being called beautiful as a greeting. It's weird.'

'Why is it weird?'

'Well 'cause, like... I'm a dude...?'

'A beautiful dude.'

Andy laughed in an odd way. 'You sure are a smooth talker.'

I bit my lip. 'Has my smooth talk worked on you?'

He paused for a moment. 'Completely.'

'Thank fuck for that!' I laughed and peered at the screen, at the picture that came up with his phone number. Andy stared back at me with a grin, the pride colours painted on his face and his arm draped around a girl with amazing lips and a stunning body.

'Who's that girl in the picture with you? The one that comes up with your number, you know.'

'Ah, that's Tess. I'll introduce you someday. She's a total blast! Did the cleavage get your attention?'

Admittedly, this Tess girl was hot. A man knows he's got it bad for his guy when firm, bulging tits and a full pair of lips don't tickle his fancy as much as the curve of his boyfriend's nose. If I closed my eyes, I could picture the warm stretch of skin around Andy's collarbones and the softness of his hair. I could feel that silky warmth under my lips and hear his rugged breathing as I licked and sucked all over his body...

'Hayden...?'

'I miss you so much it hurts,' I blurted out before I could think of what I was saying. 'I like you so much that I can't breathe, like. When you left earlier, it felt like someone had ripped off my arm. Is that normal? I don't know what you've done to me but all I do is think about you and I want...' I caught my breath. 'I want you next to me all the time. I want to feel you all night, to kiss you and hold you and bury myself inside you.'

There was a long pause. 'Andy, you still there?'

'Yeah.'

The silence stretched and I broke it. 'Say something.'

'I miss you too,' he murmured.

The need to see him was so strong that the fact that Andy

wasn't in my bed made me squirm with discomfort. I got off the mattress, taking my phone with me and my eyes went to my rucksack.

A lightbulb lit up. 'I forgot to give you your present.'

'Oh, that's alright. You can give it to me tomorrow. If you want to meet, that is.'

I strode to the corner where my bag was and grabbed it, flung the door open and shot downstairs. 'I'm coming to your place now.'

'*What!*'

On my way down, I crossed gazes with Katrina, Mum and Sophie who stood by the main door in a pool of water. They looked dishevelled, like new-born chicks; their hair was drenched and stuck to their heads, wet stains darkening their shoulders. They all stared at me with big, surprised eyes.

'Hayden,' Aunt Katrina said, 'is everything OK?'

'Yeah. I'm off out, like.'

Mum frowned. 'Where?'

'I'm going to see my boyfriend. I told you on the phone, about Andy?'

Mum's mouth opened but no sound came.

Sophie grinned. 'Oh Mum, you didn't know? They're all lovey-dovey.'

'Are you getting a taxi?' Aunt Katrina asked.

Andy said something on the phone. I pressed the screen on my ear. 'Sorry, I missed that.'

'I said there's no need to come here now! It's pouring outside, like. It's a proper storm!'

I looked out the window in the lounge. Behind the long, white curtains, the world was pitch black and angry, water drumming on the glass.

I shrugged and said to Andy, 'I've got a thick coat. I'll see you in a bit yeah.' I hung up.

I reached for my heaviest coat and slung my arms through it, kicked off my trainers and slipped on my Doc Martens.

Mum grabbed me by the arm. 'You can't be seriously thinking of going out there!'

For some reason, the fear in her eyes spurred me on to leave faster. 'I'll be alright. It's only a bit of rain.'

'But there's a yellow warning, Hayden,' she insisted.

'I can drive you, if you really need to go love,' Aunt Katrina suggested.

'No. Stay with Mum.' My tone was firm enough that it dissuaded her from saying anything more.

I tucked my phone in an inside pocket to protect it from the rain and zipped up my coat. After pulling up the hood of my sweater, I stacked the furry one from my coat over it. I secured my rucksack on my back and turned the handle. As soon as the lock loosened, the wind blew the main door open. A cold gust hit my face like the frigid slap of a wet towel, and a whirling splash of rain welted at my eyes. I laughed.

'Hayden!' Mum called after me.

I was off, swimming through the wind. I unlocked the little gate with great fucking effort and locked it behind me, because that was a step that could never be missed. My mother stood by the open door, her dark silhouette stark against the yellow light inside the house.

She hugged her chest and her hair whipped wildly around her face. 'Come back inside!'

'I'll be fine!' I shouted, and skipped along the uneven pavement, zig-zagging round the big fat puddles and running as fast as my feet would take me.

I bounced forward, smiling as if the storm was a party. I wasn't going to spend tonight alone in my room, thinking of Mum or the man with the scar. I was going to be with Andy.

My head, shoulders and arms grew heavy as the fabric of my coat soaked up the water, but I kept going. I was one with the wind, the rain, the dark night and the crash of thunder.

21

ANDY

I rang Hayden for the tenth time in a row. I waited for him to pick up but, once again, he didn't answer.

I stood frozen by the entrance door, wearing a cosy, embarrassingly bright *Rick and Morty* sweatshirt with a cold cup of tea in hand. I stared at the door with dread as if a bomb was about to explode behind it.

I put away my cup and began composing a text. *'Where are you? Are you really coming here??'*

The doorbell rang. My heart virtually bounced out of my chest and my phone out of my hands. I sprinted forward to open the front door. My boyfriend was there, leaning on the outer door frame, water running down his curls and a winning grin brightening his face.

The words left me in a burst. 'You stupid twat!'

Hayden cracked up and waddled in, bringing inside a lake's worth of water. He took off his rucksack and dropped it on the floor.

'Seriously, what's up with you?' I barked. 'Walking all the way here in this weather! There was no need whatsoever to... to...'

His cold, wet hands went to my cheeks and Hayden leaned in, shutting off my protests with the sweep of his hot tongue. He kissed me deep and slow and I went all mushy.

'At least take off your clothes, you're soaked,' I murmured when his mouth descended to tease my ear.

Without straying away from my throat, he unzipped his coat and let it drop on the tiled foyer floor with a splat. 'All my clothes?' he asked knowingly.

Phew! Was it suddenly hot in here or was it just me? Before I could think of a good answer, Hayden began stripping. He removed his thick grey hoodie and the T-shirt underneath in one go, pulling them over his head. Bare-chested, he put his arms around my waist and clamped my butt, fingers curling inside my crack. I yapped with surprise. Hayden grinned and dipped his head to kiss me again. I let my hands roam over the sturdy shape of his chest, arms and shoulders. I still couldn't wrap my head around how incredible his body was.

He pushed me against his crotch and I wasn't too surprised to feel an obvious hardness in his jeans. My dick was in the same state, stiff and pulsing.

Whatever anger or worry I'd felt melted away under Hayden's touch. Somewhere in the back of my head, I asked myself if he was with me to forget about his own worries and anger, but I pushed that thought away quickly. My clothes came off remarkably fast, and Hayden captured me in a tight embrace.

His hands stroked my back, sides and butt. He groaned against my skin and kissed my bare chest, my shoulders. He let go of me abruptly to take off his shoes, socks, jeans and boxer shorts. I gazed at the dark blonde happy trail and pubes surrounding his hard cock. My mouth went dry. Knowing what his dick felt like inside me made me pant with anticipation.

Hayden's eyes went to my pulsing erection. 'Fuck,' he said ruggedly, 'Look at you! You're leaking like mad.' He traced the tip of my cock with his thumb and brought a droplet of pre-cum to his lips, licked it and let out a deep moan. 'Man, I've gotta suck that. I'm gonna suck you proper dry.'

My heart was beating up a storm like the world outside. Hayden led me to the sofa in the lounge and pushed me on the seat, dropped to his knees on the carpet and took my cock in hand. As promised, he went down on me with the definite goal to blow me to death. He couldn't deep-throat like I could, but his thirst for cock left me speechless. His moans as he suckled on my tip were such a turn on that I couldn't do anything else but stare and gasp as his mouth plunged, fast and keen, down my shaft.

I held on to his curls and panted, 'I'm not going to last.'

He lifted his head and pushed gently on my chest. 'Lay down.'

I went flat on my back on the faux leather of my sofa, cold against my skin. Hayden knelt on the other cushion and bent over.

'Hold your legs,' he said, and as I did what he asked, he dragged me down closer to his face, my butt at his mercy.

'Oh, yeah,' he breathed over my hole and stared at it with eyes full of devotion.

I couldn't help but laugh. 'Can't say I have doubts you like ass.'

He smirked and stamped a kiss on my opening. 'I love *this* ass.'

Hayden proceeded to lick, tickle and tease my hole. He pressed his mouth on my twitching muscle and entered me with his tongue. I arched and moaned. He inserted one, then two thick fingers and slid them in and out, slow and steady. Pleasure spiked and I huffed and puffed, my body growing hot. He lapped at the stretched skin as he pressed upward and rubbed the sweet spot over and over.

Forget the blowjob, I wanted his cock. *Now.*

'Fuck me, please,' I gasped. 'Wreck my hole with your dick.'

Hayden bit his lip. 'Shit, if you ask me like that... I'll go get the lube.'

I grabbed his cock the moment he made a move to get off the sofa. His eyes met mine as I spat a large amount of saliva on my fingers and rubbed it all over my hole. I inserted two fingers and thrusted fast, stretching myself.

Hayden's mouth fell open. 'Fuck.'

I put one of my hands on his hip and tugged at his cock slightly with the other. His eyes widened even more as I guided him in bare.

'Oh, shit,' he murmured as my ass took him in, twitching and willing. The stretch burned more than usual but I loved it.

His cheeks, shoulders and chest flushed. Hayden pushed deeper and I gripped his biceps, grunting with discomfort. I could feel his naked cock inside me.

Hayden breathed hard over me, 'You alright?'

I caught my breath. 'Yes. Now, please, fuck me.' Hayden thrust hard and I shuddered. 'Don't stop.'

He fucked me raw, droplets of sweat and rainwater trickling down his chest. I hummed and gasped out my pleasure. His bare cock was inside me. Hayden was going to fill my hole with his cum.

'Oh God, Oh God,' I whimpered.

'Fuck Andy, it's so good. You feel so good.'

Pleasure coiled from within at every press of his big cock over my prostate, and gathered in my balls. I jerked off and Hayden's movements were so fast, so powerful and so perfect that my orgasm came before I was ready for it.

I gripped the cushion and threw my head back, gasping out a wordless sound. Cum spewed out of me and went all over my chest, my stomach. My hole pulsed, contracting with each wave of bliss. Hayden's thrusts became erratic. He grunted out each breath, his impossibly stiff cock rubbing over my oversensitive flesh. Before the stimulation could become too much to bear, his body tensed and wet heat filled me. I closed my eyes, relishing the feeling. Hayden slumped forward and surrounded me with his arms. He exhaled a long breath and placed open-mouthed kisses over my cheek and neck. My loud heartbeat thumped in my ears for a few more moments. I put my arms around his waist and stroked his sweat-sheened skin as we smiled at each other.

Hayden slid his half-mast dick out of me, reached to the wetness on my butt with his fingers and chuckled with awkward humour. 'I get tested regularly and the last time was when I started dating Cynthia, just so you know, and I always used protection with her. I'm saying this to put your mind at ease... the deed is done, so...' He lay next to me. 'That was quite the impulsive move, you taking me bare.'

I covered my warm face with both hands, feeling oddly shy and vulnerable. 'Yeah, hmm. Cynthia told me she asked you to get tested.'

He leaned on his elbow. 'She told you?'

'The day after we met.'

Hayden grinned. 'OK. What else did she tell you?'

What else, indeed. The memory of her latest visit was like a raw wound. I swallowed the lump forming in my throat. 'Ah... that you are very good at oral and that you have a big cock.'

Hayden guffawed. 'Fucking hell! But thanks Cynthia, I guess? She portrayed me well enough.'

I brushed his chest. 'She also said you'd never fuck me.'

Hayden's face scrunched in disbelief. 'Wha... in what context?'

'She said we'd get along because we had so many things in common but there could never be anything sexual between us. I thought you'd never sleep with me too, you know.'

Hayden snorted. 'Yeah, right. I wonder what she'd say if she saw me swallowing your jizz like I drink King Goblin on a Saturday.'

I threw a light fist on his shoulder of steel. 'Ew!'

He wiggled his eyebrows. 'Says the guy covered in cum.'

My cheeks heated. 'Anyway, I got tested too, three months ago. I haven't had sex with anybody since, aside from you.'

Hayden ran a hand over his face. 'Good to know.'

I sighed contentedly. Just then, a muffled sound came from the foyer. Hayden groaned and slunk off the sofa. He recovered his drenched coat from the floor and extracted his phone from an inside pocket. I let my gaze skate over the appealing shape of his unclothed body.

He answered the call.

Hayden's jaw clenched as he listened to the person talking on the other end. 'I'm fine, I'm at Andy's house,' he said, scratching his head. 'OK. I'll be going now. I'll be careful. Mum, I'll be alright. See you tomorrow.' He hung up and stared at his phone for a few moments, then sauntered back to me.

'Everything alright?' I asked.

Hayden sighed heavily. 'Just a bit stressed. My mother, she... needs help. My auntie is going to get in contact with the GP. I'm worried about my siblings too. Iwan has had it rough and he went to sleep over at a mate's house. Aunt Katrina is staying over with Mum and Sophie, and I wanted... I wanted to see you.'

I didn't want Cynthia's words to stick with me, to resound in my consciousness like a curse that had found its way inside me... but they did. I looked at the man I loved, at his sullen expression, as if he were lost in a lonely place and I was all he had. It could very well be that he'd walk away from me as soon as he got better, the very moment he could stand back on his own two feet. My heart would shatter for real, then. Not ache a little but mourn a loss, every beat a painful thump. Love could be as sudden as rainfall, as brief as a breath and as deep as an ocean. If any of my friends could hear my thoughts now, they'd look at me with pity like Cynthia did.

Hayden caressed me, stroked my back with his strong fingers and murmured, 'You OK?'

I nodded because I couldn't speak; I worried my voice would break. Don't leave me, I thought, the unspoken words like an earnest prayer. I tightened the embrace. Thunder crashed outside, the sky rumbling as if it was angry and shedding water as if it was sad.

'Babe, what's wrong?' he asked quietly.

I found the courage to look him in the eye and brushed my fingers through his damp hair, placing a single kiss on his cheek. In that one touch I poured all my affection, hoping it could reach him and spread like the warmth of a hearth in winter. He studied my face and I wondered what he saw, if my feelings showed.

'I wish I could take your sadness away,' I whispered.

Hayden's expression was difficult to read; it was pained but also happy. Hoarsely, he said, 'You do.'

***

My large bathtub had a jacuzzi system. When I told Hayden, his jaw dropped.

He looked at me sideways. 'You're fucking with me.'

I spluttered a laugh. 'No, I'm not!'

I ran a bath to demonstrate and stopped Hayden just in time before he could pour a dollop of bubble bath in the jacuzzi.

'You can't put soap in! The pumps are going to make it foam loads and it'll overflow. Look, I'll show you, you use this instead.' I found a packet of perfumed salts and released them in the hot water, which turned light yellow.

Hayden snorted. 'Now it looks like piss.'

I frowned. 'Yeah, it does.'

I set up my portable speakers and had music play in the bathroom.

Hayden laughed. 'This is sick as!'

I brought a few beers and savoury snacks and we were on, enjoying the moment in our golden bath that smelled of patchouli and lime. The water burbled around Hayden's torso, brushing along the dips of his abs. He grinned at me with a playful gleam in his eyes, spreading an arm round the edge of the bathtub and bringing a beer to his lips with the other.

'Why are you sitting so far away?' he asked.

I grinned back at him and sipped my lager. 'I have a great view from here.'

Hayden chuckled. 'Since when is looking better than touching?'

'Oh, I'm going to touch, don't worry. You just wait.'

Hayden slipped to the side and came over to me. He pressed his nose against my hair and murmured in my ear, 'You know I'm not good at waiting.'

My dick liked the sound of his husky voice and the sturdiness of his body. It stirred and swelled in response. Hayden slid his arm under my pit and guided me close, so that I was sitting between his legs. His hard-on pressed on my lower back. We were both erect but neither of us made a move to take things further. The music filled the room, soft and seductive and Hayden held me close. Perfection. I caressed the wet hair on his forearm as he skimmed over my neck and shoulders with his lips. We drank more beer, listened to Radiohead and let our mouths mesh into malty, slow kisses.

The buzz of alcohol, the warmth of the bubbling water, the soft music and the contact with Hayden's body lulled my senses. I was dozing off, enjoying the feel of him nuzzling my hair, when his low voice reached my ear. 'You're so smooth.'

With my eyes closed, I replied, 'Don't say it.'

'What?'

'That I'm smooth like a girl.'

Hayden chuckled. 'Not all girls are smooth.'

'Well, how would I know?' I put my mostly empty beer on the little iron stool by the tub and swirled around to sling my arms around his neck. I kissed his mouth, swept my tongue over his with deliberate slowness and grazed my teeth on his lower lip. He groaned deep in his throat and tightened his hold around my waist.

'You're seriously turning me on,' he said.

'Is my ass in danger?'

To my surprise, Hayden's expression fell. He stroked my cheek and looked at me dourly. 'I'm sorry, you know?'

I stiffened with alarm. 'For what?'

Hayden's fingers ran through the short hair at the back of my head. 'I don't know how to say this. It's... difficult.'

Is he breaking up with me already? Has he realised that he's not into me after all? Worried thoughts whizzed through my head like a tempest. I forced out the words, 'What is it?'

Hayden let out a long breath. 'I worry that I haven't considered your feelings enough. I came onto you strong and, in all honesty, sleeping with girls is all I've ever known. Being the active part comes natural to me but I know in a gay relationship that's not a set rule.'

'I'm not sure where you're going with this...'

He huffed and rubbed his eyes with two fingers. 'Look. What's the dynamic? Between us, like. We both have dicks, but I'm the only one doing the dicking. Is that how it's supposed to be? I haven't got experience with guys, so I don't know. I'm pretty clueless when it comes to gay stuff, I told you. You've gotta tell me if I do things wrong, like.'

Realisation dawned and I had to bite my lip to stop myself from cracking up with relief, as well as surprise. 'Are you worried because you've been the only one topping so far?'

'Yeah. Is that how you say it? Topping? I watched a lot of gay porn Saturday night but I can't remember all the terms. There was so much stuff I didn't know, like names for dudes' body types. Twink, otter, cub, bear... Man, that shit's weird.'

I broke into laughter, bending over to hold my stomach as I shook in amusement. 'Oh my God!'

He splashed water at me as his lips curved into a smile. 'Don't make fun of me, you knob! I'm serious like, innit.'

I caught my breath. 'You really never watched gay porn before?'

'Only whatever was included in the straight websites. Threesomes, like.'

'I can't believe it was me who awakened your gay side. How did that happen?'

Hayden gathered me closer and I sat over his thighs, straddling his erection.

'You showed up,' he said with a soft smile.

We kissed hungrily and I was in the mood to taunt him, slipping my tongue in and out of Hayden's mouth enough to drive him crazy. He bit my chin in retaliation and I stifled a groan.

'You cocky little tease,' he murmured.

'Why are you worried about me bottoming all the time anyway? I'm not offended by your preference, if that's what you're asking. Sex with you is great.'

He lowered his gaze sheepishly. 'It's not that I'm worried, just... I don't know. I don't want to be lacking sexually.'

I snorted. 'Dude, *you* and *lacking sexually* are not two things that go together.'

'I take it you don't want to fuck me, then?'

My eyes flew open and my heart jumped to the clouds and back. 'I... never said that,' I whispered.

His hand stopped on my shoulder. 'I was right then! You're not satisfied as things are!'

'I am satisfied, and I wouldn't want you to do something you might not like,' I muttered.

'Who says I wouldn't like it?'

Oh God, I could scarcely breathe. 'You... you would?'

He shrugged. 'I like the idea. Bet you could make it good for me.'

I covered my face with both hands. 'That's a lot of responsibility on my shoulders, especially seeing that my competition is you.'

'What you on about? What, is competing a gay thing then? Like, who's got the bigger cock or something?'

'In some circles, yes.'

He chuckled. 'You have a nice cock. It goes dark and leaks a lot when you're really turned on, it makes me want to put my mouth on it and lick it clean. So hot.'

My body grew warm. 'Jesus!'

He hugged me close to his chest, 'I honestly never thought I'd like the idea of getting fucked until recently, but yeah. If it's you doing it, I'd probably dig it a lot.'

'Alright...' I mumbled.

Hayden peered down my shoulder. 'Are you hard?'

'Of course I am, you header!'

He laughed and pressed himself onto my back. His stiff dick prodded at my skin and this time the air grew thick with sexual tension.

'Fancy going to the bedroom or what?' Hayden asked.

I murmured, 'Yeah.'

***

Despite Hayden's admission of liking the idea of being on the receiving end, we ended up sticking to what we already knew that night. Both of us were tipsy and the excitement of being joined without the barrier of the condom drove us wild. We fucked with abandon, taking breaks in between only to cuddle, snooze and pop to the loo.

In the middle of the night, our mutual desire rekindled. It grew between us in the form of slight caresses and heavy breathing. Every time we came together, I marvelled at the strength of our connection, at how our bodies called to one another in what felt like desperation.

At one point I was riding him, dropping down his hard cock that stretched my hole beautifully. It was easy for me to have his erection hit all the right spots in that position. I worked my dick in the meantime, though I had to take it easy stroking because the feeling of him bare inside me was close to being a sensory overload. I wanted to prolong the moment as long as I could. With Hayden, I always had this feeling that time slipped away from me a little too fast.

Darkness enshrouded my room, if not for a slit of yellow light seeping from outside through a wonky blind. The electric gleam of the lamppost outlined the sturdy form of Hayden's muscles. His warm hands cupped my buttocks and accompanied me as I descended on his body.

Our ragged breaths punctured the silence. On the street, a car swept by with a hushed crunch on the tarmac. I closed my eyes a while, focusing on the feel of our linked bodies, on the hot invasion of his dick deep inside me, on the slight dampness of his thighs and brush of body hair under me. When I opened my eyes again, I met the wet glint of his gaze.

'Are you crying?'

'It's just that you're so beautiful like this, like,' he sniffed. 'I'm so close to you now, I can feel how hot you are inside and everything. I've never had sex without a condom before today, and with you... it's like I'm melting in you.'

He took me like we did it the first time then, embraced me as I straddled his legs, hands gliding over my back. I held him close, kissed his mouth as if I could breathe only through him. Our movements grew rougher, the soft grunts turning into louder calls to the night. I took my erection and pumped it, rubbing the tip against Hayden's abdomen.

'I'm gonna...' I said breathlessly.

Hayden bit lightly on my nipple, licked it and murmured, 'Do it, cum for me, babe.'

My orgasm exploded in a rush, hot cum shooting out of me and onto Hayden's body, marking it as mine. He turned me around and pushed me on my back. His manly form towered over me, my jizz glistening gold as the light from outside shone over his torso. I knew that image would stay with me forever and I took it in, memorising everything. The beauty of it all was nearly overwhelming and I asked myself what good had I done in life, or maybe in a past existence, to deserve this gift, this person, being part of my story.

Hayden fixed his gaze on my naked body and gave himself pleasure with a swift, strong hand. The hotness of his semen hit me like a welcome blessing; an exchange of essence that went beyond what the eyes could see. I met his gaze and knew he thought it too. Both of us were baffled, awed and scared by how colossal it all felt.

What we had was immense, something that two guys in their early twenties who hardly knew each other shouldn't know, too big to handle or define. Words were useless and so we held each other for a long time instead, letting our hands and mouths speak for us through caresses and kisses.

After what could have been ten minutes or a whole hour, we were still tangled and unable to let go.

Hayden pressed his forehead to mine and spoke quietly. 'When I'm with you, when you give yourself to me, it's like I'm floating in an open sky and it's all blue and sunny and everything. It's awesome there and it's quiet, I can think clearly and be myself. I don't know what's going to happen in the future, if there's going to be bad stuff like I had in the past, but I think that after today, for sure...' He exhaled on my nose. 'I'll never regret being alive.'

'Smooth talker,' I said in a choked voice.

Hayden held me a little tighter. 'It's not smooth-talking, like. It's the truth.'

'OK,' I murmured. 'That's the most beautiful thing anyone's ever said to me.'

Hayden chuckled. 'Wait until tomorrow.'

I huffed a laugh very close to being a sob. 'I don't think I can survive this kind of oration.'

He snorted. 'Is regular oral more to your taste then, like?'

I slapped his ass and laughed. 'Sod off!'

22

HAYDEN

I was being followed by a shadow. Torn between running away from it and finding out who it was and what they wanted, I swam through a swamp of uncertainty, anger and fear.

Then I opened my eyes. A bird chirped somewhere. Andy was next to me in bed, naked and beautiful, his arm thrown over my chest and skin softer than a happy dream. My heart warmed.

'I love you,' I said quietly. Andy didn't hear; he was peacefully asleep. 'I never told anyone I loved them, aside from my family, you know. Maybe a friend or two. Anyway, not like this. This love is just for you.'

Still, he slept. I put my arms around him. Only when I hugged him and painted his face with a million kisses, did he awake. His eyes, heavy with sleep, fluttered open. So blue. Like freedom.

He kissed my lips briefly, sleepy and cute as hell. 'What time is it?'

'Don't know.'

He stretched an arm to reach his phone, rubbed his eyes and squinted up at the screen. 'Quarter to seven. That's... early.'

I chuckled. 'I get up around six to exercise, that's why I'm awake.' Andy looked at me groggily and I laughed. 'Go back to sleep.'

I was getting off the bed when he grabbed my arm. 'Will you be gone when I wake up?' He asked this with such unease in his voice and worry in his eyes that my heart nearly broke.

Covering him with my body, I kissed him and held him close. 'Of course not, babe. I'll spend today with you.'

'You will?'

'Yeah, I'm off today. In fact, I'm going to take you out for a date. Or you me. We take each other out?' I chuckled.

'Really?' His eyes sparkled. 'Where are we going?'

'We'll decide later. Sleep a bit longer, alright?' I pressed my lips to his forehead. 'I'll come wake you in an hour or so.'

Andy smiled dreamily. He took my pillow and hugged it. Pressing his nose on the fabric, he said, 'Smells good.'

A melting man. Yep. That's what I was.

As I went downstairs, I couldn't stop grinning like a twat. After my usual workout routine I decided to surprise Andy by making breakfast. I inspected the contents of his insanely big fridge. The stuff inside was a mixture of super-healthy and downright odd food, and almost everything seemed to be high-fibre. There was a little pack of tofu and a mysterious paste called *aka-miso*, macadamia milk and so on, so forth. Weird shit, like.

'Where the fuck is the bacon?' I grumbled. I found it, eventually, in the form of fatless medallions and sighed. 'That'll have to do.'

I cracked a bunch of eggs in a pan with butter to scramble them, found a stray can of beans and cooked the bacon medallions with a resigned frown. I was folding my eggs with a spatula when a surprised gasp got my attention.

Andy stood on the stairs. He was dressed, to my disappointment. 'You're making breakfast?'

'Good morning. And yes.'

His mouth widened in an ecstatic smile. 'Naked?'

'I've got my boxers on.'

'Dream-crusher,' Andy mumbled.

I laughed. 'OK, no boxers next time.'

He came by me almost furtively and inspected my handiwork. 'Looks nice.' I had him try the scrambled eggs and he moaned, '*Mmm*, tasty.' He licked his lips like a cat.

Andy and I ate our scrambled eggs with beans and the saddest-looking bacon ever on toast. We discussed where we wanted to go for our date.

'What about down the Bay? The weather's alright. We could have something to eat by the pier,' he said.

I grinned. 'That's proper romantic.'

We surveyed the list of restaurants in the Bay and decided to go for fish and chips in a popular spot that looked out to sea.

'We should go inside the restaurant. It's cold today,' I said.

'You sure?' Andy asked with alarm. 'Will you be fine? What if it's busy?'

I sighed. 'I'll be alright.'

'Hayden, don't force yourself to do things that make you uncomfortable,' he said seriously.

I put an arm around his shoulders. 'I want to get it right. Give you a time worth remembering.'

He scrolled down the screen of his phone and said simply, 'Every moment with you is worth remembering.'

***

During our drive to the Bay we played our music through the

car speakers and Andy made up some lyrics on the spot for a piece I was working on.

'That was proper awesome!' I said with a grin. 'Do you think I could record you and add your voice to the track, like? It works really well!'

Andy blushed a bit. 'It's not that good, I was only messing around.'

'Yeah, you say that, but...' I combed my fringe with my fingers, trying to find the right words. 'I've been thinking, like. It'd be nice if we worked on some tunes together. We could even make an album. It'd be a right laugh, don't you reckon?'

Andy's eyes widened. 'Under the o-Drone name?'

I shrugged. 'That, or something else. Something new. Dunno. It'd be nice to give it a go.'

Andy smiled softly. 'I'd be up for that.'

A new track trickled through the speakers. I'd forgotten I put this one in my playlist too. After getting back home and talking with my mum yesterday, I jumped on the sequencer in an attempt to get out of my emotional slump. The bass-line I'd put together was like my spirit when it fell into the grasp of fear – a low, hollow jumble. The main tune, the soft synths in a major key and the catchy percussions were my beckoning call to the light, a slit of sun parting the clouds. Eventually, the tune would grow into something more symphonic and whatever sadness there was at the beginning, was gone by the end.

Andy had found a parking space in Pierhead Street's Q-Park when the piece came to an end. He looked at me with eyes full of awe. 'Is this one of your tunes?'

Heat sidled up my neck and settled on my cheeks. I cleared my throat. 'Yes.'

Andy shook his head slightly. 'It's beautiful. Very different from your usual stuff, but still amazing.'

I watched him as he talked about my tune and told me how much he loved the cheerful beats and the scattered high notes. *Ahh, he is definitely glowing. Just look at him.*

'Does it have a title?'

Suddenly the seams of my hoodie were a strong interest of mine. 'I'm not at liberty to say.'

He chuckled. 'What, is it something embarrassing?'

I stared at the concrete walls of the car park to avoid meeting Andy's inquisitive gaze.

'Hayden?'

'Yeah?'

'It's not my name, is it?

Wow, that wall is so interesting to look at and that column... that column's so column-y.

Andy touched my shoulder. 'Is it?'

'Maybe...?'

Andy gasped loudly. 'Aw Hayden! Really?'

Shit, I should have lied. I should have said the song was called 'Total Eclipse of the Arse' or something.

Andy put his arms around me and laughed. 'You're a big softie, aren't you?'

He attempted to kiss my cheek but my hand was there, covering my embarrassment. 'Quit it,' I mumbled.

'Thank you,' he whispered. 'I haven't made music worthy of your name yet. You just wait though. It'll be proper brilliant once I do.'

I met his eyes then, and Andy had nothing less but the sweetest of smiles for me.

'Alright then, sound. I'll be waiting for it. Now, are we going to have this date or what?'

Andy chuckled. 'Let's go have fun!'

We got to the restaurant which was, to my relief, not busy at all. There were a couple of families and middle-aged friends enjoying their food and drinks. The soft clinks of cutlery and low murmurs, joined with the warm light of a descending sun suffusing the room, made me feel relaxed. Not too subtly, Andy had made sure our table was the closest to the door. He was still worried I could flip and well, I couldn't say I wasn't either. We got pints of lager and, when the food arrived, we marvelled at the generous size of the portions. I wasn't a fussy sort but even I could tell that this was no regular fish and chips; it was proper fancy. The best part of lunch was watching Andy fumble with the batter of his fish.

He met my gaze from across the table. 'What's up?' He wiped his mouth. 'Is it the tartare sauce again? Feck, it just goes everywhere.'

I broke into a grin. 'You look proper nice with a bit of white sauce on your face.'

Andy's eyes snapped wide. 'You, sir, have an insatiably dirty mind.'

I leaned over the table. 'Only just realised it?'

Andy crossed his arms, closed his eyes and took a deep breath. 'OK. Let's play a game.'

'Ohh? What game?' I asked, chewing on a big mouthful of fish.

'Whoever comes up with the dirtiest sexual scenario wins. Although, it has to be something you'd enjoy doing, not any random weird stuff that comes to your head.'

I sat back in my chair. 'Well, this sounds interesting. And it could be anything, as long as I would do it?'

Andy smirked. 'As long as you would *enjoy* doing it. With me.'

I beamed. 'OK, so what about—'

'Wait,' Andy said, looking around and glancing at the small number of people occupying the nearby tables. 'Let's do it through text.'

I flashed a crooked smile. 'Too shy to say these things out loud?'

'That, and I think...' He looked at me with a glint of mischief. 'It could get a little too heated and we'd end up having to whisper. Plus, having the fantasies written down in a message is like carving them in stone. The winner gets to decide which one of those things we should do. It's good to have all the details recorded.'

I bit my lip, my grin broadening, 'Alright then. Sound. Challenge accepted.'

***

I didn't know what to expect from my first date with Andy, but walking around the docks in Cardiff Bay with a rampant boner was not what I'd envisaged. Thank fuck my coat was long enough to cover my bulge, otherwise I might have had someone ask me if they could hang their hat on my hook. After two explicit text messages I was seriously struggling. We went to get a takeaway coffee and now here I was, was walking about with a dangerously blatant hard-on. I rested on the rail by the water and clutched it for dear life.

With a mixture of nerves and trepidation, I waited as Andy typed his message with a downright naughty expression.

I turned my gaze to the scenery in an attempt to shift my attention from Andy's tongue sticking a tad out of his mouth to the wintery vista of Cardiff Bay. A play of indigo and silver tinted the rippling water. The sky, a sweep of light blue, grey and lilac, shifted slowly as the expanses of clouds journeyed along the wind and reflected on the vast mirror below. As the clusters moved, a soft glow pervaded the bay and touched the buildings. The curved side of the Millennium Centre gleamed like the bronzed scales of a giant fish and the brick red of the Pierhead Building stood out in the quiet afternoon.

My phone chimed. *Here we go again.* I opened Andy's message and held my breath.

'*I'd let you tie my wrists, call you Master and beg you to cum all over my face.*'

The image flashed as if it was happening right in front of me. 'Jesus Christ, Andy.'

He laughed. 'Have I got this game, then?'

I adjusted the cumbersome erection in my trousers. 'Not yet.'

My excited state helped to conjure a scenario that was so dirty I could barely hold still. Maybe the day I'd cum in my pants because of sexting had finally arrived. I typed my message carefully, as if it was one of those puzzles in a videogame where, if you make a mistake, your character explodes.

'*I'd fuck you hard against the wall and, after cumming inside your hole, I'd go down on my knees and eat you out. I'd lick and suck all my jizz from your ass until there's none left.*'

Andy picked up his phone with a huge, smug grin. Clearly, he thought he had the victory in his pocket. As soon as he read my words his expression changed.

He sucked in a breath and looked at me with huge eyes and cheeks pinker than the ripest of peaches. 'Holy shit.'

I grabbed him by the hip and pressed his body against my hard cock.

I whispered in his ear, 'I don't know what you were thinking when you decided to play this game, but I'm growing a third leg here. Just admit your loss, then let's go home and fuck.'

'No, wait.' He pressed a hand against my chest and looked a little too hopeful for my taste. 'I have one more. One more!'

I sighed. 'Alright, go on then.'

Andy tapped on his phone at a galactic speed.

'Roleplay scenario: I dress up as a choir boy and you as a priest. Then I go down on all fours and you punish my ass with your dick, ordering me to ask for forgiveness while smacking my butt with the Bible.'

I cracked up laughing so hard that I almost dropped my coffee. I held on to the rail to keep steady. 'Oh God! You want me to smack your butt with the Bible? I can't breathe!' Tears streamed down my face and I wiped them off, then laughed again.

Andy chuckled. 'Come on, it's not that funny!'

'No, you're right, it's not,' I heaved.

He lifted his chin in triumph. 'Does this mean I won the game?'

'Completely! Shit, Andy, I...' I hugged him tight and kissed his cheek, heart pounding a hundred miles an hour, 'I've gotta tell you, I know it's early days but I—'

John was there.

There was a splash and Andy gasped as if he was in pain. My coffee cup had slid out of my hand and popped open by his leg.

My father stood sixty feet away, wearing a long black coat and a surprised expression. His hair was a mess of pale curls and he looked as if he hadn't aged a day. The marks of fire marred his chin and cheek. His striped scarf did little to hide the damage.

The man with the scar.

I grabbed Andy by the hand. 'Andy, he's here. You've gotta get away. Get away.'

'Hayden, what's going on? Who's here?'

My brain short-circuited. *No, it can't be John.* The man gazed right at me with ice-blue eyes, recognition written all over his face. He knew me, I was sure of it, as much as I was sure that he was about to get closer...

I ran.

A dude I crashed into fell on the ground and yelled at me but I didn't stop. I kept going, speeding through the dock, then the streets, crossing the road even though the traffic light was red and a bunch of cars beeped their horns at me.

I didn't look back as I sprinted by the Mermaid Quay building, only to find that my body couldn't take me further. The dirty pavement of a delivery zone met the weight of my limp body and my head slammed against the metal of a blue door.

He's come back to kill me. To kill Mum, Iwan, Sophie. No, no! I'm seeing shit, I'm seeing shit. But he was there! Though it can't be him. John is dead. That was someone who looked like him, yes. Oh God, I'm going to die. Andy, Andy... where's Andy?

My chest pounded with agony as I curled up in a ball of hollowness and terror. I was out of me, somewhere where I couldn't say, staring at the black walls of my mind.

A man asked me if I was alright. I couldn't answer and I didn't care to. Nothing mattered. I was already dead – my body was only an inconvenient, quivering shell moments away from cracking, shattering into nothingness.

Time passed and I breathed on.

The man touched my shoulder. 'I've called you an ambulance, mate.'

'No... no...' I heaved. The strength to speak came unexpectedly from the depths of me. '*Nooooo!*' I cried out, loud and desperate.

'Mate, calm down.' His breath stank of garlic and something else I couldn't think of.

I broke into quaking sobs and buried my face in the fold of my arms. 'No, oh no, no... Please, make it go away. Please...'

'Hayden! Hayden, are you OK?' The breathless voice was like a beam of light piercing the terrible sky of my lonely, dark place. My dearest thing was here for me and he touched my back, my hair, giving me the strength I so heartily needed.

I clung to him and cried against his chest. 'Oh God, Andy, make it go away, please!' I wept and wept and I couldn't stop.

'Baby, don't cry,' he said. 'Everything is going to be alright. I promise.'

'It's not alright, Andy! I saw... I...'

Andy looked at me with big, worried eyes.

I couldn't say it. If I did, it would become true and I *didn't* want it to be true. It *couldn't* be true and I was simply going crazy. Maybe I always had been and only now was it coming to fruition.

'Oh fuck,' I sobbed. 'I'm imagining shit. Jesus, why can't I just... be free from all this crap. Fuck Andy, I'm tired. I'm so fucking tired.'

I stayed there, cradled by the warmth of his arms. After a while, I said, 'I don't want to go to the hospital. Tell that man. I don't want... I don't want to go... please...'

Andy called the emergency number, explained I had an anxiety attack and that I was fine, that he'd look after me. He led me to his car with some effort and, once we were settled inside, he held my hand, kissed me and murmured sweet words in my ear.

I floated in a daze between wake and sleep. Andy always did so much for me and I was nothing but a weight on his shoulders.

This kind, shining human being was being dragged down into the mud because of my faulty self. That wasn't fair; I cared about him too much to give him such grief. Yet, leaving him didn't seem like an option either.

I couldn't be a burden anymore. Not today, at least.

Sat in the passenger's seat, I turned my head slowly and said, 'Please, take me home.'

23

ANDY

Hayden didn't say anything as I drove him back to his house. It was as if he'd sunk deep, somewhere where even I couldn't reach him. After a short while, he fell asleep.

The sight of him exhausted after an intense episode looked familiar. When I had to deal with anxiety, years ago, I would also shut down as if my mind had burnt itself out.

Hayden's eyes were puffy after so much crying and his cheeks gleamed with the trace of tears. He looked so vulnerable, so hurt and I could help so little. All I knew was that I loved him a painful amount. He suffered and all I was able to give was my presence, my words – I could comfort him and hold him tight. None of it seemed to have any effect.

His explosion of emotions was nothing like I'd seen before. His symptoms resembled the ones of PTSD, but it was difficult to define what it all truly was. Only an expert could say. For sure, Hayden had an invisible wound that would not heal unless he found a way to halt the bleeding.

A thought occurred and it was a horrible one. *Is our relationship his way of fixing himself?* I bit my lip hard and buried the pain the notion brought.

By the time we reached Cathays, my heart was a heavy stone and my thoughts buzzed. Cynthia's words resurfaced and wriggled inside my head like earworms, driving me crazy.

Hayden sleeps around to get over the stuff that's upsetting him... his emotional issues are too big to allow for a healthy relationship.

I'd dismissed Cynthia but, inside, I couldn't deny that her words had a semblance of truth about them.

If Hayden ripped my heart apart, there was nothing I could do because *my heart was already his.* Simple. He'd found his way inside my soul like no one else could.

I wondered about the falling-in-love process and thought of the people who said you shouldn't give your heart away so easily. I really wanted to ask them how the *feck* could you stop yourself from free-falling into the depths of love when you met someone who made you feel like Hayden made me feel. One of the culprits being Tai, another Cynthia.

Maybe I wanted to fall in love, maybe it was unavoidable. Maybe both.

In any case, when I parked in front of Hayden's house I told myself that, no matter what, I wouldn't abandon him. I brushed his cheek and Hayden roused himself.

'Mmh,' he murmured sleepily. 'Did I doze off?'

'Yeah,' I smiled. 'We're by your house.'

Hayden looked out the car window. 'It's open.'

I peered over his shoulder. 'The gate?'

'Yeah,' he said quietly. 'It always is. No matter how many times I tell Iwan to lock it, it's always, *always* open, like. How can my brother not understand that the world is a dangerous place? Fuck's sake. He should know better.'

Hayden talked about the gate but I had the feeling there was a deeper meaning behind his words. A lingering pain.

'Hayden?'

'Yes, babe?'

'What... What happened at the Bay?'

Silence invaded the car like stuffy, cold air. Eventually, he said, 'The usual thing. I disappeared. The other me showed up. That one motherfucker nobody can stand.'

'Hayden...'

He clasped his hands tightly, as if his fingers could fuse into a shield of flesh and bone. 'I told you about my mum's hallucinations, didn't I?'

'Yeah.'

He exhaled heavily. 'She told me something. She said... she said...' He swallowed. 'She said there was a man with a burn on his face who looked exactly like my old man. She said it was him but that it couldn't be. That he was like a ghost following her around. My mother doesn't know John died in a fire. It was playing in my mind, this thing. Maybe she overheard a conversation? She's imagining things, that's what I thought, but...' He looked at me gravely. '*God*. Today I... I saw him too, like. It's proper mental.'

I didn't know what to say. I stared at him, full of dread.

Hayden laughed bitterly. 'You think I'm insane.'

'I don't!'

'Don't you? Because I think I am. Deeply, fucking disturbed.'

'Stress is causing this, for sure,' I said earnestly.

'Whatever it is, I've had enough. Just...' He sighed. 'Enough. And you have to deal with all this crap, with my mental instability. It's not fair on you.'

I undid my seatbelt and wound my arms around him. Hayden hugged me back and, after a moment, I had him look me in the eye.

'You know what's not fair?'

He shook his head.

'That you should think of yourself as someone who only takes and has nothing to give. Your struggles don't make you less of a person, you hear me? Nothing about you is a nuisance, or wrong. Your body and your mind are fighting something that looks impossible to beat right now but one day, I promise, you'll look back on today and smile, knowing how far you've come. The problems of now will only be faded memories.'

In the dim light pervading the quiet street, Hayden's eyes glimmered with emotion. His voice cracked, 'Ta.'

'For what?'

'For being you.'

'Same to you.'

He held me tightly and kissed me like he never wanted to let go, but eventually we separated. Hayden grabbed his bag, offering me a soft smile as he went into his house.

24

HAYDEN

Mum, Sophie and Aunt Katrina were watching a movie in the lounge – *Night at the Museum,* by the looks of it. They sat next to each other on the throw covering the sofa, with Sophie sprawled in the middle holding a large bowl of popcorn. There were a good number of empty fruit cider cans on the floor by Aunt Katrina's slippered feet. I raised a perplexed eyebrow.

'Hey,' I said.

Aunt Katrina grinned at me. 'Hey hon! Did you have a good time with your boyfriend?' She cackled a little too loud for someone who was supposed to be in control of their alcohol. Well, at least she was sitting in the lounge at my house and not puking in the Castle grounds with a broken stiletto and no money for a cab.

'I did, ta,' I said.

Sophie's eyes were heavy with sleep and she looked as if she was trying really hard to stay awake to watch the movie but was failing miserably. In any case, she was too much in her own world to pay attention to her brother. Mum did glance at me, or rather scowled, only to turn her gaze back to the television and ignore me altogether. Obviously, she was pissed at me for leaving so suddenly yesterday, for slogging through the storm and making her worry.

'Your mum was asking me about Andy,' Aunt Katrina beamed. 'Weren't you, Grace?'

Mum pointedly avoided meeting my stare and the flashes coming from the screen brought the irritation in her eyes to the light.

'She was surprised to find out Andy was a boy,' Aunt Katrina continued, almost talking to herself, 'but then I told her how much of a sweetheart he is and showed her his pictures on Facebook! He is so lovely, isn't he, Grace?'

Mum crossed her arms, her frown deepening.

Alright, I get the gist. 'I'm gonna be in my room, if anyone needs me.'

'Alright, lover-boy,' Aunt Katrina chirped. 'And we'll be here, having the time of our lives!'

I put my foot on the first step of the staircase and asked, 'Where's Iwan?'

'Out with friends,' Aunt Katrina said, and then laughed at a funny scene in the movie.

I spotted Sophie closing her eyes, head lolling to the side a second later. I looked at my phone. It was only half past four.

'How come Soph is so tired?'

'Just a full stomach,' Aunt Katrina said. 'She had a big dinner and demolished a huge slice of chocolate cake.' She petted Sophie's hair lovingly.

Mum was looking at me again, this time with a challenging expression.

I maintained my composure. 'Watch out with the sugar, or she's going to get hyper like the other day innit.'

'How are you feeling, anyway?' Aunt Katrina asked, ignoring me. 'Have you had any more episodes?'

I froze.

Mum turned to Aunt Katrina with a questioning frown. 'What episodes?'

'I'm fine,' I muttered. 'Anyway, I'll leave you to the film. Auntie, *I'm fine.*' I emphasised the last word through gritted teeth and, maybe because of my piercing gaze or tone of voice, Aunt Katrina heeded my subtle warning.

'Oh, right,' she smiled tightly.

'I'll be upstairs,' I repeated.

Mum glanced at me speculatively and I darted away.

Once in my room, I exhaled a long sigh. That sense of being strangled by an invisible force was there again but I ignored it. Mum was going to find out that things weren't right with me, sooner or later. My episodes recurred so often recently that I was almost getting used to them, like I was expecting to drop on my knees screaming at least once a day. It was only a matter of time before it happened in front of her, but I didn't have the guts to tell her about it.

I threw my rucksack on the bed. Exhaustion pooled on my shoulders like liquid lead and I lay back on the bed over the duvet. My gaze went to the ceiling. That weird, dangling cobweb was still there, half-floating above. It was now officially part of the decor.

I decided that, since I had nothing better to do, I could get things set up for my stream. Routine was something to hold on to. I was setting up a list of tracks I was going to remix on my DJ console when Andy texted.

'*I just realised something.*'

'*What?*'

'*The present. You haven't given it to me. Again!*'

I groaned. '*FUCK! You're right!*'

Andy sent a laughing-out-loud emoji. '*What is it anyway?*'

'*I'm not telling. It's a surprise!*'

'*But I'm curious!*'

'*Stream still happening btw. Are you going to watch?*'

'*Oh gosh I forgot about that! I just remembered that o-Drone is my bf! I'm never going to get used to that.*'

I shook my head. '*You actually typed oh gosh on your phone.*'

'*Shut up LOL, half past seven right? I'll be online at my desk with a beer and my neon glasses on.*'

'*Maybe a box of tissues and lube would be better since you're going to watch me fondle my toys for an hour.*'

'*You tit! LOL*'

I smiled at my phone, imagining Andy's laughing face.

'*What was your handle on YouTube again?*'

'*Bluefox42.*'

'*I'll keep an eye for your name in the list of watchers.*'

'*I'll make sure you spot me ;)*'

I didn't have the balls to go downstairs and meet my mum's burning gaze again, so I texted Aunt Katrina like a wimpy twat.

'*Please can you remind Mum I have my weekly stream at half past seven? I'll be unavailable for an hour.*'

Her answer was surprisingly speedy. '*Sure thing babes x*'

***

Putting on my o-Drone costume was like wearing armour to battle, although there wasn't going to be any bloodshed – only awesome sounds that would destroy all that was bad in life.

I was more than ready for my weekly release, for my launch to space. I wiggled inside my white, blue and dark silver suit with all the wires dangling about before I put my head inside a painted-over diving hood and placed my immaculate, expressionless o-Drone mask over my face. Two holes for the eyes, two small windows to the internet world.

The lights were perfect, the microphones set up and my headphones steady on my head. The camera, the black unblinking pupil that would sync me to the virtual planet, was now on.

With my DJ controller I gave my tracks a new birth, a shape they never had before. I opened the DJuced software and connected it to my console, opened YouTube and clicked on the camera button.

o-Drone was a silent android who introduced himself with a stiff bow and then he was ready to roll.

I didn't waste time responding to the flood of words invading the live chat; in fact, I never paid much attention to it. o-Drone was in the zone.

'Arctic Cat' and 'High Magnetism' were going to marry in the name of the BPM, and I was the celebrant. 'High Magnetism' was a recent gem, a newcomer in my playlist, whereas 'Arctic Cat' was a classic. I was giving 'High Magnetism' good exposure by mixing it with a popular old piece. At the same time, 'Arctic Cat' could do with a fresh revival.

I matched the tempo and the sound was big, eliciting a dance from me as the notes swept me up and up. Strobe lights scrolled on the background walls in a rhythmic stream.

Sawtooth waves singed the air, the bass-line beating like an excited heart. The drums came in, bossy and sexy, like a dominatrix's varnished heels prancing over a pleading body. High notes sang a catchy tune and the music grew, passing through a brassy filter. o-Drone brought the crowd higher and higher in a place where all we could do was shake with joy. *Yeah, this is the buzz I need, this is the deal.*

I glanced at the chat and saw the flow of messages. Then I saw him. Bluefox42.

'Is this the famous Hades I've been hearing so much about? :D'

I burst out laughing, knowing that my viewers couldn't hear me.

I transitioned smoothly into something new, my track I'd called 'Andy'. Nobody had heard the piece before and I didn't want to stray away too much from the original structure. I normally published a track before remixing it, so this was an exception.

I ran some sections through a low-pass filter and added an extra beat which made the initial part sound a little less ominous. Still, the tune had a definite darkwave feel at the beginning which wasn't my usual thing. The chat went wild.

A whirlwind of growing octaves brought us sky-high and a blaring note faded through the punchy kicks, a beam of light puncturing a black horizon. The chords sang like seraphines, utter bliss brought by a trickling piano. Synths stretched and bounced around like pearls falling down a marble staircase.

The symphonics came in and the unison of strings reminded me of Andy's bright smile. The sun had risen and painted the sky with the yellows and purples of dawn.

A muffled thump came through the door. I lifted my headphones slightly to hear where the sound was coming from. A scream came, cutting my soul in half.

'I hate you! I hate you! You're just like him!' Mum cried out.

'Grace, don't be like this,' Aunt Katrina pleaded. 'Please, listen to me, we—'

'Shut up! I don't want to hear it.'

I was stunned, my feet rooted to the ground. What the hell was going on? I quickly suspended the stream.

Mum wailed and banged at my door again. 'Open up right

this minute!'

I shut everything down at the speed of light, pulled off my mask and went to unlock the door. I met my mum's teary, flaming eyes and the strength of her fists on my chest.

She hit me over and over. 'You're horrid! I thought you were better than him but you're not!'

'Mum,' I muttered, 'What's—'

'You knew he was dead! Why were you hiding it from me?' Tears rolled down her red cheeks.

The weight of the whole fucking planet fell on me. 'Mum, we were going to tell you—'

'Shut up!' She punched my shoulder and spoke through clenched teeth. 'You were making fun of me all this time, weren't you? *Ah-ah*, she's crazy! Is that what you were thinking? That I'm mental?'

'No!'

'Yes... You... Were!' I got smacked at every word. 'Everything I do, everything I say... You undermine it,' she sobbed. 'You treat me like I'm some kind of bloody nut-case! But I'm not some weak little woman, Hayden! I'm your goddamn mother!'

Aunt Katrina stepped forward and touched Mum's arm. 'Grace, calm down...'

'And you!' Mum snapped. 'You're the same, you know? I can't believe it! Of all people, I didn't expect my closest family to treat me like this, to conspire against me. You think I'm mad! But *I know* what I saw, that man is out there! I am not imagining things.' Mum shot us the coldest of glares. 'I want you out of my house, both of you.'

My stomach lurched. 'Mum, please—'

'I said *out!*' she growled. 'Pack your stuff and get the fuck out of my house! You're just like your father. A manipulator! *A bastard!*'

Her words shredded me in a thousand pieces.

My voice cracked, 'Mum—'

'*Ooout!*' She pushed me inside my room, grabbed my rucksack from the floor and threw it against my chest. 'Get your things and leave!'

She stormed out, went to her art room and slammed the door shut. Mum locked herself in loudly enough for us to hear the click.

I grabbed what I could and shoved it into my bag. A veil of unshed tears blurred my vision.

'What's happening?' Sophie enquired sleepily.

Mum's screams must have woken her. She had come all the way upstairs and now she was on the landing, in front of the open door of my room. I focused my hazy gaze on the bundle of clothes in my fist, unable to look back at my little sister.

Mum sobbed and cried inconsolably in the background.

'What's wrong with Mummy?' Sophie asked.

'Sophie, come downstairs with me,' Aunt Katrina said.

After a moment, Sophie called, 'Hayden?'

I didn't reply. I was slinking out of my o-Drone suit while immersed in a cold, lonely space in my head.

'Hayden, you're not really leaving, are you?' Katrina asked.

'You heard her,' I said shakily as I put on a thick hoodie. 'I can't stay.'

I had put more than enough in my bag – I zipped it shut and slung it on my shoulders.

I was zooming out the room when Katrina grabbed my arm. 'She's upset now. She'll come around—'

'No,' I snarled. 'And why the hell did you tell her about John? Why like this? Couldn't you wait for a better moment?'

'I'm sorry,' Aunt Katrina said with a grim expression. 'She was talking about this man with a scar who looks like John following her around. I couldn't bear hearing more. She needed to know John's gone.'

Sophie began to tear up. 'Why is Mummy crying?'

I squatted to look into her worried eyes. 'Mum's having a hard time now, but she'll be fine. She's got you and Iwan, and Aunt Katrina is with you now. Make Mum a nice cup of coffee the way she likes it, alright? I'll be gone for a while.'

'You're leaving?' Sophie asked.

'Yeah,' I whispered.

'When will you be back?' She was trying really hard not to cry.

'Soon,' I said.

'Get out!' Mum repeated from the locked room and another stream of crying followed.

I sprinted down the stairs.

Aunt Katrina called out, 'Where are you going to go? Are you going to stay with Andy?'

I went straight for the front door and unlocked it, ignoring Aunt Katrina calling my name as I stepped outside.

25

ANDY

I stared at the YouTube page and o-Drone's suspended stream with a hanging mouth. What on Earth had just happened?

A second ago, I was overjoyed because my incredible celebrity boyfriend was remixing a song named after me and broadcasting it to the world. Now I gawked at nothing. *User Inactive.*

Hayden had turned towards the door a moment before he shut everything down. My thoughts went immediately to his mother. Was she alright? What about Sophie and Iwan?

I snatched my phone from the desk and quickly composed a text message. *'Hayd, is everything OK?'*

Twelve harrowing minutes passed before my phone chimed. *'No.'*

A chill went down my spine. *'What happened?'*

The clock on my wall marked the interminable seconds that ticked by without a response.

I decided to call him.

'Hello,' Hayden murmured.

'Hayd! What's going on?'

There was only grim silence on the other end of the phone.

'Hayden?'

'Can I... can I stay with you tonight?'

'Of course,' I said. 'What happened?'

A pained sound, like a choked sob, was the only answer I got.

I grabbed my car keys. 'Where are you now?'

'I'm on Cathays Terrace, by the school.'

'I'll be there in four minutes tops!' I said, rushing to the car. 'Wait for me in front of the library across the road.'

'Thanks,' he said in the softest of whispers.

***

I spotted Hayden leaning on the metal rail in front of Cathays Library, his eyes fixed on the alphabet letters and the dragon drawn on the pavement. The pitch-black sky was clear aside from a single stretch of bluish clouds unfurling slowly above a thin moon. A tall lamppost shone a strong yellow light that cast dark, long shadows all around it and glared over his slouched form.

Hayden's curls fell over his face, hiding his expression, but the hunched shape of his shoulders told me everything there was to know about his low emotional state. My heart beat painfully for him, as it had for some time now.

I lowered the car window. 'Hey.'

Hayden looked up, his beautiful eyes hazy with anguish. 'Hey.'

The road was empty and the crossroads deserted. In fact, it was eerily quiet. Hayden walked around the car, opened the door and hopped in. I reached for him wordlessly. He threw his arms around me, enfolding me into a hug and exhaling a trembling breath on my shoulder. 'I'm sorry.'

I kissed his cheek. 'Don't be, you've done nothing wrong and there's no way I wouldn't have come for you.'

'I know,' he murmured as he skimmed his fingers through my hair. 'I know.'

We didn't speak during the drive to my house. Something terrible must have occurred but it was obvious that Hayden wasn't ready to share. I didn't want to ask anything that he wasn't ready to answer and, in his own time, I was sure he'd open up to me.

He focused his attention on a cuticle on his thumb, picking and biting at it. I glanced at him with the corner of my eye and saw that his hands were shaking. *My poor Hayden.*

I parked across the road from my front garden and he followed grimly as I walked to the main door. We went inside. Hayden waited for me to invite him to sit and, once on the sofa, he tried to occupy as little space as possible and tucked his rucksack between his feet. Darkness shaded his eyes and it was as if his whole being was haunted by a shadow.

'Would you like something to drink?' I put a hand on his shoulder. 'A hot cup of coffee?'

He nodded and I got to work, whipping up the best cup of frothy latte I'd ever made. I sprinkled it with cocoa powder and accompanied it with a pair of Biscoff biscuits. I put them on a small plate and presented them to him with the coffee. Hayden looked at my offering and his eyes widened. A tiny smile played upon his lips as he took the coffee and the biscuits. My heart squeezed. 'Thank you,' he said with a soft glint in his eyes.

I sat on the sofa next to him and turned on the telly. It reminded me of the first time we slept together. Music videos played, the colours and sounds soothing and meaningless. I wondered if Hayden would speak up soon, if he'd tell me what was wrong and would seek refuge in my arms, like he'd done before.

Was I just a haven for him? That would be OK. It would be

enough for me.

He sipped his coffee – eyes dim like hazy glass and heavy with tears he would not shed. I could see in his gaze how he held on to his pain, nursing it. I wished he'd let it go. I was there for him and I'd give it my all to make him hurt less.

'This coffee is awesome, ta,' Hayden said. 'You really know how to make me feel better, fair play.'

'I do what I can,' I said.

After a few minutes of quiet, he said, 'I'd like to try tonight.'

'Try what?'

Hayden sat up straight and glanced at me. 'I want you to fuck me.'

In a different situation this request would have excited me. Now, it only killed me. Swallowing a lump in my throat, I said, 'These kinds of things need preparation. It'll hurt if you don't take it easy. Start with fingers and toys, practise breathing slowly and relaxing your body. It'll take days, if not weeks, to get used to the feeling of penetration. Plus, wouldn't it be best to do this when you're less... I mean, you're upset.'

'I'm upset more often than not,' he said flatly. 'So what difference does it make?'

'It makes a difference to me. I don't want to hurt you.'

Hayden smiled with a glint of tenderness in his sad eyes. He put down his coffee and held me against his broad chest. Even though his body was larger and stronger than mine, Hayden felt small and powerless in my arms. It was as if I was all he could hold on to. His heart wept and his soul had lost its way.

'It'll be fine, don't worry,' he said as he peered into my eyes. 'All you do is make me feel like I mean something.' He stroked my cheek. 'That joy you give me? I want to give it back.'

'But... but you do make me happy already.' I blinked back the wetness, making my vision blurry.

Hayden kissed me. His lips brushed mine gently before he became more demanding, his touches sensual and his hands keen to explore. I loved it and resented it all. I wanted to give him what he wanted, for him to take everything I had to offer, but an uneasy feeling I couldn't ignore brewed within me.

We had a shower together. Under the warm water we did little but stroke each other's cocks and kiss languidly. Hayden insisted I told him how to make himself ready to take my dick. I washed his hole gently, feeling its tightness nestled between taut buttocks and a soft spread of hair. I inserted a soapy finger inside him and he hissed.

'Keep going,' Hayden said ruggedly, 'keep going.'

Later, we were naked and entwined passionately on my bed. Hayden's hands brushed over me and I skimmed my fingers over his body, as if our skin and limbs were waves colliding softly. He grinded against my groin and our cocks rubbed together. Despite everything, he was so hard for me and I for him. Hayden might have found sanctuary in our union but I couldn't deny that I needed this too; his touch and his gentle caresses as much as his insistent kisses.

He went down on me and ran his tongue up my shaft, taking me as deep as he could as he pressed a finger inside my hole. I shuddered with pleasure as I blew him too, making him gasp as I slurped on his thick length. Eventually, he went to fetch the lube and I got nervous. I knew what was coming. Anguish and arousal fought an unwinnable battle.

I was drawn in by his tenderness. He was so eager to do this, as if he was offering a gift, but inside I knew that this might have been his way to look away from what really bothered him.

His expression shifted between discomfort and passion as I

carefully stretched him. I took my time to work him open. He was so tight. Hayden gazed at me in the soft light of the room, murmuring how much he wanted it, begging me not to stop but I could feel his sphincter clamping against my knuckle. His tensed body arched and writhed under my touches and his breaths came out short and fast, sometimes stopping for long seconds.

'Relax babe,' I soothed.

'Fuck me,' Hayden urged as he clutched the pillow under his head.

No way I can put two fingers inside him. He's clenching around the one as it is.

'Just fuck me, please,' he panted, cheeks flushed red and eyes closed.

'I can't, you're not ready.'

'Please.' He looked at me and a slither of all he was keeping inside reached me. *Rid me of this pain,* his eyes said, *by making me hurt in a different way.*

The truth dawned and it was heavy, unbearable. My cock drooped as well as my head. I removed my finger from his opening.

'What's wrong?' Hayden asked in alarm. He sat up and touched my cheek. 'Andy?'

'I can't do this.'

'OK,' he said gently, 'Let's do it like we usually do.'

'No,' I gasped. '*This.* Sex. All of it. Something bad has happened to you and you won't tell me what it is and now you... you're trying to not think about it. Why do you want to force your body into something it's not ready for? To forget? To punish yourself?' Tears pricked my eyes. 'And I can't do this for you, Hayden. I don't care if you hurt me but I won't let you hurt yourself.'

Hayden's expression morphed into one of dismay. 'I'm... hurting you?'

'Y-you're not,' I said quickly, 'what I mean is—'

'Fuck! Is that what this is for you? A sacrifice?'

'No!'

'Then why? You've been seeing me out of what, pity?'

'Hayden, no!' I sobbed.

'What then?'

'I...' My voice caught. 'I want... I want you to be happy.'

'Knowing that I'm hurting you doesn't make me happy.'

I covered my face. 'You're not... hurting me...'

Warm, strong arms went around me. 'I clearly am.'

'No...'

'You're crying.'

Sometimes you're so upset that you can't speak. I guess that's how it was for me at that moment. Since Cynthia had come to my house I'd been stewing in doubt, worrying that my worst fears would come true. Now, as Hayden hugged me tight while I shook against his chest, I didn't know how to put into words what I felt. He held me close and stroked my hair for a while.

'Oh God, I'm so sorry,' he said. 'Fuck, what have I done? I shouldn't have come here.'

I froze. Looking up at him, I saw in his eyes that Hayden was heartbroken.

'N-no, you can come here whenever you want.' My heart drummed in a panic.

Hayden cupped my face. 'No, Andy. My life is messed up. I'm messed up. You shouldn't have to deal with it all second-hand. When I started to date you, I should have known better.'

He kissed me sweetly and got off the bed. I followed him as he started to pick his clothes off the floor. He got dressed and, when he grabbed his rucksack, I understood.

'Are you leaving?'

Hayden looked at me sadly. 'It's for the best.'

He headed for the front door and I went after him. I clasped his arm. 'You can't go just like this! Please! Talk to me, tell me what's wrong! I'm supposed to be your b-boyfriend! You pro-promised you'd make me forget about my-my ex and said you were ha-happy to be with me and instead you're just t-turning away!'

Hayden's eyes glistened like rain at sundown. 'The whole time we've been together, all I've done is burden you.'

'That's not true!'

'I didn't want to come here because I'm not the kind of person you deserve. A clingy bastard who's not right in the head! But I wanted to see you so bad, I always do. I didn't want to say anything about what happened because I don't want you to think that's why I want to be with you. I'm ashamed. This weak piece of shit, this... *carcass* of a person you see is not who I really am, but this crap is all I have to show for it.'

I took his hands. 'Hayden, that's not what I see.' He stared at the floor. 'You're an amazing person, smart and caring,' I said. 'Everywhere you go you brighten the room.'

He snorted, 'That sounds more like you.'

I hugged him. 'Please, don't go.'

Hayden's lips curved in a sombre smile. He took my hand and kissed my palm, like he often did. 'I love you, you know. More than I can say. That's why I can't stay. I need time to sort things out, otherwise it's never going to work between us. I'm just going to lean on you all the time and that's not how it should be.'

The words he'd said took a few seconds to register. 'You love me... and you're leaving me?'

Hayden stroked my cheek. 'I don't know how long it'll take to go back to some kind of normality but I have to try. Oh.' His expression brightened. 'I remembered something.'

He unzipped his rucksack, extracted a plastic bag with a wrapped gift inside and handed it to me. 'It got to you in the end.'

I clutched his present to my chest. 'Where are you going to spend the night?'

He grinned. 'Not at some girl's house, don't worry.'

'That's not... that's not what I meant.'

Hayden chuckled. 'I know.' He bent over to kiss my cheek. 'Don't worry. I'm like the Terminator, innit.'

He left. One moment Hayden was there and the next he was not. Now it was only me, standing naked in the foyer with a wet face and a plastic bag gripped to my chest. I couldn't say how long I stood there but eventually I sat on the sofa and considered my present for ages, as if it was a precious piece of my boyfriend – all that was left of our relationship.

I gathered my courage and fished the present from the bag. It was wrapped *badly*, with tape criss-crossing on every corner, as if Hayden had put it all together in a rush. The paper looked expensive and had a quirky design. There was an alien on it, in various different costumes – gangster-alien, holiday-alien and stoned-alien. I laughed, then my throat tightened with sadness.

A little envelope had a message, once again appearing to have been written speedily, that said, 'Read after you open the present.'

I tried to rip open the wrapping carefully because I didn't like the idea of ruining it. After several manoeuvres, the present was revealed. It was a piece of clothing, a hoodie by the looks of it, folded inside a plastic sleeve. This was a bit of a déjà vu.

When I freed the hoodie from the packaging, I splayed it open on the sofa and sniffed big time. It was a black Nine Inch Nails hoodie with the magenta-blue neon cover art of *Pretty Hate Machine* on the front. It was beautiful.

The first time Hayden and I met, I raved on and on about how much I liked this album.

I sobbed.

I hurried to read the card he'd attached to the present and frowned because on it was a puzzling picture of a smiling lettuce. The message inside said:

Your awesome sweater got covered in ketchup and I don't know if the stain will wash off. I thought I'd get you a new hoodie to make up for it. I'll kick my cousin's arse properly next time I see him! If you're wondering about the lettuce, well, you shouldn't. You know exactly why that's there. Hope you like the present! Love Hayden xx

I groaned. 'Salad. He's such a twat!' I sniffed again and hugged my super-lush present. 'How can you say to someone you love them and then break up with them? Dickhead!'

Was it over, though? I didn't want to believe it. It didn't *feel* like it was over, but he said he had to sort himself out, otherwise things weren't going to work between us.

I texted him, *'The present is beautiful. I love it! I'm going to wear it on our next date.'*

He didn't reply. I got myself in my pyjamas and cosy slippers, grabbed a pot of dark-chocolate ice cream and prepared myself for a long, lonely night. Hayden wanted to get better for me, for us. That's how I should have looked at it, but I was shitting myself with worry. Where was he going to go? Was he going to be OK?

Later, in bed, I couldn't fall asleep. I came up with an extremely cringe plan, which consisted of dressing Hayden's pillow with my new hoodie. I hugged the make-do boyfriend and breathed in Hayden's smell which made me think of him vividly. Result? The most unhappy erection ever. I was slowly rubbing my boner against the pillow and gulping down sobs when my phone chimed.

Hayden had sent a reply, a GIF of Arnold Schwarzenegger with sunglasses and a short message: *'Glad you liked it.'*

There was a wall between us, like that time he left my house to go home and process things for the night, but much, much bigger. I glanced at the GIF he'd sent. Before he left, he said he was like the Terminator.

Surrounded by darkness, I smiled ruefully to myself.

He'll be back.

26

ANDY

Karaoke Wednesday came around.

I looked down at my legs which were stuck inside a trap also known as 'knee-high boots'. My white patent leather shoes, lined with a criss-cross of laces and equipped with sky-high wedges, gleamed under the light of a fringed lampshade.

'How do you cope wearing stuff like this all the time?' I asked.

Crystal glanced at me, sensuous grey eyes scanning my face. 'Wearing drag is like taking cock up the arse for the first time, babes. It's uncomfortable and it feels odd, but once you get the hang of it, you're going to love it and you'll want to do it again.'

'Candid as always, Crys.'

Crystal grinned. 'That's me, hun!' They adjusted the strands of my platinum wig and kept on smiling dazzlingly. 'Look at you. You're so beautiful! God, I'm so proud! I think we're ready for the reveal time, but I say let's wait for Tai to come back, yeah?' Crystal knelt in front of me to adjust the frills of my skirt.

I'd spent the whole afternoon in Crys's bedroom, overhearing conversations between them and Tai that I decided my ears were too sensitive for. The place was an utter mess. There were clothes everywhere, shoes, scarves and make-up scattered all over Crystal's iridescent bed cover.

I was in a shit mood. Since Hayden had left my house last week, there had been a big black cloud following me wherever I went. When I told Tai that my boyfriend had decided to put some space between us, leaving me in a depressive I-don't-know-what's-coming-next state, he vowed to gut Hayden with a rusty chainsaw.

'That motherfucking misshapen cockhead!' he roared. 'He was all over you and now what? Did he get the cock-fright? Cunty bastard! Fuck!'

Once I explained about Hayden's mental health and gave him context, Tai exhaled a thoughtful, 'Oh.' Not that knowing Hayden walked away for my sake had made things a lot better. I missed him so much I was tempted to bang my head on the wall until it cracked, either the plaster or my skull, just to make the need to see him, to hear his voice, go away.

Regret, as well as his absence, made my life a misery. What if Hayden decided we couldn't be together?

Tai had tried to distract me by being his noisy self, mummying me and dragging my arse around Cardiff. Yesterday, he sat in my lounge and said, 'If you don't feel like singing with me tomorrow night I'd understand.' His dark eyes were huge with sympathy.

I handed him a frothy coffee, just like Hayden liked it. 'No. I'll do it.'

My friend studied my expression narrowly. 'Are you going to ask me to watch *Notting Hill* tonight? Or to listen to "Someone Like You" while we dance naked on the stairs?'

I blushed, because I'd done *way* more embarrassing things to cope with my loneliness before. 'I was thinking of something more like a *Die Hard* marathon.'

I spent Tuesday afternoon with Tai. We practised singing 'A

Devil in Disguise' then I put on Die Hard but neither of us seemed to care for it. Then Tai said something along the lines of, 'I know what'll cheer you up!' and put series ten of *RuPaul's Drag Race* on the telly. I spent a good three hours watching the queens performing in awkward fascination, offering the odd comment about Kameron Michaels' missed opportunity to cosplay as Sephirot. Tai didn't fail to remind me that tomorrow I'd be looking as beautiful as one of the queens in the show. I smiled tightly and *possibly* touched cloth.

This afternoon, Crystal had received us in their home with a small tray of homemade sausage rolls and tequila punch. They wore a white three-piece suit, striped with rainbow colours and complete with a top hat. It was established that Tai was going to be the first to undertake the transformation. I was intimidated and observing how Crystal turned Tai into a sexy devil-lady in just under three hours did little to reassure me. The clothes didn't look comfortable, for one. I had to confess, though – watching Tai getting ready had been a strangely fun experience.

When it was my turn to undergo the drag-magic, I was a nervous wreck but secretly curious to see the end result. Crystal dressed me, inserting padding in places like my chest and hips so that I would look less like a guy, and had me wear opaque, skin-coloured tights to hide my leg hair which I firmly refused to shave. On top of that, I slid on the net stockings and the boots.

The makeup took the longest to do. I relaxed as creams and powders were layered on my face, except when Crystal stabbed my eyes repeatedly with what they called 'my best blending brush' and glued fake lashes on my lids, almost blinding me. They said I was being dramatic. The person with the rainbow-striped suit said that.

Crys expertly created shadows on my upper chest, humming, 'There's a pair of little titties, like!'

I felt as if I was a pharaoh in the process of being mummified because, as Crystal admitted, 'that shit was going to last'.

Crys put a tight cap on my head to keep my hair out of the way and selected a platinum blonde wig from their vast collection, secured it on my capped head with an impressive number of pins and styled it. A golden halo and little white angel wings were the finishing touch and Crys helped me sling my arms through the straps. At last I was ready and as white and refined as a tray of Raffaello Rocher at a Christmas party. Halfway through my preparation, Tai went out to buy something to eat for all of us.

'Transforming into a queen burns a ton of calories,' he'd said before leaving the house in his eye-catching devil outfit.

He returned breathless and sporting a huge smile. 'Oh my God, like, you should have seen the face of the guy serving at the chippy, it was hilarious babe.'

'Where's my battered sausage?'

Tai strode towards me, taking in my new look. 'You look incredible, sweetie. Absolutely gorgeous, mun!'

'Thank you,' I said.

Crystal clapped their hands. 'Reveal time!'

Suddenly, I was terrified to see my reflection. 'What about the food? It's going to get cold and—'

Crystal and Tai sang in unison, 'Re-veal! Re-veal!'

'Alright, alright,' I conceded, and staggered on my heels to stand in front of the full-length mirror which was covered in a shawl.

Crystal sashayed close to the heavy frame, humming 'Pretty Woman' all the while. 'Ready?'

The shawl came off and an adorable angel-girl with long blonde curls gaped back at me.

'Shittin' heck!' she said in my deep, unfitting voice. Crystal and

Tai laughed and squealed with delight. The paleness of my skin and the absurd pinkness of my cheeks struck me. My lips looked huge thanks to whatever Crystal had smeared over them and my eyes were about to take over Cardiff like a pair of mutant spiders.

I frowned at the mirror and fondled my chest. 'It really does look like I've got boobs.'

'I know, right, innit?' Crystal squealed, their eyes gleaming with emotion. Then, wagging their eyebrows at me, they said, 'So, is this mysterious boyfriend of yours coming to see you perform tonight?'

I turned to glare at Tai and he gawked in dismay, fake eyelashes poking his sleek eyebrows. 'You tit!' he suddenly blurted in Crystal's direction, 'I told you not to mention it!'

Crys brought a long-nailed hand to their mouth and grimaced. 'Oops.'

I groaned and flopped heavily on the bed, make-up things jabbing my arse. 'Whatever! He's not coming, OK?' I slumped forward. 'Why did you have to bring that up, Crys?'

'Oh, I'm so sorry hun.' Crystal put an arm on my naked, shimmery shoulders. 'Come on, let's go out and have a ball, yeah?'

'Alright,' I grumbled glumly.

'Let's... take a picture together, everyone, come on, places please, bitches!' Tai said.

'Good idea!'

Crys pulled me up and squashed me into a one-sided hug. Tai pointed the phone's camera down at the three of us. Tai and Crys smiled broadly, while I tried to stop myself from crying.

27

HAYDEN

Flat on a sofa that smelt of weed *or* beer *or* possibly both, I gazed at my phone background – a picture of Andy I'd saved from his Facebook page. He smiled up at the camera, bright like the day when the photo was taken. I wanted to call him. I wanted to see him. *God,* I wanted to touch him and fuck him until the world ended. My poor cock had cried a lot in the last six days; I'd never wanked so mournfully in my entire life. And secretly. Like, in a mate's shower, when he was upstairs servicing a girl he was seeing and I was in his bathroom, pining over my boyfriend.

I put away my phone and muttered to myself, 'Fuck me.'

Staying away from home had actually been good for me. I was sleeping better and bunking at my friend's house without having to worry about my family had been especially beneficial. Did I feel guilty about leaving my brother and sister behind in a moment like this? Absolutely. Aunt Christie and I got in touch Saturday night. Mum was a little withdrawn, she had told me. She insisted she had the situation under control, although I wouldn't tell her where I was, no matter how many times she asked.

I wasn't sure I was ready to see my mum yet. I worried I'd say things I would regret. *Man,* the memory of her words burnt worse than bile. Crawling back, asking to find my place in the small, suffocating space of my room... Shit, I didn't crave that at all. So that was it. Lucas's couch was my latest stop.

My friend came down the stairs as I mused. Lucas was ready to take over the world with his sleek green coat, clinking keys and cool but astonishingly out-of-season sunglasses.

'You look like shit, bruv,' he said and blushed immediately after. Now that he knew all about my... well, my shit, Lucas realised I should not be expected to look good. His cheeks blazed red under the curve of his mocha lenses. He cleared his throat. 'I mean, you should go out for a walk, like err... whenever, bruv. Get some fresh air, innit? You haven't been out for ages, that's what I, uh, what I wanted to say.'

I smiled wryly. 'If I look anything like I feel, mate... But yeah. Guess you're right like. I should leave the house for a bit.'

Lucas grabbed a wooden chair by the table and sat close by. He sighed heavily and hooked an arm over the back of the chair. 'I'm sorry, man.'

I frowned. 'About what?'

He shrugged. 'You know, about you going through all that crap disorder shit like, innit...'

I laughed. 'Crap disorder shit?'

'Well, like, I had no idea,' he continued. 'I sent you all those pissed-off messages, like. I thought you were ignoring me just for the sake of it and the lads kept telling me to leave it alone but you're my mate, like. I didn't want to give up on you, no chance son.'

I sat up, my heart squeezing. 'Thanks, bruv. Honestly, that's sound as fuck, like.'

Lucas sniffed. He took off his glasses and wiped his eyes. My jaw dropped.

'What's up son?'

He sobbed suddenly and brought his hands to his face, shaking. 'I'm a shit friend, man! Fuck!'

'Dude! *Duuude!*' I ran to console him, patting his impressively muscled back. 'You're not a shit friend, come on!'

'But I am, like!'

'You didn't know what was going on with me until I told you! And look, you got me a place to stay when I had nowhere else to go!'

Lucas's sobs subsided. 'That's true.' He looked up at me with pink cheeks, wet eyes and a little smile, which quickly morphed into a scowl. 'You laughing at me or what?'

My face was about to rip open because of how wide my grin was. 'No, I mean, like. A bit?'

He gasped, 'What? I'm sad for you and you laugh? You're a ball-sucker!'

'Yeah. *I am* a ball-sucker,' I replied, deadpan.

Lucas's eyes opened even wider. '*Ohh fuck!*' He went on crying and I begged him to stop as I struggled to contain my laughter.

Eventually I distracted him, asking if I could borrow some clothes to wear for a jog. It was ten in the morning so I'd probably stick with running in the park. Lucas was a sweetie and got me a tracksuit with a zip-hoodie that just about fit me.

'Go like the fucking wind bruv,' he said and handed me a key.

I took it from him. 'What's this?'

'I'm going to work, mate. This is my second key. Let yourself in and out whenever, innit.'

'Are you going to ask me to marry you next?' I winked at him.

'Suck my cock nicely and I'll think about it.' Lucas gave me the finger as he left.

***

I sprinted along the artificial lake in Roath Park, cooling my blazing thoughts. The semi-circle of trees surrounding the lake cast a dark green reflection on the rippling water, meshing with the bluish-grey tint of the overcast sky. Swans submerged their heads deep to reach the murky underneath while ducks, geese, coots and pigeons crowded the bank. A few people were around, but not many, and the path was clear – though covered in bird-shit.

I grinned to myself, enjoying a surge of inner freedom. I was flying and, *damn,* wasn't I fucked in the head? I should be upset! *Upset!* Then the memory of my mother wailing in despair flashed through my mind and I came to a sudden stop. I heaved and squeezed my eyes shut.

Fuck! How am I ever going to get over this one?

I ended up leaving the park, jogging under the bridge and coasting along Cathays Cemetery, the bushy trees behind the low stone walls shaken by a light breeze. I was back in Cathays Terrace by the modest library and the red brick walls of the school. Four streets meeting in an inconsequential neighbourhood; now *that* was an accurate metaphor for my existence. Home was four minutes away, just round the corner.

I picked up my phone, seeing a barrage of missed calls from Aunt Christie, Aunt Katrina, plus loads of messages from Iwan. Finally, I noticed two missed calls from my mother. What was she thinking right now? Knowing her, she must have been feeling devastated.

Someone patted me on the shoulder. I turned around and he was there – the man with the burn scar who looked too much like my father to not be him. A glitch in the universe.

He grinned and I heard, through the music in my ears, his absurdly friendly voice. 'Hayden!'

I fell back on the damp pavement like a sack of shit and my headphones flopped off. I scrambled away as best I could.

'Dude! Dude, calm down!' he said, stretching out a hand to help me up.

I slapped it. 'No! Get the fuck away!'

'I'm not a threat, for fuck's sake!' he said angrily.

Well, he wasn't John in the fucking slightest! Now that I heard him speak and looked at his face closely, I realised it. All this time it was just fear playing with my head but... still. The guy knew my name.

I looked up at him. 'Who... who the fuck are you?'

His expression turned serious. 'Am I so much of a scarecrow? Your mum screamed at me too when she saw me.' The guy extracted a packet of cigarettes from a pocket in his leather coat. He plucked an expertly made rollie from the packet with pale fingers, tipped by black-polished nails, and frowned.

'Nah,' he said to himself. 'We need something good for the spirit.' He selected a new specimen which, from the looks of it, was a fat joint, only to put it back in the pack and look at me.

'Let's find somewhere nice to sit,' he grinned. 'And I know I'm as ugly as a ball of inflamed haemorrhoids, but Jesus, I'm not a serial killer!' He chuckled sourly and, after considering his packet of cigarettes again, he put a rollie between his lips and lit it.

***

The familiar stranger and I walked side by side for a few awkward minutes. I was as tense as a guitar's e-string.

The guy, who was contentedly toking on his cigarette, exhaled a smoky breath and looked at me with a knowing smirk. 'I knew you'd grow up to be a looker,' he said. 'That's the only good thing going in the Morris family, isn't it? And now that I've lost them, the looks, that is, I wonder if all I've got left is the bad traits.' He glanced up at the late morning sky with a wistful smile, and still I said nothing.

We went to the car park behind the supermarket in Crwys Road and sat on a low wall. Now that I wasn't running anymore and cooling down, my sweaty zip-hoodie wasn't doing a good job at keeping me warm. It didn't matter; I just wanted answers.

The man finished his first cig and, with a brilliant smile, brought out the fat joint again. After glancing around, he lit it and took a long drag from it. He closed his eyes in bliss and opened them, only to appreciate the tidy shape of his spliff as he blew out the smoke.

'This stuff is fabulous,' he said with a grin. 'I was worried the sizes were going to be shit in Cardiff, but hey, I was wrong! There are three dealers living near my flat, all busy stealing each other's customers. They all try to outdo each other so if one fucks up, the others are ready to take over right away. Healthy competition *indeed.*' He took another long draw and passed me the joint.

I hadn't smoked weed for a long time as it caused my heart to beat faster, and that could easily spiral into something nasty. Right now a panic attack was the least of my worries, though. I needed to get high, *officially.*

I took the joint from him and studied it for a moment. The man with the scar waited until I filled my lungs before speaking again.

'It's Aaron, by the way,' he said, going in for a handshake.

His fingers were really pale and so was his face, like porcelain.

We were the same height, but he was slim rather than muscular and a fair bit older than me, with light blonde curls and ice-blue eyes. *Exactly like John*, a little voice said. The burn scar snaked, pink, angry and with a raised appearance, along his neck, the base of his chin, his right cheek and ear, of which there was little left.

Aaron grinned in dry amusement. 'Like what you see?'

I looked down at his hand and shook it, my cheeks heating a little. 'Are we related?'

He laughed. 'How'd you guess?'

'What are you, like, my long-lost brother or something?' I mumbled, puffing on the spliff again.

He stared at me wide-eyed. 'You really don't remember me, do you?'

'No,' I said as I exhaled. The weed was starting to kick in and suddenly, but with a rather slow and disinterested sort of outlook, I was ready to face the absurdity of my life.

'You were a little kid when we met, I guess, but shit. I even helped you with your Pokémon game on your Nintendo, 'cause you were stuck with a challenge.' Aaron plucked the spliff from my fingers and took another drag.

A memory resurfaced suddenly. A guy in his late teens or early twenties with spiky black hair, sitting next to me in front of the flat Mum and I moved to when we first came to Cardiff. Absurdly, I remembered the challenge he was talking about. I was at the end of the game and I was trying to find the legendary Pokémon Kyogre, but was struggling to locate it. He helped me with the game and I was super happy... and yes, his name was Aaron!

I stared at him. 'Oh.'

He smiled. 'Ringing any bells?'

'That guy was you?'

Aaron laughed. 'It was fifteen years ago! What did you expect, that I'd look the same?'

A headache began to take hold of my skull. 'Alright, man. Enough with the fucking mystery.'

'What mystery? I'm only your cousin.'

'My... my cousin?'

'Yeah. I know I'm kind of scary-looking now but you guys are *really* overreacting. Even that time in Cardiff Bay, it was you, right? And you kinda sped away and I was like *fuuuck*.'

I swallowed with a dry throat. 'It's just... you look like John so much that I thought... I thought you were him.'

Aaron gawked at me. 'What?'

I nodded, stole the joint from his grasp and inhaled as much smoke as I could.

'So wait,' he said. 'Did your mum think I was John too? Is that why she was screeching like she saw a ghost when I came around your house?'

I ran a hand down my face. 'Fucking hell!' I cracked up with hysterical laughter.

'Just my luck to look like that fucking vermin,' Aaron grumbled bitterly. 'Also, your father would have been like, what, fifty? Jesus, man, I'm only thirty-four! Surely I don't look that old, do I?'

I guffawed even louder.

***

Eventually, I got really cold and Aaron suggested we go to a nearby café. We ended up having a huge all-day breakfast with the soggiest hash browns I'd ever tasted. It must have been the weed, but

I found the food delicious.

My metalhead cousin, who had unwillingly terrorised my family with his visit, had made friends with me alarmingly fast thanks to a very fat joint and generous portions of fried food.

After slurping on a burned coffee, I slurred out, 'How did you know where we lived? Like, our latest address and all that?'

Aaron chewed on a piece of bacon, eyes red and puffy with ganj-happiness. 'It's Gareth's house, isn't it? I mean, I wasn't *sure* you still lived there but uh, I guessed you might. I went to your mum's wedding. Both of them, actually, but right now I'm on about her wedding with Gareth, although I'm pretty sure you didn't see much of me that day, like... nobody did. I was totally pissed, throwing up my guts under a table somewhere. That was a tough year for me.'

'How did you know Gareth?'

Aaron leaned back on his chair, giving me a full view of his Iron Maiden T-shirt with their mascot Eddy pulling the Devil's strings. 'He was my music teacher in senior school. Gareth used to work in Bromley and I was his favourite *alumnus*.' He smirked. 'I know a lot of difficult words like that.' Aaron tapped his chin, thinking.

Odd fella. 'So... did you introduce him to Mum?'

He pointed a finger at me and grinned. 'Yep! That's it, that's how it went, sort of. Your mum came to Southampton after what your father did, didn't she?'

'Yeah,' I said.

'She told me you guys were moving to Wales and that you needed a hand getting your stuff down to Cardiff. I was around too, that time. The family was in shock after what your dad pulled. I came to offer support and I knew Gareth, who had a van. I contacted him and asked if he could help out. He said yes and it all went from there really. I think he moved back to Wales shortly after you guys did. Gareth made friends with your mum and they got together eventually. He was such a cool guy.'

'He was,' I said sadly.

'Sorry I couldn't make it to his funeral.' Aaron looked at me with regret, his scars pulling at his sympathetic smile. 'And for your loss. I never got to say it.'

Aaron stuck his fork through one of the bangers on his plate and glanced at me. 'So, I don't really know if I should be the one telling you this, but something bad happened to our dads. Your father, I mean... he did something—'

'I know. I... I am sorry for your loss too. Were you there when the brewery caught fire as well?' I cringed at my own words. 'Sorry, stupid question. It's so much to take in. Everything.'

Aaron dropped his fork and stared at me in disbelief. 'You knew they're both gone, so why the hell would you think I'm John?'

I shook my head. 'Things got spooky, it's complicated.'

Aaron nodded, his eyes wide and burning. 'Well, I'm not sure "spooky" is a good enough word. You know, my dad and I hadn't gotten along for years. He didn't speak to me for so long that I'd given up on trying to rekindle our relationship. Then he calls me, tells me he wants to meet up. I'd been working and living in central London for what, eight years? Suddenly I'm back in Bromley and Dad's hugging me, telling me he's sorry that he was a dick.' Aaron's eyes gleamed with unshed tears. 'And then John fucking shows up. He wants a job at my dad's brewery and of course Dad said no. As payback, John set us all on fire. Piece of shit.'

Suddenly, the café was colder than the frosty wind outside.

'And yeah, I was there.' Aaron stroked his scarred chin and smiled bitterly. 'I got out just in time but my dad didn't make it. Look, I moved to Cardiff because I wanted to start over. I've always liked it here and the only family I've got left... well. It's you, mate.'

I drew out a breath. 'Bruv...'

'Mum left years ago, I don't even know where she is. The grandparents are dead... I don't know. It was a bit of an impulsive move, to be honest. I lost contact with the few friends I had and nobody wants to fuck a sad sod like me. So yeah, new city. Here I am.'

I cradled my head in my hands. 'This shit's fucked up, man.'

'Oh, yeah.' Aaron took another sip of his coffee and clicked his tongue. 'Depressing stories aside, was the guy in the Bay with you your boyfriend?'

'Yeah,' I mumbled.

My cousin beamed, radiant as if the sun had risen on his face. 'Awesome! That means we both like ginger beer!'

'What...?'

'Pair of perries...?'

'What are you on about?'

'Queer,' he grinned. 'I'm gay, my man. Why did you think my father didn't talk to me for so long?'

My mouth fell open.

Aaron smacked his lips pensively and turned to face me with a bright smile. 'Well done, lad. Your boy's *really* cute.'

***

Aaron and I stood in front of my house's small gate which, for once, was locked. I smiled. *Iwan's learning, finally.*

I didn't take my house keys with me when I left Lucas's since I didn't think I'd need them. Enjoying the feeling of being an outsider a little too much, I pressed the doorbell and waited.

I glanced at the potted plant Aaron held in his hands; he'd

insisted he wanted to buy something for Mum before meeting her again.

'She'll love it,' I said. 'She's all about live plants.'

'Oh! So that's why she slammed the door in my face two weeks ago. She wasn't happy I'd brought a bunch of doomed flowers!'

I grinned. 'That *must* be why.'

The door opened and there was Iwan, dressed in pyjamas and looking rugged as hell. His eyes widened at the sight of me. 'Hayden!'

I hugged my brother tightly.

'I was super worried, like,' he said with a broken voice. 'I thought you were never coming back!'

'Course I was going to come back,' I said. 'I just needed a bit of time to sort out my thoughts.'

'Wow,' Aaron murmured, staring at Iwan. 'You look exactly like your dad.'

'Iwan, this is Aaron. He's my cousin,' I said, gesturing at the smiling man with the potted hydrangeas.

Aaron stretched his hand to shake my brother's. Iwan looked flummoxed as hell – he probably realised that Aaron was none other than the man with the scar Mum had been going on about – when Mum herself came to the door. She turned two shades paler when her gaze focused on Aaron and her mouth opened for a scream that, thankfully, didn't come.

'Hey Grace!' Aaron said brightly. 'Long time no see! Well OK, we met two weeks ago for, like, two seconds? Before that, I mean.' He thrust out the pot. 'Hayden said you like live plants. Sorry about the bouquet... oh, it's Aaron, by the way. Remember? I drove you to Gabalfa years ago, introduced you to Gareth. I was at your wedding!'

Mum's eyes opened wider and she brought a hand to her

gaping mouth. 'Oh!'

'Grace, I can't find Sophie's little handbag...' Aunt Christie put a hand on Mum's shoulder. She followed her gaze and her jaw dropped.

The situation would have been more comical if there wasn't so much depressing baggage tied to it all. Oh, fuck it! It was hilarious.

I laughed and climbed the steps to hug Mum tightly. 'I'm sorry I didn't believe you.'

***

To say Mum apologised profusely for what she'd said to me would have been an understatement. She threw her arms around my neck and snotted all over Lucas's zip-hoodie, saying she didn't deserve to have a boy as good as I was.

I didn't know how to deal with everyone crying today because, in my case, all I could do was smile. I was surrounded by amazing people who cared about me and the loneliness I'd felt for so long had shrunk almost to nothing. The day was cold, but *my* day was warmer than ever.

Aaron was dragged inside the house along with me. Apparently, Iwan and Sophie had caught a bug and were both sick at home. My cousin and I had lunch with my siblings, Mum and Aunt Christie. Aaron got thoroughly interrogated by Mum and Christie – turns out he was a music producer and composer. Un-fuckin'-believable.

Aunt Christie called Aunt Katrina and began the conversation with, 'You will never guess what just happened!'

Aaron's sudden appearance was, to say the least, a sensation. The hours following his arrival were good and weird.

We ended up, Aaron, Iwan and I, playing *Tekken 7* in the

lounge for ages, engaging in a proper little tournament. Iwan looked dreadful. He was pale, with bags under his eyes, weak and wheezy. Mum pushed a huge glass of vitamin C dissolved in water in his hands, plopped a turmeric tablet on his palm and urged him to gulp down the tablet and drink the lot. Even though he was sick, Iwan kicked both mine and Aaron's arses at *Tekken*.

The more I looked at Aaron, the more I realised he was nothing like John. Just as with Gareth when I first met him, I felt I couldn't trust him because of his appearance. Aaron was likable though, chillaxed to the extreme, and easy to talk to. Just like Gareth.

Suddenly, I had this nice feeling – like Gareth was smiling at us from somewhere up above.

His heaven might have been an old-fashioned pub hosting Jethro Tull for a live performance. I could almost hear him laugh and say with his deep voice, 'Bydd popeth yn ei le yn y pen draw.' *Everything will be in its place in the end.*

As I watched Aaron attempting to fight against invincible Iwan, a strange calm invaded me.

My phone buzzed. It was half past seven in the evening. I immediately thought it was Andy and snapped the phone out my pocket.

Thing was, I'd sent him a text that morning – a link to a cheesy synthwave track called 'Lost Boy' by The Midnight, with a message saying, '*This made me think of you. Just pretend it's not about a straight couple LOL'*, to which he didn't reply. Odd. Normally he'd answer all my messages almost immediately and I got all squirmy and excited because, yeah – that's how head-over-heels in love I was. Today? Nada. I texted him explaining I needed to speak to him, that a crazy thing had happened. Then I tried to ring several times... but his phone was off. I was starting to get anxious and was ridiculously relieved when my phone showed signs of life that had nothing to do with o-Drone's social media.

It wasn't Andy, though. The number was unknown and, at first glance, I thought the message had been sent by mistake. There was a lone picture with three girls dressed glamorously, all of them objectively hot – especially the girl with the blonde wig who...

What the fuck? I sprung off the sofa and clapped a hand over my mouth.

It couldn't be, could it? But the girl with the blonde wig was... *It was Andy!* Dressed in a sexy-angel outfit that made my head sway. The Asian chick on the left was Tai, unmistakably, and therefore *not* a chick. I couldn't recognise the person in the colourful suit on the right – perhaps a friend of Andy's I hadn't met?

'You alright?' Aaron asked.

Another message arrived from the unknown number. *'You're a bit of a cunt. Andy explained your motivations, the reasons why you're cunting away but, can I be honest with you? He deserves better than to spend his days being depressed about a... cunt? Sorry, I do actually like you but I'm slightly annoyed. Bear with me...'*

A new picture appeared on my screen. It was Andy, sitting on a bed, and the friend I didn't know the name of putting a hand on his shoulder, Andy covering his face as if he was crying. I heard the crack of my heart breaking.

'We're about to go to the Golden Cross for a Wednesday Karaoke Special. Andy and I are going to sing in front of a crowd of gay men as well as everyone else and I swear, Hayden my dude, if you don't show up tonight I'll make sure that he gets laid with at least three different, sex-thirsty blokes! It's a fucking promise!!!'

'Oh fuck!' I muttered against my palm.

'What's wrong?' Iwan enquired. He and Aaron looked at me

like I was mad.

    'I've gotta go,' I said.

    Iwan frowned. 'Where?'

    'To the Golden Cross.'

    'What, the gay bar?' Iwan grinned.

    'Yeah.' I turned to Aaron. 'You coming with me?'

    'Sure,' Aaron beamed. 'What's the occasion?'

    I shook my head and scowled in a way that made him raise an eyebrow. 'I need someone to stop me in case I lose my shit and break a few legs!'

28

ANDY

Thank God for rum and Coke.

I hid in the most obscure corner of the bar, holding the lapels of my long black coat tight to my chest with one hand and my drink with the other. I downed the remains of the booze and glanced at Tai who studied me with a raised eyebrow.

'I need another one, come on,' I said flatly.

'You've already had three and they were doubles!' Tai protested. 'Andy, I need you focused. We're the opening act, you know?'

'I can't feel my toes in these boots,' I whined. 'Seriously, how do women deal with this crap? Oh wait, don't say it. Just like first-time anal...'

Tai's mouth fell open. 'Say *what?*'

I swatted the matter aside and scoured the crowd.

Everyone seemed excited and a lot of people were wearing either devil or angel outfits, or something in between; at least I wasn't out of place. Strobe lights flashed along the tiled walls, the garish bar counter and the smiling faces of the patrons who sipped their cocktails as they waited for the event to begin.

The usual karaoke backdrop, a painting of Cardiff Castle, had been draped over with long, fringed velvet curtains and silver tinsel. There was the familiar small stage with wooden posts and red rope that separated the spectators from the performers.

'My God, it really is packed,' I said, noting how stuffy the air felt. 'We're like frigging sardines.'

Tai smirked. 'All thanks to my organisational skills, ta very much, like.'

I slipped a hand in my coat pocket and went to turn on my phone...

'*Nooo-no-no-no-no!*' Tai grabbed my sneaky wrist. 'You promised!'

'What if Hayden called? I need to check––'

'No! Listen to me, you need to play it cool! Make yourself desirable.' Tai made a gesture, like he was fanning over his beauty. 'If you're all over him he'll take you for granted, like. You'll see. If you ignore him a bit, he'll come running.'

I exhaled a slow breath. 'Fine.'

Tai tapped my shoulder excitedly. 'Here she *cooomes!*'

Lina Lovely, our hostess, sashayed up the steps of the small stage. She wore a blinding silver dress with long sleeves and a curly honey-blonde wig, the strands falling softly around her face. Her makeup was an elaborate work of art, with eyelashes long enough to cast a shadow on her glowing red cheeks. At her entrance the crowd applauded and whistled excitedly. 'Stairway to Heaven' played as she bowed for her audience and, with a deep, soothing baritone, she addressed the crowd.

'Good evening my pretty angels, devils and... everything in between.' She flapped her hand dismissively and the patrons chuckled. 'I am Lina and tonight...' she wiggled her long, drawn-in eyebrows, 'I shall be your goddess.'

Everyone cheered and applauded again.

After the introduction of the judges – the pub owners, a man called Ray Flowers and his wife, Jennifer – Lina extended a long-nailed hand in our direction. 'Give a warm welcome to our opening act, Tai and Andy, who will be performing "Devil in Disguise" by Elvis Presley!'

The crowd clapped vigorously, whistling and grinning as Tai and I slowly walked the distance to the stage.

A sea of eyes watched us and a good number of leers came our way. I was so tense I could just about put one foot in front of the other. I scanned the crowd again and, instinctively, searched for Hayden's face.

He's not here, I reminded myself, and sadness overcame me. Before I knew it, the music started.

The moment we began performing, the crowd went wild. I was a decent singer, but Tai? He was a vocal coach and was here to impress; he added a few flourishes to the song without overdoing it and moved sexily to the music, whereas I was super-stiff and about as sensual as an old bread stick.

Dots of light danced around us, streaming over the grins and gleaming eyes of the people in the bar. A yellow flash landed on a face I knew well, his gaze intent and fixed on me. The strobe lights morphed again and his lips curved under a purple glow.

My throat closed up.

Hayden and I stared at each other and my heart came back to life, beating faster and happier than ever. He was there. Right there. Did he come here to say goodbye? It was now or never.

I brought the microphone close to my lips. 'Hayden, I love you.'

Suddenly Hayden was pushing through the crowd and soon after he was climbing over the stage, shoving aside the wooden posts and the red ropes to get to me. He took me in a tight embrace of kisses and apologies.

'I love you too,' he murmured into my ear. 'Please, don't let those three blokes do anything to you.'

'What...?'

But then he was pressing his lips to mine, and all around us, the bar roared with glee.

***

'...and that's what happened,' Hayden concluded.

I listened to his crazy story with my mouth open. In front of me were my boyfriend and his smiling cousin, also known as the man with the scar.

Not long after our reunion, Hayden got a little restless because the crowded pub was a little too much for him to handle. Plus, we'd attracted everyone's attention by being all lovey-dovey on stage and the pats on our shoulders and congratulations from strangers were getting a bit overwhelming. As for Tai, he didn't look too upset that I messed up our performance. He smirked at me knowingly and I had no doubt that my cunning friend definitely had something to do with my boyfriend being here.

Hayden led me out of the pub and under the lampposts outside, Aaron came into the light where I saw him properly for the first time.

'I need to get used to it,' Aaron said as he puffed on a cigarette with a frown. 'People looking at me like that.' I closed my gawking mouth.

'Anyway,' he said, dropping the butt of the cig on the floor, 'shall we go back inside? It's cold as fuck out here.'

'I'll be there now in a minute,' Hayden said, dragging from the end of a rollie himself.

Aaron, a London soul, made a face. 'Do you mean now *or* in a minute?'

Hayden grinned, 'Yeah, like. Anything in between.'

'Right.' Aaron looked confused. 'I'll go find your mate Lucas. I'm worried he's going to get into trouble. He's a bit over-the-top, isn't he?'

Hayden shrugged. 'Not by Cardiff standards, no.'

Aaron laughed and went back inside. It was only Hayden and me now, leaning against the brown and green tiles of the outer walls.

'I didn't know you were into drag.'

I sighed. 'I'm not. This is what losing a bet looks like.'

His eyes widened. 'What bet?'

'Remember when we met by chance at the arcades?'

'Yeah.'

'Well, I'd been talking to Tai about you and insisted on saying you were straight. Tai didn't agree and told me that if you didn't whip out your cock for me the next time we met, he'd give me two hundred pounds.'

Hayden laughed. 'Seriously?'

'Yes,' I said. 'And if I lost... well, I had to do this.'

'And you did lose.' Hayden grinned. 'Massively, like.'

'Correct.'

He put an arm around my shoulders. 'Would you like to go back inside, my beautiful?'

I looked at him, concerned. 'Are you going to be alright now?'

Hayden smiled serenely, his eyes telling a story. 'Yeah, course I am.'

Inside, it was easy to find Lucas – he pulled on Aaron's arm like a maniac. 'Listen mun,' Lucas yammered, 'help me chat up that hot girl over by there. Be a good mate and give us a wing, would you? Come on, son.'

Aaron looked over to where Lucas's pint was pointing. 'You know that's a guy wearing drag, right?'

Lucas gasped. 'Really? Fuck. But she's gorgeous!'

'Yeah, I know him,' I said. 'His name's Mike.'

'Mike? Seriously? But she's gorgeous, like,' Lucas repeated wistfully as he gazed Mike's way.

Aaron grinned. 'Oh! She's giving you the eye, kiddo!'

Lucas backtracked, shaking his head. 'Nah nah nah... take me away bruv. I can't do it! I can't do it!'

Aaron cracked up and turned to Hayden and me. 'This guy is such a laugh. Well, guys, enjoy yourselves now. I'll do the same.' He lifted his lager to us and went after Lucas.

'Anyway...' Hayden leaned back on the bar counter and looked me up and down with unconcealed appreciation. 'Will you do me the honour of fucking me while wearing this outfit?'

The bartender's eyebrows shot upwards.

I should have been appalled. Instead, I got an instant boner under my frilly skirt. 'S-shut up man! Why are you talking so loud?'

Hayden batted his eyes and even brought his hands together in a pleading gesture. 'Please. I'll do anything you want.'

'Shut it!'

'I'll, like, go to church with your mother every Sunday. Literally, forever like.'

'No!'

Hayden slid his arms around my waist. 'Why not? I need your love *sooo* bad, I really do.' He whispered in my ear. 'I've been playing with my arse loads, like. I fingered my hole imagining you taking me hard and filling it with your jizz—'

I slapped a hand on his mouth. 'Hayden, seriously, stop.'

He smiled under my palm, then slowly removed it from his face and leaned over my shoulder, murmuring, 'Will you do it for me? Come on, mun.'

'Maybe.'

'Tonight, yeah?'

'I'll think about it.'

'Sound. It's a date then.'

I sighed and Hayden flashed me a blinding grin. He ordered a lager for me and ale for himself.

After two pints, the boots weren't as unbearable – the booze had effectively numbed all my aches and pains away.

The next act's performance, Rod Stewart's 'Sailing', was sung by none other than Tai's most talented pupil, Dan Devine, his slim body clad by a God-like tunic and face half-covered by a long, white beard. As soon as he opened his mouth to sing, I knew he had victory in the bag. The heavenly notes lulled us all in the bar and I turned to Hayden, whispering in his ear, 'Fancy a dance?'

He smiled and hugged me close. 'Anything you want.'

Slowly, we began to sway at the soft rhythm of the music.

'Are you really going to be OK?' I asked. 'We can go whenever, if you feel uncomfortable.'

Hayden brushed the blonde hair away from my face and spoke into my ear. 'With you in my arms like this, there's no way I could think about anything else. Right now, it's just us.'

I peered into his eyes and kissed his lips. 'I love you *soooo* much.'

'I love you too,' Hayden said with a dazzling smile. 'So much.'

Hayden and I had indeed sailed across a beautiful sea, and now it really was as if only we stood in that bar. I had the feeling that this, of all songs, was going to be ours.

When the music came to a stop, the Golden Cross erupted in applause, whoops and whistles, while Hayden and I kissed.

Printed in Great Britain
by Amazon

83310638R00187